"Fast-paced f ... ,
Bu...

"A cree... to the
urban fantasy landscape."—Tanya Huff

PRAISE FOR THE NOVELS OF KAT RICHARDSON

Labyrinth

"Richardson's once-playful Harper is clearly evolving into a supernatural force to be reckoned with." —*Publishers Weekly*

"Richardson pulls out all the stops, making this novel a fast-paced and terrifying ride. Richardson's ability to spin a complex and riveting story is undeniable, and the proof is on the page." —*Romantic Times*

"A dynamic investigative urban fantasy saga pitting ghosts, vampires, and other paranormal entities against Harper Baine—PI extraordinaire. Dark and fluid, the story line flows."
—Smexy Books Romance Reviews

"This is one urban fantasy series that is not to be missed."
—SciFiChick.com

"Harper continues her metamorphosis into a grave paranormal entity in this delightfully evolving urban fantasy. The story line is action-packed. . . . This is a complicated, superb entry in an evolving series growing stronger and deeper."
—Genre Go Round Reviews

"A wonderful, unique heroine . . . [and] a compelling place . . . a wonderfully intense ending." —Night Owl Romance

Vanished

"Full of thrills, chills, and mystery . . . easily my favorite in the series so far. Greywalker is a unique urban fantasy series that won't disappoint." —SciFiChick.com

continued . . .

"Richardson has such a natural knack for storytelling . . . completely captivating. I think Harper is one hell of a protagonist, and I can't get enough." —*CrimeSpree Magazine*

"Richardson hooks readers from the start with her storytelling talents, and offers up a multifaceted mystery that's sure to keep fans riveted." —Darque Reviews

"A terrific tale . . . the story line is fast-paced and filled with plenty of action." —Genre Go Round Reviews

"This fast-moving tale boasts lots of action, a complex plot, and meaty characters." —*Booklist*

"Richardson continues to develop strong, intriguing plots. . . . Fans will enjoy." —*Publishers Weekly*

Underground

"In many ways this is a book that brings together all that Harper has learned and felt over the previous books. She's stronger and more centered. . . . She's a very human and humane character." —SFRevu

"Following in the tradition of Tanya Huff and Jim Butcher, this is a strong addition to the growing body of urban fantasy mysteries." —*Library Journal*

"If you are looking for a new addition to your urban fantasy collection, then look no further than Kat Richardson. . . . The hair on my neck was standing up almost from the very beginning. . . . This is a tight, taut mystery wrapped in the paranormal; what more could a girl want? Ms. Richardson, keep 'em coming!" —Night Owl Romance

"This was a great addition to the Greywalker novels. . . . The actual concept of the Grey is brilliant, and I can't wait for the next novel." —The Witching-Hour Inquirer

"This powerful urban fantasy whodunit will appeal to fans of Charlaine Harris. . . . There is a lot of action as the chewing killer leaves his bite in Seattle, but the tale is character driven by the protagonist as she goes from one escapade to another, trying to end the Underground murders." —The Mystery Gazette

"Part Indian folklore, part detailed urban history, part PI procedural, part monster-from-the-depths horror story."

—*Booklist*

Poltergeist

"Richardson's view of the paranormal has a nice technological twist and features intriguing historical notes that lift this whodunit a cut above the average supernatural thriller."

—*Publishers Weekly*

"The story line is fast-paced, hooking the audience from the onset . . . and [it] never lets go until the final altercation."

—Alternative Worlds

"Gripping, stark realism . . . a truly excellent blend of detective drama and paranormal thriller." —*Library Journal*

"Richardson is really striking out into new territory with this series. . . . This is urban fantasy at its best, with new ideas, crisp dialogue, great characters, and exciting stories." —SFRevu

Greywalker

"Nonstop action with an intriguing premise, a great heroine, and enough paranormal complications to keep you on the edge of your seat." —Charlaine Harris

"A genuinely likable and independent heroine with a unique view of reality." —*Library Journal*

"Contemporary fantasy meets urban noir in Richardson's intriguing debut . . . well produced, pleasingly peopled, with a strong narrative and plenty of provocative plotlines."

—*Kirkus Reviews* (starred review)

"This book kicks ass. . . . Like Charlie Huston's *Already Dead* and Simon R. Green's Nightside series, *Greywalker* is a perfect blend of hard-boiled PI and supernatural thriller. It'll grab you from the first page and won't let you go until the last."

—*CrimeSpree Magazine*

Books by Kat Richardson

Greywalker
Poltergeist
Underground
Vanished
Labyrinth
Downpour

Anthologies

Mean Streets
(with Jim Butcher, Simon R. Green, and Thomas E. Sniegoski)

LABYRINTH

KAT RICHARDSON

A GREYWALKER NOVEL

A ROC BOOK

ROC
Published by New American Library, a division of
Penguin Group (USA) Inc., 375 Hudson Street,
New York, New York 10014, USA
Penguin Group (Canada), 90 Eglinton Avenue East, Suite 700, Toronto,
Ontario M4P 2Y3, Canada (a division of Pearson Penguin Canada Inc.)
Penguin Books Ltd., 80 Strand, London WC2R 0RL, England
Penguin Ireland, 25 St. Stephen's Green, Dublin 2,
Ireland (a division of Penguin Books Ltd.)
Penguin Group (Australia), 250 Camberwell Road, Camberwell, Victoria 3124,
Australia (a division of Pearson Australia Group Pty. Ltd.)
Penguin Books India Pvt. Ltd., 11 Community Centre, Panchsheel Park,
New Delhi - 110 017, India
Penguin Group (NZ), 67 Apollo Drive, Rosedale, Auckland 0632,
New Zealand (a division of Pearson New Zealand Ltd.)
Penguin Books (South Africa) (Pty.) Ltd., 24 Sturdee Avenue,
Rosebank, Johannesburg 2196, South Africa

Penguin Books Ltd., Registered Offices:
80 Strand, London WC2R 0RL, England

Published by Roc, an imprint of New American Library, a division of Penguin Group (USA) Inc. Previously published in a Roc hardcover edition.

First Roc Mass Market Printing, August 2011
10 9 8 7 6 5 4 3 2 1

Printed in the United States of America

IN MEMORIAM: RICHARD DENNIS HUFFINE
(1933–1989)

ACKNOWLEDGMENTS

Special thanks to Nelia Chalmers and Guilhermes Damian for their help with the Portuguese. Thanks also to my sister Elizabeth and her husband 'Tagh for help and advice about magical implements. And to all the usual suspects who make these books happen: my agents at JABberwocky; Anne Sowards and the rest of the amazing editorial and publication team at Penguin who let me keep my title and who make these books look so good; and my husband, Jim, who may never get to be a "kept man," but might get a few bon-bons out of this gig. . . .

Also thanks to the cool writers of Team Seattle and beyond for keeping my brain straight during all the insanity of the past year and a half: Cherie, Richelle, Caitlin, Mark, Mario, Nicole, Jaye, Jackie, Stacia, Diana R., and Tiffany T. And to Rob Thurman and Laura Ann Gilman for the best con after-hours ever. To David Thompson and the crew at Murder By the Book in Houston for "forcing" me to go to Texas in midsummer. To MaryElizabeth Hart for solving problems and being fun as well at SDCC 2009. To the ever-gracious Charlaine Harris. To Victor Gischler, to whom I owe a beer or three. To Ana Choi, who put me at the right table at the wedding. And to everyone I forgot: I apologize for my Swiss-cheese memory.

PROLOGUE

Maybe he should have been more worried about the ghost detector going off. At the time it had seemed pretty exciting to have it work at all, but afterward it seemed as if the squawking of the alarm had presaged something much worse than a pack of ghosts. After Harper had left town, things went to hell.

First there had been the little problem of vampires. . . . It wasn't the vampires qua vampires; it was the change in the way they acted and how many were visible. There was always the problem of vampires in the underground and hanging around the desperate and lonely looking for a snack. But suddenly there were more, and different, vampires around Pioneer Square and downtown Seattle. And they weren't subtle. They killed people and they killed one another—nothing new—but now they were doing it in public, or as public as vampires got anyway. Dead and mutilated bodies in Belltown alleys, or awash in drifts of ash on unlit corners of First Avenue or Mercer Street, and still more after a lightning-fast gunfight a block from the Moore Theater about which witnesses could recall nothing but the speed and terror of it. The cops unhappily wrote it down as gang activity with some innocent bystanders caught in the middle and survivors too frightened to talk. All right, the vampire cliques were gangs of a sort, but since most of their victims vanished into dust and ash, the real explanation was unlikely to come up in any SPD briefing. The police were still looking into it, but Quinton was certain they weren't going to arrest anyone soon.

While Harper had been in Los Angeles trying to figure out why a dead boyfriend had called her and what he had meant by "things aren't what you think," a vampire had killed another vampire under the streets of Pioneer Square and had used one of Quinton's tools to do it. Or at least something that looked a lot like one of Quinton's vampire stunners. This he had not appreciated. At all. But he also didn't understand it and that really bugged him.

Quinton liked logic; it had stood him in good stead all his life. Where things didn't add up, he'd learned to ignore what most people thought of as "common sense" and look for patterns that, when joined with confirmed facts, would establish a reasonable working hypothesis. After all, Fleming had discovered penicillin by ignoring the common wisdom of throwing out the "contaminated" petri dish, and taking a look at the mold, instead. Quinton had discovered magic. Of course, he didn't get a Nobel Prize for it.

Quinton imagined at first that someone was trying to set him up for trouble with Edward, Seattle's bloodsucker-in-chief, but nothing had come of that. Edward—never his biggest fan—seemed to know he hadn't done it and he didn't make a move Quinton could see in response to it. Not against Quinton; not against anyone. That was definitely outside standard operating procedure for El Supremo Sanquinisto. And then he had nearly begged Harper to look into a problem in London for him—another out-of-character move for Edward. Begging? C'mon. . . .

Edward's desperation had pinged Quinton's danger signals. He hadn't wanted Harper to accept the job, but it wasn't his decision and he hadn't tried to push her. Something was afoot, but whether the London job was a legit problem or just a dodge to get her out of Seattle, neither of them knew and data was too sketchy for an informed guess. It bugged the hell out of them both.

In the end, despite being busy with the investigation of her past and why she was a Greywalker, Harper had agreed to the London job. She hadn't given all her reasons, but she'd admitted that running Edward's errand would give her a chance to look into another, possibly related, problem of her own. Quinton hadn't been entirely surprised to discover another ex-boyfriend was involved—this one still alive but not in fantastic health by the time things were done in England. For a moment, he'd wondered exactly how many ex-boyfriends she had, but it wasn't any real concern to him, so he'd deep-sixed the question. He was with Harper and that was the important point to his mind.

If anyone had asked Quinton ten years earlier what he thought he'd be doing by this stage in his life, observing vampires and dating a female PI who worked for ghosts wouldn't have leapt to mind. Nor would he have said applying his skills to inventing ghost detectors or dodging monsters while living under the streets of Seattle. It's not the sort of life-ambition East Coast–born intellectuals and computer geeks generally aspire to. Even disillusioned ones who've discovered the world doesn't run on the rules taught to you in ethics class, and sometimes not on the ones you presumed in physics lectures either.

On the night before Harper left for London, the ghost detector had gone off. Quinton was pleased when his prototype ghost alarm started screeching. He had surmised that ghost activity might be rising along with the vampire activity. His working hypothesis was that paranormal activity tended to rise as a body, not just as isolated actions of isolated groups. He had expected to find a ghost or two, and here it was. Except that according to Harper, it wasn't just one ghost he'd measured; it was fifty. And they had come looking for her. Then they'd taken over the detector's speaker and blurted out the same message that had come from the dead boyfriend: "Things aren't what you think."

A few hours later, Harper was on her way to England and Quinton was ferret-sitting under the streets of Seattle, puzzling over what the vampires were up to, tinkering with the ghost detector, and wondering how his calibration could have been so far off. After that, things got seriously weird.

He and Chaos, the ferret, had been down in the abandoned sidewalks under the old part of town when push finally came to shove. They were exploring near the site where the electrocuted vampire had expired, Quinton hoping to find some clue as to why the other vampire—the survivor and aggressor—hadn't taken him out, too. The area was in bad shape, a trash-filled space that had once been a single large basement room, now partially subdivided by long-abandoned efforts to rehabilitate it into useful storage. A spill of crumbling plaster, garbage, lumber, and plain old dirt made a rat playground at one end, cutting off the small plumbing and wiring closet in which Quinton had originally found himself trapped by the vampires. Quinton was becoming paranoid and very jumpy.

Ahead of him in the darkened room, the ferret leapt straight up into the air, chittering and twisting, before she hit the ground on all fours and shot off across the rubble-strewn floor. Quinton had to dive and grab her before she made it into an unseen hole in the wall of the abandoned underground. Even wearing a harness and leash, Chaos was hard to catch. The ferret squirmed in his grip, determined to get to whatever was holding her attention. Quinton tightened up the harness, ignoring the little animal's tiny claws and teeth.

"Give it up, tube rat," he muttered. "You are not breaking for freedom on my watch. Harper would skin me if I lost you." Normally, she was a well-behaved little pocket pest, but since the first vampire incident, Chaos had been pretty spooky, suddenly taking off with no visible provocation to zoom along baseboards and floors with determined concentration, chuckling like a lunatic.

Huh. No visible provocation, he thought. With his free hand, Quinton pulled the newest version of the paranormal activity detector out of one of his roomy pockets and flicked it on. It wouldn't work very long since he'd had to trade battery bulk for portability, but it might pick up something while it lasted. He placed the ferret back on the floor, keeping a tight grip on her leash.

Chaos danced around in an angry circle of hops, baring her teeth, as if taunting some unseen foe to take its best shot. The detector chirped.

The chirping accelerated. Then the pitch changed and the detector began wailing. "Uh-oh," Quinton muttered, sweeping side to side with the device, trying to pinpoint a source direction—so he could avoid it. Fascinating as hunting ghosts might sound, he was sure that whatever was causing the aberrant response was not something he wanted to tangle with. The signal was strong enough to push the detector into a near-overload state and that couldn't be good.

He snatched Chaos up and stepped around the garbage fall with the wriggling ferret in one hand and the detector in the other. He didn't know what he was getting, but it was putting out a lot of paranormal energy.

In the gloom behind the scree of trash, a pale woman with black-and-white-striped hair and embers for eyes turned toward him and hissed like a snake. Whoa. He stopped cold. OK, hypothesis confirmed: The detector picked up more than remnant spirits because this was no ghost. His instincts screamed "Vampire!" while his mind tried to argue; she wasn't quite like the vampires he'd seen before. There was something ineffably horrifying about her and she looked . . . vaguely like a cobra spreading its hood with the way her hair fanned around her head.

Quinton twitched to the side as she charged at him.

The vampire woman passed him, then whipped around. Quinton had already shoved the detector into a pocket and snatched one of the vampire stunners as she recoiled to lunge at him again. The detector continued screeching.

She shot forward like an unloaded spring. The sound from the detector pierced upward like a needle through Quinton's spine and debilitating terror rooted him to the spot.

The ferret shrieked and bit Quinton's thumb, clawing his hand in pure panic. The pain cut through Quinton's daze, and he jerked the stunner upward at the last second.

The vampiress was on him, driving stiletto claws into his back and shoulders as he squeezed the switch, shoving the lightning-spitting head of the stunner into the monster's belly.

She fell back into the garbage. Quinton let out his breath and started turning away.

The vampiress stood up, spitting. Quinton blinked and almost let go of the ferret. The shock should have dropped the vampire in her tracks, knocked her out completely for an hour or more. He'd even adjusted the voltages up after his last encounter, not caring if he sent a few of the bloodsuckers to final oblivion in piles of ash, like the one who'd been zapped by its fellow bloodsucker.

Quinton swore and spun back to meet the vampire's next leap at him, shoving the stunner up under her chin and holding the switch down as hard and long as the sweep of uncanny fear that rattled his bones would allow. This time she fell down and stayed on her knees, quivering and making a high-pitched keen that sounded less like pain than fury. But not dead. Not reduced to smoke and a greasy spot as she should have been.

Quinton whirled and ran. Chaos approved by letting go of his thumb and burrowing into his nearest pocket with a frightened yelp.

They were a room length away when Quinton heard the vampire get back up. The pile of detritus exploded as she forced her way through it, taking the shortest route toward him regardless of obstacles.

Quinton dodged and jumped, pelting through the underground toward his bunker under the Seneca Street off-ramp. The white vampiress was slower than she had been—at least he'd hurt her—but she wasn't actually *slow*. And he could hear more bloodsuckers falling in behind her as he ran. Where were they coming from? He didn't look back to find out. He couldn't afford to waste the energy, and the fear that drove him wouldn't let him anyhow.

Except for the scraping tattoo of their steps on the uneven, gritty floors of the underground, the vampires made no sounds as they pursued Quinton. They just came on.

He shoved through his back door barely ahead of a flock of grasping hands and cutting claws. He slammed the bars and bolts home, feeling the battering of bodies against the wood.

Silence fell for only a moment before something hissed on the outside, "Next time, solo boy."

"Says you," he spat back. It was a lame response but all he could manage between his panting and shaking. They frightened him bone-deep and he wasn't used to that sensation at all.

Then something laughed and the sound made Quinton's knees buckle until the amusement faded into the distance and darkness of the underground.

He moved out of his bunker and into Harper's condo the next morning and waited for her to return from England. He didn't consider the move cowardice; it was self-preservation. Whatever those things were, they weren't your average vampires, and he didn't want to tussle with them again anytime soon.

ONE

I would like to blame jet lag for what happened when I got back, but to be honest, I just wasn't thinking. I wasn't sure of the time or how out of it I really was when my plane landed at Sea-Tac, or I might have put things off for a day, but the sense of urgency and my exhaustion worked together to convince me that getting to Edward immediately was imperative.

Bone tired is a very bad mental state for a fight. I had tried to sleep on the flight from London, but the ghost of my drowned cousin and my own thoughts about who and what I was and what I was returning home to do kept me awake. Beyond that, sleeplessness had become the norm in the past two weeks, so I wasn't at my brainy best on arrival. I tried to fill Quinton in as he drove us home, but I didn't even get to the really bizarre parts before I saw that the late May sun was setting and I felt I had no choice but to drop my bags and Quinton at the condo and head for downtown at once.

I called ahead since it was after business hours. I wasn't able to reach Edward, of course, so I called Bryson Goodall, his personal head of security. Goodall had been my contact during the London trip, but I couldn't say I was thrilled about talking to anyone other than Edward himself. There was a raw tingling in my fingertips and a muttering of the Grey's ghost song in my ears that masked my true exhaustion with a foreign irritation that seemed like attention.

I parked in the subterranean garage and took the elevator down to the cold lobby of Edward's private bunker below the building. The Grey's muttering faded to a distant whisper as the lift descended. From inside the metal box, it was difficult to see the grid of magical energy that shot through the material existence of Seattle and I lost touch with that world I'd come to accept as I plunged down.

The elevator paused at the bottom, waiting for a security code to unlock the doors. The wait dragged on. I wondered if someone was messing with me. . . .

The doors opened after a minute and Bryson Goodall stood on the other side with his security keys and card in hand. He kept his gaze just off mine, as if he feared I'd read in it what I already knew. He looked mussed, his military bearing replaced with a more casually aggressive stance and his clothes rumpled by a long day's wear, the tie and suit jacket missing. Even his strange indigo-blue aura had changed, going darker and more purple, like a bruise. I cocked my head to the side and peered at that strange energy; it looked like a tangle of dark blue, black, and ruby flames shying away from the burning crimson of the magical wards on the doors beyond him. Odd that I hadn't noticed that before, or had something changed . . . ? The layers of gleaming energy that wrapped the room seemed slightly out of alignment, too, though everything was still there. Including the clinging, stomach-tilting smell of a vampire in residence.

The next set of doors would not unlatch so long as the elevator was open, so, saying nothing, I stepped out into the luxurious lobby of Edward's underground home. The deep carpet and soundproofed walls hadn't changed in the ten days since I'd last seen the bunker, yet it seemed as if something was different, broken, or out of place. The lift doors closed behind me, leaving Goodall and me alone in the cottony silence of the antechamber. I turned my head side to side, openly studying the room and feeling jumpy. I saw a thin crack of light in the wall to my left—the outline of a previously hidden door that was now a little ajar.

He noticed the direction of my gaze and shot a glance over his shoulder before turning back to me. "Monitoring room," he said.

"You monitor Edward's sanctum?"

He snorted. "No. The rest of the building, yes."

"So you saw me drive in."

"Didn't recognize the car. Sorry."

I doubted that. If he'd been checking on me as I suspected, he knew I'd replaced my destroyed classic Land Rover a year ago with a newer, silver-gray version paid for with the windfall from a weird little job in Oaxaca. Oh, yeah, he was messing with me.

"I need to see Edward," I said, tiring of trying to analyze whatever game Goodall was playing.

"He's gone."

"I heard that. What sort of 'gone' are we talking here?" I moved toward the heavily warded doors to the inner sanctum, feeling the gruesome flare of the fell magic embedded in the carved metal panels set into the massive wooden portal. An impression of gaping, toothy jaws flickered a moment in the rage of blood magic that sheeted the doors.

Goodall moved to block my way but flinched aside with a sharp-bitten yelp as he brushed the wards. He sidled in front of me, keeping his distance by inches.

"I said he's gone. You can report to me."

I offered him a cold smile. "I don't think so. Just tell me where Edward is right now. If he's in hiding behind those doors, I still need to talk to him. And if he isn't," I continued, adding a mental push to my words, "you need to tell me where he is." I felt the spiked energy of my uncanny talent for "persuading" people to talk prickle against my skin as it pressed on him.

He gave an unconscious shiver at the contact. "No, I don't."

"But you do know."

"And I am not going to tell you. Your usefulness to Edward is at an end. Things didn't work out."

"For whom?" I pressed harder on the Grey, on the magical compulsion I was building against him. It worked even on vampires, though only the weakest of them, and Goodall was no vampire—I'd met him in the hot sunshine at Burbank's airport less than two weeks ago and I'd never seen a vampire that could stand the sun. "I know what happened in London. I did what Edward sent me to do. So who's not happy with my performance?"

He narrowed his eyes and he might have been sweating, but it was hard to tell in the eldritch flicker from the wards on the doors. "You weren't supposed to come back."

"According to whom?" I was as surprised by his words as by his resistance to my push, but I shouldn't have been; Goodall gave every indication that he'd spent some time in the hard-core military. Even in the freakish lighting, the muscles under his wrinkled shirt were solid and his stance was poised. But there was something wrong about his eyes, about the way he moved. . . . I was too tired and too focused on my own efforts to pinpoint it. I felt the sharp edges of the magical compulsion shift and scrape between us as he tried to respond to it in the most limited way, maintain his control while giving up only worthless blither.

"The plan was to get you out of the way. Make Edward feel safe. . . ."

"So you could kidnap him?"

"Wygan took him," he growled. "Not me."

"Right. And how did Wygan get ahold of him? Judging by the way you're cringing, the spells on the doors are still intact, so he didn't go through them to get Edward." I was pretty sure no one knew exactly what I could or couldn't see in the Grey, and if Wygan and his cronies thought I was more Greyblind than I was, that was fine. "You held the doors for him, didn't you?"

I pushed as hard as I dared, feeling the cold black needles of energy that formed the compulsion pierce into me as well. It felt terrible, like icicles that cut into bone and froze the body from the inside out. Goodall made a subvocal growl, grinding his teeth as he glared at me. I was getting the impression the charming bodyguard didn't like me much. "You let him in," I said. "I guessed you were the mole, but I still don't know how you got into Edward's graces."

"Things change," Goodall whispered.

"Not that fast. You didn't just decide out of the blue to be Wygan's spy. Tell me where Edward is." I already knew that Wygan, the ruler—they called him the Pharaohn—of an ancient Egyptian strain of vampire called the asetem-ankhastet, was behind the problems that I'd gone to London to solve for Edward. I also knew that Wygan had plans for me, too—something unpleasant to do with the Grey itself, that strange intersection of the here and the not-quite—and that he'd been moving toward this plan for a long time. He'd tried to force other Greywalkers to become the tool he needed, but he'd never succeeded until he got to me. I still wasn't quite what he wanted, but I suspected I was closer than I'd like.

Wygan had a pattern: He used other people as cat's-paws and leverage to get what he wanted—he almost never got his own hands directly in the dirt. Goodall must have been another of his manipulations and that must be the source of the wrongness I was picking up. I wasn't sure what Wygan wanted or needed Edward for, only that he hated him for something done long ago. But revenge alone didn't make sense of the long, complex game he'd been playing. I still didn't know Wygan's plans—didn't know *him*, come to that—and I'd have to figure them out if I was going to beat him.

Goodall moved his right hand between us, reaching toward me with the keys between his fingers like claws. "I could kill you."

"The Pharaohn wouldn't like that. Other people have had that idea; they aren't with us anymore."

Goodall winced at my use of Wygan's title. He could make of that what he wanted: threat or warning. I'd disposed of most of the London problem, but I'd also seen how awful Wygan's retribution was on those who disappointed him.

"Just tell me where Wygan has Edward."

"I can't. And I wouldn't if I could."

"Don't make me hurt you, first," I warned him, sliding my pistol from its holster at my back. I didn't intend to use it unless I had no choice; a gun should never be an idle threat but the promise of death. I didn't want to kill Goodall—or anyone. When someone dies near me, I feel it, like a blow that drives me down and tears me open. But I survive it. And I would shoot him if I had to.

I did have other alternatives, but they would tip my hand to Wygan. I wouldn't tangle my fingers into the magical grid of the Grey until I had to.

I felt Goodall shift, preparing to move in spite of the magical weight on him. I dropped the compulsion at once, surprising him. Then I rammed my knee into the side of his and slammed an elbow into his chest. I pushed him back as I spun aside, out of line with the doors.

Off-balance, he lurched back into the ensorcelled doors and then bounded away from them with a shout and a jingle of dropped keys as the magic screamed and bit at him. While he reacted, I stepped in again. I grabbed him by his left wrist, yanked it up between his shoulder blades, and put the pistol to the back of his neck. He could outmuscle me, but he didn't want to argue with a nine-millimeter bullet as I twisted his arm up behind his back. I turned him to face the doors.

Blood red flames of cold magic roared up over the warded doors as I pushed him closer. "Open it," I demanded. Through the pall of furious magic on the door, I could just make out the entry control pad with its uncanny eye above and the jagged line of invisible teeth below.

He stiffened and I tightened my grip so his arm strained in the socket and the pistol's front sight dug into the base of his skull. He raised his right hand slowly, holding his card key in white fingers. He should have been sweating, but though the tension in his body was right, not a drop of moisture rose to his skin, just an odor like burned lilies and cheap hamburger. I shoved him and his wrist flattened against the wall below the pad. The ghostly eye above it flashed wide open, but this time the sharp little teeth bit deep into his wrist. Goodall shrieked and yanked himself backward, knocking us both down as the card went tumbling away and the doors stayed locked.

We rolled apart, him clutching his unbleeding, ripped wrist, me holding tight to the gun. I was panting. Goodall just looked murderous, crouching between me and the spell-locked doors.

"You're not going to live through this," he muttered. "Just give up. It'll be easier."

"Nothing is—"

Goodall snapped his bitten arm toward my face, slapping me hard between the eyes with his limp hand. The fingertips cracked across my skin like tiny whips. I jerked back. Then he spun and bolted for the monitoring room's door.

Shaking my head clear, I turned and yelled, "Stop!" It was more a reflex than an expectation as I brought the pistol up in both hands. If he stopped, I didn't have to kill him—and believe me, I didn't want to.

He didn't even slow but slammed the white door backward on its hinges and vaulted over the mess.

I squeezed on the trigger—three fast shots at his retreating back.

Goodall jerked, stumbled, and kept going as three burned holes marred the back of his shirt. He wasn't bleeding that I could see.

I swore one sharp word as I took off after him, more angry with myself than at him. Bryson Goodall might have been human when we met, but he sure as hell wasn't now. How could I have missed it? I didn't think he was a vampire—any queasiness or the usual stink seemed to be a residue of Edward's—but I really should have put some pieces together earlier.

I jumped over the broken door and chased Goodall across the small room full of monitors. He was heading for another door on the far side. Fire stairs. He hit the bar and streaked up the steep concrete steps. He wasn't any faster than a very fit human—at least not yet—but he was still pretty fast.

No fire alarm went off as I followed him through the door. I didn't put much thought into why the alarm was dead; I just chased after Goodall. Adrenaline doesn't compensate for lack of sleep, though, so I was falling behind. In a few minutes, I lost sight of him up the cement stairwell. I was still going up, but his footsteps were fading. Then a metal door rattled and clanged, and the sound of Goodall's escape was cut off in the echo of it slamming shut.

I kept going, hoping I might catch sight of him once I reached the door, but when I got there, he was long gone. I looked out into an obscure corner of the alley behind TPM's big glass behemoth of a building with no one else in sight.

I let out a string of annoyed curses and started retracing my steps to the bunker and from there—I hoped—to the garage.

My cell phone rang. The number was my own home. Frowning, I answered, out of breath.

Quinton yelled from the phone over a pall of background noise, "Harper! Something is trying to break down your door!"

TWO

"Fantastic," I muttered. Now what? "Did you say some*thing*?"

"Yes, I did. Chaos is bouncing around the door and the new Grey detector is making noise—it's not calibrated yet, so I don't know what the signal strength is, but something not normal is trying to get in here."

I could make out the steady banging on the condo door through the phone and the electronic ping of Quinton's latest project.

"Can you see anyone out there?"

"Yeah, there's a couple of people at the door and one downstairs outside the balcony. They look mostly normal, but the detector gets louder when I point it at them."

"Do they know you're there?" I asked as I started back to the garage.

"Yeah, I'm pretty sure they do. . . ."

His voice faded away as I stepped into the stairwell, the concrete and steel of the fire stairs cutting off the cell signal. I stepped back up to the door and opened it. "Tell them I'm not there. I'll be there as fast as I can, but don't tell them I'm coming. Can't use the phone until I'm closer."

I didn't hear his response as I rushed down to get back to my truck. It was almost as difficult to get out of Edward's bunker and back to the parking garage as it had been to get in the first time. As I went back out, I recovered Goodall's keys and card from beside the warded doors—though not without a shudder as the blood magic whined and snapped at me. Without them, I don't know if I would have gotten out.

I drove fast toward home in West Seattle. The thought of strange visitors gave me the creeps after everything else that had happened. These weren't ghosts—not like the last time—or Quinton wouldn't have been able to see them. They might be some kind of vampire or something else entirely. Had they tried knocking first and asking to come in or had they just stormed my home? And if they had come on so strong and without warning, why?

From the moment I'd died, I'd been moved like a chess piece toward some hidden goal of Wygan's. I hadn't known it until my trip to London. Every step of the way things had pushed me. I wondered if this was more of Wygan's doing. Goodall had said I wasn't supposed to come back—at least not under my own power—and I was pretty sure no one had known exactly when I'd return. So if this was something of Wygan's, it had come together at the last minute, once Goodall let him know I was back in town. Of course, it could be something else. My father's ghost seemed to be involved in all this and there were always plenty of other spirits and monstrosities trying to get my attention on any given day. Where one aspect of the Grey became active, others tended to also.

I left the truck on the street and approached the condo building on foot from the western, downhill side—I live near High Point, the tallest but least trendy hill in Seattle. There used to be some wretched public housing nearby until the city bulldozed it for condo development. The neighborhood on the east side of Thirty-fifth Avenue Southwest has improved a lot since the time when I moved in on the west side. People don't shoot one another as often, and the neighbors have gotten to like their peace and quiet enough to call the cops sooner than they used to when a ruckus starts. Whatever was going on at my place needed to end quickly or I'd be up to my butt in policemen and there was one in particular to whom I really didn't want to explain anything. There was already a dog barking somewhere and someone complaining, so an outbreak of Seattle's finest might be imminent.

I saw two or three human figures in the bushes below my balcony—the shrubs made an accurate count difficult from a distance—and one near the street door. Big red-and-black auras marked them as vampires or high-level demi-vamps. I would have bet there were a couple more in the driveway or inside the garage. Crap. I paused in a shadow and dialed my home phone.

"That you?" Quinton asked, not wanting to use my name, I guessed.

"Yeah. I see three or four down here, guessing two more in the garage. How many upstairs?"

"Two that I can make out. There could be someone farther down the hall, but I don't know."

"Pretty heavy crowd. Did they say anything to you when you told them I wasn't home?"

"No. They just keep pounding on the door." I could hear it through the phone, steady as a dance beat.

The figure near my front door turned, looking for me, I thought. My breath caught in my chest as the figure rotated toward me: Its eyes, even at a distance, gleamed with an orange hellfire light. Asete. I peered into the darkness, hoping to see if any of the others had the telltale ember eyes. Given the weirdness of the situation, I couldn't be sure it was just one sort of monster prowling my place. It was difficult to be sure, but I didn't think all of them were asetem.

"Either of your knockers have kind of glowing eyes?" I asked, trying to fade back into heat blur from the truck's engine. I wasn't sure they could pick out my body heat, especially with the asphalt road still radiant from the long spring day, but I didn't want to take that risk.

"Yeah."

Two asetem at least. Wygan's people. I didn't want another fight. We just had to get out, somehow. Minimal physical contact, break through, and run. . . .

"And here's the bad news," Quinton added. "The stunners don't take that kind out. I upped the voltage, so they might go down, but they don't stay there."

I breathed out. "Shit."

"On the other hand, they seem a little slower than the regular kind."

"How—?" I started.

"Later. I left a couple of the new stunners in your glove compartment. Just in case."

"All right. We'll make a simultaneous push. But I have to make another call. When you hear my neighbor shouting, rush the door. Oh—put the ferret away first."

He chuckled. "Got her."

"Fine." I hung up and called Rick, my next-door neighbor.

"Hey, Rick. It's Harper." I could hear Grendel, his pit bull, barking.

"Hey, yeah, what the hell—"

"Rough customers. Do me a favor: Call the cops." I figured I'd rather have to explain away the mess to Solis—if he showed up—than battle half a dozen vampires.

"I already did. Should be here any minute."

"Great. Would you take Grendel, go stand in your doorway, and tell those jerks in the hall that? You may have to shout. . . ."

"Damn right I will." He muttered a few imprecations against our visitors' parentage and physiology before he hung up.

I scrambled back into the Land Rover and grabbed both the stun sticks from the glove box. I left my purse in the car and took only the keys, shoving them into my pants pocket so I had both hands free for the stunners. I started running toward the condo's shrubbery and was launching myself at the first figure in the bushes when I heard Grendel go crazy inside the building.

The psychic stink of the vampire made me gag as it turned to grapple with me. I couldn't see the eyes to know if this was an asete or just the usual bloodsucking fiend as I felt sharp fingernails cut into my upper arms, but I had plenty of movement left to punch the prongs of the device against its body and hold down the discharge button. The vampire convulsed and tossed me aside as it collapsed onto the ground, twitching into unconsciousness. OK, one plain vampire . . . though it had more the white-snake appearance of the asetem. . . .

The second one pounced and I wrenched around in his grip, barely fast enough to discharge the second stun stick into him. He jerked back, and then I was facing a fireball that scorched my face as he immolated. Ash ringed the place where he'd fallen, but of a body, there was no other trace. Well, that wasn't supposed to happen. . . . Upped the voltage, did he? So . . . what, one vampire returned to grave dust? Which made the previous one an asete that would be getting up again any second.

I heard a distant gunshot and a scream, the blip of a siren as a patrol car rounded the corner. The asete near the door took two long steps toward me, hesitated, then whipped around and joined a second fire-eyed creature as it bounded out of the building into the night. They escaped as the patrolmen came running from their car with guns drawn, rushing for the door. I heard one chattering into his shoulder-mounted radio that shots had been fired and they were investigating.

The second one paused beside me. "You OK?"

"Yeah. I live here. Was going in when those guys came out. First one knocked me down."

"Stay put."

I nodded and let them get well ahead of me before I followed them inside.

Someone was making a strange keening sound upstairs. It was an ugly noise that put a blade of ice down my spine. It was hard not to run up the steps, looking for Quinton and whatever was making that horrible sound. But I stumbled upward, keeping back so I wouldn't bang into the policemen. The post-fight burnout was making me clumsy and muzzy-headed.

I got to the landing as the cops got to my door—which was standing open, a drift of dirty white ash spread across the carpet in front of it. Quinton was kneeling down in the hallway, holding on to Rick, who sat propped against the cream-colored wall beneath a red smear. Grendel was howling in despair. The rest of my neighbors were easing back into their own homes, pulling the doors not quite shut as they spotted the patrolmen.

". . . ambulance, damn it," Quinton shouted back at the policemen.

The one cop reholstered his gun and got down beside Rick and Quinton, calling for a medic on his radio. The other took a fast survey of the hallway and open doors, making sure the place was safe before he also holstered his piece. That was the one who spotted me and came back to run me off.

I refused to leave. “That’s my neighbor. And the other one’s my boyfriend. I live in the unit with the open door.”

“Looks like someone—maybe your boyfriend—has gone and shot your neighbor.”

“Ask him.” I wanted to cry from tiredness and anger, but I didn’t give in, even though it might have bought some sympathy from the cop.

The cop left me with a warning to stay where I was this time and went over to his partner. They conferred and then the suspicious one spoke to Quinton. I saw him shake his head.

Another siren wailed and curdled to silence outside. The Medic One crew rattled up the stairs a few moments later with trauma bags and shoved everyone else aside to get to Rick. Grendel snapped and growled, not wanting to let them near his master. Rick muttered something and Quinton called the dog to him. Quinton and the dog made their way to me and we slumped down against the wall beside my gaping door.

I tried to form a question, but all that made it out was “What—?”

Quinton shook his head. “Those guys shot him when Grendel tried to jump them. I think they meant to kill the dog, but they were lousy shots. One got Rick in the arm, one in the leg. He’ll be all right, I think.”

So we weren’t going to talk about vampires with guns while the police were there. I nodded. I didn’t have enough energy left to try to make sense of any of it. We sat and looked stunned, gave our names to the cops—or rather Quinton gave our names of record when asked—and staggered into my condo once Rick was removed to the hospital and the rest of the scene was settled for the night.

The night had gone badly from the moment I’d touched down. Filling each other in on what had happened since I left for England and over the past four hours was vital. We needed to figure out what was going on and what we collectively and separately knew, but I wasn’t coherent enough right then. Quinton and I put all meaningful discussion on the back burner for the night, although neither of us was happy with that. We still had a lot to do.

Quinton dealt with the dog while I moved the ferret's cage into the bedroom. Not that Grendel is destructive; he's just dangerously curious. And we both threw a few necessities into bags and packed up anything we might need if we had to bug out. Quinton—living as he did—was better prepared than I was, but I at least needed very little that wasn't already in the bags I always kept in the back of my truck.

By the time we were done, I barely had the energy to shower. Lucky for me, Quinton was willing to help with the soaping up and so on. He was sweet to me—sweeter than I deserved, perhaps, but I was grateful he was there, as always. As much as I tried to go it alone, I knew I was better with Quinton than without him. We were good together, and not just at the horizontal bop. It was nice to have someone to give up to once in a while, to show your weaknesses and not fear injury. It frightened me a little: Weakness and dependence are dangerous. I worried that he might be hurt by my need, by my relying on him, hurt the way Christelle had been. She'd worked for my dead father and for her loyalty and proximity had come to some still unknown, but probably horrible, end. Thinking of it, I fought an impulse to cry, feeling it in my throat like a lump of clay that even the soothing touch of hot water and soap had difficulty washing away.

We got into bed about one a.m. while Grendel snored outside the bedroom door. Quinton would have liked to do something a bit more athletic than just sleep, but my energy was shot, and we curled together like exhausted puppies. I sank into a dreamless torpor as he pulled me tight against his body. The snowfall-flutter of moths under the streetlamp outside was the last thing I saw as my eyelids closed and the world fell away at last.

Too few hours further into the morning, Detective Rey Solis rang through from the front door until I couldn't ignore it any longer. I cursed the dogged policeman and his sunrise-loving ways. At this rate, I thought, I might get some decent sleep sometime after Satan opened an ice skating rink.

I'm sure I looked like something that had been extracted

from under a thorny bush when I answered my door in dirty jeans, a Noir City Film Festival T-shirt, and bare feet. Grendel the pit bull completed the ensemble, gluing himself to my leg and staring at the detective as if measuring him for a side order of fries.

I glanced at Solis from between puffy eyelids. The man isn't very tall or very wide, and he looks like he's made of gouged and pitted leather, but he projects a quiet solidity that gets a lot of suspects talking just to fill the silence and get out from under those unblinking black eyes. I'd have liked to wait him out on principle, but I didn't have the patience. "Don't say Rick died."

"No. Your neighbor is doing well this morning. He requests that you look after his dog."

I pointed at Grendel. "Got it. And Rick's all right?"

"Yes. He should be released tomorrow."

"So what . . . you got demoted?"

"Eh? No."

"Then what brings a detective from Homicide to my door if the guy who got shot is fine?"

Solis made a small shrug, his round, impassive face remaining blank while his close-clinging corona of energy flickered yellow and gold. "Courtesy call."

"Bull."

"May I come in?"

The living room gave ample evidence that something was up, piled as it was with bug-out bags and Quinton's electronic and computer gear. I didn't want Solis to start speculating but I didn't want to have a conversation about what had gone down the night before while standing in the hallway. I didn't want him to catch sight of Quinton either, whom he had known as Reggie Lassiter ever since our run-in with a monster on Foster Island. Complex as the situation already was, I wanted to avoid any additional conversational land mines, like . . . "Why are you still hanging out with that guy from the marsh?" or "Seen any monsters lately?" No matter what I did, this was not going to go well. . . .

I made up my mind and stepped back to let him walk past me. "Sorry about the mess. I just got back from a business trip last night and I haven't put anything away except for shoving stuff the dog might eat into the closet."

Solis grunted. "Ah. Where had you gone?"

"London."

The detective looked at the pile of electronic equipment on my dining table. Then he shifted his gaze over the rest of the room. "How long were you there?"

"About five days. A week with the flight time. Why the cross-examination?"

"Only curious."

"No, you aren't."

He shook his head and shrugged. "You are, again, in the center of a most curious circumstance."

"My neighbor got shot by some thugs. That's nothing to do with me."

"They were knocking on your door."

My turn to shrug. "I wasn't here. I came in with the first responders."

"Your . . . roommate—"

"House sitter," I corrected.

Solis shrugged. "Your house sitter was here. Could this have been connected to him?"

"No."

"You're very confident." I didn't think he meant that as a compliment. "And where is Mr. Lassiter?"

"At work."

"Mr. Lassiter is unemployed."

So Solis was still suspicious about the whole incident and everyone connected to it. He could worry that bone all he wanted; it wouldn't get him anywhere on this case and the other was no longer his to pry into. There might be hell to pay for it another day, but not today.

I just smiled back at him and went into the kitchen to start some coffee. "You are a nosy bastard, Solis."

"I am concerned."

"Why? Probably just some wannabe gangbangers raising Cain. It's the sort of thing that used to happen all the time around here. And how is a nonfatal shooting in Southwest district the concern of Homicide?" The coffee machine made burbling noises as I turned back around to look at Solis. I leaned on the counter and waited for his reply.

"There is a pattern of crimes recently that have drawn our attention. This incident, though not fatal, fits into that pattern. And there is you."

"Me? How? I know you seem to think everything weird in Seattle—"

He cut me off. "No. I do not think it. It is a fact. When cases go strange, you are in the thick of it."

I poured myself a cup of coffee. "That's a bit much."

"Do you think so?" He started ticking things off on his fingers. "In the matter of Mark Lupoldi, at the end I find you and his killer—a young man gone completely mad—in a place neither of you should have been. In the matter of the homeless deaths last year, wherever I turn, there you are, and again, it is you who brings the killer to us—just as the case is classified by the government." The energy around his head and body began to jump and form spikes of frustrated orange and burning yellow as he continued. "There is the matter of the museum that burned down; and the man who assaulted you two years ago; and the business with the sunken ship, and of the poisoned child, and the lost brooch. . . . Oh yes, there is also the disappearance of Edward Kammerling, whom you had gone to see just before this incident last night. Shall I continue?"

"That's quite a catalog." I thought about what he'd said and a few of the items took me by surprise: I didn't know he'd made any connection between me and the museum fire, and what had happened to the guy who'd killed me? He seemed to think I knew, but I'd never followed up on that—I'd been a little busy. But funny that it should come up again since Alice had mentioned him to me in London. I would have to find out. . . .

"Hardly complete."

I made a face and offered him a cup of coffee. This might take longer than I'd thought; might as well keep him happy—or at least confined to the kitchen.

Solis accepted the mug I held out. He stared at me over the rim as he sipped, waiting for my reaction to his recitation.

I heaved a long breath. "Look, Solis, you know my cases get strange sometimes. It's not as if you haven't benefited from that. I turn over cases that go hot—like the poisoning case. I play fair with you and the department." Well, as much as I could. "If you think I've done something criminal, find evidence and arrest me. I don't know what you're talking about on some of those points of yours. The rest is nothing but coincidence and bad luck. Kammerling hired me for the London job. I just got back and was trying to check in. I didn't even know he was missing. And what was that about the guy who assaulted me? I haven't had any contact with him."

"You didn't know Todd Simondson came out on parole last week?"

"Why would I? The parole board doesn't have to call me in—it was a plea bargain. Time served, we're done."

"So you did not know he died two days ago, either?"

That startled me and I spilled a bit of coffee on the counter as I twitched in surprise. "What? No. Of what?" I didn't like the sound of that. . . .

"Most mysterious circumstances . . ."

"That's not a cause."

He shrugged.

"Don't say you suspect me. . . ."

"It fits."

"Not unless you believe in bilocation. Two days ago, I was on a nonstop flight from London to New York, and then on the connection from JFK to Sea-Tac. I spent fourteen hours in transit and I have boarding passes that prove it."

"Do you?"

"Yes!" I stomped into the living room and dug my passport and airline folder from my bag and brought them back to him. I shoved the lot into his hand. "Unless you think I have a secret identity and had someone else fly under my name while I snuck back into the country and murdered the poor bastard. But I'm sure the security cameras at Sea-Tac have tape from the Customs area that you could check if you don't choose to believe me."

He studied the papers, his aura drawing in but getting no less orange and frustrated. He huffed and handed the pages back to me.

"Thank you for not arresting me." Maybe I was a little snippy as I said it, but damn. . . . "So what happened to Simondson? And don't stonewall—you owe me."

"Looked like a hit-and-run," he admitted. "Maybe a beating."

"'Looked like'? Was it or wasn't it?"

"No one knows. No witnesses. The body was already in rigor when found."

That struck me odd: Solis wasn't the sort to reduce a victim to a mere corpse and dismiss it. "Where did this happen?" I peered at him, looking for a change in his energy that might give me a clue what he thought. Or what he was fishing for.

"He was discovered at the old brewery buildings in Georgetown—the demolished end."

I noticed Solis didn't claim the death itself had happened on the same site, but all I said was, "Hardly seems like his sort of neighborhood." The man had been white collar all the way; even the fraud I caught him at that led to his murderous rage was genteel stuff.

Georgetown—a former independent city of farmers and brewers that had been eaten up by the combined appetites of Boeing and the City of Seattle—was mostly industrial with a few isolated houses and clusters of shops among the warehouses, light manufacturing, and so on. It lay sandwiched between I-5 as it cut below the cliff of Beacon Hill on the east, and the mucky, muddy waters of the Duwamish River a few blocks away on the west. Cases I'd had down there had been connected to industrial accidents, theft, and that sort of thing. The area had made a stab at bohemian trendiness a while back when most of the old brewery and cold storage buildings had been converted into offices and studio space for artists, but that attempt had centered on the streets near the old brewery and hadn't penetrated much farther. The brewery area housed a lot of funk in a few square blocks, not to mention a metal club named Nine-pound Hammer. It wasn't the kind of business neighborhood in which I'd expect to find a former estate embezzler with anger management problems hanging out.

The bare dozen blocks of houses still standing in Georgetown were mostly farther south, right across the road from the airfield—single-family structures from the first third of the twentieth century being renovated by hopeful yuppies who were not likely to take in guests from the parole board. Up by the old brewery where Simondson's body had been found, only two blocks of old wooden houses stood in domestic isolation west of the freeway off-ramp, and I doubted most of them would have suited his taste.

Solis continued. "He was staying at a cheap motel near the airport." The coincidence that I'd been in the area just hours after the man's death was disturbing: Georgetown lies eight miles due north of the airport on the route to Seattle. The cheapest airport hotels with weekly rates were mostly on the north end of International Boulevard, where it passed a cemetery and approached the new light rail station next to the freeway. Neither was the sort of place in which Simondson would have willingly spent time before his incarceration, and I couldn't imagine Boeing hiring him on straight from jail. Georgetown was a bit rough but hardly Blood Alley, so any nonindustrial death there was remarkable. I didn't buy the coincidence any more than Solis did and the timing was more suspicious than he knew.

About four days ago in London I'd been told that my assailant had been seduced and manipulated to kill me. The next night, I took out the vampire who'd done it and wrecked Wygan's plans for London and myself. Even vampires can use a telephone or e-mail, so one of the asetem in London had let their Pharaohn know things had gone bad and how. I could guess which white-skinned monstrosity that had been. I'd tied off my own loose ends in London, Wygan had tied off some of his here, and all the oddities of timing were no more coincidence than I was a pastry chef. Wygan didn't want me to talk to the man who'd killed me. Too bad for him that I wasn't inclined to be pushed any further. I'd just have to hunt down the guy's ghost instead.

"What's the autopsy say?" I asked, reclaiming my coffee cup.

"No report yet."

"You think the body might have been dumped?" Because if it wasn't, what had brought Simondson—middle-aged and conservative—into Seattle's post-grunge bohemia in the first place?

Solis shrugged. "Perhaps. I may not have time to follow up until the report is in. While you have been gone, the homicide rate doubled."

"You can't blame that on me."

"Not legally. Not logically. But it feels right."

"Gosh, thanks. Now I'm home, it might go back down." But I wasn't betting on it.

Solis didn't seem inclined to bet that way either, but he didn't say anything. He took my flippant attitude and pointed look as a hint that I wanted him to go away since he couldn't arrest me. He put down his mug and walked to the door without my having to push him.

"You shall let me know what you discover."

"Of course. And you won't try to arrest me for every weird occurrence in King County."

He raised his eyebrows as if I shouldn't count on that. "Stay out of trouble. Or at least off my case load."

"I don't intend to land on your desk or Fishkiller's slab, thanks."

"Ah, but the best of intentions . . ." Solis said, waggling his hand dismissively as he strode out into the hall and to the elevator without looking back.

I frowned after him as I retreated inside and locked the door, thinking that if I were Wygan, I'd have put my pet security guy on the job of tidying up: It kept him too busy to wonder what the boss was up to, and Goodall was strong, ruthless, and smart enough to know the moves without the disadvantages of the usual vampire time limits during summer hours. It also had that classy "I'm one step ahead of you" touch that's so endearing when you deal with psychotics and megalomaniacs.

Now that I'd had coffee, it was unlikely I'd fall back asleep for a few hours. As long as I was up, I thought I should feed Grendel and take him for a walk before he decorated the kitchen floor. I also thought I'd let Quinton get a little more sleep—at least one of us should, and he could play doorman and guard later so I could catch up on the doings in the land of Nod, myself. Grendel was more interested in the food. I put on a jacket against the exterior chill as he devoured his breakfast.

I'd never had a dog of my own as a kid—no pets at all in fact after the disaster of my mother's first post-Dad boyfriend and his dopey Labradors. It hadn't occurred to me, until I moved in next to Rick, that happy pit bulls, by nature, are just as playful and silly as any other well-trained dog. Grendel didn't look too scary most of the time, grinning and wagging and doing the play-with-me bow. But in defensive mode, he was a terrifying bundle of crushing teeth and hard muscle. That's what the asete and his plain-vanilla vampire buddy must have seen last night when Rick came out into the hall: eighty pounds of pissed-off pit bull. But they hadn't dominated the dog or frightened it. They'd shot at it. And they were pretty lousy shots—not that I was surprised about that.

Vampires think of themselves as top predator and they aren't afraid of much at night, not even mean dogs. They generally don't carry weapons since they think they don't need them. But the specimens in the hall had been packing guns. That seemed kind of odd to me. I thought about it as I walked Grendel twice around the water tower green space, stopping several times while he left various doggy messages.

The vampires had come to my door. They hadn't just wanted in: they wanted to raise a ruckus. They didn't come with just their natural weapons, so they hadn't come with the intention of killing— No. Wait.

They *had* come to kill me. But it would have to be the right kind of kill since the whole point of pushing me close to death was to bend me into the Grey form Wygan needed for whatever plan he had in mind. And the more trouble the whole scene caused, the more likely I was to be forced out of my home if they weren't entirely successful. Wygan wouldn't want them to bite me, just in case someone was a little too thirsty. He couldn't risk my not being in his control by being blood-tied to another vampire—if that was even possible. It also wouldn't be difficult to explain the wounds on any bystanders who caught a bullet, unlike the classic broken necks and gouged throats of the usual vampire victim.

Solis had said violence and homicide were up, that the crimes fit a pattern, but he hadn't said exsanguinated bodies or unexplainable wounds were part of it—Simondson had looked like a hit-and-run but I was pretty sure he was a vampire victim one way or another. The pattern of last night's crime looked like thugs with guns who'd left some odd piles of human ash scattered around. That might be strange or creepy, but from the reports, the police were already thinking of the uptick in violence as weird gang crime with some bizarre ritual or marker. Witnesses wouldn't be too eager to say they'd seen something as crazy as one apparent gangbanger roasting another into a pile of ash in the space of a few seconds. That's nuthouse talk, and vampires are damned good at leaving only foggy memories in the minds of survivors. If anyone had been talking, they'd only say what the vampires wanted them to say—or something so crackpot the cops wouldn't pay attention. The SPD gang unit was still based in West Seattle, even after the biggest gang problem was cleared out by the demolition of the projects. If they had related crimes downtown, they'd be working with Solis or one of his colleagues, which explained the detective's swift appearance. Quinton had mentioned vampires making trouble downtown, including some shootings, while I was in London, but that had been centered on the clubs and bars around Belltown and the financial core—the vampire neutral zones where faction fighting was supposed to stay off the streets and not attract the attention of the sheep. But if it was part of the pattern Solis had noted, that would connect last night's mess to his cases and to me by way of Simondson, the dead guy.

The possibility of a wider pattern explained another curiosity: the vampire who'd cooked another vampire with something very much like one of Quinton's stunners—probably the same thing I'd done to the vampire last night. That first incident must have been a test run. Once the vampires with the stun sticks knew what effect they had on others of their kind, they could take out their rivals in a more public place than usual—someplace most vampires felt safe—so long as they sprayed a little lead around to cover the scene and make it look like a gang war. It also created panic and fear—emotions that the asetem fed on. Edward had kept his position partially by leaving Quinton alone so no one would discover he was as vulnerable to electrical disruption of his nervous system as the rest of the blood-sucking pack. Except that asetem weren't as susceptible, according to Quinton, and they weren't afraid of carrying the stunners around either. I'd just gotten lucky with the one I'd zapped the night before.

There lay an unhappy thought: vampires who weren't as easy to knock down or kill as the usual kind—which wasn't a waltz with Fred Astaire to begin with—even if they were a bit slower. And they had weapons to take down their vampire opponents as well as any human in the way without having to close to biting range. I hate it when the monsters get clever. Damn Wygan.

Grendel and I headed back to the condo as I kept thinking. If I were Wygan, I'd keep the pressure on and try to drive me out of my safe zone so he'd have a better chance to catch me and then do whatever he needed to do to me at his leisure. He'd want to keep me off-balance and tired so I'd keep on making mistakes like the ones I'd made with Goodall. On the street alone I was vulnerable; I had a much better idea of what I was and what I could do than ever before, but I still didn't know enough about what was coming next. I quickened my pace and Grendel loped beside me with a huge doggy grin all over his face. Wygan knew I'd come to him eventually: He had my dad's ghost captive; he'd taken my employer, too; and he'd teased me with information he knew I couldn't resist pursuing and then killed off the man who had some of it—assuming Simondson did. But Wygan hadn't tried to isolate me, hadn't gone after Quinton. . . .

The thought galvanized me. The grid of power seemed to hum louder and with a discordant note as the shape of the world blazed for an instant, too bright. I burst into a full run, Grendel loping happily beside me as I pounded down the hill toward my place with the conviction that all was not well at home.

THREE

Smoke. I smelled it before I got there, before I saw the dark wisps coiling into the sky. The fire alarm in the building was shrieking loud enough to be heard on the street even over Grendel's excited barking. A guy with a garden hose was already trying to douse the burning shrub under my balcony, but not all the smoke was coming from the landscaping. I cursed the security door and wrestled my way through it, tugging the dog behind me as he tried to go after the stream of water from the hose.

We galloped up the stairs, my chest tight from the whiff of burning and anxiety that made a high metallic ringing in my ears. It almost sounded like distant fairy voices screaming.

From the landing, I saw my door engulfed in yellow flames sprouting from a bundle of black cloth stuffed against the bottom. Someone had added two fresh, bloody handprints to the stain left on the wall the night before. Nice. As I crouched and ran forward, the bundle of burning cloth tipped away from the door, propelled by the tip of a yardstick poking out through the gap between the door and the threshold. I ordered Grendel to sit and stay while I yanked off my jacket and started beating the flames out.

Quinton ducked through the open doorway with the fire extinguisher from my kitchen and killed the flames in a powdery stream of chemicals. The oily wad of rags smoldered a bit, but didn't reignite.

Reaching up with the yardstick, Quinton poked the

alarm's reset button. There was still one squalling from inside my condo, but as we stood in the hall it wound down and stopped with a sad whine.

"You all right?" he asked, looking me over.

I stooped to pick up my ruined jacket. It was a good thing I'd bought another one in London, since I seem to be death on outerwear. "Fine. But we're going to have to get out of here."

Quinton looked around the hall, silent now as the neighbors were all off at work and the smoke had begun dissipating. "Yeah, I guess that wasn't too subtle."

I peered at him, not quite sure in my dopey sleep-deprived state if I'd understood him.

He poked the partially burned rags and gave the stains on the wall a significant look. "The goons are rattling your cage."

"And I need some quiet if I'm going to stay out of their hands. And keep you out of them, too."

He considered that before heading back into my condo. "You think they'll try to split us?"

I nodded and followed him inside. "It's in their best interest to keep me isolated and off-balance, even to grab whatever leverage they can get."

"We need to talk."

"We do. But not here. They'll keep coming at us so long as we're someplace they can find us."

"You think so?"

I nodded, feeling dizzy from the motion. At least my ears had stopped ringing and Grendel was acting subdued, sticking close to us but not begging for attention. The smoke seemed to have damped his spirits as much as it had ours.

Quinton took my steel wastebasket and swept up the mess in the hall as I started pulling out the bags and the ferret's traveling kit. The living room reeked of smoke.

As I put the necessary pet supplies together, Quinton returned and poked at some of his equipment. "Slag," he muttered.

"Huh?"

"This stuff near the window. The smoke got in it. Most of it's kacked. Including my Grey detector. Well. At least that's something less to carry." He sighed. "What's the plan, then, supergirl?"

"Bug out, find a safe place, get some sleep. Then go after them while they think they have us on the run."

"Risky. What if they grab you? I mean . . . they do intend to grab you, don't they?"

I shrugged. "Yeah. But I don't plan to give them any more chances. I'm making mistakes, but if I can get some sleep before they can catch up to us, get some information, then I may have the upper hand. If I move fast."

Quinton nodded, starting to smile. "We'll attack them first—gives us the options to act while they only have the option to *react*. I definitely like that scenario. Much better than the alternative." He picked up a pair of bags and slung them up onto his shoulders.

He threw a handful of objects into another bag and zipped it up while I snatched my one bag and the animal kit. I went back to the bedroom to fetch the ferret and returned to see Quinton grabbing the handles on his last bag with one hand and Grendel's leash with the other.

"What are we going to do with the dog?" he asked.

"Ben and Mara have a yard . . . and I want to talk to them anyway." They'd been my first instructors in dealing with the Grey, and their home would be more than just a place to hide; I was pretty sure I would need their knowledge and help before this was done.

Quinton looked thoughtful. "Wygan must know you're friends with them. And their place is close to the broadcast towers."

"It's the best I can come up with. We'll just have to be careful."

"It's worth a try." Quinton twitched the dog's leash and Grendel trotted out like he'd been Quinton's pet all his life. Dogs seemed to do that for him; I guess they knew he loved them.

We secured the condo and bundled our gear downstairs and into the truck. I only wished I'd had the energy to move it into the garage the previous night so it was less obvious to any watchers that we were leaving, but that couldn't be helped. If we grew a tail, we'd lose it, and there wasn't anything in terms of electronic tracking they could do that Quinton couldn't defeat.

We drove away from my building and I wondered if I'd ever see it again.

FOUR

It took more than forty minutes to get to the Danzigers' house on Queen Anne Hill. We had to shake off a tail and check the truck for tracking devices once that was done. Then we were able to continue, but we knew we'd have to check for anyone watching their house. I didn't know how many resources Wygan had to throw at surveillance and for causing me trouble, but I assumed it was plenty. I didn't want to draw his attention to the Danzigers if it wasn't there already. Mara was good at protecting the house with her magic, but the whole family couldn't just stay home for as long as it took me to wreck Wygan's plans.

Total destruction was my goal. Even in my bleary, sleepless state, my mind was clear on that. Whatever his plans were, the consequences wouldn't be pleasant for anyone and I couldn't let him win.

We both checked the area for watchers, Quinton by eye and scanner, me sinking into the Grey and looking for signs of energy out of place, ghosts, or the ashen signature of those who consorted with vampires. I found one harsh sigil on the sidewalk just outside the reach of Mara's own protective spells. I left it intact so as not to alert its caster and circled around through the silver mist and ghost light of the Grey to the back of the house. The alley had a few shreds of deep-red blood magic, hot with anger, festooned across the back gate. It was amateur work, done in a hurry and easy to bypass. I wished I could show it to Mara and see what she thought, but I'd have to unmake the nasty little screamer spells to get past them. Whoever had set them hadn't bothered—or hadn't known how—to attach them to the grid so they would let him know if they were taken apart. They only went off if tripped. I'd just have to not trip them.

I fetched Quinton to watch my back while I went deeper into the Grey to dismantle the spell. I'd taken Grey things apart before; spells were generally out of my league, but these were rudimentary things and I didn't have to work too hard to sort out the one thread of magic that held the things together. I grabbed on to the kernel of the thing in the Grey, feeling the muttering of the grid and the hot/cold burn of it through my bones as I did so, and pulled with an even, firm pressure. The fury of the spell ripped along my nerves like a spray of decompressed Freon, and the strands of magic fell apart. It wasn't too bad, but I stumbled a little as I reemerged back into the normal world.

Quinton caught me. "You all right?"

"Yes." I tried to brush him aside, but he wasn't having any. "We can go in now."

"Maybe we should catch our breath first. You look a little . . . pale."

I might have looked something worse than pale, like maybe not quite solid. Maybe it was just fatigue, but that worried me a little. I only got ghostly when I was very close to the Grey, and here I believed I was all the way out. I brushed the thought aside and let myself through the gate to the Danzigers' backyard. The gate gleamed with a tracery of pure gold energy I recognized as part of Mara's magical perimeter. I guess it was used to me after all this time since it didn't do anything as we stepped through its complex lattice. I heard it whispering pleasing lullabies as we passed.

I'd never seen the back of the Danzigers' house before; I'd always kept to the interior rooms. The big pale-blue house had a wide, slightly wild back garden, a little tamer than the tumbling wilderness in front, overlooked by a full-width screen porch that overhung the deep stone foundation. The yard was quiet, though we could hear some domestic noises from the house. Quinton tied Grendel to a tree that supported a half-built play platform and we finished the trek across the yard alone.

Mara was standing just inside the screen door when we climbed the back stairs. "Good morning to y'both. Have y'brought us a dog, then?" I'd never been able to read Mara's energy, and today her face was just as difficult. She wasn't ready to show me what she thought of our appearance at her door. Our friendship had been a little cooler since I'd nearly gotten her husband eaten by a monster, even if it had been more than a year ago.

"Only temporarily," I replied. I wasn't surprised she'd known we were coming. Mara is a witch, after all, and her spells on the house were more sophisticated than they looked.

She opened the door to let us pass. "Did y'take down that wretched blood spell on the garden gate? I thought to do it in a bit, but I wanted to see who'd be coming along to trip it. Not surprised as it's you."

I entered the house, hearing the muttering of the grid fade to a distant water babble. The magical calm inside eased an unsuspected tension from my shoulders and I took a deep breath of the quiet. "Good guess."

She scoffed. "Hardly much of one: You're the only person we know who consorts with vampires."

"So you saw them cast the spells?"

"No, but I've developed a nose for 'em." She looked at Quinton and cracked her blinding, infectious grin. "And how is it with you? Are y'keeping herself here out of trouble?"

"Don't seem to be."

"Ah. I see. Well, come inside. I've some coffee and scones on—if y'can get them before Brian."

Brian, the Danzigers' three-year-old son, was scaling a chair beside the long kitchen counter as we entered. His mother snuck up and tapped him on the shoulder. "And what is it you're playing at? Hm?" she asked as he jumped in surprise.

Brian turned to face her and bit his lower lip, his eyes huge, shifting side to side as he tried to come up with an excuse. "I sawed a mouse."

Mara didn't look convinced. "You *saw* a mouse on the counter?"

Brian nodded with vigor and tried to look sincere. "Yes, Mama. Big mouse. It was gonna take the scones." Brian's *s*'s came out a bit lispy through a gap between his front teeth.

"Oh, I see. A very large, black-haired mouse, I suppose. And was this very large mouse named Brian, by chance?"

"Umm . . . no. . . ."

Mara raised her eyebrows and fixed a stern look on her son. Brian deflated and looked at the ground with a sigh. I gave him another two years to figure out that his mother really did know everything—at least everything he didn't want her to. There was no longer a ghost in the house, spying on every move, but that didn't mean there weren't other ways for Mara to get information.

Mara straightened up and took a small biscuitlike thing off a plate, wrapped it in a paper towel, and handed it to Brian. "You may have one scone—just one, mind. You may take it out to the back garden to eat it and then y'can play with the dog."

Brian's face lit up. "Did we get a puppy?"

"Mara . . ." I started. "Are you sure . . . ?"

She gave me an arch look. "Now y'wouldn't be bringing us a vicious killer dog, would you?"

"No. . . ."

"Then we've nothing to fear."

I still wasn't sure sending Brian out to play with Grendel unsupervised was a good idea. The boy was rambunctious and I didn't know how the dog would react without someone he already knew around to cue him. I saw Mara whisper something over Brian's head and draw a quick shape over him with her finger.

The charm dissolved into a rain of tiny blue stars that seemed to stick to him as Brian turned and charged for the back door, shouting, "Hi, Harper! I'm gonna see the doggie!"

"No scone for the dog!" Mara called after him. Then she looked a bit worried. "I suppose he'll be all right a moment. . . ."

Quinton glanced at me. "Grendel doesn't stand a chance," he muttered. "I'm betting on the kid."

Mara stuck her head out the kitchen doorway and called

out to her husband. "Ben! 'Tis Harper and Quinton. Come down, can you?"

We could hear him clumping down the stairs from the attic, the old wooden steps musical and echoing under his tread.

A shriek came from the backyard. Quinton, Mara, and I bolted back out to the screen porch and stared out at the yard. I don't know about them, but I figured Grendel—the appetite on legs—had eaten Brian by now. But no: The boy was rolling around on the ground all right, but the dog was prancing about, wagging his whole butt in the air as Brian guffawed in whoops and gales like the maniac version of his mother's own laughter.

Brian rolled onto his belly and, as we stared, Grendel trotted over and shoved him onto his back again, licking his face and nuzzling at him. Brian pulled himself up with his hands locked around the dog's powerful neck and Grendel just stood there, grinning. Grendel received a lot of pats and scritches that rendered the dog a wiggling mass of glee.

"Oh, yeah, the dog's a goner," Quinton murmured in my ear as Brian and Grendel started chasing each other back and forth across the yard.

"Hey, when'd we get a hellhound?" Ben Danziger asked from behind us. We all turned around—perfect synchrony that would have made Balanchine proud—and stared at him as he stood in the doorway from the kitchen and gazed over our heads at the yard beyond the screen. "Well, it doesn't have three heads, so it can't be Cerberus," he added.

"That's my neighbor's dog, Grendel," I said. "And no, he does not have a cat named Beowulf."

Ben broke out laughing and almost fell, stumbling on the threshold plate of the doorway.

"We're dog-sitting. My neighbor . . . got shot last night."

Ben's laughter cut off short and Mara looked alarmed.

"He'll be OK," I assured them, "but he can't look after the dog for a while. And since it's my fault he got shot—"

Quinton cut me off. "No, it isn't. They were trying to kill the dog and Rick was just in the wrong place. That's not your fault."

"I told him to take the dog to the door."

"You didn't tell him to let it off the leash."

Mara made sharp cutting gestures at us. "Stop it, the both of ya. I assume you'd not be here, arguing in my home, without a good reason. So. Whyn't ya sit down and start tellin' it, soon's I've brought out a bit of food? I'll not be listenin' to such bickerin' before breakfast." She shooed us into wicker chairs around a wooden table and dragged Ben with her back inside to fetch and carry. Quinton and I kept eyes on Brian and the dog, but they only continued to play as if we weren't there.

I refused coffee once it was offered, which got me some raised eyebrows, but I'd already had more caffeine than I needed if I was going to get any sleep soon. I played with a couple of the small biscuitlike scones Mara put in front of me along with a glass of water. It wasn't that I didn't want to tell the story—that was a big part of the reason we'd come—but I needed to put my thoughts in order before I started in. Quinton wouldn't tell the tale for me, even if he'd known it all. It was an insane story, if you considered it. It was only because it had all built up over time, a bit here and there, that I could believe it myself.

"There's a bit of a problem at my place and . . . I hoped we could presume on your hospitality for a day or two," I started, keeping my voice low so as not to alarm Brian. "I haven't had a lot of sleep lately and my condo isn't safe for us to stay in right now. We need someplace secure to catch up and do some planning until things get better. I can't imagine any place safer from Grey things and I don't think we led any here. The spell on the back gate didn't get a chance to alert its caster when I dismantled it, so no one should be coming to check, either."

Mara made a face. "So things are bad, then."

"If the normal level of 'bad' is something like 'oh darn, we've blown up the house,' this bad comes with its own small but unattractive mushroom cloud. I'm kind of behind on the news in Seattle since I've been out of town, but a little Colombian birdie came by this morning to tell me that the homicide rate in town doubled in the past two weeks and I hear there's been a lot of purported gang activity downtown, which probably isn't really gangs. Our favorite vampire king, Edward, has been kidnapped. And it all comes together in some unpleasant plan with me as the bow on the package."

Ben scowled. "I'm sorry—I think I'm missing something. Is this related to the ghost you were trying to find, the one you called us about a couple of weeks ago?"

I nodded, keeping my gaze on the plate in front of me. "That was my dad."

"Your da?" Mara questioned. "I thought he died when you were small."

"It turns out," I said, feeling something cold and miserable knot up in my gut, "that he blew his brains out. I didn't know this. I thought it was an accident. I was twelve. But . . . well . . ." I stopped talking. This wasn't going well at all: I felt like crying. Just tired, I told myself. Just too damned tired.

I lifted my head. They were all watching me, and you'd think after more than a decade of professional dance and almost as much in surveillance and snooping, I'd shrug it off, but this time I froze.

Quinton pushed his knee up against mine under the table and dropped his near hand to rest, still and warm, on my leg. "Maybe you should start with the phone call," he suggested.

The Danzigers huddled closer to the table and leaned in as if I were about to tell a ghost story around the campfire. In a way, I suppose I was.

I shifted my gaze away from them, unhappy about this necessity, and started in. "All right. About three weeks ago I got a phone call from a dead boyfriend. He said things weren't what I thought they were and that there were . . . things lying in wait for me. Since he died in Los Angeles eight years ago, I thought that might be the place to start looking. It seemed to me that whatever he was talking about must be related to my past—and to my abilities as a Greywalker—since I couldn't imagine anything else a dead guy might think I needed to be warned about. So I went."

I glanced around to see how they were reacting. Quinton knew this part, but the Danzigers didn't. Mara looked wary, her head half turned so she regarded me sideways with narrowed eyes. Ben just looked intrigued. I stifled a yawn and went on.

"I thought I should visit my mother and see if she had any ideas—though of course she doesn't know about the . . . paranormal connection. A lot of what she revealed isn't relevant, but she is the one who told me my father hadn't died in an accident, as I'd believed, but had shot himself."

Mara flinched back into her seat, catching a sharp breath through her nose. She looked out into the yard, watching her son a moment before she spoke. "Had she any inkling why he did it?"

"That's the creepy part. My mother claimed he was depressed, crazy, and having an affair with his receptionist. She said he'd been kind of crazy for a long time and finally, he just . . . lost it. But she let me look through his things, including his old diaries, and . . . at first I thought he might just be nuts, too—those diaries are pretty freaky." I didn't say his suicide note had been addressed to me; that just seemed too personal and gruesome, even for this group, and especially with three-year-old Brian playing nearby. "It was obvious that he had some kind of contact with the Grey, although he didn't understand what it was or what was going on. It was upsetting him even before Wygan started prodding—"

Ben cut in, staring. "Wait a minute. Wygan? The DJ on Radio Freeform?"

I nodded, catching each pair of eyes in turn. "Vampire. He's the one who stuck the knot of Grey into my chest two years ago. You remember."

Mara and Ben nodded, recalling, I imagined, the long, uncomfortable session in their kitchen when Mara had tried to untie it from me. Quinton looked quizzical. It wasn't a point of my history I'd discussed with him since we hadn't been close at the time. I caught his eye and gave a minuscule shake of the head. I'd explain it to him later. He returned a quick, reassuring smile.

Ben was scowling. "You mean, right up the hill . . . ?" I knew he was thinking of the proximity of the broadcast towers on the crown of Queen Anne, just about fifty feet straight up and a hundred yards over from where we sat. I caught his gaze also creeping toward his son.

I nodded. "Yes. But he's not the same type of vampire as Edward and his bunch. He's the Pharaohn-ankh-astet."

"What?" Mara let out a startled squawk.

Ben was appalled. "Asetem? Here? But . . ."

"What? They shouldn't be in the New World, or something?" I asked.

"Well, basically, yes. I mean . . . at least according to legends, they're rare and very clannish. Why would they be here?"

"Because I am."

FIVE

They all stared at me again and their collective expressions, ranging from confusion to disbelief, made me a little sick to my stomach. I hated this and wished I could just go to sleep and somehow dream it all away, never have to talk about it, never live through it again in speech or nightmares. Or at least be able to magically give them the skinny on the situation without having to think about it, sort and select relevant facts, shape it into coherent speech, and blurt it all out. Just the act of speaking made me weary and I wasn't sure I was making sense.

"I didn't know Wygan was any different from any other vampire," I explained. "I mean, I knew he was different, but I didn't think it was something like this. While I was in London—"

Mara shook her head. "London? When was that?"

"Last week. I just got back yesterday and I went to see Edward . . ." I realized I'd lost them all completely. The Danzigers didn't know I'd been in London or why and Quinton had no idea what the asetem-ankh-astet were. I'd told him to be careful of Wygan, but I hadn't had time to explain why. I shook my head, more to clear it of the muddle I was making than anything else. "Let me try this again." I was making a hash of this. . . .

The Danzigers nodded. "Yes, do," Mara requested.

I concentrated on her—it was easier than trying to keep my eyes on all three of my audience. "All right. My dad killed himself because he was a Greywalker—I didn't get this until I was in London, though I feel I should have figured it out earlier. He didn't know what was going on. He didn't have anyone like you to help him. He never did know what he was, but he did figure out that something unnatural was happening to him and that it was being *done to* him by someone. That someone was Wygan. It took a while for me to put it together and I didn't get all the pieces until I was in London and in some serious trouble. I'll get to that in a minute, but the important thing is that my dad wasn't really going crazy; he just wasn't handling exposure to the Grey well. When he figured out that Wygan—he called him the White Worm-man—was trying to force him to do something that was probably terrible, he killed himself so Wygan's plan would be ruined. Unfortunately, all he did was put things off. He thought he was protecting me, but what he did was put me in his place.

"Wygan has a long-range, overarching plan—I don't know what it is yet, but I'm pretty sure it's not good for anyone but Wygan. Anyhow, this plan of his requires a Greywalker with very specific powers. Wygan has figured out how to force that Greywalker to develop. It took him several tries. I got this information from one of his failed experiments, another Greywalker I met in London—a creepy son of a bitch named Marsden. Marsden wanted to get rid of me so the plan would collapse, but we ended up working together instead, and he explained a lot of this. That story's strange stuff and not entirely relevant, so I'd rather just let those details slide for now. That OK with you guys?"

I finally looked around at Quinton and Ben. Ben, naturally, seemed a little disappointed. Quinton had a grim expression, but he nodded. Mara's manner had slipped from a narrow, concentrated stare to wide-eyed horror. I took a couple of long breaths before I went on.

"So. My dad didn't know the whole plan initially and he didn't understand what was happening to him, but he knew he was changing, and to keep him in line, Wygan and his minions threatened him and his family. I'm pretty sure they killed his receptionist or gained some kind of magical hold over her so she'd spy for them or hurt my father in some way. Dad destroyed her—I met her ghost—and he killed himself so he wouldn't become a monster. That's what he thought was happening to him, that he was turning into some kind of monster. But taking himself out of the equation wasn't enough. I'm next in line and Wygan's been working on shaping me into the tool he wanted my dad to be. Every time I die a little, I change. So . . . he's been making sure I die. I'm still not quite what he wants yet, but he's going to try to gain control of me and kill me again because the final stage of his plan is now in motion."

Quinton and Ben both yelled over me, drowning me out as Mara frowned.

"What is he doing?" Ben demanded.

Quinton clutched my arm. "Kill you? What the hell—"

I wriggled out of his grip as I tried to wave Ben off. "Stop it. Stop it! I don't know!"

Mara sat back, making a thoughtful moue as I quieted the men. "Hm. Something that needs a special type of Greywalker. . . . Well, that can't be good." She got up and started twiddling with a pile of odds and ends on one of the unused chairs nearby, touching them absently as she thought. "So, your father was a Greywalker, you're a Greywalker, and the only way out is . . . to kill yourself? I can't say I like that." She turned back to study me, scowling with unhappy thoughts as she leaned against the back wall of the house. The protective magic wrapped around the building made a worried murmur.

"Actually, death won't get me out of it," I replied. "That's more like a . . . reset button of sorts. If I die in a way that doesn't destroy my brain or body, I come back, but each time I die there's a window of opportunity to push my powers as a Greywalker into a new shape, or to let them reshape themselves. Most of the time. According to Marsden, there's a limited number of times I can die and bounce back. At some point, I'll just stay dead. According to my mother, I died once when I was a teenager. I didn't remember it until, at my mother's house, I saw a photo of my cousin Jill. We drowned together one summer. I came back; Jill didn't. I don't know if Wygan engineered that or not, but while I was in London, I found out my death two years ago wasn't just a bit of bad luck either. Alice—you remember Alice?"

Mara nodded and I could see Quinton from the corner of my eye, mirroring her.

"Alice didn't die in the museum fire. Wygan got her out and kept her. . . ." I couldn't bring myself to describe the ghastly and extreme measures he'd taken to heal Alice and keep her alive until he needed her again. I shuddered in spite of myself. "She was working for him. He sent her to London earlier this year to disrupt some business of Edward's and lure me away from Seattle so Edward could be attacked and Wygan's plan could begin to move into its final phase—and no, I don't know why he needs Edward either. When I met Alice in London, she told me the man who killed me did it under her influence. I had every reason to believe her."

"Is she still out there, then?" Mara asked.

I took a couple more deep breaths before I answered, tamping down a sudden spike of nauseous memory. "No. I killed her. I dropped her head into some kind of magical hole and left the rest to rot. I don't feel bad about it: She helped kill me and she helped keep my dad a prisoner."

Mara shook her head, her coppery brows pinching together. "You've lost me. When was your father a prisoner?"

"He still is. Wygan has his ghost in some kind of magical . . . oubliette—sort of a one-way prison hole. Two birds with one stone: leverage against me if I refuse to do what he wants, and a chance to torment Dad for kicking over the traces in the first place. Wygan's like that: He carries grudges for a long time. This business with Edward seems to go back to something that happened between them in England two or three hundred years ago. When I called you guys from Los Angeles, I was trying to find my dad's ghost, but all I could get was the ghost of his receptionist and a big, fiery hole where Dad should have been and a really pissed-off guardian beast running around it whenever I got close."

"*The* Guardian Beast," Mara said in an absent manner, biting at her lower lip and staring into nothing.

"Pardon me?" I asked.

"If it's running around something like that at the edge of the Grey, it's not just any guardian beast; it's *the* Guardian Beast, protector of the Grey."

I felt my own eyebrows draw down as I peered at her. "I thought there were a lot of guardian beasts."

"In general, there are," Ben put in. "Lots of them. Lots of types of them, too, guarding all sorts of things. But as Mara said, there's just the one for the Grey. At least that's what my—our—research shows."

Out of the blue, Mara asked, "How do you know your father's in an oubliette?"

That startled me a little. "I was told, but the hole I found at the site where he died kind of reminded me of the place Marsden tried to shove me into—the same hole I dropped Alice into."

"Hm. I can't say I'm knowin' enough about how the Grey works to tell you if such a thing is possible without a spell in place, but a spell can be undone."

"The one I found in London wasn't created by a spell. It was more like a . . . black hole: Things around it had warped the magical landscape until it sort of folded on itself. It was kind of a magical vortex around a tree in a graveyard."

"Hardy's tree?" Mara asked. "At St. Pancras Old Church?"

I nodded. Being from Ireland, Mara must have at least heard of most of the magical oddities in the British Isles, even if she hadn't seen them herself.

She pursed her lips. "Oh. Yes. Something like that is going to be a lot harder to extract anyone from."

"Yeah, but I suspect Dad's not locked down quite as thoroughly as Wygan thinks."

She raised her eyebrows into quizzical arches. "Oh? Why ever do y'think that?"

"Because I keep getting hints. I've had several brushes with—not really ghosts, but energetic things like poltergeists and collective entities. They keep calling me 'little girl.' That was my dad's nickname for me, and crazy as it sounds, I think he's been trying to warn me in whatever way he can. I have a feeling that if I can get to him, he might know something about Wygan's plans and how to stop them."

"If that's so, then you'll have to be findin' a way to your father's ghost."

I nodded. "I don't think that's going to be easy, what with the Guardian Beast around and that . . . fiery whatever in the way, but I would guess that the guy who killed me two years ago might have a few clues. He's dead, too, and it sounds like more of Wygan's minions at work."

My announcement didn't come as a surprise to Quinton—he'd eavesdropped on my conversation with Solis, after all—but the Danzigers both looked taken aback. I was getting used to the number of dead people around me aside from the ordinary run of ghosts. I didn't care for it, but it was a fact of what I was and how I'd gotten that way that death seemed to litter my background landscape like so many rocks in a floodplain. It even showed up in family photos as smudges and phantoms that weren't just dust and lens flare.

I explained. "Todd Simondson—the guy who killed me two years ago—may be a little easier to get to than my father. I suspect he was killed by the same people, so he might have useful information, and if I can get anything out of him, that may help me get to Dad."

Mara seemed to approve of my ill-expressed logic. "And from your father, perhaps a way to put paid to whatever the Pharaohn-ankh-astet is plannin'. It's got to be nasty, whatever it is. . . ."

Quinton was the only one left out of that reference. He turned a quizzical expression on me.

I sighed, feeling drained by the long recitation with still more ahead. "Lost?" I asked.

"A bit. You mentioned the asetem last night, but you didn't say what they were. Some kind of vampire, but . . . what's the deal? Aside from the spooky eyes and their resistance to stun sticks."

"They're Egyptian," Ben started. He was in full lecture mode. "According to the legends, the boy-priest Astet was killed but didn't die. He was so perfect in his devotion to the gods that they allowed him to live, even though they couldn't restore his life—if you get the fine distinction. He was the undead, being on earth but existing in the afterlife as well. Very interesting stuff for a people who believed the afterlife was the perfection of earthly life, complete with food and sex and so on. So a cult formed around him, and his closest followers also became the undead. How is a point of debate, but the upshot is it's a lot harder to get to be an asete than a regular vampire—kind of an exclusive afterlife club with fringe benefits in the real world. It's a pretty early version of the vampire myth. Some claim it's the earliest, but the Assyrians have one about as old and the Asian vampire myths go back before that."

Quinton looked a little doubtful. "Do you think there's a real vampire for every myth?"

"Not all of them, perhaps, but some."

I'd have been willing to bet against that statement: my experience had been that whatever humans believed strongly enough had form in the Grey. The only question would be how far those things projected into the normal for ordinary people to perceive and be tormented by.

Quinton took it all in like a sponge. "All right, so we have the asetem—these glowy-eyed creepazoids I've been seeing around—and they have a . . . what did you call it?"

"Pharaohn," Ben said. "The ruler of the asetem is given the title Pharaohn-ankh-astet—God-King, Life of Astet—like the ancient pharaohs of Egypt were thought to be direct descendants of the god Ra. His subjects are the asetem-ankh-astet, or roughly translated, 'descendants of Astet who are the life of Astet.' They believe they are the children of the blood and soul of the immortal boy-priest. They're a bit different from the regular kind of vampire: They're emotion-feeders, not just blood-feeders. Supposedly they're not as fast as Western vampires like Edward's people, but they're natural magic-users, which most Western vampires aren't."

"I can vouch for the speed," Quinton said.

Ben perked up. "Really?"

"Yeah. They were showing up downtown and around the underground before I moved out. I got chased by a bunch of them the night I figured I should move someplace safer. If they'd been as fast as the regular kind, I'd be dead. Or shambling around after dark, looking for bums to make a withdrawal from."

"Why did they chase you?"

"I'm not sure what started it. I saw one of them about a week ago take out a regular vampire with a sort of homemade Taser—knocks them out, but if you keep the voltage on, they go up in a fireball. I found another one snooping around where I'd seen the first one a couple of days later. That's when I found out the zapper doesn't work on these asetem. A discharge that should have turned one into a smoking pile of ash just knocked this one down for a minute. Then it got back up and came after me. I barely kept ahead of it, and it started calling in buddies to chase me. They tailed me to my hooch. It wasn't safe to stay there after that, so I bugged out to Harper's. If those things had been any faster, I'd have stood no chance. As it was, the fact I knew the area and they didn't was about all that saved my ass."

"Ahhhh . . . so they aren't locals. . . ." Ben murmured, scribbling notes on a napkin with a finger dipped in coffee. Mara clucked her tongue and plucked a yellow legal pad from her pile of junk. She tossed it onto the table with a proper pen, and Ben snatched them and wrote in rapid, spiked shorthand, nodding as he did. "Did they look different from a regular vampire?"

Quinton sent me a bemused glance. We were all used to Ben's research obsessions and it was easier to humor him most of the time than try to restrain him to the topic at hand. Unless the topic *was* at hand, red in tooth and claw. Then things could get intense. But at least this was useful. I now knew what had driven Quinton out of his hidden home and he had a better idea of how bad these creatures we were tangling with truly were.

"The ones I saw had either white hair or streaked black and white. Their skin was pretty pale, but it's hard to tell under the street what color 'pale' is. From most angles, their eyes glow orange—fiery orange—and there's something . . . kind of snakelike about them."

"Their skin has a faint scale pattern to it," I put in. "Sekhmet referred to them as having 'fine, white cobra forms,' if I am remembering the conversation right, and they do look a little like hooded cobras when they get annoyed."

"They hiss," Quinton added into the silence as Mara and Ben stared at us.

I stared back. "What? You don't think they hiss?"

Ben started, excited. "Sekhmet is the Egypt—"

I cut him off, not wanting to risk the goddess's attention. "I know what she is."

Mara seemed frightened more than amazed. "You ... met her? In London?"

I bit my lip. Time to sound crazy. . . . "Yes. Sort of. Not so much in the flesh ... in the Grey form, I guess you could say. We had a rather disturbing chat. The asetem aren't much liked by the other vampires in London, but there's a sort of truce ... or there was until Wygan got Alice to kick over that apple cart. That was what caused Edward to send me to London in the first place."

"Why ever didn't y'say something to us if you knew there were asetem involved?"

"I didn't know. I didn't know they existed or what the problem was. I just went where I was told to go and did what I had to do. And I don't care to repeat that conversation—it wasn't pleasant—but it did put me onto Wygan and Alice. They were undermining Edward, partially to get to him and partially to get to me, but Alice thought it wasn't good enough, so she kidnapped Will Novak, too, and that's when things started to get really strange—but it doesn't matter! The point is this: Wygan is moving forward with a plan that has something to do with Edward, and with me, and with the Grey itself. Whatever it is, I don't want to be part of it, but more than that, I don't want it to go ahead at all. I intend to put a stop to it, but it has to be my way.

"Wygan has been attacking my home, trying to get at me, wear me down, keep me off-balance I'm guessing. I can't let him do that. I have to be free to move or I'll end up doing what he wants. And I have to get some sleep so I don't keep on making stupid mistakes because I'm too tired to think more than a single move ahead." I was losing my cool and I knew it, but I just didn't have the energy to be more subtle. I took a few long breaths that turned into yawns before I could continue. "That's why we'd like to use your basement for a day or two. Lie low long enough to get some sleep and plan. We can leave the dog with you until things are less dangerous. Grendel is a great protection dog. Wygan likes to grab people and use them as leverage against others and I don't want him to get you or any of my other friends. I know you can take care of yourselves, but . . ."

Ben and Mara exchanged a worried glance, and we all stared out into the yard, watching Brian gambol with Grendel. The dog was jumping around and knocked the boy over. All of us got to our feet, poised to run to the rescue, but the pit bull just held Brian down for a moment and slobbered all over his face, making happy wuffing sounds through his nose while the boy shrilled his pleasure. Boy and dog got back to their feet and Grendel herded Brian around the yard for a while as we watched. I noticed the dog somehow kept himself between Brian and the blood red stars of the malefic spells scattered along the fence. Maybe all animals had a touch of Grey vision, like the ferret seemed to. I hoped so.

"It won't be for long," I said. "Just until I can get into a better position against Wygan. I'll have to free my father from him somehow and I'll have to figure out what he's doing so I can stop it. I have to take the offensive or the game is lost already. Please . . ."

SIX

It took a little more talking before the Danzigers felt they knew enough to let me head for bed in the basement guest room. Grendel, the fuzzy bodyguard, turned out to be our ace in the hole: Brian's immediate response to the idea that we might go and take his playmate away was to throw his arms around the pit bull's neck and literally dig in his heels. "No! Doggie stay!" he insisted. The plight of adults being a bit too abstract for even the brightest three-year-old, he went for the most important thing to himself: the pet. Ben and Mara exchanged a rueful glance and gave in, which earned a delighted squeal from their offspring. Rick was going to have a hard time getting his dog back.

Quinton had gotten a lot more sleep the previous night than I had and elected to stay up for a while and help the Danzigers out with some household projects. I suspected he wanted to pick their brains a bit more about the situation we were getting into, and Ben had looked more than happy for the opportunity to do some picking of his own, too. Whatever work Quinton did for the Danzigers would mitigate some of the obligation we both felt for the safety and quiet they had extended to us. Some, not all. I knew I was probably dragging them into the enemy's sights and I didn't like it, no matter how much they protested that they wanted to help. Quinton, too, come to that. It seemed that this had become his fight as well, whether I liked it or not.

I fell toward sleep wondering why Simondson had ended up in Georgetown. . . .

As I slept, I dreamed I was sitting at the bottom of a

swimming pool, trying to make sense of conversations going on at a party above the surface. Distant, burbling sounds that were almost words floated in and out of my ears, and I could see them darting through the water like glittering, colored fish. My dead cousin Jill swam by, her long hair forming a blond cloud as she paused to look at me.

"This time, we'll use the back door," she bubbled. In the drowned light, her pale, dead skin looked blue. She swam away, dissolving into a school of neon-bright tadpoles that broke into sudden shapes and began spiraling around a single, flame-filled bubble. When the gleaming creatures reached the middle, they doubled back and swam out again: an endless gyre of brilliant flecks going in and out, round and round. . . .

A randomly bobbing conversation bubble popped, releasing the words "phone box" to rise to the surface and burst into the air as a disjointed gasp of sound. An effervescence of englobed words rushed past, swirling through the tangled net of light that the waves cast onto the bottom of the pool. A few bubbles collapsed, letting their syllables out into the water: "rosaceae," "polyphony," "etrier," and "fur." The glimmering tadpoles darted apart and away, fleeing the sudden voices and dispersing the dream into blank sleep.

In spite of the weirdness, I slept well once the dream left and woke feeling more clearheaded than I had in a while.

Quinton had stretched out on the bed beside me while I slept, still dressed and dozing only lightly. As I started to sit up, he rolled over and looked at me, propping himself up on one elbow. "Hey, how are you feeling?"

"Well enough to go hunting for ghosts."

"Should we grab the dog? If we can separate him from Brian, that is."

"I'm sure Ben and Mara have the parental equivalent of a crowbar somewhere. It can't hurt to take the fur-covered assault weapon along. If nothing else we can always tell any busybodies that we're taking Grendel for a walk. And who'd argue with that?"

"Only the suicidal."

As if she knew we were talking about some other trouble-making animal, the ferret began to rattle her temporary cage's door. We both looked at her and she gave us the imploring ferret look.

I let Chaos out to romp while I put on fresh clothes. "That reminds me. While I was in London, Marsden told me ferrets seem to have an affinity for the Grey. How, I don't know, but it would explain her craziness around the vampires and ghosts."

"Then we'll take the carpet shark, too."

It wasn't too hard to get the dog to ourselves: we just had to wait until Brian went to bed. We took a lot of precautions as we left, looking for observers and tails, checking for tracking devices both technological and magical, and paying attention to the reactions of the animals—just in case.

The sun was still up but starting to slant a bit, lengthening the shadows around the old brewery as we passed it. Where the southern brewery building had stood until a few years ago, there was now a neatly paved parking lot, devoid of the chain-link that had once held back the rubble from the street. I'd read that the old building, not originally built for cold storage, had chilled the ground enough to form a ball of filthy ice as large as a house. The current owners' plans for redevelopment of the lot into shops and apartments had come to a standstill while the site was dug out and thawed. The remaining walls of the stock and brew houses had been shored up with cement blocks and steel posts, leaving two walls of the shell standing empty, boarded doors and windows gaping in the upper stories between brick scars where the floors had once been. The ghost shape of the original building flickered in the Grey, silver-touched with persistent lines of blue energy as if the magical grid had risen into the walls and was crumbling back to ground at a glacial pace. I shivered as I saw it and drove on, looking for a less exposed place to leave the truck.

I wanted to walk the neighborhood a little. If Simondson had been dumped at the brewery rather than killed there, I suspected he hadn't been moved far. Wygan couldn't have thought I'd miss the news that my assailant had died by violence, so chances were good that the location wasn't a fluke.

We parked a few blocks away near an off-ramp and a playfield that sprouted artificial grass. A row of old-fashioned clapboard-sided houses in varying states of refurbishment or decay faced the field. A swaybacked house in the middle of the block hosted an elderly man with a Santa Claus beard and crow-sharp eyes who sat on the dilapidated porch. He didn't stare at us as we got out of the truck, but the curious, blue-green energy around his head reached out, as if scenting us, then pulled back once satisfied we had no interest in him.

Grendel wanted to investigate the playfield but lost interest once he realized that only the grass near the bleachers was the real thing. Instead, he peed on the leg of a bench and then looked up at us, satisfied and ready to walk on. Chaos was happier to ride in my purse with her head sticking out the top. We passed under the freeway ramp and across two sets of railroad tracks within a block. Except for the cars parked at the curbs, the street we walked on looked like something straight out of the Old West: Buildings of corrugated tin, clinker brick, and horizontal boards crowded the narrow sidewalk leading toward the long brick-and-sandstone wall of the brewery's late-Victorian buildings. Even with the sun still up in the long summer twilight, I could see wisps of ghost-stuff and bright scribe-lines of energy that chattered like squirrels. The Grey was as noisy as a train yard in this low-lying stretch of ground between the bluffs and the river. The animals seemed unaffected, except that they glanced around more than usual—like kids in a new neighborhood. This all struck me as odd, but I didn't comment—it would do no good to discuss the strange degree of activity until I had a little more information, and it might be nothing more than the residue of a still-busy settlement that hadn't been buried and remade like much of Seattle had over the years.

We stepped out onto Airport Way at the north end of the former brewery complex and turned south to reach the partially demolished buildings Solis had mentioned. I thought I heard something muttering in my ear, but there was nothing nearby, even in the Grey, besides Quinton and the animals.

Ghosts grew thicker as we moved along the sidewalk on the brewery side, mostly men in work clothes and teams of horses pulling wagons piled with grain, hops, or barrels. I could smell the horse dung and sweat, the sharp, bitter memory of fresh hops, and the sweet odor of boiling grain mash. The weird muttering was drowned in the harsher, louder cries of workers, the snort and whinny of horses, and the heavy roll and thump of barrels being loaded.

Quinton's hand closed on my upper arm. "Harper?"

I shook myself. "What?"

"Just making sure you're still here."

I felt my brows pinch down in a scowl. It wasn't quite a slip, but I shouldn't have been sliding into the Grey like that. I wasn't tired, so that wasn't the cause now, but I didn't see any other reason I would have gone a bit ghostly. I concentrated a little harder as we walked on.

The long buildings were pierced by recessed, black-painted doors and windows with sparkling-new glass, and odd ramps to old loading doors swooped here and there. Finally we reached the end of a building with two walls of soaring, arched windows and impressive double doors that faced a driveway and another building on the other side. A covered iron walkway crossed the driveway at the third story and a gate stood closed across the passage. Through the chain-link gate we could see a huge brick chimney near the train tracks on the far side.

The partial shell of a building on the other side of the driveway had a sandstone foundation that had been eaten away at the corners and mortar joints until it looked like rotting teeth holding up the charming brick edifice with carved stone signs above the big, boarded-up doors and windows that read "Brew House" and "Stock—" Just beyond the truncated stock house sign, the wall ended abruptly and the black expanse of the asphalt parking lot stretched to the south nearly another block to run up against the former brewery office building that now stood alone under the pylons of yet another freeway ramp. We'd arrived and, naturally, it was the spot with the aberrant lines of Grey energy that had given me the willies on first sight.

We stepped around the broken wall, over a parking bumper so new it gleamed white, and turned to look into the gutted remains of the stock building. A chill cut through me as we crossed the gleaming Grey power lines in the memories of walls that had once stood there, but the feeling faded as we left the ghostly walls behind.

A bit of tattered yellow crime scene tape still fluttered from one of the massive iron pipes that had been erected to brace up the remaining front wall. Sand, scrub grass, and tumbled bits of stone and garbage were the only floor the old stock house had. The brew house still had one complete room, but the jagged edges of more rooms that had once stood beyond the front one ran like raw wounds in the towering brick walls. Ivy and grass had rooted in the back wall of the brew house along a jerry-rigged plastic downspout that had broken apart halfway down. The stock house walls grew a thick coat of some horrid yellow spray foam at the second floor, but nothing else. Straight down from the foam and in the corner of the last standing walls, I could see a thin red smear of remnant energy—not a ghost but the mute energetic residue of something angry and violent.

The noise of the grid increased as I got closer, whining and rattling like blues guitar feedback on a cheap amp. I'd never heard so much local disturbance from the Grey's power grid before. I wondered if it was an artifact of the asetem's involvement, but I didn't recall any such thing from London. . . .

There was no roil of vampires, nor the gut-blow of death lingering over the site, not that I'd expected it, but it might have explained the spine-crawling racket of the grid at this spot. I stepped up onto the sand mounded where the building's floor must have been. Chaos made a chuckling noise in my purse. Grendel watched me with his ears pricked up and his shoulders a little hunched, as if his hackles might start rising in a moment. Pretty strange body language for a dog, I thought. Quinton held on to the leash and followed several paces behind.

I looked toward the yellow scrap of crime scene tape and guided my gaze along the line from pole to pole, searching for another bit of yellow or some indication of exactly where the body had lain. A second tag on the boarded doorway to the brew house and a small dark patch on the sand near the smear of red energy led me deeper into the site. I didn't have to look hard for signs once I got close;

the red haze resolved itself into the misty wire-frame shape of a human curled on the ground in a semi-fetal position. The dark patch, predictably, was blood, though very little and mostly smeared on the sand, not soaked in, where the body had lain, battered but not bleeding out. Either he hadn't bled much at all, or, as I'd suspected, he'd been dumped on the sand after he was too dead to do more than ooze a bit.

I crouched down and put my hand on the bloodstain. The world seemed to drain away into silver mist and the screech of metal tearing apart under massive strain. I hadn't meant to sink into the Grey, but the bloodstain had drawn me in. I started to back out, afraid for a moment that I had fallen into some kind of magical trap, but the Grey was no less fluid than usual. I wasn't imprisoned, just sucked in. I took a few deep breaths and let myself fall all the way in.

My heart caught on a barb of sudden pain as I went and my breathing faltered as if I were feeling the distant echo of Simondson's death but not the man himself. "Where did you come from?" I muttered as I looked around in the fog-built world, trying to pick up and follow with my gaze the miserable red thread of energy that marked Simondson's temporary resting place. I concentrated on it and it got a little brighter, a weak tendril raveling toward the south until it broke off and died out. I dug my hand harder into the ground, a little frustrated that I couldn't pick up more, and felt a piercing electric thrill in my palm, as if the dormant line of energy had suddenly gone live. I gasped a startled breath and heard the ferret chitter in alarm.

I shot a glance over my shoulder, staring down the length of the vanishing red thread, and saw a faint ghost resolving out of the Grey mist, walking toward me in jerks and starts, the thread seeming to haul it along. I grabbed on to the thread and reeled it in, yanking the reluctant ghost closer. He stopped on top of the spot where he had lain dead and glared at me in resentful silence.

As vague as his image was, I could see that his jaw was still square, his hair still blond, even though it was showing some gray at the temples. But he wasn't looking as sleek as the last time I'd seen him; his residual self-image seemed to have skewed into an ugly awareness of what his greed had lost him. He looked like a stockbroker who hadn't weathered the crash. Angry self-pity rolled off him in sickening waves. I stood up and hooked my fingers into his substance before he could escape. "Hi, Simondson. Remember me?"

Someone growled, but I wasn't sure whether it was the ghost or Grendel. I shook Simondson a little. "C'mon, I know you can talk. How did you end up here?"

"Fuck off."

"Nice. You haven't gotten any sweeter now that you're dead."

"Which is your fault, you nosy bitch."

"It's my fault you're a foulmouthed ass with a bad temper?"

He tried to spit, but it's not an impressive gesture from a weak phantom. "I died because of you."

"Like I haven't heard that one before," I muttered. "Why does it always have to be someone else's fault with you, Simondson? It was your dead wife's fault you robbed her daughter's inheritance. Now it's my fault you're dead. Me, I'm betting on greed, vanity, and plain old-fashioned stupidity—your usual motives."

He started to object and I rattled his vague substance in an offhand way while rolling my eyes. "Oh, please. Try something new. The truth would be good. Let's start with the woman who convinced you to beat the living hell out of me two years ago."

"Claire?"

Interesting: I knew her as Alice—I was pretty sure we were talking about the same female. "Petite thing, ruby-red hair, sharp teeth, smokes like a silent film star . . . ?"

The ghost nodded. He looked tired, as if whatever had befallen him at the end of his life had been exhausting and death wasn't any more restful. But, of course, I had come along and made him wake up from whatever brand of eternal sleep he might have been enjoying. Or not. I felt no shame: This man had beaten me to death and I felt he didn't deserve much respect from me now that he'd joined the post-life crowd himself. "You didn't know me from a hole in the ground, so how did your Claire talk you into knocking my head in?"

The ghost wavered and blinked, seeming to cringe and fold into a smaller shape. "Can't think," he moaned.

"Try harder. How did she compel you to attack me? Who killed you? How? Tell me. Tell me any of it and I'll let you off the hook." I needed everything I could get to fight Wygan. . . .

I yanked Simondson a little closer, studying the thickening mist of his form as he tried to remember. When he seemed nearly corporeal, he began shaking, a choked squeal of pain singing out of his mouth in a red cloud. I sank deeper into the Grey, looking at the tangled skein of energy that was Simondson's ghost. Red, a hot red that deepened to a bloody claret color at the core. I touched one of the swirling strands of his energy, hooked it with my finger, and pulled with a firm pressure.

The hot color leapt off him, running up my own arm like flame and nerve gas. The wretched arc of agony made me buckle and cry out. I nearly let go completely. Voices from everywhere and nowhere shrieked and gibbered in my head. I backed away from the deep level of the Grey, shaking. Simondson panted, a remembered response to surcease, and trembled.

I kept one hand on him, but I relaxed my grip, pushing him just a bit away from me in the depth of the Grey, letting him drift into a less corporeal state. He shuddered and breathed a blue gust, almost sexual in the quality of its release. Repelled, I had to force myself to keep him present.

He caught a breath he didn't need and sagged a bit in his respite. "Let me go," he murmured. "I can't help you and it's torture when I try to remember. . . ."

"I can see that." I didn't want to investigate the how of it—I knew I'd have to eventually, but not this second. For now it was enough that I thought I had the principle of it. I guessed that this was something akin to whatever torment Wygan had my father tied up in: The Grey was in large part memory in various forms; when the memory was strong, the spirits were more corporeal, but as they became stronger and more "there," they were also more subject to pain. Wygan had done something . . . horrible. A spell or binding of some kind that looped back through memory as agony.

Ghosts didn't experience sensations like a live person, but they remembered them as if they were real and that was what Wygan had tied him to, somehow. As Simondson—or my father—tried to remember anything or act, he became more solid . . . and so it went in spirals of suffering: remember and be tormented, move toward presence and become engulfed in pain. It was better to fade down to the merest whisper of what you had been, to a shade and a shadow, and remain mute, stupid, and inactive. Unable to help anyone or even yourself until Wygan was ready to use you for his own purpose. Best, by far, to go away forever, if you only could.

Simondson groaned again, almost crying. "Let me out of this. Please."

I could let Simondson go. I was sure of that, though the process of tearing his shape apart and out of the weave of the Grey would be miserable for us both. But I needed him. I needed his knowledge and I thought I might need him just because he was connected to me and what might happen next. But keeping him in this state—as I had no doubt my dad was also kept by Wygan—was cruel. Letting it go on sickened me, left me feeling like I was collaborating in the horror.

But still, I said, "No."

SEVEN

I wavered when Simondson howled in rage at me. I wasn't intending to torture him, but I couldn't let him go yet. There were still too many answers missing. I had an idea and I hoped I could make it work.

He clutched at me with incorporeal hands that still had the power to do me hurt. His fury and pain were a whirlwind around me, tearing and pulling at my own substance as if he could rend me to pieces and scatter me to the etheric winds of the Grey.

Faint and distant noises intruded and became recognizable: Grendel growling and barking, Quinton calling to me, Chaos chuckling like something demented. The thread of their familiarity kept me anchored against the storm of noise and emotion. I backed further out of the Grey, not quite gone—still present enough to keep a hand on Simondson but much harder for him to harm. I needed a container, silvered if possible. . . .

"Stop, Simondson!" I yelled, crouching. "I'll let you go, but you need to do a few things for me, first."

"No! Why should I?"

"Because I can let you go and no one else who can will. I'll set you free when I'm done."

"How can I trust you? Why would you do it later if you won't do it now?"

I put out my hand, slipping it into the tangle of his angry energy. I ached like the bones of my arm were burning, but I did it, working into the weft of his shape and pushing a bit of it aside, loosening his form for a moment. Then I just held still as long as I could stand it, letting him sigh and dim in relief. Something of his mind brushed against mine and I shivered, gagging a little at the sensation, but it should have been enough for him to know what I was thinking. Ghosts aren't psychic, but if they can crawl inside your skin for a while, they can seem that way. I concentrated on my intentions and hoped he was picking it up.

"I will let you go," I said between clenched teeth. The red storm of his emotions was tearing across my nerves. "I swear. But you'll have to come with me. I swear it," I repeated, feeling my legs tremble with the effort of remaining upright.

He eased back, the ire of his presence draining away. I crouched down, putting my hands to the ground as I slipped back toward the normal. I clenched the bloody sand beneath my palms into my fists, feeling Simondson's presence as a dull heat in the compressed grains.

As soon as I was back in a more visible state, Quinton and the animals converged on me. "Stop!" I yelled. "Don't touch me yet. I need a metallic container, a shiny one. Any size."

Quinton scrabbled through his pockets, displacing the ferret, and dumping a handful of mints out of an Altoids tin. He buffed the interior quickly with a handkerchief and held the tin out to me, open.

I dumped the handful of stained sand into the tin. Then I reached back into Simondson's tangled, dim form, and twisted off a thread of his energy, which I shut into the tin with the sand. As long as it stayed closed, I should have a way to call on Simondson's spirit for a little while at least. Simondson and I both breathed easier then. I slipped the tin into my pocket, careful to keep it closed.

Quinton helped me to my feet. I shook my head before he could start asking questions. I still had a few things to do while we were here. The rest could wait, but not this.

"Simondson," I started, "show me where you died." He grew hotter and the humming pain around him increased. "No. No, don't think of it. Just go there. Go slow enough for me to follow. Don't think, don't remember, just move."

The ghost drifted back the way he had come originally,

south, across the parking lot that was now pitch-black between the scattered bars of light falling from the freeway and the cones from rare streetlamps. His color flushed and faded again and again as he moved, as if he couldn't stop the sparks of memory that haunted him with pain. Stumbling a little on my still-trembling legs, I followed him. Quinton and Grendel stayed by my side while Chaos crawled up into my collar, as if she meant to comfort me by her presence. Or just lick the sweat off my neck—who knows?

At last, Simondson stopped and flared bloody red before his shape darted through the brick and glass of the nearest building. I could see that he'd stopped inside, but he was fading now, his energy ebbing. Even ghosts need rest. "All right," I murmured to his thin shade. "I'll take it from here." He dimmed into the raw sparkle of the Grey.

As soon as he was gone, I plopped down onto the steps of the building he'd led us to. It had a covered porch with a short set of marble stairs on each side. The brick-and-stone porch led to three arched windows with French doors in two of them. I wasn't quite high enough up the steps to look through the glass. I hung my head a moment while I caught my breath.

Quinton must have been studying the building. "It's the old brewery office."

I raised my head, shaking it a little to dispel the tinnitus that had started up—my descent into the Grey after Simondson seemed to have muffled my hearing, as if I'd gone swimming and now had water stuck in my ears. Quinton was looking past me into the darkened building.

"Looks like the tenant left in a hurry; the carpet's been torn out. I don't think that's the latest in corporate decor, though it looks like someone's been using it for something."

"How can you tell?"

"Footprints in the dust and lots of power cables on the floor."

I put one hand on the brick wall beside me so I could stand up and then jerked away from the building as the energy streams running through it snapped at me like static. I peered at it, glancing sideways into the Grey to see what was going on.

Coils of red power encircled the base of the building, crosshatched in blue, as if someone had erected a kind of magical insulation between the interior and the rest of the world. I couldn't be sure of the magical nature of whatever had been going on without more information, but the gory crimson lines gave me the impression vampires had been involved. Not too surprising, since Simondson had died inside. Taking care not to touch the walls again, I walked up the short flight of steps and looked through the glass panes of the nearest window.

Squiggles of industrial glue and motes of sand and sawdust defaced the once-gleaming marble floor. Black and orange snakes of electrical cable ran across the mess, disappearing through the doorways in the white-plastered walls. Glancing up, I could see a chandelier that had captured shreds of translucent plastic and white gauze on its curled arms. I would have bet the missing carpet had a hell of a bloodstain on it and more than minor traces of Simondson's DNA. Solis hadn't mentioned the office building. I guessed the police were still trying to get a search warrant, even though an office wouldn't seem much like the site of a hit-and-run, and Solis hadn't been entirely sold on that idea anyhow. The right kind of beating might look a lot like a car accident until the autopsy report was in. . . .

A year or two earlier, I might have been perversely mollified by the manner of Simondson's death, if my idea was correct. Back when the damage he'd inflicted on me was still fresh and seemed to be nothing but mindless fury unleashed on my undeserving self, it might have seemed poetic justice. Now it left me stunned and angry. Yeah, he'd killed me, but he hadn't done it strictly from his own desire; he'd been led to it, tricked and used like everyone else Wygan had touched in his scheme. Not that I was feeling sorry for Simondson; I just didn't feel the need to cause him any additional hurt anymore.

"I should go in there," I mumbled, trying to convince myself.

Grendel whined and shifted to stare toward the street. The ferret was more interested in the building as she wormed her way back up to my shoulder. The scrape of footsteps on the gritty sidewalk pulled my attention around in the same direction as the dog's.

A police officer on foot, his light-blue uniform shirt glowing under a moving shaft of light from the freeway, strolled toward us. He checked his radio on his shoulder and I spotted his partner coming across the street from the direction of Nine-pound Hammer. Both cops kept their hands in sight, not worried about us, just keeping an eye on things.

The first one called out as he came close. "Evening, folks. How y'doing?" He might have thought we were drunks who'd left the club to get some air, except for the dog. Quinton twitched the leash and the dog sat down to his whispered command as the two cops got within talking range.

I knew Quinton didn't want to chat with them. I didn't either, but chances were good they'd make a note of our presence and Solis would see it, so I leaned out the nearest arch in the front of the dark office porch and returned the greeting.

"Hi, guys." I didn't recognize either of them and they didn't seem to know me, which was fine.

The first cop noticed Grendel, who was cocking his head and looking at the dark legs of his uniform trousers with some speculation. "Nice dog."

"Yeah, except for all the peeing," I replied. "I swear he has to sniff everything and leave a puddle every fifty feet."

The second cop laughed, casually hitching his thumbs into his equipment belt. "Mine's the same way. Gotta read his pee-mail and leave a reply, I guess."

The first officer was looking us over but seemed satisfied we were just a couple out walking their dog. I was grateful Chaos was keeping still in the darkness under my collar—no one would believe we were out walking the ferret. We needed to keep up the illusion and negate their interest by moving along. Investigating the site of Simondson's death would have to wait.

I glanced at Quinton as if I were irritated by the delay. "Is he ready to go?"

"I think he's done for now."

I nodded and walked down the other set of steps, the one

farthest from the cops and more shadowed by the freeway ramp overhead. "All right, then. Let's go."

Quinton shrugged and twitched the leash again. Grendel stood up, wagging his tail at the prospect of moving; his doggy grin broke out and he panted in excitement. Quinton just nodded to the cops and walked past to catch up to me, the dog trotting alongside. We strolled off under the freeway as the patrolmen gave us one last look and dismissed us from their minds to go back to their beat.

EIGHT

As we walked away from the policemen, I felt the hot/cold presence of Simondson's ghost in my pocket, thrumming in the metal box. Grey things whispered in my ear, not quite comprehended, not quite ignored. "Are we clear?" I asked Quinton.

He bent down and adjusted the dog's leash, shooting a look back toward the old brewery under the cover of his long coat. "Yup. They're checking out the bar up the street."

I lifted the ferret out of my collar and she made a disgusted chittering sound. "Don't give me that, you furry knee sock. You almost got us in trouble."

"How?" Quinton asked. "I didn't see her doing anything."

"She was wiggling down my back trying to get into my pocket with the box full of ghost." I put my free hand into the pocket in question. As my fingers brushed the metal surface, an electric shock ran up my arm and with it came a shriek of sound. Chaos made a high-pitched bark and twisted in my hand as I jerked, consumed in the moment of noise.

My grip failed and Quinton grabbed the ferret, tucking her into one of his own pockets before reaching to catch me as my knees buckled. I pushed him away, afraid the shattering noise in my head would envelop him, too. The shouting, muttering cacophony meant nothing, a jumble of sounds and words running over one another, breaking apart in my mind like exploding fireworks. I pulled my hand out of my pocket, clasping both of them together at my chest, bending as if I'd been punched by a heavy fist. The sound fell away slowly, leaving a single word in its fading echo in my mind: "*maiandros*."

Quinton hooked his arm around me against my will and hauled me upward, the dog dancing alongside us. I braced for another blast of uncanny sound, but it didn't come as he moved me along. "Are you all right? Can you breathe now?"

I sucked in air, stunned to realize I was almost faint from lack of oxygen. I'd blown out my breath when the sound hit, as if I had, indeed, been physically struck in the gut. I nodded and settled my breathing into a normal rhythm, pulling out of his arm to walk on my own. But I stayed close. "I don't know what happened. Did you hear anything?" I asked.

"No. What did you hear? I mean, that is what happened, isn't it? You heard something . . . weird?"

"More like I got hit by the sound, but it doesn't make any sense. What I heard doesn't mean anything to me. It was just . . . words and noise. . . ." I had a feeling, a certainty. . . . "We have to go back and get into that building. There's some . . . information there."

"How do you know?" he asked, but he turned around with me and started walking back to the brewery office with Grendel's leash in one hand and the ferret peeking out of his pocket under the other hand.

"I just do. It's . . . like the sound told me something I know but can't understand in words. It makes my head ache, though." I rubbed at my right temple, feeling a low throb in my skull like a migraine coming on. Was there something dire about Simondson? Was his ghost some kind of trap set by Wygan and his minions? It didn't seem that way, but . . . the discomfort, the creeping sense of hidden knowledge ticking like a bomb at the back of my mind gave me pause. Not enough pause to stop my progress to the office, but enough that I frowned over it all the way back.

The cops hadn't come back around on their beat yet so we had some time, though we didn't know how much. I took a moment to steady myself, get my mind back on the task at hand and not on the freakishness of what had happened a few minutes earlier. Then I turned to Quinton. "You should go on without me." He started to object but I cut him off and continued. "If the cops come back, you shouldn't be here. They'll recognize you and Grendel. I'll be inside, and while they might recognize me, they'd have to get close first. I can meet you back at the truck."

"What if something else happens to you? I don't like leaving you without backup. Things seem a bit off the rails, here."

I waved his last comment off and addressed the rest. "I still have my cell phone, and if I don't call or turn up at the truck within thirty minutes, you come looking for me. But you won't be any help if you get arrested for trespassing or run off for loitering." Then, just because she'd been so jumpy about it, I put out my hand for the ferret. "I'll keep Chaos with me. She can raise the ghost alarm if something's too close." I didn't like endangering the little animal, but I needed any edge I could get and she'd reacted faster to the presence of whatever was ringing my ears than I did. Without Quinton around to spot for me, I'd have to rely on Chaos and my own skills—which weren't inconsiderable but currently left me a little confused.

Since London, I'd noticed subtle changes to what I could do in the Grey and with what ease. I'd flicked a ghost away like it was no more than a wisp of smoke and torn a piece from Simondson's substance without stopping to think if I could. Wygan's goal was to make me into something new, and it seemed that, even without his hands-on interference, I was changing whether I liked it or not. I'd learned that I couldn't fight being part of the Grey, but I still didn't like these new powers—they worried me when I thought of what they might mean to Wygan's plan. Didn't mean I wasn't going to use them, for now at least.

I checked the area for anyone who might be freaked out by what I was about to do and then watched Quinton start away. He moved reluctantly, looking back over his shoulder twice before Grendel decided to bolt after a rat that had scuttled out of a brush of wild fennel growing from the packed dirt of an alley.

Chaos had been into the Grey once before, so I thought

she'd be all right to come along, so long as she was all the way inside my clothes. I tucked her into my shirt as I went up the office steps on the darkest side. I slid into the Grey and felt my way through the layers of time until I found one in which the office was occupied and its doors stood open to a long-ago afternoon's hop-scented breeze.

Once inside, I checked for the ferret and she chuckled at me, apparently feeling no ill effects of passing through a physical barrier. Well, at least I now knew it worked, though not the parameters and limits. I let her crawl up and poke her head out of my collar. I began walking around the shadowy edges of the first room, looking for signs, either normal or paranormal, of what had happened to Simondson.

The main floor was broken into two unevenly sized rooms with a small atrium and staircase between them. There were more rooms upstairs and at the back, I assumed, but the ground floor was what interested me at the moment. The more northerly downstairs room was open all the way to the second-floor ceiling with an open gallery around the back and inside wall. It was this room we'd looked into from outside, where we'd seen the marks of industrial glue on the floor. Nothing seemed to excite the ferret and I wasn't getting much of an indication of activity, except in a vague way as the ghosts of a generation or two of clerks went about their business without a care for us. The other room, the southerly one, was slightly smaller and completely closed up with blinds and white paper on the windows, hiding any activity within. Chaos wriggled and made her angry chuckle, wanting down onto the floor to explore for herself. I kept a tight hold on her as I looked around.

Here the carpet had been pulled up as well, leaving the same sort of mess: loops of glue marks on the floor, gummy with dirt and something like sawdust; broom marks in the detritus; and snakes' nests of black electrical cable connected to nothing. I looked at the mess through the Grey, hoping for something more useful and trying not to leave any fingerprints or other evidence that might link me to the scene whenever the cops got in—as I was sure they would eventually. Ferret footprints might be a little less conspicuous than human fingerprints, so long as the forensic technicians thought it was just the track of a rat or two, but I was still reluctant to let Chaos down, just in case.

The cold washed over me and with it the strange chorus of babbling and shrieks that had plagued me since I'd returned from London. I tuned it out as best I could and looked around. Near the interior wall, farthest from the windows, I spotted a formation in the Grey, like a field of broken stone thrusting up through age-old peat and fog. I moved closer to it, keeping to the upper levels of the Grey, wary of being sucked into anything before I knew what it was. Chaos let out a fierce chitter as we advanced, just as intrigued as I was.

Drawing near, the cold of the misty world between the worlds fell away and a tingling heat bled out from the strange structure. It looked like . . . no, it *was* a ring of shattered temporaclines, shards like mirrored glass tipped and ruptured from their proper places. Rifts of motion and memory skittered across the ghostly surfaces of the broken layers of time. As I got closer, the temperature rose and Chaos seemed to pull away from it, sniffing and going still. It reminded me of what I'd seen at my father's old office, a ring of unearthly fire standing around the place his ghost should have been, an impenetrable darkness at its center and a fury circling its edge.

I turned my head, searching for any sign of the Guardian Beast. It had rushed to harry me at the border of the zone in Dad's office, but here there was no sign of it. Whatever had happened here didn't seem to threaten the Grey directly as the other incident had. I reached for one of the broken shards of time and felt a jolt of electricity at my fingertips as I touched it and it came away in my hand.

I'd only once held a piece of the material Grey before: when I'd grabbed and used a ghostly knife in the underground cells of an abandoned prison beneath the streets of London. This was like holding on to electrified ice. It crackled and sizzled with cold that arced up my arm. The moment of time contained in the shard replayed like a broken film as I stared at the shattered piece of memory: twenty seconds of Simondson cowering in the corner while two figures stood in front of him holding heavy objects I couldn't quite see. Something white moved behind Simondson, coming into view for only a moment. "Break the spell." The voice was Wygan's. Then the vision broke off, sharp as the shattered edge of the temporacline.

I snatched at the next shard of memory, hoping for more information, but all I got was the same wrecked moment of time from different angles, as if the broken temporacline was a hologram, smashed into a dozen pieces but showing the same thing, no matter where you looked. There had to be more. . . .

I pulled Chaos out of my shirt, holding her tightly by the harness. The ferret looked around, her whiskers twitching. I studied the area where I had no doubt Simondson had died cornered and beaten, cocking my head side to side as I looked for ghostly traces in the unsettled mist. I'd rarely seen temporaclines less than two decades old and the residue of broken time struck me as something else done by Wygan and his minions. It didn't have the same impact as the hole left at my father's office, so I guessed it wasn't the same thing. This wasn't something locked up and hidden; it was just someone's way of removing evidence. The void of Grey information was just a convenient side effect for whoever had broken the plane of time. If that was the case, they might have left a few other things behind. . . .

Chaos jerked and tried to jump from my hands to the floor. I knelt down, keeping a grip on her as she began wiggling like a mad thing and chuckling to herself. She wrenched out of my hands and dove through the mess of broken temporacline, dancing in fury over a tiny spot on the floor and snapping at something dark and gleaming near the corner.

It was a tiny loop of black energy almost invisible against the filthy floor and the heavy mist of history that lay on it. Black. Dead. The ferret stopped dancing and watched as I reached through the knife-edged circle of shattered time and hooked the thread of Grey energy onto my pinkie, trying not to leave a fingerprint on the dusty floor as I did. The remnant of some lifeless thing unspooled at the speed of chilled molasses, reluctant to reemerge from the grid of Grey energy beneath the city.

I persisted, standing and pulling with a steady pressure until it came free and cast up a pall of memory and a loop of remembered action. It wasn't Simondson or his ghost, just a bit of the building's recent cache of time. The scene unfolded and spread into the corner, playing forward like scratched film, the sound thin and partially covered by the squabbling whisper of the grid that had invaded my head and the noise of the ferret scrambling back into the safety of my shirt.

Simondson stood in the corner. The light in the memory of the room seemed to flicker and change at random times, as if it were changing color, though to me it was all a dim silver and gray, like an old black-and-white movie on a dirty screen. Two male figures faced Todd Simondson, vampires I thought, until I recognized the stance of one: Bryson Goodall—whatever he was. Even in the loop of memory, pale and shuddering as it was, I could see something magical clinging to Simondson, glittering in the silvery mist like a rage of moths. The sound cut in and out as the second villain swung a long, heavy object into Simondson's side.

". . . know why you did it . . ." That was Goodall, I thought.

Simondson buckled and cowered into the confluence of the walls.

Wygan walked past, barely casting them a glance, his mouth moving. ". . . the spell. She'll sniff . . ." I thought I could fill in the first part since I'd already seen it. He was telling them to break the spell. Perhaps whatever it was that had compelled Simondson to attack me . . . ?

Goodall reached out, curling his free hand around Simondson's head. "Jackass . . ." Then he pulled his hand back, closing his fist and yanking the glimmer away. He flinched a little as the web of spell-stuff tore and came dangling and dying into his grip.

Simondson screamed.

". . . rid of him." Was that Wygan who'd spoken? I couldn't tell with the sudden howling of Simondson coupled with the garbled muttering in my ears.

Goodall and his companion belted him with their blunt weapons. Simondson collapsed, but the careful beating went on and the scene darkened, as if someone had turned off the lamps. I thought I smelled something burning—like circuit boards and wires smoldering into flame. I heard a rattle and a roar that chilled my spine. Then the image shuddered and started again.

I watched for another moment, compelled to learn more even as I felt sickened by what I saw. Until something buzzed and burbled against my hip, insistent and getting louder. . . . I shook myself, dropping the loop of memory. It whipped away into the floor, fading until I could no longer see it in the mist that was receding as I struggled back to normal, pestered to the surface of reality by my cell phone vibrating in my pocket. Chaos rumpled about in my shirt as if she, too, had been shaken from a daze.

I took a few cautious steps away from the corner death had occupied, groping for my phone as I set my feet only where they would leave no significant marks. I squatted down and answered.

"Yeah?"

"Where are you? You're running late. The patrolmen are heading back around your way."

It was Quinton. I took a couple of relieved breaths before I answered. "How long till they're here?"

"Five minutes to sight of the office, I'd say, coming from the north on the opposite side of the street."

"OK. I'm on the way out. See you at the truck."

If I got out fast enough, I could stay to the darkened side of the building below the freeway ramp. They wouldn't see me until I crossed the street.

I wanted to look around more and try to figure out what the electrical cables were for, but that was not an option: I didn't know if the cops would inspect the office building again, hang around the bars across the street, or what. Quinton was taking a risk watching them at this point. They'd notice him if he kept it up. I had to be gone before they came down to this end of the block. I slipped into the Grey and found my way out through another balmy ghost of a summer day, onto the darkened asphalt beneath the freeway.

I strode out, keeping the building between me and the

path of the policemen until I was a long block down. Then I crossed the road, timing myself between two trucks that rattled along the dray-haunted street with the sound of a dozen car wrecks. I nipped down the block until I was below the old Georgetown City Hall building and checked back up the street for the cops.

No sign. They must have stopped in a shadow or a doorway farther up the road—probably talking to the bouncer of one of the clubs. I made my way around by the long route to the lonely row of houses facing the plastic playfield.

The old man was still on his porch, but he didn't pay me any mind this time, his odd aura keeping close as I made my way to Quinton and Grendel, strolling along the edge of the fake grass. The ferret took the first opportunity to abandon the snug confines of my clothing for the luxurious complexity of Quinton's coat pockets.

"Find anything?"

"Some pretty disturbing stuff," I replied. "Not something the cops could use as probable cause for a search, though. And," I added, casting a glance toward the strange old man, "I'd rather discuss it elsewhere."

Quinton nodded and we piled back into the Land Rover and headed away from Georgetown, looking for sign of any tail as we went.

NINE

"Let me drive."

"Huh?" I replied, glancing at Quinton.

He raised his eyebrows at me. "I said, pull over and let me drive. You're thinking too much."

I'd been letting my mind churn and was paying less attention to the road than I should have. But I still didn't like the implication. "Are you saying I'm driving badly?"

"No. I thought you might prefer to do just one thing at a time. Although with these two along, shotgun has to play battlefield negotiator too," he added, scritching Grendel behind one ear as the dog stuck his head through the gap between the front seats to sniff at Chaos for the dozenth time in as many minutes. The ferret made a hissing noise and gaped her teeth at him.

My face felt cramped from the depth of my frown. Maybe I shouldn't drive after all. . . .

I pulled over and traded places with Quinton, taking the ferret and putting her into my purse on my lap, which made her bolder. Chaos crawled out at once and up onto my shoulder so she could lord it over the dog from the height of the backrest. Strangely, the dog seemed to think this was much better, too, and lay down with his head on his paws, heaving a sigh. Apparently Grendel was perfectly happy not to be top dog, so long as he knew who was. That reminded me of the vampires' pack mentality and I felt myself scowling again.

Quinton put the truck back in gear and pulled into traffic. We hadn't even discussed where we were going: We were just driving.

"So what is it you're thinking?" he asked.

"That I caused Simondson's death."

"What? I'm sorry you think so, but that's a load of crap."

"Maybe, but it's still what I'm thinking."

"You are not responsible for the death of anyone who ever touched you or knew you. People die. You aren't responsible for your dad's death, or that cousin you mentioned, or your ex-boyfriend who called up and put the current game in motion—"

"Cary did not start this. He's not even involved."

"Except to call you and say cryptic things."

I stared at him. "Are you jealous of a dead man?"

"No, and that's not the topic. The problem is you sound as if you're blaming yourself for this guy's death."

"I am."

"Don't. You didn't do it."

"But he wouldn't be dead if he hadn't been involved with me."

Quinton made an impatient noise. "He wasn't involved with you. You were investigating him and he went off the deep end and beat you."

"But he wouldn't have done that if he hadn't been . . . bespelled and coerced by Alice and Wygan."

"I don't necessarily believe that."

"I saw a loop of memory. I saw Goodall break the spell."

"But can you be sure the spell compelled Simondson against his will?"

"Yes!"

"I don't think you can. You don't know what that spell did, only that there was one. And are you certain that any spell could compel a man into an action that is totally against his nature and inclination?"

"I've pushed on people myself, compelled them to answer questions and even pushed them into actions—"

"That they already had reason to do, or words they were already thinking, or ideas they had already formulated."

And I suddenly wasn't so sure of my guilt or of the things I'd done. What *had* I done?

"This guy wasn't the nicest, straightest shooter to begin with, you know. What were you investigating him for again?"

"Fraud—which is not a violent crime."

"Was that all he did?"

I had to think back a bit to remember—two years had passed since then, after all. It hadn't been a major case in my mind at the time. Not like a pretrial investigation for a murder case or a rape.

Todd Simondson had embezzled from his dead wife's estate, stealing from his stepdaughter's inheritance. He'd done it for years after his wife died—longer than he'd had any legal right to be administrating her estate—by intimidating and manipulating his stepdaughter so she never challenged him. He hadn't been a nice man; he'd been vain and greedy and emotionally abusive, for certain. But off the top of my head, I couldn't remember if my client had ever said he'd struck her. She'd implied that he'd hastened her mother's death, but there'd been no evidence of foul play; the woman had died in the hospital of a blood disease. The sort that creates bruises and freakish bleeding. I creased my brow as I thought harder, wondering if some of the bruises might have had some help in getting there. Simondson had certainly kept his stepdaughter quiet for a while and perhaps his methods crossed over into the physical. Maybe he hadn't been entirely against solving his problems with women in a violent way.

If Wygan, through Alice, had led Simondson to believe that I and my investigation were a physical threat to him, that I was dangerous, that it was all right to fix the problem by putting me in the hospital . . . maybe he hadn't been disinclined to do violence and the spell upon him had only encouraged him to go too far once he started. Most people, no matter how pissed off, wouldn't have slammed an antique elevator's security gate on another person's neck. Especially after they'd beaten that same person's head against a wall first. He hadn't seemed like a violent guy when I'd approached him, but I hadn't been looking into his proclivities in that direction; I'd just been looking at his creative financing.

I still had some doubt. I didn't want to think that I'd been the cause of his death—no matter how deserving—or of anyone else's. Even if it might be true once in a while, I didn't think I could live with myself if I thought I had the literal touch of death.

"So, you don't think it's my fault, even though Wygan and his crew killed Simondson," I said.

"Did they?"

I nodded. "Yeah. The bit of memory I got to see definitely showed me Wygan and Goodall were involved. I don't think Goodall was in at the beginning—he wasn't even around that I know of—but he's playing on Wygan's team now. And there's something really weird about him. . . ."

"Aside from the vampire thing?"

"Well, he's not a vampire, at least not any type I recognize. But he's something close. And there is something very odd about his energy. I think," I added, considering the way I'd seen Goodall rip into the web of magic on Simondson, "that he's got some kind of power. I'm not sure what he is or what the magic does, but I saw him touch the spell and most people can't even see them. But I don't think he cast it in the first place. . . . I don't see how that works, timing-wise, since I never met him before a few weeks ago. If he'd been in the mix then, I'd have expected to at least stumble across him back when—"

"You were killed."

I took a couple of deep breaths before I nodded. "Yeah." Now I was confused. I wished I knew more about the spell that had been on Simondson and what Goodall had done to remove it. It had hurt and that didn't seem to be true for most spell-destruction. At least it had never seemed to be the case when I dismantled a spell, but I rarely had anything to do with spells cast on people, so I wasn't sure. I needed to talk to Mara; she could tell me more about the spells and maybe what Goodall was.

But that wasn't going to solve the question of my guilt in Simondson's death. And regardless of that, it was still Goodall who'd been the direct cause. I wanted to get my hands on Goodall and Wygan, not just because of what they were doing to me but also for what they'd done to Simondson and my father. And wherever I found one of them, I was pretty sure the other would be nearby.

"Umm . . . why do I think you're planning something dangerous?" Quinton asked.

"Because you've gotten used to the face I make when I'm pissed off. I have to go after Wygan and Goodall. The sooner the better. They might not know I've gotten ahold of Simondson, and the faster I move, the less time they have to guess what I'll do."

Quinton pursed his lips, but didn't say anything about how stupid I might be or what the risk was. That was one of the things I loved in him: He didn't lecture me or tell me not to dive into things. If he had information or questions, he spoke up. Otherwise he let me do what I had to.

"You want me with you?"

I shook my head. "No, it's strictly my gig. I wouldn't mind having you nearby, but the Danzigers' is close enough and we need to go there anyway."

"We do?"

"Yeah. We need to drop off the pets before I go do something stupid."

TEN

Quinton drove in loops and meanders up to Queen Anne Hill, checking for anyone watching the Danzigers' house or the approaches. "You're sure you don't want us along?" he asked.

"Sure? No. What I'd like is an army at my back, if I'm being honest. But that won't really help and it will help even less if I lead the only people who can save my impulsive ass into a trap with me."

"*Do* you think it's a trap?"

"No. I don't think Wygan and Goodall have had time to adjust to our disappearance. They know I'm out here somewhere, but vampires—especially Wygan—are arrogant and they may not have any contingency plan in place for my coming to them so soon without having been nabbed by their cronies first. Also—" I cut myself off.

"Also what?"

"I don't think they know."

"Know what?"

I waved my hand through the air as if wiping my words out. "Sorry, I'm going to hold that for now since I'll have to explain it to the Danzigers, too. Just bear with me a few minutes."

Quinton shrugged. "OK."

We found a safe place to leave the truck, in a small parking lot near a tiny grocery store, and walked the rest of the way. There was a slight risk in our walking together since either one of us was probably recognizable to most of the vampires in Seattle by now and both of us together was a sure ID. Still, we were better as a team in detecting the bloodsuckers from a distance: I could see and smell them and Quinton had been tinkering with yet another Grey detector system. We had to go a bit out of our way but once again made it through the back gate to the Danzigers' house safely—at least as far as I could tell. No one had renewed the spell I'd defused earlier, so the way was open.

Brian was still abed, so there was no noisy reunion between boy and dog. Grendel looked disappointed as Mara met us at the back door.

"Ah, you're back in one piece I see."

"For now," I replied. Grendel whined to come in and find his playmate, but we left him to guard the backyard instead. Bowls of food and water quickly replaced the boy in his affections—at least for a while.

Mara led us through to the living room where the drapes were, uncharacteristically, drawn closed. Ben was seated in a comfy chair, reading a thick tome in German. I know less German than I do Spanish—which is about enough to curse at people and ask for a beer, the bathroom, and my hotel keys—but I could still recognize the words for "ghost" and "paranormal" so I assumed it was more research for his book. He looked up as we entered.

"Hah! I found a reference to the asetem outside Egypt! So this is not the first time they've gone afield. But here's the interesting bit: They never travel without the direct order of the Pharaohn and they always have servants."

"Yeah," I replied, "I've noticed most vampires have servants of some kind to protect them during the daylight hours. I met a sort of . . . fish man in London who was enslaved in some way to the vampire I was looking for."

"But most of those are servants of opportunity—demi-vampires and the like. The asetem make theirs quite specifically."

"Are you talking about the kreanou?"

"Kreanou?" Ben frowned. "I'm not sure. . . . What is that?"

I blinked at him, surprised I'd come up with something he didn't know. "They're, uh . . . sort of super-vampires. They're incredibly fast, single-minded, and vicious. They can change shape, too, a little. But they are driven to hunt and destroy the vampire who made them. Some kind of rare mistake, I gathered. Sort of fury incarnate that dies once it kills its creator."

They all stared at me. "Well, that doesn't sound like a useful servant at all," Mara said.

"No. I think they're usually something vampires fear," I added and explained the kreanou I'd encountered in London.

Silence ticked a moment after my tale ended. "Uh, no, I don't think this is the same thing," Ben said. "The book calls them 'ushabti'—it's the same word as the funerary statues of servants meant to attend the dead in the afterlife—and attributes some magical powers to them—limited, but still powers. Did I tell you the asetem are magical?"

"Yes, you did. What kind of magic?"

"Mostly small magic, illusions and emotional manipulations, but the Pharaohn has a few bigger powers, chiefly generative. He's the only one who can make another asete or an ushabti."

I narrowed my eyes in thought. "What are these ushabti like?"

"Unfortunately the book isn't specific about that except that they can move around in the daylight. And it doesn't say how they're made or destroyed, just that they are 'servants by life and by blood.' Or that's the best translation I can make. This is a pretty old book and the writing is a bit . . . eccentric."

"So the asetem and their servant went to Germany once?"

"Looks that way. You know the Nazis were big collectors of antiquities, but they weren't the first group of Germans to be interested in that sort of thing. Various Germanic states and institutions stuck their paws into the collection of ancient mystic artifacts. Apparently one prince or another . . ." He looked down into his book for a moment for more information but had to shrug and continue after a fruitless moment. "Well, it's a little unclear who, but someone managed to piss off the Pharaohn and he sent a small cohort into the area to exact revenge, with an ushabti to protect them. According to this book, the asetem did it in remarkably bloody style—even for vampires—which isn't too unusual for them since they thrive on strong, negative emotions like fear and panic. They did things like flaying people alive and killing their children while they watched—"

I felt sick and, judging by the others' faces, I wasn't the only one. I held up a hand. "I get the idea. They committed atrocities."

"In a word. And when they were done, they packed up and disappeared."

"Literally?"

"Well, no. They went back to Egypt. The Pharaohn doesn't squander his people—they're too rare. But they probably didn't worry too much about their ushabti once they got home since he wasn't an asete—at least if I am reading this correctly he wasn't. And I don't see how he could have been; the asetem don't have any daywalking abilities among their magical powers and they wouldn't convert one of their own and then throw him away."

"But their servants do have some powers? How does that happen if the ushabti aren't asetem? Regular vampires don't usually wield any magic. How do these guys rate?"

"One skill the asetem do have is sensing magical ability in others. Which might explain how the Pharaohn found you and your father in the first place. The . . . subject's powers remain intact after conversion to asete, apparently."

I was getting an idea, but it was also confusing me on another point I'd thought I had. "So they know what powers people like me have?"

"I don't think so. I think they just know there's a power there. To know which one, they'd have to observe for a while. I'm guessing here, but that seems the likely scenario."

"And that would also explain why Wygan didn't make a move to force me into his plan earlier. He had to wait until I did something he recognized. It also confirms something I was thinking—" I turned and glanced at Quinton. "This is what I didn't say in the truck—I don't think most vampires have any idea what powers I have or that I even have any at all. I don't think Edward knew what I can do until he got information from others and made guesses that were often incomplete and presumed more on my investigator's skills. I don't think the asetem—or even the Pharaohn—know exactly what I can do. Wygan only knows what direction he's pushed me in and he won't be certain he's succeeded until I show him or he pushes again and sees what I do."

Quinton closed his eyes and nodded, putting the pieces together to his own satisfaction.

"Carlos is probably the only vampire who has any idea at all. And I have no way of knowing how good his idea is," I continued.

"So y'need him as an ally," Mara suggested.

"Let's hope I don't. I'm not sure how safe I'd be standing between Carlos and any offer of power."

"True," Mara agreed. "He can be a right greedy bastard."

I grunted in thought: These ushabti had some kind of magic. They weren't vampires or asetem, but they had some traits in common; they could walk in the daylight and were the servants—tied by blood and life—to the Pharaohn and his asetem. A servant . . . I knew who that had to be. "So . . . that would make Bryson Goodall Wygan's ushabti. But I don't think he always has been. Edward wouldn't have let him close." Now I thought I understood why Goodall had said, "Things change." Not just things but him, too.

The Danzigers looked puzzled and I had to explain who Bryson Goodall was.

"Certainly if he was workin' that closely with Edward, he couldn't have been Wygan's ushabti," Mara said.

"But he was Wygan's spy. So maybe the ushabti thing came later," I suggested.

Ben looked crestfallen. "I don't know how the conversion is done or what state the candidate has to be in first. . . ."

"That doesn't matter right now, but the fact that I know it might."

In spite of my long rest earlier, I felt a little tired either from my exertions at the brewery or just in anticipation of what I was yet to do that night. I sat down on one of the pale green couches near the hearth. No fire was lit, but it was the most Grey-silent part of the whole room where the only ghostly noise was the distant electrical hum of the power grid. Quinton sat down next to me and slipped my closest hand into his own warm, grounded grip. I took a slow, clearing breath, savoring the moment of peace.

Mara perched on the arm of the chair next to her husband and they leaned together without thinking. A small, pink corona swirled between them. I hated to break the surface of contentment, but I spoke up anyway, knowing I had to get on with my plans soon. "If Goodall is Wygan's ushabti, that would explain how he was able to pull away the spell on Simondson. Or rather, he's Wygan's ushabti *because* he could do so, once trained." Mara and Ben looked startled. Quinton just squeezed my hand a little. "I think Wygan's been a busy master while I was in London."

I explained what I'd seen at the brewery office, how Goodall had been present at Simondson's death and what he had done. "If he's the ushabti, then his ability to break the spell—even knowing it was there to break—makes some sense it didn't before. He didn't seem very comfortable with it, though I'm not sure if that's lack of experience or what. I would like to know what the spell was doing to Simondson before it was removed."

Mara frowned. "Without seein' it myself, I can't say."

I shook my head. "That's not quite what I mean. What I'm really interested in is whether the spell could have caused Simondson to do something that was entirely against his will and inclination."

"Some can. But it would have to be a very powerful compulsion indeed. The greater a subject's resistance, the more force must be applied."

"Like the inverse-square law?" Quinton asked.

"Well, perhaps not quite quadruplin' the force as you halve the distance, but 'tis something like that, yes." Mara smiled a little. "But a working that compelling would be complex and not so simply torn away when y'were done with it. It would need dismantling."

Quinton turned his gaze to me, but he didn't say anything. Certainly not "I told you so," and yet I didn't feel much better about Simondson.

"It didn't look complex. Maybe I only saw the end of the

process. We don't know that Goodall couldn't have taken a more complicated spell apart."

"That we don't," Mara agreed, "but 'tisn't likely. If he had such skills, surely you'd have noticed. And I'm thinkin' Wygan wouldn't want an ushabti with too much power runnin' about while he's dozin' of a morning. Bit of a paranoid control-freak, isn't he?"

That I would have to concede. "But the hole in the temporaclines—doesn't that argue for some greater power? I've never seen them just broken up like that in a recent timeline. Someone tore that bit of history out of the Grey there."

"Not necessarily. Was the Guardian runnin' 'round it?"

"No. There wasn't anything there except the *absence* of anything."

"If it wasn't attractin' the Guardian's attention, then it's only a local break, not a chronic one. More likely the effect of someone bein' hasty in the Grey while tryin' to cover up their mess in the normal world. Settin' the garden on fire rather than pullin' up the weeds." She snorted in disgust. "The Grey'll repair itself there, in time, but they've made a bloody bags of it in the meantime."

That, at least, made me feel I might not be walking into a nest of vipers—just one really big snake and his pet asp. "So you think," I started, "that he might not really know what he's doing . . . ?"

"He must know he's touchin' magic, but he may have been ignorant of what or how he's usin' it. Judgin' by the wreck you say he's made, he's not experienced at the very least. Likely he's just followin' Wygan's instructions and muddlin' through on instinct. If he never knew he had any touch of the Grey before this, it must be comin' as a bit of a shock now. Just think of yourself two years ago."

I nodded. "All the better reason to move now, before anyone gets wiser."

"Move?" Ben interjected, twitching hard enough to dislodge Mara from the arm of his chair.

I patted the air, trying to calm Ben down, but I knew it was useless. "Yes. Simondson's ghost gave me a clue about what might be happening to my dad. And if I can figure it out, I can let both ghosts go free. So I'm going to go up to the station and see what I can get out of Wygan and Goodall that might help me find my father and Edward and ruin whatever plans the Pharaohn has for me. Right now they think they have all the cards. If I can surprise them, shake them up, I might be able to get some information out of them before they can do me any serious harm."

"'Any serious harm'?" Mara repeated. "Y'can't mean to confront them so soon—y'don't know anything, certainly not what they're up to."

"I do know that if they were ready to capture or kill me, they'd have done it earlier. Right now they only want to manipulate me and keep me off-balance. If they had grabbed me, they'd have to keep me, and that means guards and magical restraint and keeping me isolated and under control. Obviously they can't or aren't ready to do that yet. Probably they're spread thin with other preparations. So I still have some grace period. If I hit them now, they won't expect it and they may tell me something useful, if I can shake them. Maybe I can even do *them* a little damage for once. If I keep dithering around until the conditions are perfect, they never will be. A preemptive strike makes more sense in this situation than waiting. I will not allow them to think they have the upper hand."

"You're mad!" Mara protested. "Y'haven't even got a plan what to do when you get there."

"I can't have much of a plan since I don't know what they are doing. That's the point. If I shake them now, I may be able to find out or even stop them. But if I just sit here and let them do whatever they like, they remain in control and I have no choice but to be driven where they want. I will not let them do that any longer. I'll find out what I can, by whatever method I can."

Ben chimed in on the same tune with Mara, squelching by sheer volume my attempts to tell them I wasn't crazy, just willing to take a risk now, while the odds were not so stacked against me in exchange for a better position later.

Before the noise could wake Brian, Quinton pulled me around to meet his stare. "I'm going with you."

"Oh, no, you aren't. I already told you"—I shot a quelling glare at the Danzigers, too—"I'm not taking my backup into danger with me. That's why you're called 'the backup.' You stay out until I need you."

Quinton grabbed on to my shoulders so I had to focus on him. "*They're* the backup; I'm the partner. And I *am* going because I have the key."

ELEVEN

"What? A key? To what?" I demanded.

"To the radio station," Quinton replied. "You may be sneaky and ghosty and all that, but you still have to get past the gate and into the building without setting off any alarms, magical or mundane. I can work the mundane side, which leaves you just the magical side to worry about. And I can take care of myself even with the vampires and ghosts, remember? I did it for years."

"The asetem aren't your regular vampire. Didn't we just discuss that?"

"Yes, we did. That does not change the tactical problem of getting into the bastard's lair, just the details. You are not going to play Rambo—even if you *are* a lot better looking and smarter. You don't have to go alone and there's no advantage to it, so you won't be doing that."

The Danzigers were both giving me pointed stares, plainly on Quinton's side now that he'd spoken up.

"You're making a hell of an assumption."

"Yup. I'm assuming you haven't totally lost your mind or your sense. And, well . . ." He blushed and his gaze cut aside for a moment before returning, softer, to my own. He continued in a whisper. "There is that I-love-you thing. . . ."

My throat tightened and I felt tears prick my eyes. I couldn't get words out of my mouth; they just knotted up on my tongue.

"I didn't just say that to get you home. I mean it. If you are determined to do something crazy-ass stupid because you have to, I won't be a macho jerk and try to talk you out of it. But I'm going to do everything I can to keep it from killing you. If staying here really would make you safer, I'd stay put. But it won't. Greasing electrons and lying to locks might. So I'm going with you."

"Quinton—"

Mara cut across my protest. "He's right. Aside from your being utterly barkin'—and I still say you're madder than a March hare—you have no hope of this plan workin' without help. Your wantin' to protect us has gotten ahead of your sense. You won't be any safer keepin' us *all* behind the barricades and Quinton does have skills you could use."

"So do you."

"But you don't need them. Anything I could be doin' for this situation, you can do yourself. I truly am the backup."

"I don't think you should go at all," Ben added. "Why should you? You could set a trap and wait for them to come to you. Bide your time, stay safe."

"Ben, you haven't listened to a word I've said. That only buys more time for *them*," I retorted. "I cannot let them have any more advantages. It's risky for me to walk into Wygan's lair, but if I'm bold enough and fast enough, I can keep them off balance and possibly get through to my father, get some information, or break Goodall's loyalty to Wygan. Any of these would be worth the risk."

"What if they're already waitin' for you?" Mara asked.

"I'll burn that bridge when I come to it and call in the cavalry: you."

"But you *will* be takin' Quinton along, shan't you?"

I looked at Quinton, who gave me half a smile that was more rueful than smug. I guess he didn't like having contradicted me in front of other people, but I could live with it. I've had worse, usually from my mother.

"Yes."

"Good. We'll give you an hour and if y'haven't called or come back, we'll come after you both. Shan't we, Ben?"

He nodded, adamant and a bit tense. "With the dog."

"Maybe you should leave the dog to Brian-sit," I suggested, hoping to lighten the mood.

"Better than the ferret, I suppose," Mara added.

Ben refused to laugh, though we could all see his mouth twitch.

There was a bit more discussion, none of it really going anywhere, before I put the ferret into her cage and walked out of the house, heading uphill toward the broadcast towers on the top. Quinton strolled along with me, holding on to a paperback-sized silver box containing his latest Grey detector.

"Not seeing anything here," he muttered.

"Not surprising. Wygan won't have staked out the whole route—it's pretty public—only the Danzigers' and the station. Nothing else is really important and would spread his resources too thin."

Quinton grunted acknowledgment. "Sounds like he's got a limited supply of cronies."

"Limited numbers, yes. Unfortunately, his assistants *aren't* limited to the asetem and Goodall. Any vampire who's not aligned with Edward could be working for Wygan. I don't know how many vampires there are in Seattle, or how many might be persuaded to come from somewhere else, if that's possible. So I admit I'm only making a best guess based on the activity I've seen and what you've reported."

Quinton sighed. "I hate Heisenberg. We can know where the vampires are but not how many."

"Not that it matters. We will get in one way or another. Or I will. If things go pear-shaped, you get the hell out and fetch the Danzigers."

He nodded and we walked on in silence, each scanning for enemies or pitfalls but finding nothing. Even outside the station, in the darkness at the edge of the parking lot, there was nothing to find except the uncanny blood red trace of vampires past.

We went around and came up on the tower from behind, pausing in the shadows of overgrown hedges that skirted the now-abandoned parking lot of the old Queen Anne High School gymnasium across the narrow road on the east side. The gym building was locked, the nearest doors secured with a loop of chain and a padlock, keeping them closed in spite of evidence of recent vandalism. The windowless concrete refugee from the 1970s was the ugliest building on the whole hill—and would have been standout grotesque almost anywhere—but it was still unusual to find any sort of petty destruction or tagging in the area that was sometimes called Nob Hill. But the snippet of narrow road we stood on was rarely traveled, even sitting as it did across from a newer school building and next to a graciously renovated old one. The odd isolation of the old gym made it a perfect target for anyone angry enough to kick in the doors. I took it as a sign that the area wasn't too well patrolled at night or monitored by any video cameras, which was good news for us.

There was a bit of open park on the west side of the tower and some impressive houses across the main street running in front. Nothing but trees and bushes to the north. The chain-link fence around the tower and its building was pierced by gates on the front and side. The side gate, facing us, stood open.

"Seems too easy," Quinton whispered.

"The bad stuff's inside."

"Yeah. . . ." He studied the rear door with a monocular from where we stood. "Looks like one old-style CCTV security camera on the door and an electronic combination lock. Bit behind the times, technology-wise."

"I don't think Wygan is too worried about that sort of thing."

Quinton snorted. "Makes my job easier." He scrambled in his pockets and brought out a small flashlight in place of the monocular. "Do you see anything in the Grey between here and the door?"

"Nothing significant."

"Then get ready to run when the next car comes over the hill."

We both crouched in the shadows of the plants at the edge of the street and waited. After a few minutes, an SUV came up the road, its headlights momentarily flicking upward and over the building as it crested the rise. Quinton flicked on his powerful flashlight, aiming for the camera and flooding the lens with bright white light under cover of the headlights' glare. We bolted forward for the few seconds that the camera was blinded and stopped directly under it, where it had no view. Whoever had set it up had assumed that no one inside wanted to see the lock keypad or the intercom as much as they wanted to see the face of someone standing on the porch to use them, leaving a nice human-sized hole in the view if you stood right under the camera or up against the door. I took the door position so Quinton could work on the lock, putting my back to it and scanning the area in the Grey, just in case.

An unusual number of ghosts seemed to wander near the building, thin vaporous things even in the Grey, loops of memory drained of all intelligence, but lingering. Or perhaps drawn in, I thought as I peered harder at one: the ghost of a railroad worker, wearing an antique coverall and cap with the Great Northern's mountain goat logo on the front. What was he doing here? What little I could make out of the rest was equally hodgepodge and as I started to examine them the ringing in my ears returned, rising to a whining chatter. I shook my head.

"Not ready?" Quinton whispered.

"Huh?"

"I said I'm done and you shook your head. Aren't you ready to go in?"

"Oh. Yes, I think it's safe to open the door and see what's on the other side."

Quinton quirked an eyebrow at me, catching the pun. A heavy click sounded from the lock mechanism and, remaining crouched outside the threshold, he pushed the door open. I looked in through the Grey.

Just beyond the door, the hallway to the broadcast booth looked like a red-and-black version of a funnelweb spider's trap. I could barely spot a surface on the walls or floor bigger than my hand that wasn't thick with the filaments of magic. They caked the narrow corridor, converting it into a tunnel that led to the monster's lair at the center of the web: the booth where I'd first met Wygan.

My stomach heaved and a flash of hot fear broke a sweat on my skin that went instantly clammy. I had to go ahead, even though my mind and body balked. In all the rushing to examine my past and the why and how of my Greywalker status—even though I knew it would come to this—I hadn't considered the visceral horror that returning to confront Wygan here would hold for me. In this building, at the end of the spell-hung hall, was where he had broken me, where I'd been forced to knowledge I didn't want.

The buzzing in my ears crescendoed to a screeching of ghostly voices calling out to me: "darling," and "Harper," and "monster," and "bitch." They cried for my attention in every way imaginable, pleading, cursing, cajoling, flirting, and even in the din a thin voice called me "little girl" and sent a flare of dying fire scurrying toward me on the spider's web of magic. That was my father—this time I was sure—and he was trying to reach me. I'd hoped there might be a way to him if I was close to Wygan and it seemed I might be right. And no matter how half-formed my plan, now I had no choice; I had to go to him, somewhere ahead in this web-bound maze.

The tangle of energy that festooned the hall pulled away from the weak flare, making a path too narrow and coiling to tread but pointing the way deeper into the heart of the gyre. I could see there were other holes in the uncanny fabric, now that I was looking for them. A difficult string of stepping-stones, rising normal and dry in the flood of Grey energy. It was going to be tricky, but I thought I could do it. . . .

I braced myself, catching my breath and straightening my spine as much as I could. I hadn't been *en pointe* for decades and I didn't have the shoes for it, but I still knew how to move with the precision and balance required. I hoped. I shed my boots and socks and started to step over the doorsill.

Quinton caught my near elbow, steadying my movement. "You're going?"

"Yeah," I whispered back, digging in my pocket. "Here, hold on to Simondson while I'm gone. I don't want Wygan to sniff him out."

Quinton accepted the tin that held the thread of my dead assailant and tucked it away, adding, "Forty minutes and I'm coming after you."

"You damn well better."

I took a long, storklike step into the thick nest of magical threads, arching my foot into a slender point that slid through a hole in the crimson tangle until I could touch the floor. As I stepped away from Quinton, I eased deeper into the Grey, becoming less solid, more fluid, and closer to death. I lost contact with his warmth but didn't look back as the sound of the Grey roared in my head.

Tunnel-like, the center of the hallway was clear enough for me to stalk down without much bending to avoid the energy threads. I plotted each step with care, certain that like a real spiderweb, one inappropriate twitch of the magical mesh would bring its master rushing to capture me. It was difficult finding the right spot for each step, but the thin, blazed trail of my father's sending remained, though slowly closing, hinting at the way ahead and leaving clear spaces on the walls to put down an occasional steadying hand.

Progress was slow and miserable. Each step sent a new shout of sound through my head, as if I were treading on unseen wounded beneath the fire and fog of the Grey. I controlled a shudder and went on toward the chromatic flashing of lights at the end of the hall.

I remembered that light from the first time I'd met Wygan: a rack of simple, colored bulbs strobing random combinations of blue, red, and yellow. I didn't understand it then, but now I knew the Guardian Beast had difficulty with certain colors of light and shied away from them, confused that they looked like magic but didn't act like it. Wygan, plotting something it wouldn't like, had learned the trick of hiding himself from the Beast with the random lights. But it meant he couldn't go far without risking its attention. No wonder he'd sent Alice to England: He couldn't leave Seattle unless he took his light show with him. I nearly stumbled as I thought that perhaps he'd needed them two years ago to keep the Beast away as he'd planted a piece of the Grey in my chest. And now he was too far advanced into his plan for the Beast to ignore him. Which meant that killing Simondson—for which he'd left his lair, at horrendous risk—had been the last stage before he became an active threat to the Grey. Now I knew what the coils of electric cable in the brewery office had been for:

to run the light show under which Wygan hid from the retribution of the Guardian Beast. Whatever I was going into, it was extremely unpretty.

As I neared the door I began to see hints of a dark-blue thread in the red-and-black warp of magic in the hall: Goodall was nearby or had had a hand in making the web. Either way, it seemed likely I would find him in the room with Wygan. I wondered how long the funnel web had been in place and what it meant. It could have been a trap just for me, but it had the feel of something built up in layers over time.

I paused at last before the door, standing in a void of the web just a little bigger than a shoe box. Music I couldn't identify muttered from speakers over the door, mixed with the whispering of the grid. The sound made my head ache. My bare feet were cold—so was the rest of me—and I wasn't sure if I should pull the gun or not. It wouldn't do much to Wygan I was sure, but it did seem to distract Goodall, who wasn't used to being bulletproof yet.

To hell with it: better one distracted than none. I went for the gun. Sometimes I have difficulty holding on to normal objects when I'm deep in the Grey, so I pushed myself away from it, becoming as solid as possible as I slid my hand into the small of my back, gripping the pistol at the back of my hip and sliding it free of the holster. Then I threw my shoulder into the weak side of the door and bulled my way into the room, bringing the muzzle up to sweep the area as I ducked and dove in.

Wygan might have been on me by the time I came to a stop, except that Goodall got in the way. He wasn't as fast as the Pharaohn-ankh-astet, but he happened to be standing between us and he was both surprised and pissed off at my entrance. Goodall lifted his arm to grab me, pivoting on the leg I'd knocked in earlier. He wobbled a little but he didn't buckle, so the vampire recuperative powers were working. This time I didn't kick his knee; I shot it.

He shrieked and spit a string of epithets as he went down. So far, so good.

Wygan seemed to vault over the other man, reaching for me, but I was already crouching down to avoid him, and the white-haired vampire ripped the air just above my head. I pushed the gun's muzzle into the hollow below Goodall's chin and forced him back to his feet with the pressure as Wygan spun to take another swipe at me. I kept the pale vampire in sight and turned Goodall to face him. "Keep coming and you'll be shopping for a new minion."

Goodall made a coughing sound as he rose. "Unholy bitch . . ."

"You can blame your master for that."

Wygan had stopped on the far side of the room, keeping the broadcast control console between us—more of a barrier to me, with my limited human strength and speed, than to him. In the normal he didn't look any different than he had when we'd met two years earlier: heroin-addict thin, shoulder-length white hair rock-and-roll wild to hide the strange long shape of his skull, and still no sign that he was older than thirty-five at the most, though I knew he was ancient.

" 'Arper Blaine. Wot an unexpected pleasure." His Cockney accent was as broad and fake as ever.

But I *had* surprised him—how nice for me. I kept my mouth shut and my gaze steady on his body, avoiding his snake-eyed stare—funny how they didn't glow like those of his underlings—and watching for any shift of muscle that would telegraph motion. I took in the room from peripheral vision and replayed my memory of it, comparing the changes. There wasn't much that was different from last time, except that the broadcast booth was plainly doing double duty now as Wygan's lair and the old light array he'd used to keep the Guardian at bay was now much larger. There was also a dark spot of energy that coiled on itself like a gleaming black Orouborus, hanging unsupported in the air near what had been the disk racks. Now the rack was empty of all but a glimmering curtain of magic and that dark circle. The discs and my unschooled state must have hidden the circle from me before. Or maybe I just hadn't noticed.

"You don't 'ave to threaten Mr. Goodall, love—'e's not doin' you any 'arm."

"But you're planning to and I don't see why I should

suffer for your benefit alone. I'm not interested in playing games I can't win."

"Games?" Wygan snorted, his accent fading away to an angry hiss. "You don't have a proper appreciation of necessity. My goals are far grander than some game. Ascension requires sacrifice."

"So far, I doubt you've been the one to make any; you just coerce other people into giving up their lives for you. Aren't sacrifices voluntary? It looks like you had to kidnap Edward, and did Goodall volunteer to be your lackey and spy or did you trick him into it? And you haven't been so very clever at getting me to do what you want, either. Batting zero on cooperation, Wygan."

"Yet you are here, Greywalker."

"Right—with a gun to your ushabti's head. Is that really the way you thought this was going to go down? You've been playing hardball to get me into your clutches for a while—years now—but I don't think you're as much in control as you pretend. Do you intend to keep playing me until I just happen to fall into the right place, the right shape? That doesn't sound worthy of you; that hardly sounds like a plan at all, really. Unless it's such a bad idea that you know no one would participate willingly. You couldn't get my father to do it. You couldn't get Alice to stick to your plan—I'm sure your minions in London have told you how she fucked up and went rogue. You're the Pharaohn-ankh-astet—you're supposed to be the baddest of the bad—but you don't seem to be holding the reins as well as you should and you don't have the confidence in your own plan to sell me on it."

Wygan narrowed his eyes but kept silent. I imagined I'd hit a nerve there. He was hesitating and that was to my benefit. All I needed was for him to show me my father, or Edward, or slip up on even the smallest hint of what he was up to and I was sure I could work out the rest from there. That was all I needed: one admission, one clue. I was willing to walk dangerously close to the line to get it, but once I did, I was gone. I hoped. Though I might need all my cavalry to pull me out. I was cognizant of how little plan I had and how thin what there was of it looked.

Goodall twitched in my grip and I squeezed on the pistol's cocking lever so it made a quelling click. He seethed and held himself stiffly against the pain in his knee and the indignity of having been held at the point of an uncocked gun. "You're not worthy," he muttered. "You don't deserve it, you weak, mercenary little bitch."

I ignored the insults—it's not as if I haven't been called them before. "Deserve? There are a lot of things I don't deserve—like having my head beaten in, or my relatives killed and friends terrorized. Whatever the Pharaohn's plan is, I doubt he's got anyone's interest in mind but his own. If you believe otherwise, you're deluded." I wondered if Goodall hated me for some other reason or if he thought he could take my place. . . . "If he wants me to play along, he's going to have to make it worth my while one way or another. And that starts with a little information."

"You have no idea what is in store," Wygan whispered, "what you can do. . . ."

"No." The whispers of the grid roared in my head and seemed to push out of my mouth as an echo of some other mind: "I am the gate, the bridge. Mine is the power to cross the gap—" I broke through the rushing voices and regained control of my words. I had no idea of the meaning of what I'd just said, but I wasn't going to let on. "So why not tell me the rest? I'm sure Goodall is dying to know, too. After all, he already sold his soul and he doesn't even know what he'll get for it. Me, I prefer a more equitable exchange."

Goodall shifted his eyes to Wygan. "You can't trust her. She's a weak vessel, like that whimpering thing you keep in the blackness. She's not interested in anything but destroying you and keeping the world as it is. She's on Edward's side."

Now I wanted to know what the thing in the blackness was, but I knew better than to let Wygan know that. It might have been Edward or my father, but it was something Goodall disdained and that might make it something I wanted. I barked at him, "I'm on my own damned side and I'm not giving anyone anything for free. Edward tried to push me and I didn't bend. I went to London when he gave me something I wanted, not because I'm his lackey or his hired gun."

"He gave you money," Goodall sneered.

"He gave me an excuse to do what I wanted to do anyway." I dug the gun muzzle into his neck harder. "You want to give me another one? You think I didn't enjoy taking Alice's head off?"

Wygan laughed and a sensation like knife-edged shards of ice ripped down my spine. "I know what you want. Equity, knowledge, justice . . . yes, those are the currencies that move you, Greywalker. But not all. You have the weakness of loyalty, a useless emotion. The fury in you, the anger . . . that I can use."

I could feel imminent motion building in the room like a static charge. I wanted to get closer to the hanging coil of darkness that might contain my father or Edward. I shifted the pistol so I'd have a better arc of movement and Goodall started to duck away from me. Wygan lunged forward, making a shrieking noise that should have frozen me in place like a jacklighted deer, except that the noise in my ears cut across the sound and kept me moving, though trembling.

Ahead of me, the oily magical curtain billowed as if in the wind of Wygan's passage. The normal world fell aside, letting the Grey flood the room, lit with fire and neon. Goodall tumbled away, pushed or falling I didn't know, as I toppled the other way, toward the gleaming void.

Wygan's claws pierced into my upper arms. As at the first time we'd met, his true form showed through in the Grey: white and scaled, with a long, ophidian skull topped by a ridge starting above mesmerizing, pearl-black eyes. And like the first time, I screamed, feeling something ancient and awful cut into me. With time, the memory of his soul-chilling touch had softened and made the terror bearable, but it rushed back and once the air had fled my lungs, the deathly cold of it suffocated me.

"Remember this world, remember what I showed you," Wygan hissed. "I taught you to see. Now learn it all. Take it in, gather it to you, let it rush into you, the sound, the feel. . . ."

I just had to concentrate on getting to that dark ring

within the magic, certain that something I needed lay beyond it. I didn't want to touch it or take it in, but I was hearing far more than he knew. He wouldn't have wanted me to listen to the voice that worked its way through the crystalline cold of his words. . . .

"Harper, I'm sorry. I didn't think it would come to this."

I gulped for the wisp of warmth his voice brought. "Dad?" It wasn't even a sound, just the shape of the word cracking against the ice. I tried to look for him and spotted a ring of dark fire around the black center of the gleaming nimbus of void. I struggled to turn toward it, to move into that familiar silent flame I'd first seen around the hole where my father's ghost should have been.

Wygan pushed me forward, toward the blazing grid of magical energy that roared up in the Grey. Twin fires leapt as my head and shoulders crossed over the black edge of the ring—cold flame edging the oubliette while the hungry, singing power of the grid flared with surreal color. Agony raced over my nerves, wrenching another soundless shriek from me and turning the world black at the edges. I felt twisted, immolated like a tree writhing in wildfire.

"It's knowledge you crave," Wygan cooed at me, stabbing my heavy, ice-bound limbs with his claws. "Here is knowledge. Is that not an equitable exchange? Drink it in and know."

His voice flayed me and I gagged, struggling to wriggle free even as the sensation worsened with every second I resisted him. I was half in, half out, held on the brink by Wygan's bitter grip. I couldn't stand it. . . . It felt as if every molecule of my body was tearing apart from the rest, exploding from the sound and power at the black edge.

The other voice drifted to me. "Don't fight yet. It makes the pain much worse. Slide, go limp."

That's what I'd seen happening to Simondson; when he fought, when he moved toward the memory of life, he was burned and tormented. It felt like my brain was bleeding, my limbs charring into brittle sticks. No, I thought. I can't give in. I will die. I'll become what he wants; he'll win!

"It's not so simple. Listen to them, little girl. Let them in."

It wasn't Edward and it couldn't be my father. He'd killed himself to keep me safe, so how could he tell me to give in? He wouldn't! It was a trick. It was something of Wygan's to pull me into the Grey beyond redemption, beyond my control. This voice was a monster that wanted nothing less than my soul—if I had one.

The cacophony of the grid sang and boiled at my brain. Snatches of words fluttered in my ears with a whisper of moth wings and the screech of magic. The sound tore at my mind and burned into my body like acid. Shrieks of pain and terror snuffed to whimpers as they caught and burned away in my throat.

My father's voice continued in swift blasts of soft air against my face. "It's everything. That's what he wants. He doesn't need me, only you. You have to listen. The song will tell you. There's a back door. Use the puzzles to open the way. Shape the key to the lock and open the maze. Each puzzle is a door. The doors are always at the center. From center to center you can cross to me. From the center you're in the Grey, but you're not really here. You'll be safe if you come through the maze. Find the labyrinth—the first maze. Open the right door with the key."

Things were starting to fade, a darkness like fever sleep closed in as the cold and anoxia shut me down. The ringing in my ears, the screeching and muttering, became a shouting chorus of voices tumbling over one another into babble. I felt myself going limp, the pain easing back but not helping me stay alive.

"Not like that, little girl. I said not to fight; I didn't say to give up."

Wygan's voice floated over the top of my consciousness, crooning, "Yes, yes. . . ."

And in counterpoint, the voice from within the void continued as if from another conversation. "You'll have to come back for me later. He can't know I have any strength or he'll destroy me and . . . then I can't help. Listen, listen. . . . I remember your mother. . . . I remember the time she bought you those red tap shoes so the blood wouldn't show. I was so angry with her! So angry . . ." Dad's voice slid upward into a spine-jarring shriek of anguish I could feel through my whole body, like the cutting agony of those horrid crimson shoes. The angrier he got, the more I thought I could see his shape in the darkness, nearly there, nearly solid and writhing in torment with every word. His pain seemed to infect me. A scarlet rage of suffering ripped through me, shouted into my head on the voice of the grid and I jerked away from Wygan's grip.

The frigid ivory knives of his claws slid out of my flesh and blood washed onto my skin, warm and sharp with the scent of life. I rolled onto my back, the floor unexpectedly solid beneath me as the Grey pulled away, recoiling as if in shock. The room flushed amber as the lights in Wygan's rack shifted to keep the Guardian Beast at bay.

They were all I could see and all I could think of to buy time to escape. The echo of the grid's refrain vibrated along my nerves as if the energy of the Grey were powering my limbs and not the weak impulse of my own battered brain. Wygan swooped to grab me once again and I clutched my hands together over my chest, feeling the hard shape of my pistol between my palms.

I squeezed and shot. Again and again. The gun kicked against my sternum as each light shattered and the room went dark with the roar of the Beast descending.

I rolled again, the ringing of the gunshots in my ears deafening me, and started crawling. . . .

TWELVE

It didn't matter now if I touched the red spiderweb lines that coated the hallway. Wygan and Goodall already knew I was leaving, but there was nothing they could do; they were too busy with damage control and keeping themselves out of the jaws of the Guardian Beast. I didn't doubt they'd survive—it couldn't be that easy to stop the Pharaohn-ankh-astet or someone would have done it long ago. I dragged myself down the darkened corridor toward the exit, a growing square of distant, white light.

Even crawling, I felt I was staggering, swaying unsteadily from wall to wall and losing my focus under bouts of nausea. Yeah, that was familiar. But this time I didn't feel like a rape victim. This time there was some hope under the ache, horror, and disgust. Also a hell of a lot of fear, but I wasn't listening to it gibbering in the back of my head; I pushed it down and dragged onward.

The light grew painfully bright and ran toward me, making a sound like wings. It started dipping toward me, that light, and a gold thread of a voice called out from a distance, "Not yet! You don't know what they've done."

The chorus in my head shouted through my efforts to shut it up, like a dog barking to greet its master, cutting through the physical ringing of my shot-damaged hearing. I stifled an urge to puke from the pressure of the noise.

Something shiny and pale blue whirred through the air and settled on me, prickling on my skin like sleet and covering me in a glittering reticulation of energy. It had no weight, but it pushed me to the ground and I sprawled onto the streaked linoleum, sighing out the breath I barely had. "Know the song—"

Someone scooped me up, bundling me over their shoulder with the urgent speed of a fireman exiting a blaze. Jouncing miserably, I was carried outside and into the dimness of the dark streets behind the radio tower. That was when I gave up and vomited.

The jarring, rushing trip continued, down a hill and across broken fields of light and darkness. Feet pattered behind and ahead, and something snorted a hot breath onto my ankle.

"Grendel, sit." It sounded like I was underwater again but at least my normal hearing was returning.

All right: That was Quinton. And the dog. And I thought I saw Mara . . . so . . . Ben had to be around somewhere. . . .

I still couldn't put the images together but I heard the bang of the Danzigers' back screen door and the light around me became a soft, silent yellow. The chattering Grey sound in my ears faded back to the most distant of whispers as the screen door slammed again, leaving only the lingering high-pitched whine of fading gunshots.

This must be the kitchen. I tried to raise my head, but it was difficult and Quinton hefted me higher on his shoulder, knocking the air and the fight out of me. In a minute, he rolled me onto the bed in the basement bedroom and sat down beside me.

"Hey, Harper. Hey, can you hear me?"

"I'm dead, not deaf," I moaned. "At least not permanently deaf."

"Not dead this time," Mara said, her voice drawing closer. She sounded annoyed. "Quinton, you've sick on your coat. You might be wantin' to clean that off."

"It'll wait."

Mara cleared her throat. "It shan't. Go upstairs and wash. Ben'll help you while I take a cloth to Harper. Off with ya."

Quinton's weight shifted away and the slighter one of Mara took his place at the edge of the mattress. I pried my eyes open to see her bending over me, scowling.

"You look bloody mangled."

"Thanks."

"I mean it. Burns, blood, scrapes. What happened to ya?"

"If I knew I'd tell you." I could feel the press of her frown. "Really."

"Well." She took a deep breath. "I hope y'aren't over-fond o' these clothes. They're beyond salvage. I shall have to cut you out or risk tearin' off your head to get the shirt off ya."

"Go for it," I muttered, lolling on the bed, feeling like my bones had been removed.

She stripped off my upper layer and swabbed at me with a wet cloth. I tried to figure out how my body was doing beyond the feeling of having been put backward through a wringer.

"So, was it worth near-dyin' for?"

"Huh?"

"Goin' in there. Whatever y'got. If y'got anything." Angry red and orange sparks danced around her head. I couldn't recall ever seeing anything like that with her before.

"Yes. There's a back door. A way in. I heard my father. I didn't see him, but I knew it was him. He told me about the door."

She made a muffled snort. "Quite sure it wasn't a trick of Wygan's?"

"I thought so at first . . . but he's not that brand of subtle. I didn't get any idea about Edward, though. Or Goodall, except he didn't make any magical moves while I was there." Talking helped to straighten the ideas in my head, but I was still a little confused.

"And has the Pharaohn gotten what he wanted of you, too?"

"I don't think so. He didn't kill me—he didn't really try—and except for this damned ringing in my ears, I don't feel any different."

She sat back, her eyes narrowed. "But would y'know if he had . . . bent you?"

"Yes. I think I would. He hurt me, but not more than that. He said he wanted to give me some kind of knowledge. . . . He tried to force me to listen to something, but I was too busy screaming. What brought you in at the right time?" I asked, hoping to redirect the questions before I had to say anything about the unsettling whispers of the grid. And I didn't mention my far-too-narrow escape.

Mara glared. "You were over time. When I got up the hill, Quinton said he'd heard gunshots and reckoned that was as good a signal as any that y'might be in a bit too deep this time."

"This time? What the hell . . . ?" I levered myself up, feeling a little dizzy but not too wretched, and rested against the headboard so I could look at her without straining. "I'm always in too deep with this stuff. What's with the inquisition?"

She frowned at a spot on my shoulder. "I've always seen us as friends, but there are times I'm unsure what's the cost of that friendship. Or what you really are. I'm always here for you. Always. But you're keeping secrets from me and you make me doubt my own judgment. The business with Albert hasn't done my confidence any favors. I could have lost my son."

"That was more than a year ago. And you didn't have any way to know."

"Hah! I've always read people very well. But I didn't read that right. And maybe it wasn't Albert. Maybe it's you."

I shook my head, thinking I couldn't be hearing this clearly. "What? You think I made Albert do the things he did? He was a bad guy, living and dead. I didn't make him that way. This isn't some experiment where observation changes the outcome."

"That is not what I mean! Some people change things—it's a trick they're carryin' with 'em like luck or disease. With you there's always damage! We met because you'd been damaged, but when it's not you, it's someone else: my son, your da, my husband, Will. . . . What's going to happen, now, hm? Just look at ya. I don't know what you *are*!"

I was so startled, all I could do was stare and shake my head. I hadn't changed into a monster in the past ninety minutes, hadn't grown an extra head, or fangs. . . .

Mara could see I wasn't understanding her. She pointed

at my shoulder and pushed her finger hard into my flesh. It hurt, but not enough to make me wince. "Look: You're healin'. I've seen that before, but not like you're doin'."

I glanced down, tucking my chin so I could see the shoulder Wygan had sunk his claws into. The deep gouges and pits were smeared with blood that had soaked into my shirt and dappled my skin with scarlet and dried brown. It wasn't disappearing or soaking into my flesh, like you'd see in a movie. The holes weren't pulling themselves closed; instead they were weeping light that slowly choked off as the ragged openings dilated shut. They looked like shining, eerie eyes, closing for the night.

"You left here tired and still injured from what happened in London. You came back pukin' ill and bleedin'. But y'aren't now. And how long have we sat here? I'd wager y'don't feel like a woman's just done battle with an asete. Do ya?"

I flexed my hands into fists and ground my teeth, watching the smallest of the bright little wounds wink out and vanish. "No," I replied over the swelling roar of the Grey in my head. I ached and felt burned and bruised, but I didn't hurt like I had in the radio station, or as I lay over Quinton's shoulder being sick from it. Even my ears had stopped ringing.

"Then what happened to ya?"

That was a very good question and I, of course, had no answer. I realized that Mara wasn't angry; she was scared—well, perhaps a bit angry. I had brought a lot of distress into her home and now I was freaking her out. I was freaking me out a bit, too.

"I don't know. I don't feel different. . . . Trust me: I've got a pretty good idea what dead feels like and this wasn't it." I poked at my shoulder and smoothed a finger over one remaining cut. It felt irritated and raw, and the rate of healing had slowed down to a crawl. It was creepy. "As I understand it, I have to actually die—not just come close—to make any changes, so whatever happened isn't a final change. He said he was giving me information . . . no, knowledge. Someone said I should know the song. . . . Huh . . . all I got was this noise in my head and I've had that off and on since I got back from London. There is something . . ." I thought aloud.

"There's something going on that just hasn't crawled up to the front of my brain yet. . . ."

"And that's all? That's the payment for whatever you went through?"

"It's not payment. It's just another block in Wygan's construction."

"Of what?"

"Some kind of gate . . . I think."

She snorted. "To hell I hope, and then shove him in."

"I'll do my best."

She made a face but looked less pinched. I guess I scared her less when I made bad jokes. "Mara. Are you still angry at me about Ben?"

"Angry? Y'mean about the swamp? No. . . . Well, perhaps a bit. Y'really shouldn't have—"

"Taken him where he wanted to go? Mara, could either of us have stopped him once he knew there was a monster to interview? Maybe I shouldn't have asked at all, but it was Ben's choice and I needed his help. The same way it was your help I needed and your choice to come with me to the Madison Forrest House. I do ask too much of you guys. I know I do. Thank you and—" There was that word I rarely used, hanging in the air like a sword, like "I love you" and all those other things that are hardest to say when you mean them most. "I'm sorry."

She huffed in surprise, blinking. "You are. Well." She stood up. "Next time we'll know better. You should be after a wash and brush-up. Y'still look like you've been run down on the road."

"I doubt I look that good," I replied, heaving myself to my naked feet and heading, still unsteadily and stabbed by sudden knives of pain, to the bathroom.

She left me to it and I stepped under the flow of hot water, relieved by the warmth and the sense that water washed away the horror as well as blood and physical discomfort. As the character of my pain shifted from uncanny agonies of fire and cold to ordinary aches of aftermath and injury, sleep nudged at the edges of my mind. I felt soft and dopey by the time I got out of the tiny shower.

Quinton was sitting on the bed, dressed in a clean T-shirt

and baggy pajama bottoms, when I came back into the basement bedroom.

"Hey," he said.

"Hey, yourself."

"You look better than I thought you would."

I made a face at him. "Thanks."

"No. I mean that I thought you were in pretty bad shape, but looks like I was wrong."

"No, you weren't. Mara said I looked like I'd been hit by a truck."

He got up and put his arms around me, squeezing gently. "You look great." He kissed my neck and worked his way up toward my ear. "You feel better."

"Then you forgive me for barfing on you?"

"It washed off. You only ralph on the one you love, right?"

"Or the one who's crazy enough to put me over his shoulder like a sack of flour."

"You are much sexier than a sack of flour." He went back to nuzzling my neck.

"And you are big, goofy geek-boy."

He raised his head and grinned at me. "Yes, but a goofy geek-boy with taste. And excellent timing."

"It was pretty good."

"Only pretty good?"

I shrugged. "You could have come a little sooner."

"It's hard to detect gunshots from a soundproof booth. What were you shooting at anyway? It was dark as the inside of a whale in there."

"Lightbulbs. To let in the Guardian Beast." I wasn't sure that made sense, but it came out anyhow.

Quinton looked puzzled. "How would that work?"

"Colored light confuses it. I shot out the bulbs and it got in. It doesn't like Wygan or whatever he's up to, so it attacked him. I think. I didn't stay to watch." I yawned and felt my legs go weak.

Quinton kept me upright. "Ah-hah. I see. So what did you get?"

"Hints and clues. Talked to Dad. And got a headache that mutters."

"Interesting collection. Was it worth it?"

"Mara asked that. Some hints from Dad about how to get back to him. And some kind of . . . knowledge I can't process. That's what I got. I know it's in my head but I don't know what it is. Except it makes me bleed light. Or that's what I think. 'Cause I wasn't weeping lumens when I went in. . . ." I was just mumbling, blurting out whatever came to mind. I was too tired to filter it. "It's loud in here, in my head. I know that's something . . . and the light thing. Must be related. . . ."

"Wha—?"

I shook my heavy head. "I don't know either. I healed up on my own. But it's creepy. Like little eyes all over. . . ." I couldn't help but shudder. "It's just little hints and clues, little bits and pieces. About Dad and Wygan and something magic. . . . I need more. I need to know about Edward—I never saw a sign of him, or what Wygan wants him for, but he must be around. . . ." Something more than the oceanic whispering in my ears was growing in my mind. Some idea . . . something about bits and pieces . . .

"Quinton, what happened to the boxes I sent from England?"

"They should have come to the condo, but I was out picking you up at the airport and the FedEx guy left a note. They must be at the depot."

"We—" I started, yawning myself silent. "We'll go get them. There might be a clue there."

He shut me up with a kiss. "In the morning, sweetheart. They aren't open and you aren't dressed for more burglary."

"I could be."

"Sleepwalking doesn't become you. And I don't think there are a lot of vampires working the day shift at FedEx, so it might be safer to wait."

"You think?"

"Uh-huh," he murmured, brushing another kiss onto my lips as he scooped me up. This time he didn't throw me over his shoulder, just snuggled me into his chest for the short walk to the bed. . . .

THIRTEEN

Seattle's FedEx World Service Center is deep in the industrial district, just north of the train yards from Georgetown and a short drive from both airfields. The bland, two-tone gray structure looks like a collection of giant shoe boxes, featureless except for the huge purple-and-orange logo on one end. I figured any building that determined to be boring was probably full of troublemaking gremlins or some other supernatural pest equally determined to play havoc with the system from sheer perversity. I didn't see any, but it seemed like their kind of haunt.

Probably because they'd been sitting for several days, the boxes took a few extra minutes to locate and extract from the delicate architecture of shipping crates into which they'd drifted. Once I had them, I didn't want to wait to open them any longer than it took to haul them to the Land Rover.

"What's in these?" Quinton asked as we carried them across the parking lot.

"Stuff of Edward's. Mostly paperwork and files, but there are some loose things in one of the boxes that might be useful. . . ."

I'd mailed the two boxes from England before I left. They weren't mine, but I thought Edward wouldn't mind if I scoured them for tools or clues since I meant to use whatever I found to get him away from Wygan. And me back to see my father so I could stop the Pharaohn-ankh-astet permanently.

Inside the truck, safe behind its locked doors, I slit open

the packing tape on the smaller box. The contents had shifted since I'd packed them, and the collection of animal teeth and bones had drifted to the top of the other, heavier bits, tangled in the loops of a black silk scarf. Maybe it was the luminosity of the fabric or just the way it lay, but Quinton and I both paused and stared into the carton, disquieted.

"It looks like a cat," he muttered.

"It almost looks like it's breathing, the way the light moves on the silk," I added. The thin filigree of smoke-colored power that lay over it all only added to the unsettling display in my eyes. Just because it was there and kind of creeped me out, I reached out and tapped the thing lightly, giving it a tiny stroke about where the top of its head would have been. "Good kitty. No biting."

Quinton shivered. "That's really disturbing." He bumped the box with the edge of his hand, and most of the bones slid across the slick surface of the scarf, scattering again into the depths of the junk. The skull lodged in a corner and directed its empty eye sockets at us, as if waiting for another pat or a treat. Probably a finger.

I felt a touch queasy reaching into the box past that bony remnant. I half expected the thing of bones and mist to knit back together and attack me. But it didn't. I lifted the skull and scarf out with care and settled it on the dashboard in the sun with a few of the bones. As I dug through the container, I found more bones and put them onto the scarf with the rest. Don't ask why; it just seemed the right thing to do. I added some teeth as I found them, too. More than enough bits to make a cat and a half at the very least, though the teeth clearly hadn't come from anything as small as a domestic house cat. Meat eater? Yes. House cat? Not on your life.

"You're giving me the creeps, which I do not say lightly," Quinton commented, watching me.

"Why? What's so creepy? It's just a bunch of bones."

"It doesn't seem that way when you touch them. And did you notice you've laid them out in a skeleton? Kind of a freaky one, but, still . . ."

I looked at the pile and saw he was right. "Ah. I don't know. It just . . . seemed the right thing to do."

He peered at me. "That's an odd thing to say. How do you get that impression? I mean you don't usually do that sort of thing."

I caught an annoyed sigh—I wasn't put out with Quinton, but something was digging at me, and that scratched at my short temper. "Wygan said he was going to give me knowledge and ever since it seems like there's something lurking, just at the edge of my understanding it. Like a shadow at the corner of a building, but I can't see what's making it. I have an urge to make order out of things. I keep thinking I can figure out what it is if I just clear away everything it isn't. Does that make sense?"

"Mostly. But can you stop with the bones? There really is something . . . unsettling about that thing."

I looked at it again, tilting my head to a better angle on the Grey without slipping in. The two-headed cat hissed at me from its disparate mouths. "Ugh," I coughed, sweeping the bones into a single pile and shuddering as I touched them. "All right. No more skeletons right now." I turned back to the box, more mindful of what I touched and how I laid it aside after that.

The carton yielded up a small trove of broken or orphaned jewelry—including a single garnet earring with an aura of outright malevolence clinging to it—a scatter of antique tarot and playing cards that didn't make up a full deck of either, a few small cloth bags of plant matter that had dried to unidentifiable dust long ago, keys singly and in bunches, a stained leather glove so old and dry it had cracked across the knuckles, three knives of various materials and types, a tiny silver mirror in a carved mother-of-pearl frame, broken sticks of colored chalk, various candle stumps, a book no larger than my palm that had rotted into a lump and crumbled at the edges, and a leather bag containing a few old gold and silver coins whose origin I couldn't guess from the misshapen portraits on the front.

"Any bells going off?" Quinton asked, watching me.

I slumped a bit, disappointed. "No. The bones, the knives, and that earring are the only things sending off anything I can pick out from the general clutter of Grey coming off this box in the first place. This stuff's been sitting around, going quiet or mixing with the rest for a long time. If it were just one or two objects, or if they'd been isolated from one another, the auras would be stronger. I could tell more about them. But this is like . . . soup. It's been cooking together so long it's hard to figure out which flavor came from what ingredient."

"But it's all got some magic remnant?"

"Seems that way."

"So maybe it's a box of tools and supplies for some kind of magic. Maybe someone cleaned them off before they packed them up originally."

"They're all dirty now." I paused to think. "But someone might have tossed something else in the box, later, that infected the rest. . . ."

I began picking up each item and trying to feel or scry some information from them.

Quinton put his hand on my arm. "That's going to take a while. What can we eliminate? Anything too old or rotten to have been added late is probably not the thing you're after. What was on top the first time you saw the box?"

I closed my eyes and tried to conjure a picture in my mind. The insistent muttering of the grid complicated the process, intruding as static yelps and stutters as I concentrated on remembering the box as it lay in its vault below London. "Shut up," I muttered, pushing the sounds aside with a will, and dredged the memory into my mind's view. "Umm . . . the scarf. The garnet earring. A couple of teeth. A knife. The scarf covered everything below it and those few items were on top of the scarf."

"Start with those. The scarf seems to be the dividing layer. Whoever packed the box may have used it to protect the lower contents."

"So what's on top is most likely to have been added later," I finished for him. We didn't think alike—his different perspective was one of the many invaluable things about Quinton—but we did understand each other's way of thinking. It circumvented a lot of confusion and argument. When we didn't *want* to argue, that is; we didn't agree on everything, after all. Who does?

I did not wish to pick up the earring. I'd touched it once

already and that had been unpleasant, but concentrating on it sounded like a bad idea. I put it aside for last and began with the teeth, picking them out from the pile of bones and disturbing as little else as possible.

They weren't human teeth, so at least I wouldn't fall prey to whatever intelligent horror might have held the creature when it died. I curled the half-dozen bits of rough ivory and enamel in my fist and closed my eyes for a moment, trying to settle my noisy mind before attempting to "read" them. I opened my eyes and my hand again and stared at the hard white objects.

There were five of them and they shone in each of the primary colors, plus one blue-green and one pink. Not black as I'd half expected. I didn't know for certain what the colors represented, but they didn't seem sick or warped. They didn't send off much feeling either, at least not as a collection. If I separated them and concentrated on just one at a time, they sent out varying sensations of chill or warmth, sharp tingles or smooth hums, but that was all. Someday I was going to have to make a better study of the colors I saw in the Grey and figure out what they meant. I guessed most of the time based on how I felt or on other clues, but that was the best I could do.

I put the teeth back down.

Quinton raised his eyebrows. "Nothing?"

"Nothing interesting. I think they're some kind of elemental icons. You know: earth, air, fire, water . . ."

"That's only four."

"Yeah. Well. They could be emotional icons instead. That pink one, that's . . . love." I felt a little nervous saying it. I'm not a romantic, moony person and I've never looked good in pink. "But I'm not sure. They aren't giving off much. No clues. Let's try something else."

Quinton started to reach for the earring. I pushed his hand aside.

"Not that. Not yet. Hand me the knives."

"Which one do you want first?"

My eye fell on the one with a missing tip. I recognized the odd shape of it from the first time I'd looked into the box, like a long leaf with a dark channel down the middle, and it was made of a curiously dull and heavy metal or some cold, homogenous stone that shone with a frigid darkness. The handle was wrapped in stained leather, bound on with gold wire. "That one—with the broken tip."

He handed it over, giving a slight, unconscious shudder. I closed my hand on the knife and felt a shock through my whole body, like I'd been stabbed in the chest with lightning.

I must have gasped aloud and started to crumple in my seat; Quinton grabbed on to my shoulders to hold me upright, then jerked as if he'd touched a live wire. I dropped the knife to the floorboard and batted him away, breaking the connection between us, between the scene rapid-spooling forward in my mind and the remembered horror of the first time I'd encountered it. Only this time it hadn't been at a storyteller's remove but first person and intimately dreadful. I gagged and gasped for breath; only the fact I hadn't eaten in a day kept me from throwing up again.

"What the hell—?"

"That's Carlos's knife," I gasped.

"What? What are you talking about? What happened?"

I drew several long breaths, trying to steady myself and doing a half-assed job as the voices of the dead shrieked in my ears. I raised my head and looked him in the eye. "Quinton, did you see something? Did you feel anything? What did you just experience?"

"To hell with me. What about you?"

I caught his reaching hands and pulled them down to the console between us. My heart wouldn't stop racing, but I tried to pretend I was calm, that I hadn't just experienced the deaths of a score of innocents, hadn't felt the very knife I'd held plunge into my chest and shatter. . . . I kept my grip on his hands, comforted by the touch, and hoping he felt that reassurance too. "I'll tell you in a minute, but I need to know what just happened to you. How bad is it?"

"Just painful, just . . . confusing. It was as if I'd grabbed on to an ungrounded electric cable when I touched you. And I thought—I swear I heard half the world screaming in my head. Jesus . . . what happened?"

"It's over. It was more than two hundred and fifty years ago. Those voices are just ghosts. Just ghosts in my head."

"Harper!" He put his hands back on my arms and I let him. Without the knife in my grip, I thought it was as safe as it was ever likely to be. I still heard them, the voices of the two dozen men, women, and children, dead and crying out as they were murdered a second time, their spirits ripped from the vessel they'd poured into at the instant their life-blood flowed out. I thought Quinton would not also hear them now. They screamed their shock only in the memory forced into my mind by the knife and by a tale I'd heard two years before. Quinton wasn't psychic, didn't share my mind. Thank the gods.

I caught him gently once more, putting my hands over his. "It's all right. I've met them before. They'll stop in a minute. It's just a memory."

He was aghast. "But of what? Do you go through this all the time? Is this what it's like?"

I shook my head. "No. This is different. It's . . . unusual. That knife, though. That's what I need. I think that's what the scarf was for—to wrap the knife so it could be handled by someone who could see what it had done."

Quinton glared down at the fallen blade, his head wreathed in furious red and orange spikes: he loathed it.

"It's just a thing, sweetheart. It's not bad or dangerous on its own, but it can help me and I need it. There's a paper bag in the glove compartment. Put the bones in that and then give me the scarf so I can pick up the knife."

He didn't want to look away from me, but he did what I wanted and handed me the black silk scarf, dusty from the bones and teeth and bits of chalk that had fallen on it. I bent in the seat and scrabbled blindly to catch the knife in the folds of silk, avoiding touching it with my bare hands. Once again, it wasn't that I knew the silk would insulate me from it; it just felt like the right thing to do. And the whispering voices of the grid seemed to sing the action to me, like the chorus of some surreal ballet.

Even through the silk, I could feel the vibration of the tale, dread music sung in dead voices. I folded another layer over the knife and wrapped it tightly in the black scarf before I tucked it into the pocket of my jacket for safe-keeping.

"So what is it?" Quinton asked when I paused, putting my hands on the steering wheel.

"Let's get away from here first. We've been here awhile and I think it's best if we move."

He shrugged, not happy with my stalling, but not objecting. Yet. I started the Rover and pointed it toward the loneliest place I could think of nearby.

Carkeek Park tumbles off the top of a steep, tree-thick ridge in the upper-middle-class neighborhood of Broadview and drops into Puget Sound beside the railroad tracks that run from the aircraft plant at Everett, south to Boeing Field. Expensive homes overlook the park at a distance but see little through the rolling acreage to the small lawn at the cliff edge. A mile down the coast lie the busy locks and marina at Ballard, but you can't see a sign of them from Carkeek. On a weekday at midmorning, few people stroll the park and even fewer cross the pedestrian bridge that spans the railroad to descend steep steel stairs to the ragged spit of sand at the bottom littered with driftwood as large as cars. It's a landscape of tree-crowded emptiness above desolate sand, and the isolated park that used to be a sewage treatment plant has hosted more than its share of assaults and dumped bodies, even a murder or two in the steep little canyon that cradles it. It is lovely now, but it's not a place to drive; it's a place to walk and possibly to disappear.

I parked the Land Rover as close to the cliffside strip of grass as I could. Then I donned my leather jacket against the chilly wind from the Sound and led Quinton down the lawn to the railroad bridge. We crossed down to the deserted swath of sand and sat on a sea-scoured tree trunk facing the cliff. Only a fish could sneak up on us from there.

I took the black package from my pocket but I didn't unwrap it. I let it rest in my hands between my knees; it was heavy beyond its size with my knowledge of its past. "You know Carlos," I started, looking up from the silk wrapper to glance into Quinton's eyes.

He nodded. "Yeah. He was the extra crispy we stashed at the Danzigers' after . . . what happened at the museum two years back."

I nodded, too. "Yeah."

"Scary customer. Even by bloodsucker standards."

I looked back down at the hidden knife. "More than you know. He's, uh . . . well, you know how Mara and I are always a little reluctant to deal with him. He's, well . . . literally power hungry. He's a necromancer, which is kind of unusual for a vampire. Dangerous stuff, sucking magic out of death when you're dead yourself. So, he's always tricky about dark power sources and I have to approach him carefully every time."

"He's kind of unpredictable."

"Yes and no. You can bet if there's magical power to be gained, he'll want it, and unless you can hold him off or persuade him not to take it, he will. I've seen him do it and couldn't stop him nearly killing someone for it. But, see, there's more to the problem—the immediate problem—than that. He's got a . . . an issue you could say, with Edward. They aren't friends. They used to be, about two hundred and fifty years ago. I think they might have been the very closest of friends then, but Edward did something . . . just phenomenally stupid and greedy." I felt increasingly constrained and physically uncomfortable telling him these things, even though I'd never been bound not to. But the sounds in my head and the humming of the grid sang a spell that dragged on the words and squeezed the breath from my lungs. I labored to bring each sentence into the air. "Edward wanted power, but to get it, he had to kill a lot of other vampires. It was easier to do it in one big cataclysm, so he persuaded Carlos to help him cast a spell that would destroy the homes of his enemies. It took out most of Lisbon in an earthquake back in 1755."

Quinton whistled. "Hell of a spell."

"Well, Carlos is a necromancer. He's good at killing people. He gets his energy from death and this needed a lot of death. About twenty people, I think he said."

I knew what he'd said, but it was too bad and dreadful to admit. I could hear Carlos's voice as if he were beside me: ". . . two dozen men and women—all children of the streets, the unnoticeables, the lost—knelt on a platform, bound within the machine . . ."

"They killed them and powered the spell, but it wasn't really enough for Edward. He wanted more. I guess there's some kind of special magic in killing a mage or killing your lover or maybe both," I lied. I knew well enough from Carlos that it was a vampire's blood that was precious in this case, but that I could not say. I had promised that. "So, Edward stabbed Carlos with this, making the spell into something worse. He left him to die as the earthquake brought the building down on him. Carlos couldn't do anything about it but hide from the sun and hope to survive."

Quinton blinked as I paused and looked over at him. "That's . . . extreme. But—"

"Why didn't Carlos go after him?" I finished for him.

"Yeah. Neither of them is the forgiving type."

"He couldn't. Edward did something extra so Carlos couldn't hurt him if he happened to survive the earthquake and the morning sun. Edward broke off the tip of this knife in Carlos's heart. As long as it's there, Carlos can't touch him. He can't hurt him. But he can't help him much either. And I know the one thing that Carlos would do anything for is the chance to be free of this knife."

The dual memory, Carlos's evocation and my new experience of the story, brought up the echoing sound of Edward's cruel anticipation in the depths of the long-ago carnage as he knelt over Carlos in the pool of blood and bodies. "I shall always be in your heart. . . ." And I shuddered with his receding laughter, feeling myself in Carlos's battered flesh, oozing the stolen blood of the murdered and knowing despair and betrayal so dark and bitter it made me blind.

I blinked and shivered, shaking the impression away as if it were offered poison.

Quinton didn't respond at once. He looked out to sea over his shoulder. Then he gazed up at the heights of the cliffs above us and along the crumbling edge. His glance came back down, studying the sand, and only very slowly returned to me. "So you're going to use that as a lever to get Carlos to help you find Edward and figure out what Wygan's doing."

I nodded, making a grim smile as the pressure on my

chest eased. I was done; the voices couldn't stop me once the words were already out. They were angry, though. The noise in my head turned to rage and storm, unintelligible and violent.

I squeezed my eyes shut and tried to argue it to silence. It ebbed down only slowly, peeling into layers of discord that fractured and fell away in snatches of borrowed conversation.

"You won't be safe with him," Quinton said. "There will be nothing to restrain him if he gets free of that." He pointed to the black thing in my hands.

"That may be true, but I think I can persuade him that stopping Wygan's plans is worth suspending his revenge on Edward for a little while. Once this is over, I don't care if he wipes out half the vampires in Seattle."

Quinton made a skeptical frown. "Yes, you do. You're tough but you're not callous, and I don't believe you'd let whole rooms full of people—if you can call those red-handed bastards people—die if you could avoid it. Not to mention the stink it would raise with your cop friend. He already thinks you have something to do with everything freaky that happens around here."

"Yeah. I noticed that."

Quinton cracked a smile. "He's not that far off, you know: You attract the weird."

I grinned pointedly at him. "Yes, I know. Lucky me."

His smile, though crooked, widened and he slid his nearest arm around my waist. "Better than boring, I guess." He tagged my cheek with a lightning-quick kiss.

I snorted. I had missed him horribly while in London. I had been too busy running for my life or someone else's to notice most of the time, but every pause had brought it back to my mind. I hoped whatever happened next wouldn't tear us from each other. I put my head on his shoulder a moment, resisting the insidious whispered urge to hurry, hurry, do something. . . .

I wanted to hiss back at it, "Shut up. Leave us alone for a while. Just an hour, half an hour. Go away!" But I kept my mouth shut and shouted only in my mind.

FOURTEEN

There wasn't much we could do with the long summer day that would help my crusade. We could only wait it out until the sun went down and the vampires got up. Until then, I tried to put my mind to the other odd little mystery my father had given me—something about keys, mazes, back doors, puzzles. . . . It was like a maze itself, trying to unwind the possible meanings of all his hints. I knew he'd tried to be clear, but he hadn't succeeded.

We couldn't go back to my condo—it surely was still being watched—nor could we further endanger the Danzigers by returning there unless it was unavoidable. They were literally on danger's doorstep and I'd put them at enough risk already. I hoped they'd take good care of the ferret and Grendel a while longer. Even my regular business routine seemed risky: Every Grey thing in Seattle knew what I did for a living, and it wouldn't be hard for them to report back to anyone willing to pay for the information if I were spotted at the records office or my own.

It is very hard to break yourself of routines and places. When you have nothing else to do, you fall back to the familiar. What we needed was to run forward into the unsuspected.

What we did was take the ferry to Bremerton—a one-hour trip across the widest part of the Sound. Vampires, I'd noticed, didn't like crossing water—and the longer, rougher, and saltier the stretch, the less they enjoyed it—so pockets of isolated vampires or their minions weren't too likely to be watching out for us anywhere on the Kitsap Peninsula or tiny Bainbridge Island, which hung off the northeastern corner like a bud waiting to flower.

Off the ferry on the Kitsap side, I drove north along the rocky Soundview road from Bremerton, heading slowly for Poulsbo and the long span of the Agate Pass Bridge that crosses the rushing narrows between the peninsula and Bainbridge. The scenery along most of the route was breathtaking, and we stopped once or twice to stare at it, breathe in the salt smell of the Sound, and think. I'm not sure what Quinton thought about, though he did sometimes write frantically in a notebook he kept in his pocket. Me, I thought about my father and his riddle.

I was sure that the key to which he'd referred was the little wire pocket puzzle I'd found in his effects. With the help of Marsden, I'd discovered it was, in fact, a kind of magical skeleton key. It didn't seem to work on real-world doors, only on Grey ones, but it was very effective. If that was the key to use on the door, what were the mazes he'd referred to? It seemed as if he'd equated mazes and puzzles, puzzles and doors, and they all opened to a key I already had. I just had to find the mazes. He'd said to find the first maze—no, a labyrinth—and that would lead me to a back door. . . .

So I was looking for a labyrinth. The only one I knew of was the one on the floor of St. Mark's Cathedral in Seattle, but I was reasonably sure that wasn't it—it would have been near impossible to open any magical device inside the cathedral without someone noticing. No matter how I may feel, personally, about any religion, wherever belief in something paranormal is strong enough, Grey things take shape or show up, and it was a sure bet the cathedral was thick with magic that would have a dampening effect on anything that didn't belong there. There must have been other labyrinths. . . . I'd have to do some research when I got back to a computer.

We were sitting on a bench someplace north of Illahee looking up the bay toward Agate Pass with the sun high overhead as I thought about this. The bridge in the distance looked like a long-backed dinosaur stretching its neck toward Bainbridge to take a nibble of the island's robust greenery.

"Do you suppose there's a Radio Shack in Poulsbo?" Quinton asked.

I was shaken out of my thoughts by his non sequitur. "Huh? Why?"

"I want to make a change to the detector circuit, but I need some parts I don't have in my pack. We could go all the way down to Renton for them, but that's a long drive the wrong way from here.

"Oh. Well, I guess we could look. And have lunch," I added, noticing a pang in my belly.

"I like that idea."

We killed most of the rest of the afternoon looking for parts for Quinton's project and finding places for him to work on it and that was fine; electronic parts stores were certainly the last place any vampires would be searching for us. Quinton continued to surprise me with the things he could produce in a pinch. By the time he was satisfied with his tweaking and tuning, it was late enough to head across the bridge to the island and take the return ferry from Bainbridge back to Seattle.

Finding Carlos without getting nabbed by any agents of the Pharaohn was going to be more of a challenge. Wygan and Goodall were probably furious with me and they'd have set every demi-vampire, minion, cat's-paw, and informant on the alert. I tried calling the sex shop Carlos owned, but no one admitted to his presence or the likelihood that he'd turn up. I had to leave a message with Cameron, his apprentice of sorts, and hope he hadn't disappeared or changed alliances since the last time I'd seen him.

Cameron's had been my first paranormal case and he my first vampire: a missing college student who'd turned up in more trouble than anyone could have imagined and with a problem beyond just being a bloodsucker. I had liked him then. Now I didn't know how undeath might have changed him. He'd also had reason to hate Edward, but unlike his mentor, he didn't seem to, though time and familiarity might have altered that. I wasn't even sure that Cameron was still under Carlos's tutelage or, if he wasn't, that they still were in contact: Vampire protégé is not the most stable position in the world.

But the relationship must have been good enough. A little before ten o'clock, as Quinton and I lurked in a diner near Green Lake, watching the last of the evening joggers make their endless circuits of the walking path, Cameron called back.

"Hi, Harper." His voice was very soft, not whispering, just without any force.

"Hi, Cam."

Cameron gave me an address near Northwest Eighty-fifth Street and Greenwood Avenue North. Northwest of the zoo and our current location, it was a place I wasn't familiar with off the commercial streets nearby. "Carlos will be there in ten minutes. He says you should be alone." The destination seemed close enough to make it in time, but I'd have to get moving.

Invitation issued in the third person morose. It was disquieting.

"Why?"

Cameron paused almost thirty seconds. I wasn't even sure he was still there and nearly hung up. Answering my question, his voice took on a slight tone of anxiety. "He's . . . nervous. About someone."

"Me?"

"No. No, no. Someone worthy of distrust. No friend of yours."

"Ah. Well, then I'll see him soon." I assumed that meant not Quinton.

"Will you call me afterward?"

"If you want."

"I do. And . . . be careful, Harper." Then he disconnected without another word, as if someone might overhear him if he lingered.

I put my phone away and turned to Quinton. "Mysteries on top of enigmas. Apparently I'm to meet Carlos alone. He doesn't feel safe otherwise."

Quinton frowned. "Don't like the sound of that. What freaks out a vampire necromancer?"

"Wygan, I'm guessing. Hoping at least."

Quinton chewed his lower lip. "Where?"

I paused before I answered. "This time, I think it would

be better if I didn't say. But I trust Carlos's paranoia to make sure the place is safe. I'll be all right."

"I'm less worried about the place than Carlos. People don't act rationally when they're scared. I don't imagine vampires are better about that."

On consideration, I imagined they were so rarely afraid of anything that fear might be a bit of a thrill to some vampires: the undead equivalent of adrenaline junkies. Carlos didn't strike me as the type for it, but I hadn't thought he'd take pleasure in driving anyone insane, either. Maybe I should have.

"I *will* be all right," I repeated. I culled my memory for a safe meeting place unlikely to be on any vampire's rounds. "I'll meet you in the bar at Louie's when I'm done. If the bar closes and I don't show, call me." There couldn't have been much less likely to hold attraction for the undead than Louie's Cuisine of China in Ballard—a nice working-class neighborhood's idea of a nice family night out since back when there were still beavers along the shore of Piper's Creek.

"What if you don't answer?"

"Then you should take the ferret and run like hell."

"Harper," he started, reaching forward as if he meant to grab me.

The whispering in my head got loud and ran along my spine and into my brain with nasty spike-heeled fears and incomprehensible gabble. I gave him a wary look. For a moment, I thought he was going to get all stupid, macho male on me and tell me not to go. In which case I'd have to deck him. Or start screaming to make the noise quit.

He didn't stop reaching, but he just put his hands on my upper arms and stroked lightly down until he caught my hands in his. "I'm an impatient bastard now that I've got you, and I don't want to stand here and wait like a navy wife on the shore. I don't care for the idea of taking out the whole vampire community of Seattle by myself, but—I'm sorry—if you don't come back, I'm not running. I did that once: It kind of sucks. And didn't I already tell you I'll always come after you? Day later doesn't change that."

I blinked at him, mentally shoving the voices down,

though they fought and made sounds like feedback in my head. "Oh. Yeah." I smiled, a quivering expression that threatened to fail at any second. Why was I so afraid? I was not a weak and cowardly creature, yet the past few days had left me with a sense of growing horror for no reason I could name. It hadn't been that bad . . . had it? Maybe it was the cacophony in my head, those unending babbling voices, just below hearing. . . . "I'll be all right. I don't think I'll need the cavalry this time."

He tipped my chin a little and kissed me on the lips. "Get going. I'll meet you at Louie's."

The crazy tangle of streets around the lake made it faster to separate than for me to drop Quinton off and double back. I headed back to the Rover while Quinton walked south toward the bus line on Forty-fifth. The drive up to Greenwood wasn't far, but without knowing exactly where I was headed, and with no time to scout, I had to move quickly and hope for the best. With such a short lead time to get there, no one could reconnoiter and prep any surprises except Carlos, and I suppose that was the point.

FIFTEEN

I drove up to Eighty-fifth and turned west for a few blocks. The address I wanted would be somewhere behind the strip mall that faced Northwest Eighty-fifth Street at Greenwood Avenue North. The area was residential, and once you got beyond the cheesy facades of the old shops on the main street, it was obvious that the gentrification that was barely started in Georgetown had settled in here a while ago.

The houses were nearly all from the early 1910s, with a handful of exceptions: a modern-art box featuring a white slab facade in front of hard angles in polished wood, a 1920s Spanish bungalow with smooth plaster and a red tile roof, and the ubiquitous block of condos under perpetual construction. Most of the buildings were wooden cottages with clapboard or shingle siding and a few larger Craftsman or Eastlake bungalows. One tiny house and matching garage had been painted the same deep purple as the foliage on the aging ornamental plum tree that sprawled in the front of the lot, though most homes were in subtler colors and none were falling down or flaking. Minivans and pickup trucks dominated the parking along the curbless edges of the road. I had to park a half block from the address Cameron had given me and walk. Just as well: It gave me a chance to look for hiding places and alternate routes out if anything went wrong. Not that I was having an easy time of it—concentration was unexpectedly difficult here from the moment I stepped out of the Rover.

The air seemed to tremble as I walked, the Grey flickering and moving in front of me like a heat mirage. The uncanny whispering in my ears became a rumpus of voices arguing and cajoling, crying and shouting. I could see long, thick grid lines of red and yellow, and one wild blue leyline, surging through the Grey at a slight angle to the middle of the street and sending abrupt feelers of color toward each house along the way. Most cut off abruptly, leaving the shadows of squares and half circles behind. Odd colorless shapes like tiny hunchbacked dogs crept across the lawns here and there, disappearing into vapor and sparkles of light. My skin crawled and my heart sped up, anticipating something horrible as I went on.

The house number I wanted hung in cool black iron figures on a weathered wooden gate gone silvery with age. A high, thick hedge of small-leaved, thorny branches cut off the view of the house beyond and gave refuge to a flock of tiny gleaming eyes. Whatever owned the eyes chittered and hissed to itself as I approached. I was panting as if I'd run to the gate rather than walked. I glanced around, looking for anyone or anything else that might be watching and waiting for me, but only the hedge eyes blinked back. The ground beneath my feet was like jet in the Grey: black earth sparkling with the cut edges of black grass and black roots growing out of the silver-green mass of the hedge. The thinnest red line, braided with obsidian gleams, outlined the edge of the gate and its threshold.

"Break it, break it!" something urged in my head.

Whispers and shouts of "Defile, destroy!" and "How dare they?" and the miserable shriek of an infant while someone sobbed without relief racketed in my mind with sparks of color bursting across my vision like flashbulbs.

"Shut up!" I snapped. I looked for ghosts but didn't see anything more substantial than the searing power lines of the grid and the misshapen horrors that crawled across the ground. I pressed my hands over my ears for a moment, feeling my fingers quake against my skull as I squeezed my eyelids closed and tried to imagine the calm blue lines of the grid washing over everything like water, washing the sounds away as I breathed in and out for two long, slow breaths. "Be quiet," I muttered. "Not now."

The volume of the noise seemed to ebb back to a murmur and I reopened my eyes, reaching out, still shaking, to open the gate. I touched it with care, letting my fingers just brush the black iron latch handle, testing for a magical current before I took a stronger hold and pressed the gate open.

The red-and-black line around the gateway flexed a little, then reshaped as the gate opened, making a doorway within the doorway. Looking straight through the opening, the little buff-colored house in the garden beyond appeared entirely ordinary and quiet. From any other angle, it was wreathed in inky flames and scarlet coals. Hoping I was interpreting the invitation correctly, I stepped through, keeping my focus on the charming little house and the ordinary brick path to its porch.

The gate clacked shut behind me. Under my feet, the path stayed clear, but to each side, beyond the edge of the bricks and the low border of plants filled with still more gleaming silver eyes, the black fire raged across the whole breadth of the yard. All right then: Stick to the walkway. I stepped forward with more confidence than I felt—the hellish panorama in the garden and lawn only adding to my fears—and made it onto the porch in a sweat.

The front door was painted a cheery blue outlined in black, as if some dread magic oozed through the narrow gap in the frame. I really didn't want to knock. . . .

The door swung open before I could tap or ring, quiet but for a slight shushing as the bottom weather stripping brushed the hardwood floor inside. Carlos stood just inside the entry, glowering, the dark cloud of his power riding on his shoulders like a storm rolling up from black waters. He had always seemed large to me and now he seemed huge, looming in the opening like a giant from a monstrous fairy tale, a study in darkness: dark hair, dark eyes, dark beard masking his olive skin. He looked more like a jungle predator patiently waiting for his prey than most people's idea of the undead. He cocked one eyebrow slightly and moved aside to let me in. "Blaine."

I gave him a small nod and stepped over the threshold, keeping my teeth set against the ice that seemed to slice through me as I moved inside. The sensation left an impression of maggots and knives across my nerves that almost made me gag until it faded away a second later. Carlos pushed the door closed again and it made a surprising chime of crystal notes that shimmered blue and white in the interior darkness for a moment, reducing the noise in my head to a low mutter and leaving my skin goose-bumped with uncanny cold. I could barely see him or the room now as anything but gray shapes in the gloom.

"You'd prefer some light, wouldn't you." It wasn't a question.

"I haven't grown cat's eyes yet," I replied, "so, yes, I would."

He humphed a little as if amused by my human weakness. A quick shuffling sound preceded the brightening of the room, and as the lights came up, I glimpsed the same small, humped mist-shapes I'd seen creeping over the lawns outside now scuttling away from candles and oil lamps—there was no sign of electricity—throughout the visible rooms. Whatever they were, they'd lit the flames and now seemed to shy from them.

I caught my startled breath. "What are those?"

"Névoacria—the mist things."

"I saw them outside. Are they . . . yours?"

"I use them. They grow here of their own accord from the displaced spirits of the dead. This ground was once a cemetery."

That startled me, yet it made sense of the feelings and strangeness of the area, the hazy blackness of death on the ground and the deeper shades that held sway within the house. I hoped I'd never have to come here again, into a place the dead could neither find nor leave. A perfect place for a necromancer to work, I thought, and had no doubt the quaint little house had hidden Carlos's secrets as long as it had stood. I pushed the sickening thought aside, cleared my throat, and asked the first seemingly safe thing that came to mind.

"And the eyes in the hedge . . . ?"

"Seraphi-guardi. That I did place there. It keeps watch for that which should not approach this place. The Guardian does not mind if I borrow some of its mille occhi for such a task."

That made me blink. I'd heard the term "mille occhi" before—I couldn't hang around people like the Danzigers without picking up a few words in Latin, Greek, and other languages—and knew it meant "a thousand eyes." My father had written in his journals about the "Thousand Eyes" as if it were a single horrible creature that would swallow him for his misdeeds. I hadn't had much time to puzzle that one out, nor had I cared much at the time with more immediate problems and threats to deal with. But now that I knew my dad had been a Greywalker, pieces fell into place. He had seen the Guardian Beast just like I had, but he had seen a different manifestation of it. He had seen the thousand watchful eyes of the Beast and known from the beginning that it hated the creature he'd called the White Worm-man: Wygan, the Pharaohn-ankh-astet. I wished I had known that.

Wygan's approach to Dad had been too direct and had brought down the Guardian's attention. So the Pharaohn had taken a more oblique approach to me, staying out of sight, using unsuspecting tools and cat's-paws until I'd foolishly stumbled into his own hands.

Carlos was frowning at me. "Something bothers you?"

I shook my head. "No, just . . . lining up the pictures."

He raised his chin a bit, half an acknowledging nod. "The coil is coming together."

"Or just tightening around our necks."

He narrowed his eyes as if considering his inclusion in the noose with curiosity. Then he turned his back and moved deeper into the house. "Come in and say your piece."

Having no choice, I followed him into the living room. The furniture looked as if it had come with the house when it was new, but while the house had aged and darkened over a hundred years with whatever magic had soaked it, the furnishings had remained untouched—not even dust marred the upholstery and gleaming wood. Maybe the névoacria played housekeeper as well as lamplighter here, but it felt more like a stage set that no one lived in. Only the crammed-full bookcases that lined the walls looked used. Some of the volumes seemed to drip black and red gore that vanished into the charcoal haze over the hardwood floor. A darker shape of lines and curves radiated through the boards from below, incomplete to my eyes and incomprehensible with a baffling obsidian shine.

Whatever lay below sent a deep vibration through the house that twined into the remains of the voices in my head and made me dizzy. I reeled a little as I dropped into a chair in the deathly sterile sitting room.

Carlos sat down slower, watching me. "Something has changed in you." He reached for me, one of his massive hands coming toward my face.

Faster than I could think of it, I knocked his hand aside. The crack of our bones against each other was sharp and red in the air. He froze, his eyes glittering. Then his hand went limp and he led it back toward my face by the wrist, leaving himself vulnerable to my grip if I chose. I steeled myself, but I didn't stop him this time. The back of his hand barely brushed my cheek. Then he pulled his hand away and it seemed to drift through the dim light as if it wasn't his at all.

"Changing, but incomplete. Where have you been, ghost-girl?"

"Where I've been isn't as important as where I'm going. And where I hope you're going to help me."

"I warned you that further favors come with a price."

"I think I have something you want."

"Indeed. Which one will you offer?"

Fear chilled my bones and made my heart beat out of time. If I was miscalculating the importance of the knife, if he'd misled me or I'd misunderstood the complicated relationship between Carlos and Edward, I had nothing else to bargain with. At least nothing I was willing to give. I could try to draw him out and see if my guesses were good, but in the end it would come down to the heavy, silk-wrapped bundle in my jacket pocket, one way or another.

I felt queasy as I drew it out, the sudden protest of ghost-voices clogging in my throat as I choked them down. Carlos jerked back in his seat as I flipped the black covering away from the knife and the blade gleamed oily-black and radiant. Its exposure to the stygian air wrung a cry from the house, and the whole structure trembled, real and Grey, shivering in colors more numerous and flickering than the eyes of the seraphi-guardi. Carlos's gaze locked onto the shadow-glowing broken blade with such intensity that, if he had not already been sitting down, I thought he would have fallen. The strange sound of the house echoed out of his mouth, strangled and horrible.

He stood up in a rush, the house howling and buckling as if with rage and anguish, though Carlos now made no sound at all. He snatched my wrist into his grip and hauled me forward, yanking me out of the writhing room, through a twisted doorway, and down a flight of unyielding stone stairs into the basement: the black heart of the house. I was completely in his territory, his power, and yet he let me go, dropping my arm as if I were made of fire and stepping away. "Put it down," he demanded, pointing to the center of the cellar floor. "Throw it there!"

The basement was built of gray-and-white stone that looked charred, becoming glassy black as it met the floor. The floor itself was matte black, as if a smooth surface had been etched with acid and left blurred and rough. Lines and curves of glossy jet and carmine joined and crossed, containing and elaborating one another into a complex sigil on the floor. Some kind of magic circle, it was the actual version of the vision I'd seen upstairs, the shape that had shone through the living room floorboards. It radiated black and red energy straight upward, strong but incomplete, waiting, throbbing with potential, for something to close the circuit and make the circle whole.

"No," I shouted back.

"Put it in the circle or the house will come down on our heads!" he roared. He didn't touch me, didn't move toward me, only pinned me in his black stare and shouted.

The house moaned as if it were collapsing. I tried to slide into the Grey, to slip sideways and out, but the house was solid in both worlds and still writhing as if in pain, no matter how I turned. At the center of the magic circle I could see a pool of calm that never moved or flickered, not a void like the emptiness at the center of the Hardy Tree or the hole where my father's ghost should have been in Glendale, just stillness.

The little singing voices in my head bent themselves into a single melody and urged me toward the stillness—not the raging voices I'd been hearing off and on but the more cohesive chorus of something else.

A section of the subfloor above cracked and fell, collapsing against the stone walls of the foundation with a reverberating crash. I hoped I wasn't making a mistake. . . . My heart raced so fast I couldn't feel my legs and I stumbled into the circle, rushing for the center of calm. The lines on the floor burned and sent fire up my body in midnight sheets and spikes of scarlet that jabbed through my limbs and I staggered almost to my knees. I caught my balance and took two more steps, into the quiet at the heart of the circle.

The house went still and sighed. I stopped, relieved and slumping slightly as the charge of fear shook my body and burned low. Carlos leaned back against the closest wall. "Leave it there and come out."

My silence told him I didn't like the implications of that option. I had no doubt it would take him only a second to close the circle behind me and keep the knife inside if he wanted.

"Then put it away, for the love of life, but choose!"

Quivering, I rewrapped the knife in as many folds of the black silk scarf as I could make and tucked it back into my pocket. I edged out of the circle with care and a wary eye on Carlos. He didn't seem angry, but I wasn't sure what he was feeling or thinking and I didn't trust him. Once I was out of the circle, he kept his distance, as suspect of me as I was of him, I thought.

He pointed into a corner where a table and two stools lurked in the shadows. "Sit down, Blaine, and I will tell you what you've brought into my house."

I backed into the corner and onto one of the stools, not looking away from him. "I already know this is the knife Edward stabbed you with in Seville."

"It is considerably more than that. I had been told that someone else had it. I would gladly sacrifice numberless virgins and goats to any god or monster you care to name in thanks that *that* is not true."

SIXTEEN

Under any circumstances, perching on the stool in Carlos's cellar would have been uncomfortable and creepy. In the present ones, it was surreal. The post-adrenaline burn left me feeling wrung out, but I didn't want to lean against the stone walls of the foundation for support—knowing what they contained and what they kept out made me certain they wept invisible horrors the same way water condenses in a cold room. I hunched on the backless stool, keeping my feet off the floor, too. The darkly shining shapes of the magic circle etched into the surface gave me chills.

Carlos had no compunctions on either score. He leaned against the wall nearby, eschewing the other stool, with his arms crossed over his chest. I watched him as he started speaking but he didn't meet my eyes. Every other time we'd talked he'd stared at me, unblinking, his gaze boring into me as if he could capture my will or my soul by the pressure of that glance. "Don't misconstrue this place, Blaine. This is not my home. This is my workshop, my . . . house of labor." He flexed his hands into and out of fists. The house rustled above us and the fires of the magic circle surged as if a wind fanned them. "Where one finds peace, that is heart and home. But this . . . this is my blackened soul."

If he'd still been alive he might have drawn a breath or two, but he paused and frowned, darkening the room with his expression. I thought I could hear the névoacria crawling across the floor above us and shivered.

"That object you brought here has wreaked more death

than a hundred years of warfare. I was dishonest when I called it a mere knife."

"I can tell it's a magical implement. Like an athame?" I asked, trying to understand. It didn't seem quite like a dark artifact, but I wasn't sure what else it was. I don't know much about magic-working—I don't do magic—and I only had vague ideas about the tools required from Mara and some of my past cases. Sometimes it's better to play the fool than be one.

"No!" he barked and finally he looked at me, his dark eyes glittering with the same black fire that rose off his magic circle. "An athame is a witch's tool, ceremonial, dull at the point. They are not meant for bloodletting. *That* is the Lâmina que Consome as Almas—" He cut himself off and shook away the name, infuriated at his slip. "It is a blood blade for black work. Meteoric iron, its source rained destruction and death on the world millennia before men put their puny feet to the ground. It was forged in a fire of human bone, quenched in clay dug from blood-soaked ground. It was mine. I killed for it. The man I murdered had slaughtered a whole village for it. And so on, back and back to its first forging. It hungers for blood, for death. It *wants*, but nothing so much as it longs to be whole again. Do you understand?"

His voice rang on the stone foundation and played on my bones, rousing the chorus of the Grey in my head as he continued, echoed and amplified by the singing of the grid. The other sounds of the house in the former graveyard fell away.

"That was Edward's mistake: He didn't understand the instrument he stole. Had he chosen any other knife, it might have destroyed me. Had he not broken the blade in my chest, I would have expired in the wreckage of Seville. If the fool had understood *anything* of what he did, we would both be long quit of this world. The blade would have killed him also if he hadn't locked it away—he could not have controlled it for so long otherwise. But luck favors fools. We both survived."

I shook myself from the disgust that wove around me—I couldn't afford to be squeamish or delicate about this. "Are you saying that the knife has some kind of will or . . . sentience?"

His voice dropped a little, no longer ringing the room with its resonance but still deep enough to throb in my chest. "It has purpose. You've seen this before. You were the one who brought me to the organ. . . ."

"That artifact had a ghost—*he* had the will," I said.

"But the organ contained and channeled it. This knife has an owner and a desire. Brought naked into the heart of my power—this place that sings with the essence of what I have given myself over to—it longs for that which it lost. It pulls on the shard, compels it to rejoin the whole."

I scowled. "You don't want the broken tip out of your heart?"

"I wish it gone. But the blade does not have a mind; it does not know that rejoining the pieces by force will rip me apart. If they are brought together again, without control, that I would not survive. I am not ready to end this existence."

"Then—" I started, but he pushed himself suddenly off the wall and leaned over the table between us, staring hard at me, cocking his head as he did. The reek of death and blood, the nausea that vampires always cast over me, was much worse with Carlos. It made me wince and pull my knees up as if I could roll into a protective ball around my churning guts.

He ignored my reaction, studying me with a stare as penetrating and precise as a laser. In the past, he could see things about me that even I didn't know; what did he see now? "You could do it," he muttered. "Not yet, but very soon. You are growing together."

Shocked, I blurted out, "I'm what?"

He hesitated for a tense moment. Then Carlos grabbed on to both my shoulders at once, without any word or sign of what he intended. His violent twitch at the contact rocked us both and I felt like I'd been wrapped in a live wire. My hair rose on my arms and the buzzing sensation of electric shock crawled over my nerves and every inch of skin and bone as my muscles spasmed. Air bound up in my chest and I felt that I was choking. Panic surged over me and something that felt like resurrection and clear water flowed behind it, bursting outward from my core.

I flung myself backward, jerking my knees to my chest and lashing forward with both booted feet at once. I shouldn't have had the strength to hurt him with such a short kick, but he ripped away and stumbled back to the wall he'd come from. I fell off the stool and sprang back to my feet with my back against the cold-burning foundation stones, gulping in breath that tasted like tombs.

I reached for my pistol, but stopped my hand on the bundled knife instead. "Don't try that again."

Carlos wasn't looking at me but at his hands as he brought them away from his gut. He straightened up, frowning. I didn't see anything wrong with them; they weren't bloodied or burned as I'd almost expected from the force. "Very close," he murmured. "So that's what he wants. . . ."

"What who wants?" I demanded. "Wygan? What pieces are you putting together, because I want to see that picture, too."

He raised his eyes to mine and I could see them smoldering red and yellow within the wide irises. "I'm certain that you do. The Pharaohn. His ruthless monstrosity, Goodall, came to bargain with me recently. The whelp didn't seem pleased. . . ." Carlos tilted his head and looked me over again. "I should have given in to impulse: He would have made a pretty home for maggots." Carlos seemed to enjoy my shudder at his image. "Edward did not know the viper he coddled. Now Goodall's master pretends to cajole my assistance with a plan unnamed in return for my freedom, though in truth so long as he controls Edward and the knife, he commands me. But he does not have the knife."

I wanted to know more about Goodall, but there was something more pressing and I asked about that first. "But so long as you thought he did, why wouldn't you help him? I presume he made some offer to set you free from Edward in exchange for help with whatever he's up to. You're no friend of Edward's. Why would you balk?"

He almost smiled, but what he said seemed disconnected from his expression. "I would rather lie buried alive ten thousand years than see any world the Pharaohn would build. Edward bred our hatred—mine and the Pharaohn's—by what he made of us, by his . . . stupidity, for his ambition. What he sowed now comes to reap him. But our tie is a tangled thread and if one of us can use it to his advantage, the others are compelled to his purpose. Wygan now has the whip hand and plans to use it. Unless the cord can be cut."

Now he did smile, a terrible thing of predator's teeth, lit by the unholy fire in his eyes. "You're hovering a hair's breadth from the great weft of magic. If you reach for it, you can bend the shape of magic itself."

I shook my head. "I'm not a mage or a witch. I can't use magic."

"I said you could bend it. Or you nearly can. That is not use, only ability. With that power, you could remove the blade's shard from my heart and make the knife whole. Then I would not be subject to the whim of either Edward or his captor."

I started shaking my head. "I don't—I don't think I can do that. . . ."

He stared at me like a collector evaluating a piece. "You have no idea. What you 'know' is a handful of salt in the ocean. I don't guess this, Blaine. This I know. But I *can* guess why the Pharaohn would find such a skill useful, given what else he now commands."

I looked at him as narrowly as he had inspected me and saw the black aura around him shaping itself into sharp spikes whose tips reached deep into the Grey, like rigid fingers seeking a grip on the grid. "What does he command? Do you have some idea what his plans are?" I demanded.

"I do."

I was drawn toward him but held myself back after a few steps. "Then you must understand why I want your help."

He leaned in again, lowering over me. "But the knife alone is nothing—more likely to destroy me than aid you. Agree to do what I ask, and I will help you."

"The help I need is not half-guessed plans or horror tales. I need to stop Wygan. I have no intention of being his pawn."

"You could simply flee. How could he compel you?" He

was playing with me; he knew there was more at stake and was pushing me to say so.

"Aside from not letting him rule the world, or whatever he's after? Shouldn't that be enough for anyone?"

"Perhaps once. But I can see your white honor crumbling. There is something more personal for you now. Darker."

I squeezed my eyes closed a second so I didn't have to see the certainty in his eyes. "He has my father."

That wretched eyebrow rose and his mouth quirked into half a cruel smile. "Your father died when you were a child. What part of him does the Pharaohn hold?"

"His ghost. He has him trapped in a sort of magical cell—an oubliette—and he's discovered a way to . . . torment ghosts."

Carlos focused past me, thinking aloud. "Interesting. . . . I wouldn't have thought he had the skill. Oh, but he has his ushabti."

"This trick predates Goodall—he wasn't Wygan's ushabti two weeks ago."

Carlos waved that aside. "He hadn't made the final offering, but he was the Pharaohn's man. Once the Pharaohn knows the thing can be done, he need only teach each ushabti how. Generations of his servants could have known it."

"Wouldn't you have heard of it before if he had?"

"That is not important at this point. His plan and your place in it are what concern you. And me. All else will fall in the scope of that. His plan depends upon you and Edward—who stupidly put this train in motion. He has Edward. Even if you run, it matters not to him: He will keep Edward prisoner until he captures you and forces you to do what he desires."

"And what does he need you for?"

Carlos gave me a sly look. "I am merely convenient. He controls Edward, Edward controls me, and I have skill to do something the Pharaohn needs. There is another with the ability, but the Pharaohn has no leverage on that one. He would have to bargain with something more precious than threats and torment. He would rather press me into service than deal with the other. And so would you."

Carlos knew me too well. I wanted to tangle with some unknown mage even less than I wanted to deal with him. And he'd confirmed something I'd suspected since Edward first asked me to go to London: There was a powerful blood mage somewhere in the area—one strong enough to have controlled and installed the ancient blood-worked panels on Edward's bunker doors. The price for those services might be as awful as whatever Wygan was already planning. Better the devil I knew.

And he knew it. Carlos gave me his wolf smile and chuckled; the house shivered. "When the power comes to you, then you can relieve me of the knife."

I was not letting him off easy. I pushed through the Grey, pushed on the blackness in the cellar and made a geas that thrust its spines into us both. His surprise quivered through the iron-hard shape in the Grey. I stared him down before he could recover, trying not to cringe from the pain and the cold. "And if I help you get free of the Lâmina, you will take my side in this confrontation with the Pharaohn. You'll tell me his plan so far as you know it and you'll do all you can to help me stop it."

The death-cold fingers of the compulsion and bond pierced into me. I could see the dark magical form, a barbed helix, coiling deep into both of us. Carlos resisted and I stopped breathing as the geas surged and throbbed a moment, cutting me with such chill agony that tears sprang from my eyes and ran in viscous, icy trails down my face.

He threw back his head, eyes shut. "Yes." He gave in and the cold pressure of the geas collapsed, dissolving into us in a shimmer of black threads. "I will." He brought his head down again, making a small, respectful nod. But his glance was wary and appraising. "You do not need to bind me."

I caught my breath—I didn't care if he saw I was shaken—and wiped the back of my hand across my cheeks. "Oh I do. I remember the last time you helped me."

He made an ingenuous face. "I only advised—"

"In the Wah Mee," I said, my voice like acid.

He gave a dismissive shrug and looked aside. "I didn't kill the boy."

"You absorbed his life and drove him insane."

He glared back at me, his chin down and only his eyes showing between the dark swaths of his hair and beard. He was angry and it shivered in his voice, growing louder as he spoke, making the creatures of mist and shadow scurry a scratching tarantella on the floor above. "An unhappy consequence of his own design. He intended your death as well as others; it reeked on him like sweat. I only showed him his own mind. You required my assistance and there is always a price. You could not pay, so I took what I needed from him—he will toil in his madness a shorter time for that. Is that not *mercy*? Insanity was his fate, but *you* stopped him from practicing it upon others. Is that not *righteous*? Has not *justice* been served?" he roared. "Are you dissatisfied with your role, *Paladin of the Dead*?"

I reeled under his fury and a slap of self-loathing: I was guilty of thinking only *I* could do right or bring justice to the dead and the things of the Grey and I had been secretly relieved to see Ian Markine sent to the prison wing at Western State and not escape justice for what he'd done. I could have left it to Solis to solve, but I hadn't; I'd gone out to capture him and I'd taken Carlos with me to make sure. I had hated the way it happened, but I had caused it and I had been glad of the end result. Now I saw myself as a hypocrite for it.

The shocking strength of Carlos's anger and my disgust with myself sent me stumbling back against the wall as the building seemed to shake. I wanted to scream or cry, but I choked it off. I slapped my hands against the stones to keep from falling and felt something brush past my palm with a wet, sticky sensation. One of the névoacria slipped away, leaving a crimson trail on the wall that the stone seemed to drink. I twitched away and stared down at my hands, appalled with what I had done and horrified by what I saw.

The backs of my hands were streaked red where I'd wiped away my tears: half-frozen, bloody tears that now ran bright across my knuckles as they thawed. No. No, not this too . . . I wanted to flee, to hide. What was happening to me . . . ? Denials crescendoed in my head in mocking, shouting chorus. . . .

I didn't realize I'd given voice to those fears until I felt

Carlos touch my hand. I hadn't even seen him come close and reach; it was the softer chill of his finger sweeping across my hand that startled me back to sense. I gasped and jumped away from him, but there was no place to go. He wasn't going to hurt me; he couldn't—we were bound together to a purpose—but I was still afraid and my stomach knotted, twisting in my gut and freezing the air in my lungs.

I was panting as Carlos backed off a step. "How long have you wept blood?" He wasn't shouting or angry but curious.

I shook my head too rapidly and caught myself. I bit my lip and breathed through my nose until I calmed enough to speak without shaking, but I wasn't doing well. I let out a laugh edged in hysteria. "I don't know. I don't know what's happening to me. I bleed light and cry blood. Since I got back. Since London. Since . . . I don't know." I really was losing it if I was confessing my fears to Carlos. But the words tumbled out, echoing inside my head, and I couldn't stop them.

"Hm . . ." He drew a shape in the air between us and it shimmered red before fading to gold and drifting away like dust. He looked me over, frowning. Then he pointed just to the left of my breastbone. "What dead thing made that?"

SEVENTEEN

I looked down and saw a thin red line shining through my shirt and jacket. It was right where Norrin had slashed through my skin. "I was . . . cut by a ghost—a wraith. In London."

"Ahhh . . . I see. You become more intriguing with each meeting. What was the circumstance?"

I felt exhausted and he could tell; he pushed the stool toward me. I took it and sat. I was too tired to argue or to tell him off. And I needed his help. So I told him about Alice, the vampires of London, and the wraith in the wreck of an abandoned prison beneath the streets of Clerkenwell; how the ghostly blade the thing wielded had cut into me; and how I'd grabbed the incorporeal knife and turned it on the specter. I would have gone on, but Carlos laughed then.

Not a pleasant laugh, but one of discomforting satisfaction. "The Pharaohn doesn't know. . . ."

"What?" I stammered.

"That he succeeded. It was meant to happen much faster; you should have died, bleeding too fast to stop, until there was nothing left to sustain you but the magic. That cut should have been deeper, slashed from throat to thigh, through the heart. He didn't expect you to have a more tempting target with you to distract the wraith. That cut is still enough: You bled into the magic and it bled into you. You can't stop it: You're growing toward the weft—the great, flowing web of magic."

"But I didn't die, and if it worked, how come Wygan didn't notice?"

"When did he have the chance?"

"I saw him last night."

He raised an eyebrow. "Indeed? What did he do?"

"He pushed me . . . toward the grid."

Carlos looked puzzled for an instant. Then his expression cleared. "The grid. That is how you see it. I perceive it as an endless tapestry, color swirling through this woven darkness of magic. I stand on the warp and draw my threads through the pattern, while you reach toward the weft and change its shape and color."

"No. I don't. I don't touch magic. I see it, but no more than that."

"You will. You held Norrin's knife. You pulled it from the weft because you knew its shape in the blood you spilled on it. If this continues, you will not have to know a shape to draw it. That is the power the Pharaohn desires in you. I don't know what use he has for it, but I see the pattern of his plan."

"Then tell me." I tried to concentrate on that, hoping the knowledge would settle me and keep me in my own troubles enough to solve them, and not go shrieking mad with the impossibilities thrust upon me.

"Like us all, he sees the magical world differently than you or I. He lives much closer to it, needs it—the strength and frailty of the asetem-ankh-astet—more than we ever will. He is in the real as a near exile. I would pity him for such loneliness if either of us had a heart for pity. As it is, I hope for his most hideous and eternal isolation. Once he was worshipped as a god—the White Worm-man, the great snake of the desert—but as the world changed and he was forgotten as a god, he chose to take the form of a man rather than fade into the darkness. He found followers with what magic he still had and he made them his children. As he became more human, his powers ebbed and it drove him a bit mad. His followers fell away and he faded from a god to a mage, trapped in this world but remembering the glory of the other. He is quite insane and he dreams of his old world endlessly. More so than all his children, he is a shadow in this one. Were it not for Edward, that would not be true."

I knew they were enemies; I knew from our first meeting

that Edward had done something to Wygan that had caused the other to hate him with a cold fury. The asetem lived closer to magic than most vampires, so perhaps that had something to do with it. Wygan and Edward had almost been allies in London at one time, if the story I'd had from the London vampires was true. But then a rift had emerged and Edward had been forced to flee, all accord between him and the Pharaohn reduced to bitter wreckage. Yet Wygan's overarching plan continued, in spite of—or maybe enhanced by—that destruction. Something Edward had done to Wygan two hundred years ago or more had sealed his own fate in the icy hatred of the Pharaohn-ankh-astet. "But what . . . ?" I muttered. "Why?"

Carlos tilted his head. "I don't know what occurred between them, but somehow, by his overweening ambition, Edward . . . pushed the Pharaohn deeper into the shadow, into the warp of magic. He is a creature of magic, but he could not live as he was and he is too powerful to die, so . . . he is evolving. Toward what I do not know, but it draws him back, away from the world of his children and their service, which gives him life. Whatever the details, his plan must be to change that. He will need Edward since Edward was the trigger for the change that makes this possible—and, in the Pharaohn's mind, necessary, not only in whatever design he practices but in his vengeance. He is not the magus he once was, so he must have another to work the spell—whatever it is. That is his role for me with freedom from the Lâmina the poisonous bait to bring me to heel. He has long sought his Greywalker, and now, seeing you as you are becoming, I know what he means to do: to break the curtain of the Grey so that he and his tribe might wield more power, live more fully, in both worlds."

"He can't!"

"With you under his sway, able to shape the weft, he could."

I shook my head as much in negation as to shut the persistent, echoing song of the grid out of my head. "The Guardian Beast won't allow that."

"Then he must have a plan for the Guardian that we don't yet know. Perhaps Goodall is meant to hold it until there is nothing the Guardian can do." Carlos made a wry face. "Such a selfless task seems out of character for Goodall—perhaps he doesn't know the whole of his master's plan yet, either."

"Too much guesswork," I muttered. I couldn't go forward with such a vague idea. "I need to talk to Dad."

"Why? If the Pharaohn controls him, you cannot speak to him without risking your liberty. I assure you, if you come into the Pharaohn's hands while I am still in thrall to the knife's tip in my heart, I will not be able to help you. You will be at his mercy."

"I can. If I can find the back door to him. My father said there's a way into his prison—this magical oubliette—and something about puzzles and keys. He said I need to find a labyrinth. That a song would tell me. . . . No, he said '*the* song.' 'Know the song.' Which song I don't have any idea, but I have a key. If I can find the right maze, I can find the back door. My father must know what Wygan is up to—he tried it on Dad first. I get to him, I get the plan."

The rumble of Carlos's amusement made the floor quake. "Your father is a better man dead than he was alive."

I went cold, everything hardening within me to icy fury. My eyes narrowed to slits and I found my feet braced on the black ground as if I meant murder, my hands fisted at my thighs. "Never say that."

This time, both his eyebrows came up and Carlos stared at me with plain surprise. He resettled his face into its usual silent glower in a moment and said, "I meant you no disrespect, Blaine. I have touched a million of the dead and find suicides are rarely men of courage. Father, like daughter, astonishes me. Accept my apology."

I wanted to kill him—the muttering in my head sounded like psychotic ranting urging me on—but I knew I needed his help; I needed him on my side. What was I thinking . . . ? I tried to shake it off but this time it wasn't going. The sound swelled in screams and I felt sweat break on my skin—don't let it be blood this time, gods, not this time. Something brushed my right leg. Another of the névoacria. I kicked it away in disgust, the thing of mist and shadow surprisingly solid on my boot.

The urge to do harm slid away, the raging in my head spiraling down to a whisper of nonsense: "a rose by any other name . . . superior, orientalis. . . ." I shuddered and looked down. A crimson line swept across the floor beside my right foot. A piece of Carlos's circle. I had been standing on it; the feelings that had overwhelmed me were not mine but those of the circle's voice and victims. I swallowed hard, tasting bile in the back of my throat as I edged away.

"Perhaps this place is no safer for this conversation, now that the knife is put away," Carlos suggested, remaining still and waiting for me to move first.

"Yes. That is, I agree. But I . . ."

"You tire."

I closed my eyes for a second. They were gritty and I did, indeed, feel tired. "There's so much . . ."

"Yes, and you fight it. You can't. It will come. You will change. Learn it."

"That's what *he* said. Wygan," I spat.

"Better to know the tool you have been given than become one yourself. If you hope to stop him, you must use every weapon you have at your disposal. And we must not let him know of our . . . agreement. If he cannot hope to control us through our friends, the Pharaohn will destroy them. He must think us alone and powerless until the last minute." He waved his arm toward the doorway and looked the question at me.

I nodded and swayed a little. Then I let him lead the way back up to the sitting room, muttering to myself as I went, "I have to get to my father. I have to find this labyrinth, this back door . . ."

"The back door . . ." Carlos echoed, his voice soft in thought as we came to the top of the steps. "If there is such a thing, and it leads to your father's prison, then it also leads to the lost passages of the Grey, places that have been sealed away or broken beyond repair. That would be the place to make the knife whole again—where no one but you and I could see. You have a key?" He turned back to me, standing in the doorway of what started as the kitchen—a room I didn't want to examine any closer after what I'd felt elsewhere in this house.

"Yes, my father's key," I explained. "It's a kind of puzzle. Puzzle . . . I have another puzzle. . . . Maybe. . . ."

"Yes?"

"It's crazy," I objected, shrugging it off.

"Would any of this have seemed sane to you two years ago?"

I hacked a bitter laugh. "No."

He gave me that damned look with the raised eyebrow again.

"All right," I conceded. "I'll think about it."

"Look for the connections. Don't reject what seems completely mad."

"As I seem headed that way myself, I guess I shouldn't."

He nodded and walked me to the door. He watched me pass him but remained inside, in the shadow. Even in his death-black sanctuary, he was cautious. "Take care, Blaine, but move with speed: Our days are numbered."

I would have turned back, but the door clicked closed behind me. This time I couldn't hear it chime. All I had ahead of me was the narrow path. I put my hands in my pockets, disliking the thought of touching anything by accident in this garden of hell. The bundled knife lay like an uncanny weight beneath my fingers. I hated to touch it, but I couldn't let it go, afraid to lose it.

The eyes of the seraphi-guardi blinked at me as I passed, and its rustling hisses sounded like whispers in the night. I wanted to hurry away from the silvery stares, but I walked forward with care, trying to keep my thoughts from breaking on the whispers and muttering of the grid. Forgetting, forgetting . . . there was something in the noise that haunted my mind. I was forgetting something.

"Goodall." Damn it, I hadn't figured him out yet. How had the Pharaohn's ushabti come to work for Edward? Carlos had almost told me, but I hadn't pressed and now I didn't know. Maybe it didn't matter, but it worried me nonetheless.

I made it to the end of the walkway and pulled the gate open. The road outside was as it had been before, still hot with energy and silvered with the mist of the Grey. But at least it wasn't the black flames that burned ceaselessly behind me.

I stepped out and began to retrace my steps to the truck, forcing myself to think of something other than my self-righteous past. I thought about Goodall. Carlos had said something about a final offering. . . . It must have been a complicated ritual, whatever it was, taken a step at a time. Something like the demi-vampires, not quite vampires yet but only a bite or two away. . . .

EIGHTEEN

I stopped on the sidewalk, still about half a block from the truck. A cluster of névoacria paused in the yard beside me and waited for me to go on—some kind of honor guard sent along by Carlos, or just spies?

The whispers in my head were loud in the former graveyard. I didn't want to hear my own reflections on what Carlos had accused me of. They were too dreadful, and anything, even the shredded and stinging melodies of the Grey, had to be better. It was hard to sort them, to concentrate, but something seemed to answer my question. I could hear it; like someone singing very far away, it dipped and swelled through the mist and magic, buzzing with energy. I closed my eyes and tried to listen for that one line in the clashing harmonies of the grid.

Not an answer, just another question: What if the origin is different from the end? Huh. That didn't make a lot of sense, but it gave me something else to occupy my mind for the rest of the distance, and that seemed to help push the noise back a bit.

The creeping things of mist and shadow followed me, some coming when others vanished but always there until I reached the edge of the road by the Rover and let myself in. Then they sparkled away.

It was much quieter in the truck. Something about the heavy steel and glass filters out most of the ghosts and lowers the effects of the Grey. That had contributed to my decision to replace the old Rover with another despite the cost. Even so, I didn't want to linger in Carlos's neighborhood.

I started the truck and drove, glancing at the clock in the dash. It was eleven thirty. The bar at Louie's didn't close until one, but I would have to rush a little if I wanted to spend any time there with Quinton—and I did want to.

But the question in my head started me thinking as I drove, and I poked the last-number redial on my cell phone and put it on the console while I waited through the rings from the speaker until Cameron answered.

"Harper?"

"Yeah. I've seen him."

He didn't say anything for a moment, the silence growing long and sad.

"He's all right," I said, finally getting it.

"Ah. Good."

"I have a very rude question for you."

"OK."

"Becoming a vampire. Is that . . . umm, that is, is it a one-shot kind of process or does it take a few steps?" It was hard to talk like a normal person; the strangeness lingering in my head made me want to scream or babble or just curl in a corner and rock while I muttered to myself. I hope I didn't sound as unhinged as I felt.

"There's a lot to it. Over time. It's . . . complicated."

The memory of the singing voice pushed me on, as if it were still moving in my head. "I don't need to know the details, but here's the real question: What happens if the vampire who finishes the process isn't the one who started it?"

"That can be a bad thing. Usually you just die . . . pretty horribly. Sometimes other things result."

"Like the kreanou?"

"No, they're a different problem. But, yeah, there are bad results, depending on the details. We don't do that. The . . . umm, community agrees not to. It's too dangerous."

"When you next hear from him—you know—ask him if that's what caused Goodall. He'll understand. It's not important, but I'd like to know just the same, and there wasn't a good chance to ask."

"Oh. All right." He paused, but I could hear his fingers

rubbing against the surface of the phone, making papery noises. "Harper. Thank you."

"Don't. I've started something terrible and I doubt you'll thank me when it's done."

"You don't know what you're doing."

"In a nutshell, yeah."

"No. I mean, there's a lot more going on and you're affecting it more than you know."

"Gods, I hope not because I really *don't* know what I'm doing. I'm just improvising as fast as I can and . . . hoping it's the right thing."

A car braked hard in front of me to let a couple of kids dart across the road. I tromped on my own brakes and fought the wheel to keep the Rover straight. The rear end tried to slide to the left and I let up, steering into it and re-braking as I cleared the other car, trying not to hit the running teenagers as they bounded across the road to the sidewalk. My cell phone and purse tumbled off the seat and into the footwell as the truck lurched to a halt.

The other driver accelerated away without a glance. I found the phone under my feet, but the call was dead and Cameron's phone was off when I tried again. I didn't leave a message. He'd call me when Carlos answered the question and then I could ask him about his portentous words. I had had enough for one night: I was creeped out and all I wanted was a drink in the unhaunted dark with Quinton. I turned the Rover back into the lane and drove with that as my only focus.

Louie's is not a real late-night place and the lingering crowd in the lounge was small and quiet. Three regulars huddled at the bar, chatting up the female bartender, while Quinton had a tiny table—and the rest of the room—to himself. The place was dark and done in moody browns and golds straight out of the 1970s. The dim steam-shapes of ghosts and the colors of the grid made the place a little cheerier as livelier times replayed in silent silver loops.

I waved to Quinton and stopped at the bar to order a drink before I joined him. He looked relieved at my appearance, though he gave me a puzzled look as I sat down.

"You look odd."

"In what way? Do I have blood on my face?" Why did I say that? I didn't seem to have control of my mouth at the moment.

He scowled and shook his head. "No. Should you?"

"I hope not."

The bartender strolled over and put down a couple of glasses: a whiskey, neat, for me and a beer for Quinton. We paid up and Quinton glanced at the drinks.

"It was like that, was it?"

I picked up my drink and sipped it, though I had the urge to bolt the alcohol and hope it masked the cacophony in my head. "Yeah. That kind of night. Kind of like last night, but without someone actively trying to kill me."

"Passively trying to kill you?"

"No, nobody trying to kill anyone, but a lot creepier: I cry blood."

"That is creepy."

I nodded and took another drink. "Carlos is going to help me with the Pharaohn problem, but I have to figure out the way to my father first. That's the back door and that gets me into the Grey without being in someone's sight. Which would be a good thing since the someone still wants to kill me 'cause he doesn't know he doesn't have to. It seems I'm already developing the power he wants; I'm just doing it slower. And I have a better idea of what's going on but not the details. The usual sort of evil villain, rule-the-world stuff, except this is my world we're talking about, not some comic book."

I think I got a little shrill there; Quinton put his arm around my shoulder and pulled me against him. He kissed my temple. "We'll stop them. Don't worry."

"What if we can't? It can't be just stop them for now; it has to be stop them forever. And it's all so complex that it ought to be easy to break it down, but he's got control of everything. No one can help me until I break that control, and if I can't . . . then what?" I lowered my voice to a whisper, partially because I knew I was too loud and partially because I didn't want anyone else to hear what I was about to say. "He used to be a god. How do I stop that? How do I stop a god?"

Quinton kept his head next to mine and whispered back. "He's not a god now. You've done harder things than undermining the plans of a megalomaniac."

"But there's more. Cameron says there's more going on and there is: I haven't even looked at what else is happening. The crime, the killing . . . there's a blood-mage somewhere out there. There are turf wars between the vampires. With Edward gone, they must be falling apart. And magic is . . . loud. It's like someone turned the volume up on everything Grey and it won't shut the hell up! How does Mara stand it?"

"I don't think she has to, Harper. I think it's only you who hears that."

"You think I'm imagining it?" I felt defensive and I didn't know why; I knew Quinton wasn't saying I was crazy, but that didn't stop me.

"No. You see things others don't—even Mara—so why shouldn't you hear things they can't? If your antenna's more sensitive, you pick up more signal. But with more signal there's also more noise."

"It sounds like voices. It sounds like something singing, but I can't figure out the lyrics. And I need to figure out so much. My father said the song would tell me something—that I need to 'know' the song—but if it's this song, all it tells me is that I'm losing my mind."

"Stop thinking that. You're perfectly sane."

"I don't feel sane."

"If you thought all of this was normal, then I'd be worried. Why don't you finish your drink and we'll get out of here? There are a lot of other places we could cuddle up and defy the darkness, and most of them don't smell of chow mein."

I backed off and frowned at him. "You are a sex fiend."

"I'm a pragmatist."

"How is that? I'm worried about monsters and gods destroying the world as we know it and you want to shag."

"Well, yes. If the world's going to end, I'd prefer to go out with a bang." He grinned and winked at me.

I sputtered. Something about his stupid jokes always disarms me. "All right, Roger Rabbit," I said, finishing my drink.

"Roger Rabbit?"

"Yes. Don't you remember why Jessica said she loved him?"

"Um . . . no."

"Because he made her laugh."

"So this is why statuesque beauties fall for geeks. Hm . . . I'll take it."

I stuck out my tongue—yeah, very mature of me, I know—but at least I was smiling, and I thought I'd forgotten what that felt like.

Quinton caught my hand and squeezed it gently as we headed for the door. "I love you even when you don't make me laugh."

That made me feel like crying and my smile got a little crooked, because running blood red tears was the last thing I wanted to do.

Quinton had barely touched his beer, so he got to drive. I had to talk. Concentrating on something and forcing it into a neat procession of thoughts and words helped keep the noise from overwhelming me.

"All right. So," I started, organizing my thoughts as much as I could. "There's a back door into the Grey according to my dad as clarified—sort of—by Carlos. This door leads to Dad, but it also leads into the Grey in a way that keeps me hidden from Wygan. Dad probably knows exactly what Wygan has in mind—after all, there's no reason to hide that information from my father and every reason to torment him with it, and Wygan likes to make people squirm. So, have to get to Dad, have to find the back door.

"Dad said something about keys, puzzles, and labyrinths. I need to find a labyrinth. But I have a key and a puzzle—a puzzle ball actually, but it's kind of Grey, so it seems like we ought to start there."

"Maybe it's not a physical labyrinth but a magical one," Quinton suggested.

"Possible. Dad said the puzzles were doors. Maybe the puzzle ball and the key make some kind of door into the labyrinth."

"Worth a try. Where are the puzzle ball and the key?"

"The key I have with me. I got it in Los Angeles and I've

been carrying it ever since. It was my dad's. It looks like one of those pocket puzzle things—the wire kind—but when I shuffle it around, it sometimes becomes a sort of magical key. I used it on a door in the Grey while I was in London. A prison door. I had a run-in with a ghost there. It . . . stabbed me."

"Stabbed you? How?"

"I don't quite understand it myself. It was a wraith, really, so kind of a special case, and we had to be in the Grey to get out of the prison—it's condemned now and the only way out from where we were was blocked in the real world—so . . . a little Greywalking was in order."

"Who is 'we'?"

"Marsden and me. And Michael."

"Michael Novak . . . can do that?"

"No. Not normally. But I guess when you have a critical mass of Greywalkers and enough plain old-fashioned fear behind you, you can drag someone normal into the Grey. Kind of. Enough at least. I wasn't stopping to analyze it at the time. Maybe it was Marsden's ability—I don't know. Apparently I have the gift of persuasion. People and things do what I want—at least more often than usual."

"That's useful. Go on."

"So we needed out and the door was locked—"

"No, about being stabbed. I get the rest. This ghost cut you."

"Wraith. Not a ghost of a person, really. A kind of evil remnant of something. A Grey thing. Anyhow, yeah, it cut me with this knife it made out of the Grey, and apparently that's all it took to start . . . infecting me."

"With what?"

"According to Carlos, I can—or will—bend magic. I don't *do* magic; I just might be able to move the conduits of it around. Shape the weft, he says. And that, according to him, is what Wygan is after. It makes sense to me as much as anything since Wygan clearly wants some kind of power and is doing something the Guardian Beast opposes—it attacks him whenever it can—so it has to be something in or affecting the Grey. He's figured out how to confuse the Beast by using colored light. That's why I shot out the lightbulbs in the studio—those were the gunshots you heard."

"All right. So you're getting more powerful in the Grey, and you have some ability to shape things, even if you don't actually cast spells or anything. And this is useful to Wygan in whatever his plan is. So you want to know the plan before you get stuck in it and that means talking to your dad . . . who is in some kind of magic prison Wygan made?"

"Basically. Not precisely, but close enough. If I can find this back door, I can get to Dad. But I need the puzzle ball. Which is in the condo."

"Well, that's going to be fun."

"We'll have to break in."

"You have keys: You don't have to break in."

"I'm sure there are still asetem watching the place."

"For you, yes. Not for other people."

"But they will be watching for you, so no go on that idea."

"What about your neighbors?"

"Rick's probably still staying at his sister's."

"Other neighbors?"

"Not really friendly with them."

"Friends you could ask?"

"Not many. The Danzigers are on the watch list, too, so that's them out of the picture. And there aren't a lot of other people I trust in my home . . . except Phoebe." My shoulders slumped a little and I sighed. "She's not going to like this."

Phoebe was my oldest friend in Seattle. I'd met her on a rainy afternoon when I'd hidden in the back of her used-book shop to look through the rental listings. Short and round and fierce as a mother wolverine where her friends and family were concerned, she'd kind of adopted me on first sight. I still had no idea why. We'd had a rough time of our friendship when I'd ended up investigating the death-by-poltergeist of one of her employees, but she was still the closest nonmagical female friend I had.

"She'll do it, though," Quinton said.

"Yeah, and if she has any trouble, I'll hear all about it."

"Yes. But she'll still let you come to dinner because that's how she is. You should call her."

I was doubtful and frowned. "It's pretty late." And I was both tired and afraid I'd babble something inappropriate.

Quinton shot me a disbelieving glance. "It's Friday and the shop stays open all night. If anyone's up keeping the drunks from sleeping in the Sociology corner, it'll be Phoebe."

I know when to stop fighting and, well, he was right. Unless she was sick or mourning a dead friend, Phoebe never missed Friday Happy Hour at her bookstore, Old Possum's Books and Beans. I hunted my phone out of my bag and poked the speed-dial button for the shop.

Of course, it wasn't Phoebe who answered the phone but one of the minions; Phoebe was busy stalking the stacks. I waited on hold for a minute or so, trying not to listen to the whispering chorus in my head.

Phoebe's words danced out of the phone on an island rhythm. "Hey, girl! Where you been? Poppy told me t'have you come t'dinner last week and you weren't home."

"I was in London on business."

"So, you back now. When you comin' up here?"

"Uh, well . . ."

"Don't be sayin' you're not comin'—and you bringin' dat man of yours, too. Or Poppy's gonna skin us both."

"I would love to accommodate your father, but I am currently in a bit of a jam."

"Oh? So you're callin' me to get you unjammed?"

"Yes, I am. See—"

She cut me off. "No, no. No, you don't. You come up here and ask my face. I'm not lettin' you sweet-talk me over the phone. 'Sides, I got some things to show you anyhow."

"All right. We'll be there in . . ." I glanced at Quinton, not sure where we were.

"Fifteen minutes," he said.

I told her.

"All right then. See you *both*," Phoebe answered before hanging up.

"She's in a mood," I warned.

"I guessed. What's up?"

"I have no idea. So long as it's not vampires, I think we'll be OK."

"I haven't heard of much weirdness in Fremont—beyond the usual kind."

I hoped that was true.

We looped around and got back to Fremont in a reasonable time, but finding a parking space on a Friday night was a bit trickier and we were a little late. Phoebe wasn't in a condition to notice, though: She was glaring at a guy in a trench coat and blocking the door when we arrived—she's not very tall, but Phoebe's evil eye can stop rampaging elephants in their tracks.

"You callin' me a liar, Mr. Thief?" she demanded. "You sayin' you ain't smugglin' some pussy in your coat?"

The patrons of the shop giggled and the miscreant blushed in shame. He wasn't very old and I guessed he was a college student doing something foolish on a dare or a drunk.

Phoebe softened her scowl and put out her hands, beckoning with her fingers, palm up. "Hand it over, before the poor thing suffocates."

Slump-shouldered, the guy pulled a black-and-white kitten out of his pocket and gave it to her. Phoebe snuggled the kitten, who was purring nonstop, and stood aside to let the cat-napper make his escape. "Next time, try da pound!" she shouted after him.

She saw us standing outside and waved us in. "Come on in da back," she said, handing off the kitten to the minion behind the counter. The kitten was shelved in "returns" and went back to purring mindlessly between the books as we followed Phoebe into the back of the shop, toward the espresso machine.

Phoebe's accent was thicker than usual from her annoyance. "I swear, dem boys steal anyt'ing and Beenie's too stupid not t'go along. He been in dat boy's pocket twice now. Usually dem snatchy-hands jus' take da books—now dey takin' da cats, too!"

She stopped at the espresso machine and grabbed three cups of coffee off the back counter, muttering to herself. She shoved two of the cups at us. "You're late, so it's cold."

It wasn't very cold, and I decided I didn't care so long as it was coffee and took the closest chair in the nook. Phoebe plopped down into another beside the fake fireplace that hid the door to the office. Quinton seemed to think standing was safer and kept on his feet. None of us doctored the coffee.

I waited for Phoebe to settle in and calm down before I said anything, but she beat me to it. I suppose she wasn't quite so angry about Beenie's near kidnapping as she seemed. It only took her two long sips before she asked, "So, what sort of trouble you want me to get you out of?"

I had to swallow quickly to reply. "I need someone I can trust to go fetch a puzzle ball from my place."

"And you can't go . . . why?"

"Because some guys I really don't want to tangle with are staking the place out, waiting for me. You they don't know, so they won't give you any hassle if you show up."

"You think they aren't gonna notice some black woman ain't you sneakin' into your place and not think that's kinda strange?"

"They aren't watching the inside of the building, just the outside." I hoped. "They won't know which condo you go into."

"Uh-huh. They any kind of observant, they *will* notice I wasn't in there very long."

"They won't care. You could be any one of my neighbors or one of their friends dropping something off. Take a box of books with you and leave it if you think that'll fool them better."

Phoebe looked thoughtful. "Hm . . . I could do that. I could take the safes."

"The whats?" I asked.

"Safes. That's what I wanted to show you. I got a bunch of these 'book safes'—they're those hollowed-out books that people hide stuff in—in a box of books I bought at a big sale on Capitol Hill. Some of the book safes have things inside and I thought you might help me find out who they belong to. No one from the sale knew. So. I help you out and you help me."

That was a no-brainer. "OK. I'll give you my keys and if you can go tomorrow, I'll meet you here when you're done."

"Fine. I'll leave the safes at your place, say . . . tenish. Where's this puzzle ball?"

"On a bookshelf by the TV. It's wood, about eight inches across. You can't miss it: There's only one." I handed over the condo keys, showing her which one was for the exterior door and which the interior.

Phoebe took them and nodded like the deal was done. "Dinner next Sunday. And you're both comin' or Poppy's sendin' da braas for you—don't think he wouldn't."

Intimidating as they look, Phoebe's brothers don't scare me except in terms of sheer bulk. Phoebe is the oldest but she's also the smallest, and you could lift three of her for one of her brothers. But the oldest brother, Hugh, would do anything for her, so I like to stay on his good side. And Poppy's, because I sometimes suspect he sees a lot more than he lets on.

"Sunday. All right," I agreed, hoping I'd be alive to see it.

NINETEEN

I did not sleep well that night in the Danzigers' basement. I might have been sending Phoebe into danger and I hadn't been honest about it. I couldn't get the sound of the Grey out of my head, nor could I push aside my own internal voice that worried at the things Carlos had implied about my own motives. I felt bloody and raw inside and even my dreams were haunted by that voice. My brain was as loud as an asylum without drugs and even Quinton's attentions didn't push it back far enough.

The ferret tried to haul me off the bed in the morning by biting my toes and heaving backward with all her two-pound might; she didn't quite shake the turmoil from my mind, but she did get me upright.

"Stop that!" I snapped, flailing the air as I tried to catch the escaping miscreant. She danced backward, chuckling and flashing her teeth until she fell off the bed and had to retrench underneath it.

"I thought you were going to sleep all day," Quinton said, watching me from across the room at his makeshift worktable. "Not that what you were doing was really sleeping. . . ."

"What was I doing?" I asked, shooting him a questioning glance and grabbing the nearest clothes my size.

"Mostly muttering and thrashing around. Mostly."

"And when I wasn't?"

"That's when you scared me. About four a.m., you made this gurgling sound and went rigid. Then you stopped breathing. And when I touched you, you gasped, whipped around, and kneed me about . . . here," he added, pointing to his navel. "I'm really glad I'm shorter than you. After that, you scrambled over me and when your feet hit the floor, you went limp. It was fun getting you back into bed. But you slept a little better after that."

I bit my lip and frowned in confusion. "I don't remember any of it."

"You weren't exactly awake when it happened." He looked back at his work and picked up his soldering iron, prodding something with the hot tip. "I don't know what you'd call it. It's not really sleepwalking; more like . . . sleep-fighting. I figured you were dreaming and the cold floor shocked you enough to stop but not enough to wake up."

I sat back down on the edge of the bed with my clothes half on, trying to remember what I'd been dreaming, what might have made me act like that in my sleep. I studied his half-turned back, watching him for a moment. His posture was a little odd, as if he were pulling his shoulders in. Defensive. He wasn't telling me something.

"Did I say anything?" I asked.

"I'm going to kill you."

"What?"

"That's what you said: 'I'm going to kill you.' "

"You don't think I was really talking to you. Do you?"

"Well, I admit, I wasn't sure. It was very clear and your voice was very cold. It's a little freak-worthy when someone stops breathing, says something like that, and then attacks you. I'm not even sure how you managed to say anything when you weren't breathing—holding your breath, maybe?"

I felt something well in my eyes. "Oh, no . . . Quinton. . . ." My chest ached and it was hard to breathe around what felt like a rock in my throat. I got up and rushed toward him but stopped short of the intended embrace. My vision was going blurry and red, and I sank to my knees, wiping my eyes while I bowed my head. I felt an unusual stickiness against my skin and knew it was blood.

I didn't want him to see it and tried to turn aside, but I felt his arms come around me as he slid down onto the floor. I kept my face down and pressed it into his shoulder. Oh, gods, I was going to stain his shirt. . . .

He stroked my hair, shushing me as I hiccuped on the tears I tried to hold back. "Hey, hey . . . it's all right."

I let the awful feeling go, let it roll out and over me and tumble away on a series of shaking breaths. "Y-you know I didn't mean it. I didn't mean it," I cried.

"I do. I know."

"You're afraid of me."

"I'm not. I'm not."

I raised my face. His eyes flashed wide and he jerked back a little before he caught himself. He blinked a few times. "All right . . . that's disturbing." He took a deep breath. Then he shrugged and pulled me back into a hug. "You know, in horror movies that's usually just a picturesque trickle. . . . You kind of look like someone broke your nose."

I mumbled against his chest. "Oh, thanks."

"Do you remember what you were dreaming?"

I shook my head. "No." It wasn't like the disturbing dream-sendings I'd had about Will; this was a regular dream, if a horrible one. Pieces came back as I thought about it, but not the whole and none of it made sense alone. The only thing that seemed clear was the lingering sensation of electricity across my fingertips and a soreness at my neck and shoulders as if I'd been hanged.

"Maybe you should take a shower and then call Phoebe back," Quinton suggested. "She left a message on your phone."

"Oh, damn. What time is it?"

"After ten."

I cursed and scuttled for the bathroom, confusion and upset pushed aside for more practical concerns. I focused on the routine: wash, brush, dress. . . . I extracted Chaos from my right boot, from which she was trying to remove the insole, as I simultaneously juggled the phone to make the call.

"Hello, Harper."

"Hi, Phoebe. Did you get the ball?" Chaos gave me a dirty look as I took the insole away.

"Yes. And I want to get rid of it fast as I can. Somet'ing 'bout it make my skin crawl."

That made me frown as I stood up, watching the ferret attack my reassembled footwear from the outside. "I can be down at the store in about twenty minutes—"

"No. I'll bring it to you. I just want this t'ing gone."

Her response surprised me, but I gave her the Danzigers' address and she hung up.

Quinton watched me. "So she's bringing it here? Is that safe?"

I bit my lip before answering. "I hope so. I mean, it should be safe for Phoebe. If she's being followed or something, it's not so safe for the rest of us, but she was adamant about getting rid of the ball as quickly as possible."

"That's weird."

"Yeah," I replied, thinking. Was there something I'd never noticed about the puzzle ball or was it something about Phoebe? Or maybe something about the ball had changed since I'd seen it last. . . . I scooped up the ferret and went upstairs to find Mara. Quinton followed.

It was Saturday, so there were no classes to teach and the Danzigers were both home, entertaining Brian. Or rather, watching Brian be entertained by Grendel in the backyard. There was a lot of running in circles and rolling on the ground going on, in spite of a lingering morning cloud cover that kept the day unusually cool for late May. The adults wore extra layers, but Brian made do in just a shirt, jeans, and sneakers—little boys being their own heaters.

Mara looked up as we came onto the back porch. "Morning. There's coffee and brekkie in the kitchen if y'like."

"Thanks. I'll get it in a minute," I said. "My friend Phoebe wants to drop something off for me here."

"That'll be fine."

"She may be here pretty soon and I hoped you'd take a look at it when she arrives."

"Oh?" Mara looked curious. "What sort of thing is it?"

"It's a puzzle ball—a large one that used to be on a newel post in an old house. It might or might not be part of a back door into the Grey."

"Now that's an odd sort of thing to have layin' about."

"Will gave it to me. Phoebe picked it up from my condo

this morning, but she says it gives her the creeps. It's never bothered me, but . . ."

"You're wonderin' if there's more to it."

"Yes."

Now Ben was watching us too. "You think it could be dangerous?"

"I never thought so, but my place has been empty for a few days and I don't know what's been going on while we've been gone."

"Ah. All right then," Mara said. "We'll take a look." She stood up and started inside, tossing one end of her woolen shawl over her shoulder. "Let me get a few things. Ben, don't let the mud monster into the kitchen without a rinse down."

"No problem. I have the hose right on the porch."

I started to follow her and Quinton caught my eye, raising a questioning eyebrow. "I just want a second with Mara," I whispered and passed him the ferret.

He nodded and sat down near Ben, watching the boy and the dog out in the yard, while the ferret took possession of the table and went hunting for crumbs. I headed for the kitchen.

Mara was climbing a step stool to get to the top of a cabinet. Even with her height, the shelf was well over her head in the lofty old kitchen. "If I toss this down, will y'catch it?" she asked, without turning her head. It was disconcerting that she always knew when I was in the room.

I stopped next to her. "OK."

She dropped a round black thing about the size of a salad plate toward me. It was heavy and I almost dropped it in surprise. It was a thick disk shape with some kind of black cloth stretched over it and a stubby handle on one side. She made a sling out of her shawl and piled a few more things into that before she stepped down.

I held up the disk. "Why couldn't you put this in the shawl?"

"Shouldn't mix with the herbs. Devil to clean off, and if it's dirty, it shan't shut down."

"What is it?"

"It's an eye. Sort of a magic magnifyin' glass. But like a convex lens, it can concentrate light and energy. Tends to set things on fire. You can see why I keep it as far from Brian's busy little fingers as possible."

"Mara . . ." I started.

She stepped off the stool and laid her hand on my arm. "Don't vex yourself. I've been thinkin' on what I said before. After last night, it seems to me it's a bit of omelets and eggs. Things will get broken when there's wicked magic afoot, and you've been the one to take the brunt when it must be done, but it will splatter about sometimes. I don't say I like it, nor that it's all right, but 'tis better you do the things you do than that you stand aside and let worse happen."

This was about 180 degrees from what Carlos had implied. Or was it . . . ? I found myself frowning and shaking my head.

"Never mind. You'll do what you have to."

I would have asked her what she meant, but the doorbell rang and, still carrying the eye, I followed her into the front hall. Mara opened the door and started to say hello.

Phoebe, holding a sack and looking horrified, lunged forward, knocking us both down as a shot cracked off the door frame. The open portal flushed red, the house rang with an alarm, and the door tried to slam closed. Mara and Phoebe were scrambling on the floor to clear the doorway. I was to the right of the frame, on the knob side, and I grabbed Phoebe, the closer of the two, and hauled her to me along the polished floor. Mara rolled away and the unobstructed door snapped closed as a second shot made an odd crackling sound against the scarlet haze between the lintels.

Brian shrieked in the backyard. The house was still making noise. I reached for my pistol, but it was not on my hip. I cursed: I'd left the gun downstairs when I finished dressing.

Mara snatched the eye off the floor where I'd dropped it and pulled the cloth off it as she flew to her feet and charged toward the kitchen. I jumped up to follow her and something crashed against the front door.

"Dat's him," Phoebe croaked, her voice and accent so thick with fear I could barely understand her. "Dat mon what was in your house. He say he gwine t'kill you."

I pointed at the basement steps. "Go down there and lock the door. No one is killing anyone today. There's a gun on the bedside table. You hold on to that until I come downstairs for you." The door bulged and cracked as something rammed against it. "Go!" I gave her a shove along the floor and Phoebe scrambled the rest of the way on her own.

I had no idea what I was going to do. The alarm was still howling and there was noise from the backyard that I didn't have time to investigate. I cast a quick glance sideways into the Grey and saw the shape of the house touched in crimson at the front and back, wavering as something attacked it both physically and in the Grey. To the rear, two small black shapes wrestled in the center of three white ones with one more white shape and a tower of emerald green bearing down on them. Outside the front, something indigo and red reared back to make another strike at the buckling door.

I crouched, tight as a spring, wrenched the door open, and leapt forward, keeping low and ramming my shoulder into Bryson Goodall's midsection. He lurched backward into the porch rail. I ducked down and yanked his legs upward, sending him over the barrier and into the rosebushes below.

A pitiful scream came from the backyard and the alarm shut down. A moment later a stink of singed hair rose on the wind as I stepped down to haul Goodall to his feet.

He was hard to see: He'd learned the vampire trick of sliding into the Grey so his normal shape was dim in the real world, but see him I did and I reached for him in a hot rage. But I didn't grab him by the shirt or shoulders. Instead, I let my hand pierce through the shell of his thrashing, thorn-pricked body and into the whirling colors of his energy corona. I don't know what I did or how, but I closed my hand around the core of his strength and yanked him upright by it. I didn't think it would tear away and it made as good a handle as anything.

He made a strangled gurgling sound and I shook him

like a rat. I felt like I could have snapped his neck with a flick of my wrist and I dropped him only long enough to change my grip to his throat. The shouting chorus of the grid roared in my ears like a conflagration. The voices were obscured individually, but their collective urged me to go ahead and kill him. I quivered, resisting. I wanted to, but I knew I shouldn't, though why was lost in the crackle and gust of noise. I shook him again. He clutched my forearm and I shoved him back toward the street, watching the flashing, writhing threads of his power try to crawl up my arm. I flicked them off with my other hand and squeezed his throat.

"Harper, don't."

I ignored the voice behind me and kept pushing Goodall backward, cutting off his air as I went. He glared pure hatred at me and clawed at my arms, but the dark blue of his aura didn't move so strongly this time; it only flickered at my grip like the tongue of a dying snake. I could just take that energy, I could push it into the earth like a grounded wire. . . .

"No. Harper, don't do it. Let the creep go."

I knew that voice. . . .

"Harper . . ."

I'd pushed him almost to the arch of roses at the peak of the stairs leading to the sidewalk. A gun—a stubby, small-bore rifle with a collapsing stock—lay across the top step, just outside the weak gold line of Mara's magic. That made me angry, but it was my own, pure anger this time, not something pouring into my head from the Grey.

I opened my mouth to speak and the voice that issued out of me echoed with a dozen strains and cries. "Tell your master I'll come when I'm good and ready." The voices in my head changed pitch and volume, singsonging "alone, alone, alone . . ."

I let him go, dropping him, staggering, onto his feet at the stone landing. I was just about to give him a push when a bright bolt of light flashed past me and hit him in the shoulder, setting his shirt on fire. He slapped at it, turning and letting out a gasping cry as he stumbled down the stairs.

"And don't come back, y'feckin' bastard, or I'll burn y'to a crisp!" Mara yelled from the porch. She had the eye clutched in her hands, the disk flashing and smoking as the sun touched it. Her shawl was gone, her hair was wild, and her face was streaked with black. Quinton stood beside her with a bucket. Behind them, just inside the doorway, Ben, shocked pale, held Brian against his chest. The boy had turned his face away from the scene and buried it in his father's jacket.

As Goodall escaped down the street, Quinton took the eye from Mara's hands and dropped it into the bucket, where it sizzled and hissed with a watery splash. Mara sat down in a boneless heap on the porch. I picked up the rifle and started back up the walkway. I climbed the porch steps and handed the gun to Quinton. He dropped the magazine, cleared the chamber, and slung the rifle over his shoulder like he'd been doing it all his life. I sat down next to Mara.

"Hell of a morning," I said. "And nice shooting."

"I thought y'were gonna kill him."

"I thought you were."

She shook her head and looked queasy. "I think I'm gonna be ill." She threw herself full length across the step and vomited into the battered rosebush. We gave her a minute to finish and rinse her mouth with a handful of warm water from the bucket and then Quinton and I helped Mara up and back into the house. She flopped again into the first couch in the living room and Ben sat down beside her with Brian still in his arms.

The three of them curled into a shivering ball as Quinton and I retreated to the hall.

"What happened in the back?" I asked.

"A couple of . . . I don't know. Stumpy little doll-like things tried to grab Brian. The dog got one and Mara got the other. Or maybe Ben did. I don't know if it burned up or if Ben kicked it to death. They must have jumped in at the same time that shot went off out front. I guess Mara's perimeter wasn't designed for a coordinated attack from multiple points. What about Phoebe?" he added, stooping to pick up the paper shopping bag that was lying on the entry floor.

"She's downstairs. Goodall was at the condo when she

got there, and I'd guess he made her call and then sent her to the door to lure me out. He tried to shoot us, but Phoebe knocked us down. The spell on the house might have bent the bullet's path, but Phoebe probably saved our lives."

Quinton looked into the bag. "She brought the puzzle."

"She's going to be really mad at me this time. And she's got a gun."

"Excuse me?"

"Mine is down there. I told her to take it—in case anyone made it through."

He sighed and then gave me a quick, soft kiss on the lips and glanced at the basement steps. "You want backup?"

"Want? Yes. Taking? No. She's my friend and it's my fault she's scared. I'll take care of it."

He nodded and let me go.

Phoebe did not shoot me, though she was very jumpy when I knocked on the basement door. She let me in, looking over my shoulder and all around for any new creeps who might do something nasty.

"It's all right," I said, taking the pistol from her gently and putting it back into the holster that should have been on my hip to begin with. "We sent him packing. I'll talk to the cops about him later—I think I know who he is. How are you doing?"

She was still a little shaky, but she drew her shoulders back and stood up as tall as possible. "I'm OK. Not happy, but OK. Store's been robbed before. That ain't the first time some no-good waved a gun at me."

"I'm sorry." I was saying that a lot lately. "I wouldn't have asked you to go if—"

"I know that. Now you tell me what that man wants with you. Why he's willin' to shoot three women in plain sight."

I shook my head. "It's complicated, but . . . he works for someone who wants me to do something pretty bad. I mean, he wants me to do something that might hurt or kill a lot of people. I won't do it. I guess that's not the answer he wants to hear."

"You aren't gonna change your mind?"

"No. And I'm not going to let it happen, either."

"What are you gonna do, then?"

"I'm working on that. I need more information first and that puzzle ball may help me get it. Then . . . we'll see."

"'We'll see'? That's a plan?"

"Not by itself, but there are other considerations." I thought for a moment about how much to tell her and what might help keep Phoebe safe and sane. "That man may have helped kidnap Edward Kammerling of TPM, but since Kammerling's still missing, the situation's delicate."

She goggled at me. "I knew he looked familiar! I saw him on the news: He's that security guy! He kidnapped his boss?"

"Helped. Probably. And he thinks I know something or have something he wants."

"Why?"

"I just got back from doing some work for TPM in London."

"And do you know something?"

I cocked my head over and made a disapproving face. "Phoebe," I chided. "You don't want to know that."

"Oh, all right." She started for the door, then stopped and turned back to me, still a little pale. "You think it's safe? To go back home?"

I nodded. "Yeah. I think it'll be fine. So long as you stay away from my place and stay away from here, no one should bother you any further."

She made a dismissive grunt in the back of her throat. "Better be right about that. Or I'll tell Poppy to poison your food on Sunday."

"Tomorrow Sunday?" I questioned, thinking there was no way I could risk going to the Masons' family dinner at this point.

"No, not this Sunday. I said next Sunday, didn't I? Don't you know the difference between this Sunday and next Sunday?" She snorted and tossed her head. "Next Sunday." Then she turned and marched up the stairs. I followed her back into the entry hall.

She paused and pointed at Quinton, who was still standing near the door. "Next Sunday. Don't you let her forget, or I'll find someone to put a curse on you both so bad your hair'll fall out."

Quinton nodded. "Yes, ma'am."

"Don't you 'ma'am' me! You just be there," she shouted back and stomped out.

Quinton gave me a wide-eyed look. I only shook my head. Phoebe was dealing as well as I could expect with what she'd been through, especially since she hadn't seen anything that couldn't be explained as ordinary violence and human action. She'd be all right. I was a little less sure about the Danzigers.

"We had better find another place to stay," I suggested, taking the bag full of puzzle ball from him.

"Why?" Ben asked behind me.

I spun around, startled by his unexpected presence in the hall.

"Why what?"

"Why would you leave now?"

"Why not, after disrupting your home and your life so badly? Mara's wards are a mess and Quinton says there are a couple of dead somethings in your backyard. You do not need me here, making your family and your home into targets."

"We also don't need dead friends on our consciences. We know what's at stake. Really."

Brian came galloping into the hall and grabbed at the bag I was holding. "Gimme!"

"No," I replied pulling the bag away.

Brian jumped and snatched for it. "Mama says gimme! Wanna see the zuzzle ball."

"Yes. As I've killed something for it and set someone else alight, I'd like to get a look at the infernal thing," Mara added, leaning in the living room arch. She looked wan but less upset than I'd expected.

I looked around and saw they were all staring at me. I raised the bag higher out of Brian's reach. I felt lame saying, "You do not get to touch it until your mother says it's safe."

Brian stuck out his lower lip and looked more pugnacious than tearful. " 'Snot fair."

"Get used to it," I shot back.

I handed the bag to Ben since he was the tallest person in the room and most likely to keep the thing out of Brian's clutches. We all trooped into the living room, Mara in the lead and Brian scampering around, eyeing the bag with a calculating expression. We distributed ourselves on the twin couches, except for the boy, who dragged a child-sized chair up to the coffee table from beside the hearth and plopped into it.

Mara took the bag from Ben and peered inside. "Ben, would you get the eye out of the bucket? It's on the front stoop. There's a pile of clean washin'-up towels on the kitchen counter. Someone fetch those, too, please."

I went for the towels and met Ben in the hall to wrap up the dripping disk he'd fished out of the bucket of water. Mara dried off the eye with care and looked it over. Brian stood up and leaned as close as he dared, almost breathing on the object his mother had.

"What is it y'think you're doing, little man?" she asked.

"Lookin'," Brian replied.

"Did I say you could? What's the rule?"

"'Don't touch the magic things 'less you wanna wear the warts.' But I'm not touching it!"

"If you were any closer, you'd have your nose on it. And a warty, warty nose it would be, too. Now, go into the hall and fetch mama's shawl and the things she dropped with it."

"But—"

Mara made a sharp little humming noise and glared at her son. "Fetch, boy-o."

Brian bit his lip and trundled off. Mara sighed. "Troublesome little mite."

I glanced at Quinton with a sudden flare of alarm. "Speaking of trouble . . ."

He unbuttoned one of his pockets and Chaos stuck her head out, making an uncomplimentary grumbling noise. "And the dog's OK, too," he added. "I went out to look while you were downstairs."

I nodded, relieved the only serious injuries seemed to be the opposition's. Brian returned, hauling the bundle of shawl, and heaved it up onto the coffee table. In spite of his earlier demeanor, he seemed quite pleased with himself for returning successfully.

Mara thanked him and opened up the shawl. The contents were a bit of a mess—several of the packages had spilled and the contents were sticking all over the fabric—but she sorted out enough of the various herbs to satisfy her needs and ground them between her palms. Then she dusted them over the flat sides of the disk, which took on a gleam like glass as she muttered and spread the crushed herbs over the surface. The object was still opaque, but it looked shiny.

"Right, then. Harper, you hold the ball."

I dug into the bag and pulled out the wooden puzzle ball, seeing the thin Grey sheen that seeped from its seams. I didn't see anything else and it didn't feel any different than it ever had. But it wouldn't: Phoebe's saying it was creepy had been directed by—or at—Goodall. I held it at arm's length, hearing something rattle gently inside, and Mara moved the eye over the ball as she stared at the surface.

Quinton and Brian both stared at the eye in fascination. As Mara moved it around I could see why: When you looked straight down at the arcanely shining surface, what you saw was an enlarged section of the object below, but glowing with colors and shapes in a strata of glittering dust.

"Ooo," Brian sighed. "Pretty animals."

Mara laughed and looked up from her work. "Not animals, y'silly boy: *anima*. It's girly magic," she added, glancing at me.

I frowned. "I don't get it."

She put the eye down in her lap and began wiping the surface clean. "Some things, some types of magic, are gendered. I don't mean that only men or women can do it, but that there's a tendency or bifurcation that's analogous to gender."

I rested the ball on my knee; my arms were tired from holding it out while Mara inspected it.

"So," Mara continued, "either that puzzle was made by a woman, or for some very feminine purpose, or there's another part that's the complement to that one. A masculine part with an *animus* type of magic. There's something inside that's not radiating at all, so no concern here. Oh, and it's quite safe. You can put it down if you like. Aside from the gendering, there's not much there. Something compacted but neutral, and a partner strand, which I assume is linked to the other-gendered part of whatever that's supposed to do."

"Supposedly, it's either a labyrinth or a door to a labyrinth. I have a key, which is probably the male half of the equation." I pulled the small wire toy from my pocket and held it up. It didn't look much like a key at that moment, but I knew what it could do and they didn't.

"Keys would seem pretty masculine by nature," Ben observed, studying the twisted wire thing in my hand.

I made a dry smirk at him. "Ha, ha."

"I'm serious. Keys tend to be masculine objects."

"Magic isn't subject to concepts like political correctness," Mara added.

"All right then," I said, hefting the ball in one hand and the wire puzzle in the other. "Door, key. Let's see if they work."

"Just a second," Quinton broke in, putting his hand over mine. "How big a door, or whatever, do you think that thing opens? Just from a physics standpoint, if the area or pressures aren't the same on both sides, there's going to be a mess in here when you open it up."

"It's magic," Ben said. "Physics doesn't enter into the equation."

"Yes, it does," Quinton argued. "So far, everything I've observed says that there are still working laws of physics, like the conservation of mass and fluid dynamics, in play with magic. So if you open an area of different pressure into this room, there's going to be displacement of whatever fluid you have—be it air or water or giant Cthulhuan horrors from the slime dimension—until the pressure is equalized. Do you really want to risk psychotic killer jellyfish swimming around your head?"

Ben looked at Mara. "Maybe the yard *is* a better place. . . ."

TWENTY

It took a while to get the backyard into the physical and magical condition that satisfied all of us. Mara was most concerned about reinforcing the magical wards and clearing off the remains of the blood-magic charms and alarms the vampires had left behind. We all figured it wouldn't surprise anyone by now if they were removed. The men wanted to clean up the yard, burying the scorched and trampled remains of whatever nasty creature Goodall had set on them, while Brian wanted to get the dog to safer ground. I really did start to think Rick was never going to get his pet back at this rate.

Mara and I also cleared off a bit of ground for a containment circle, marking the area with various signs and symbols as she directed, so if anything did come through the door, it wouldn't get far.

In the end, it all proved pointless. I shuffled the wire puzzle until it clicked into a formation that chimed and hummed when brought near the ball, but when the two were put together, the key sinking into an invisible slot and twisting with an ease that surprised me, there was only a breath of hot, plant-scented air and a sound like something heavy settling into the earth at a distance. A small object dropped out the first time, but nothing else happened. Mara and I tried several configurations and spells, weaving various bits of magic together and trying to cajole the puzzle to work, but the effect only got slightly more fragrant with the odor of flowers and a rustle of invisible leaves that almost covered the persistent muttering in the back of my head.

We gave up and returned to sit on the back porch. Mara took the key from me and looked it over with the eye as I bent to pick up the thing that had fallen from the puzzle: it was a garnet earring that looked familiar to me. Mara finished her inspection of the ball and then pointed at the bauble in my hand. "May I look at that?"

I handed it over. She inspected it with the eye before shaking her head. "Neither of these is the second part," she said. She handed the earring to me and I pocketed it.

The men had gone out into the yard where we'd cleared the circle and, at Brian's insistence, were playing a complicated game involving a soccer ball, the dog, and two goalposts erected hastily between the side yard fences. I watched them for a moment, trying to figure out what they were doing. "It's not the second part of what?"

"The key is not the second part of the mechanism," she explained. "Nor is the earring, incidentally, but that's a bit off the point since it seems to be here almost by accident. This key isn't actually *animus*. It's neutral. There's another part somewhere. But beyond that, this puzzle ball seems to be keyed to a location."

"Meaning . . . ?"

"Y'have to use it in the right place. So, y'need to get all the parts, mate them together, and then use them in the correct location, or nothing happens. Or nothing much."

I blew a silent whistle. "Well, we wouldn't want this to be easy, would we?"

"Certainly not. Consider the potential: If the complete mechanism *does* open a way into the Grey that is invisible to the Guardian Beast, unregulated, and accessible to folk who've had no prior contact with magic at all, it could be disastrous. Imagine the cataclysm one ignorant action could set in motion. Whoever made this was remarkably careful, though why they didn't destroy it when they were done, I can't guess. It hardly seems the sort of thing y'leave lyin' about."

"They didn't. They put the pieces away carefully, somewhere most people would never look for them: in plain sight."

Mara frowned at me. "I don't follow. . . ."

A memory jogged loose in my head and I pointed at the puzzle ball, which was resting on the table. "That was one of a pair that came from an old house that was torn down or damaged—I forget. Anyhow. Will got it from a friend of his who dealt in architectural antiques. He said the other one was stuck. But what if it wasn't? What if the pieces are nested and to get the second one open, you have to open the other one first?" That jibed in a way with something my father had said about doors inside doors. Or was it mazes inside mazes . . . ? Whatever the case, I thought I was onto something. "Maybe whoever made it wasn't sure he'd ever need to use it again, but he doesn't want to risk just throwing it away—maybe he knows there's going to be a need for it someday. So he puts the parts away and he gives the key to someone he thinks no one will ever associate with him: a kid in Montana, or a dentist in Los Angeles. Someone who has no apparent link to him."

Mara nodded thoughtfully and went on with the idea. "Except that the magical world is really very small, so . . . it's not entirely surprisin' that the key ends up with a Greywalker."

"The key and the first part of the machine—whatever it is."

"Seems obvious you'll have to get the rest of the pieces and take them back to wherever they came from. That should be where the mechanism comes together and where y'can activate it once you have all the parts."

"That's not going to be so easy: I got the ball from Will Novak and the last time I saw him, he . . . wasn't doing very well."

She asked and I had to tell her what had happened in London and how I had last seen William Novak bloody and broken, raddled by the horrors of imprisonment and torture at the hands of vampires and their pet sorcerer. By the time I was done with the tale, Ben, Quinton, and Brian had given up their game and come up onto the back porch. Grendel flopped at the foot of the steps, tired out and with tongue lolling. Ben took Brian inside to wash up and avoid the more graphic parts of my description.

"So they're still in England?" Mara asked.

"I think not. The only thing Will was clear about was that he wanted to come home. The doctors didn't want to release him, but even if his mind was going, his desire to get away from London might have been enough to motivate someone to let him go. So he and his brother could be stuck in England or back in Seattle. It's been almost a week since I saw them and I just don't know."

"You could call Michael and find out," Quinton suggested.

"Yes, but it's Will who knows where the puzzle balls came from," I replied.

"No, Will knows who had them last. That guy would know where they came from. Michael might know which of Will's friends that is."

I conceded that. I wasn't sure my relationship with Michael Novak was any better than my relationship with Will was after what had happened, but I could try. The only number I had for him was a London mobile, but I thought it unlikely he'd already have replaced the phone if they'd left England. It was hard to remember that I'd seen him less than a week ago because it felt like more.

I called, half expecting no answer, but Michael picked up and spoke from somewhere so loud it was hard to hear him. Clanging metal and shattering glass punctuated an erratic symphony of mechanical roars and human shouts.

"Michael," I started.

"Hang on!" I could hear him moving around; then the noise faded down a bit. "Whatever you want, Harper, make it fast—have to get back inside before he notices I'm gone."

"Who?"

"Will. He's totally lost it since we got home. Come on, come on! We've got about a minute."

I would have asked what was going on or where in Seattle he was, but I could tell he didn't have time for that. "What is the name and business address of Will's friend here who breaks down antique houses?"

"Breaks—? Oh. Charlie Rice. Rice House Antiques—it's under the viaduct on Alaskan Way. Not the aquarium end of the row, but the ferry dock end. Big warehouse space. Look for a red London phone box on the loading dock."

Something hard crashed against something made of wood and the background noise rose again. "Gotta go!" Michael shouted and cut the connection. I blinked at the ground in a fog of sudden disquiet while a bitter sensation curdled my stomach. Something was askew with Michael and Will. . . .

As I worried that thought, Quinton dug a small device out of his pocket and detached the clinging ferret, which he handed to me. Chaos wriggled into my shirt and went back to sleep, while Quinton flipped the little box open and turned it on: some kind of tiny palmtop computer.

"OK, what did you get?" he asked, poised to type on the miniature keyboard. I told him, and he had the address and map location in seconds. "Should we just go, or should we call first?"

"We?" I asked. It didn't sound like a dangerous trip, but I was feeling off-kilter and wasn't sure I should drag anyone else deeper into this mess if I could avoid it.

"You, me: intrepid investigator and faithful sidekick—who still has the keys to the truck."

"Ah. Well, in person is usually better."

"Then we'd better pack our stuff into the Rover, just in case there's a hot lead to follow up."

I pointed at the ferret in my shirt. "What about the furry knee sock?"

Quinton and I both looked toward Mara. She shrugged. "Another day or two with the weasel won't hurt us. Brian's too taken with the dog to bother her much and she hasn't been any trouble. Except for the smell and stealin' shoes."

"Wait until she notices the key chains and cell phones," Quinton said.

It took us longer than expected to get things into the Rover and clear off since we had to scout for any remaining friends of Goodall's and any new spells that might have been laid. We got down to the waterfront near Rice House Antiques about forty minutes later.

The building was an aging brick warehouse a block from the seawall and just at the edge of the tourist zone. I'd been there back when I was more active in hunting up interesting old things for my place, but the average size of the inventory items—from carved entryways and massive chandeliers to whole fieldstone fireplaces—was too large for me and I'd taken the place out of my mental directory. The loading area under the viaduct faced the old, disused municipal dock that lay just south of the ferry terminal across the double row of city parking under the elevated roadbed. Rumor had it the old stacked highway was going to be replaced with a tunnel someday, but so far, the crumbling concrete structure was still in place and still dropping bits of cement and road dirt at irregular intervals. The location had a lonely feel, despite traffic near enough to see; even the glow of the grid seemed a bit tired here.

Rice House Antiques was painted once-cheery yellow and green that made it look like a faded and forgotten carnival building. An old red British phone box stood on the loading ramp, adding another splash of aging color to the frontage. Quinton and I left the Rover in a parking space beside the loading ramp and walked up. Being nearly noon on a Saturday, the business was open—literally. One of the two huge freight doors was rolled all the way up to expose some of the treasures inside. But of customers, there wasn't a sign.

Once inside the door, we could hear someone talking and moving around near the back of the shop, but the words were indistinct, muffled by racks full of carved doors and leaded windows between the massive pieces of architectural whimsy. Failing to see anyone else, I headed for the sound. Quinton trailed a bit, staring at the odd collection.

I came around a corner to a room that was built of antique half-glass doors—they looked a lot like the door to my own office—and could see someone moving around inside beyond the frosted glass, between hazy shapes that stood here and there inside. "All right, all right . . . it's got to be here. . . ." It was a masculine voice, but not one I recognized. Elderly and quavering.

I rapped lightly on one of the doors that seemed most likely to be functional and not just nailed in place. The man inside scuffled around and pulled the door open.

He was stocky, shorter than average, with round, heavy shoulders and legs slightly bowed. His thin gray hair was brushed down more in hope that it would cover his scalp than with any real expectation. He jumped a bit at seeing me and blinked hard, making a chewing motion and a snort. He stayed in the doorway with one hand on the door and the other on the frame as if he thought I was going to rush inside if he didn't. The energy around him was a nervous shade of orange shot with green.

"What? Hello. What can I do for you?" he asked, his voice was low and scratchy, like a conspirator's.

I matched his volume—there was no need to be louder standing so close. "Are you Charlie Rice?"

"I—yeah. Yeah, I'm Charlie."

"I wanted to talk to you about a pair of puzzle balls you had about sixteen or eighteen months ago. They came from a house. . . ."

Rice scowled. "Don't have 'em."

"Yes, I know. I have one of them. I wondered where they came from and what happened to the other one." My eye was caught by something else moving inside the office. Something tall and thin. A cold feeling bolted through my gut, stopping my breath. I felt a warm thing looming behind me as well, but I kept my eyes forward.

He blanched. "*You* have one? Oh, God—"

The shadow inside leaned toward Rice's head and I started to reach for him, to pull him away, but the door jerked open, yanked out of Charlie's hand, making him stumble a bit.

Will Novak stood just behind Rice's shoulder, the door creaking as it swung wide, nearly off its hinges. "Harper!" He clapped Charlie on the shoulder with one crabbed hand covered in livid scars and scuffed bloody across the knuckles. "See: I told you she'd come."

I was shocked to see him.

Will looked horrific. For a moment I couldn't believe he was there, much less upright in such a state. He hadn't regained any weight—possibly he'd lost even more in the week since I'd seen him last. His skin was slack over unpadded bones and it had a raw, dry look, as if it had been scrubbed too much. He hadn't replaced his glasses and his eyes glinted out of shadowed pits beneath his brow without seeming to blink. Energy rioted around him in clashing colors and sparks with no cohesion or harmony except for a single black line that ran steady and unmoving through the mess, more like a lack than a presence. A spike of fear—for him or of him, I wasn't sure—struck through me as I looked at him.

A shrieking disharmony of voices battered inside my skull, and I had to concentrate on calm, on normalcy. "Will, what are you doing here?"

"Wanted to see you."

"You don't need to see me right now. You need to rest and get better." But I feared he was never going to get better, that his broken, sickening discord was permanent, and that twisted in my gut. "How did you even know I was coming?"

His aura flickered with antifreeze-green lightning. "Michael told me."

The mad chorus in my head chimed, "Liar, liar . . ." as Will drew his hands together, rubbing the bruised knuckles of one hand in the cupped hollow of the other. A prescient flash struck me like a physical blow. "You hit him."

He blinked as if wounded. "He wouldn't have told me otherwise. And I needed to see you. I owe you . . . everything. Everything."

The worshipful sound in his voice sickened me. "No, you don't. All I did was get you in too deep in the first place."

He shook his head. "No. No. You saved my life."

I felt myself growing remote and cold against my will. "Michael saved your life. He found you, he carried you out, he took you away. Not me." My spine seemed to vibrate and ring with the shouting of the Grey voices, and I almost choked on the sound.

Charlie Rice tried to slip away while Will's attention was on me, but Quinton sidled over and caught him. "Where did the ball come from?"

"Leavenworth," Rice whispered back, shooting nervous glances at me and Will while trying to move farther away. "Old house in the orchards, but it's gone. Nothing left but the foundation. . . ."

"Did this house have a maze or a labyrinth, a pattern on the floors—anything like that?"

Charlie shook his head in a spastic way without letting Will and me out of his sight. "Don't know. I just—" He seemed to catch himself and change his mind before he said, "I just cleared the wreckage."

Will stepped toward me, reaching with his bent, mutilated hands, his stride crooked and off balance. "I need you, Harper." He glanced toward Quinton and Rice, his aura flashing orange, followed by green and red. "The new guy doesn't need you. Not like I do." I felt repelled in a way I couldn't explain, as if Will had become poisonous. Sensations of pity and horror fought with the frigid resistance that welled up in me as if I were splitting in two. This icy disgust wasn't like me. . . .

Quinton's shoulders stiffened and he turned a little more in our direction. "No. I don't *need* her. I don't need her to be anything or do anything. I only want her to be what she is."

"See?" Will implored, laying his wrecked hands on my shoulders. "I need you. I'll go with you."

His touch was hot and cold, sharp as electricity; it roused the chorus and made me want to scream with them and shove him away. I gulped in air and swallowed the voices. "No, you won't. Not there. It won't be safe—there are monsters in labyrinths, don't you remember? You're only safe here, with Michael. Not with me."

Rice turned to escape again, but Quinton sprang after him and snatched him to a halt nearby, asking, "Where did the other ball go? Who has it?"

"I . . . might have the receipt. . . ."

"OK, then. Let's look at your records."

Rice leapt at the chance to get away from Will and me and dragged Quinton back into the office, snapping the door closed after them and leaving us outside in the strange assembly of broken houses. Will tried to grip my shoulders and draw me closer, but his hands felt like giant crab claws and they had no strength to hold me. I slid free, guilty at my relief.

"Will, please. You don't understand how unsafe you are with me. I didn't save you from anything; I put you in danger."

He shook his head and his eyes were bright with an unreasonable adulation. It made me feel sick and I wanted to cry over it, but that was the last thing I would do. "It's not true," he whispered. "I love you. You love me; you came after me."

My voice came out cold. "I came after some work. I found you entirely incidentally. It was luck—mostly bad luck."

He made a small smug smile and shook his head again. "You can't get rid of me by lying. I know what you really feel."

I sighed. "Oh, no." I tried to turn away and come back later, figuring Quinton would get the information I needed for now. But whatever else I did, I had to get away from the mania shining in Will's eyes. It tore me into pieces to see it—to see him like this—but still the sensation of being coated in emotional ice deepened.

Will hooked one of his hands under my arm at the shoulder and tugged me back. "We need to be together, Harper. I won't let you go. I'll come with you. Trust me."

There was no way I could. The little voices trilled and chattered: "Touch him, touch him, make him go."

For a raw, heartless moment I did not resist them. I turned back, letting my body roll into the compass of his arms, not like a lover but like an enemy ducking under his guard, and putting out my hands so the tips of my fingers brushed across his chest. It felt like I'd touched a corpse. I let my hands slide up to frame his face, feeling the rippling colors of his chaotic aura like currents of hot and cold water and sudden spikes of electric shock. I tangled my fingers in the energy strands and wondered if I could do something. . . .

I leaned on all the persuasion I had and tried to *think* his aura to a calm shade of blue. I doubted it would work, but anything was worth trying. "You don't need to come along now. You need to sleep. And I'll be back soon. Just sleep." No luck: Nothing was happening and, if anything, Will only seemed annoyed by my attempts to calm him down or persuade him to give up.

"Don't coddle me, Harper." His tone was sharp with sudden anger.

I stiffened and would have replied, but the opening of the office door cut me off. Quinton popped out, stuffing something into his pocket and closing the door behind him, leaving Rice alone inside. Will glared at him as Quinton eased next to me and put his left hand around my waist, pulling me back from my former boyfriend. I felt something nudge against my side as I dropped my arms and stepped back next to Quinton, but I couldn't look down. "You ready to go?" he whispered.

I nodded and we started to turn away.

Will stepped forward, trying to reestablish his hold on me. Quinton gave him a narrow look over his shoulder. I risked a glance down and saw that Quinton was pressing the hard handle of a stun stick into my hidden side, offering it to me underhand, as he turned halfway back to say, "Let it go."

"You don't understand—" Will started.

"I do. But Harper can't save you; you need to start saving yourself. And you need to let her go and do what she has to do."

Will glared at him and brushed past to pull me to his chest again. I snatched the device into my fist as Will yanked me away from Quinton.

"Oh, man. Don't do that," Quinton said.

"Will, don't," I echoed, stumbling forward, turning the hard shape of the stun stick around in my hand. "Just let go of me. Go home to Michael—"

Heavy footsteps thudded on the wooden floor, drawing closer to the rear of the shop.

"Michael can't help me—he doesn't know how!"

"Neither do I!"

"Yes, you do! Yes, you do! You're the only one. I need you! I'm going—"

He cut himself off as two cops came around the end of the stack of doors and windows. These weren't slicked-down, tourist-friendly bike cops; they were old-fashioned beat-pounders in full gear. They glanced at Quinton and then at Will, then back to Quinton, their shoulders tensing as they took in Will's grip on my shoulder and Quinton's protective arm at my waist, masking the object I now held.

"Mr. Rice?" one of them inquired, but they both kept their eyes on Will. I knew they couldn't see the madhouse colors around his head, but they still had cop instincts for trouble. Neither reached for his gun, but their hands touched their belts. One of them hung back while the other stepped toward us. "Is one of you Mr. Rice?"

The office door creaked open on its damaged hinges and the owner stuck his head out. "I'm Rice."

"What's the problem, Mr. Rice?"

Rice's voice quavered, but he answered strongly enough. "Mr. Novak is frightening my customers. He should be at home—he's been in an accident and he's . . . not himself. I—please. Would you help Mr. Novak get home safely?"

Will whipped back to stare at Rice. "Charlie! No! Don't do this to me!"

"William, you're not well."

Will made an irrational growling sound and released me so he could grab for Rice. The violence of his gesture spun me toward the nearer policeman and I ducked to avoid hitting the man. The cop sidestepped me and lunged forward to catch Will by the shoulders.

In a second, the two cops, Will, and Charlie Rice were a scuffling mass in the office doorway. Will shouted and thrashed, doing more damage to his reputation than anything else, though he did manage to break Rice's nose with one flailing elbow. The splattering blood sent Will into fits, and he threw himself back from Rice and the cops, exhausted and terrified beyond all reason. Making shrill screeching sounds, he lurched backward into the half-glass doors and tumbled through one of the upper panes with a crash.

The cops and Charlie Rice ran into the office to retrieve him and Quinton put his hand back under my free elbow, urging me forward. "C'mon, let's get out of here before this gets crazier."

I was still at war inside: A part of me said I should stay

and try to help Will, but I turned with Quinton and we zigzagged our way out of the antiques warehouse and back to the Rover. I hoped that Will was all right—or as all right as he was likely to be—and that Rice's nose wasn't too badly wrecked, but I didn't go back to find out. We bailed into the truck and abandoned the situation to the cops.

TWENTY-ONE

We reached the West Seattle Bridge near the container yards before I broke down. I felt as if some fortress of ice had surrounded me and now shattered, letting the horror and despair I should have felt before rush out. I had to pull over and stop the truck as my vision flooded with wavering crimson.

Quinton drew me into his lap and pressed a paper napkin to my cheek to catch my running red tears. "It's OK, babe. It'll be all right."

"'Babe'?" I sniffled, pulled out of my confusion, upset, and pity by the oddity of the word.

He shrugged. "I'm terrible with synonyms. I'm a science geek, not an English teacher, you know."

I blotted up the bloody mess and blew my nose. "'Babe' is what you call women with more boobs than brains," I said. "And I may be acting stupid, but given how little bust I've got, it doesn't say much for what's north of my chin."

Quinton made a bemused face. "I am not going to try to unravel that. But regardless of whether it's your boobs or your brain you're insulting, you're wrong: They're both magnificent."

I poked him in the shoulder. "What are you on? I feel like I've got a sieve full of Jell-O in my head. Oh, gods, poor Will. . . . I shouldn't have left him like that." And why had I? Why had I gone so cold . . . ?

"It was Rice's call—he thought the cops might be the best solution. He's known Novak for years and he's just as worried about him as you are. He'll be all right."

"No, he won't." I squirmed around so I could see Quinton better. "Maybe you didn't notice—"

"That he's lost it completely? Yes, I did. But it wouldn't be diplomatic of me to say it."

"You just did."

"Yeah. . . ." He bit his lower lip and looked away. "I'm sorry."

"It's the truth, so . . . you shouldn't be. And I feel there's nothing I can do. I wanted to—I tried . . . but it didn't work. I felt like it was too much to care for. . . ."

"You can't fix everything. You try too hard to fix too much of the world as it is. And don't start saying that what happened to Novak is your fault: It isn't. No one could expect him to keep his head on straight after being kidnapped and tortured by things he thought only existed in horror films and pulpy novels. This is one thing you're going to have to let go. You can't help Novak. You *can* help a lot of other people by completing the task you already set for yourself. You have to stop wasting your energy on what you can't change."

I narrowed my eyes at him. I wanted to be angry or, better still, to be as cold and remote as I'd felt at Charlie Rice's warehouse—it would hurt less than the horror and sorrow that now pressed on my chest—but that, too, wasn't working. Quinton dropped his forehead onto my shoulder for a moment and took a deep breath before he looked up again.

"Harper. I'm not saying it's wrong to want to help, but you can't do it all, and some of it is simply not doable. Someone said, 'Pick battles small enough to win, big enough to matter.' You need to pick the one you can win."

"How do I know which one that is?"

"You know. You just don't like thinking you're abandoning someone. Especially someone you went back for once already. But that's not the job you're on now. It's up to Novak and his brother to take what you gave them and do their best. Like it's up to you to do your best with what you have in front of you right now." He pulled a piece of paper out of his pocket and spread it on my thigh. "I have the address in Leavenworth."

My heart stuttered. "For the maze?"

"No. For the other puzzle ball. Kind of a funny coincidence that it went right back where it came from, yeah?"

I felt a tug of curiosity and a touch of premonition. My brows drew down as I thought about it. "Probably not a coincidence at all. . . ."

Quinton hugged me suddenly and with unexpected power. "Glad to have you back, sweetheart."

I slumped into him. "Have I been missing?"

"A little. Off and on."

I shook my head. "I'm hearing things and I can't seem to . . . feel what I ought to, as well as all the rest. I feel pressed for time and anxious to get this over with before things get worse. As if I even knew what sort of worse they might get. And yet part of me is growing remote, as if none of this matters."

"It does matter. You're just overwhelmed."

I took that in with a nod, though I wasn't sure I believed it.

"You're hearing things?" he asked, looking concerned.

"Yeah. Singing and voices. From the Grey. Not ghosts, something more . . . endemic. Sometimes it says things I need to listen to, sometimes it seems to move me, but most of the time, it's just noise. Intrusive, implacable noise. Like the audience at a rock concert without the music."

"Do they have lighters?"

"What?"

"Lighters. You know: The sappy ballad dedicated to some dead band member starts up and everyone flicks their Bic and holds it on high."

I fixed an incredulous stare on him. "You have a romantic streak as wide as a hair."

"I am very romantic—I brought you flowers for your birthday."

"No, you didn't."

"The ferret ate them."

I glared at him.

"All right, she didn't eat them. She pushed them on the floor and broke the vase and I had to throw them out, but I did bring them. You just weren't home to appreciate them. See: That's romantic, even if it's kind of messed up. But that rock concert thing is sentiment, of which I have almost none."

I continued peering at him, though I did feel a giggle tugging at one corner of my mouth.

"I traded it in," he explained, "for an oscilloscope—it was a pretty nifty one, too."

I snorted a laugh. "Goof."

"Yup. Big goofy geek-boy here. I'm working on that 'he makes me laugh' thing because, you know, Roger and Jessica have it all over Rhett and Scarlett."

Now I laughed out loud and Quinton had to shut me up by kissing me, which I didn't mind at all. It wasn't that I was happy about what had happened at Rice House Antiques, but I no longer felt too awful to go on or too cold to care. Quinton was right in saying I couldn't do anything for Will—at least not right then—and there were more pressing things on my agenda. I did feel terrible for the brothers Novak, but I'd have to make some kind of . . . amends later.

It's about a three-hour drive to Leavenworth from Seattle if you don't pause for much. Most map searches will tell you it's two and a half, but even in the best weather the roads through the mountains in the final third of the trip don't encourage driving over the posted limits. The surfaces themselves are fine, but the twists and turns with precipitous drops into rivers and ravines just a few feet aside aren't. Ribbons, rock piles, and occasional plaques mark the places where the road and some of its drivers parted ways. We took the northern route through Monroe, but I had to ask Quinton to take the wheel once we passed Skykomish. Even with the filtering effect of the Rover's steel and glass, the sudden flashes of accidents and ghosts racked me with shocks. We were almost out of the pass when I spotted the last shadow of a fatal accident on the route: Two women and a young boy in 1940s clothes stood at the outside edge of a bend that hung over the Wenatchee River below. They were dripping wet and looked frightened and confused. Even the small black dog at their feet seemed disoriented by what must have happened to them all. I had to turn my head away from their imploring stares.

"Bad?" Quinton asked.

I just nodded.

About ten minutes later we came out of the pass and started the last short downhill to Leavenworth, a mock-Bavarian village beside the highway surrounded by a larger town full of retirees, orchard keepers, and railroad workers. The traffic was thicker than I'd expected for so late in the day—it was after four o'clock already—and we slowed to a creep as we entered the city limits. A soft, floral smell spiked with the odors of greenery, manure, and beer slipped into the truck's vents and invited us to roll down the windows, even though the air outside was crisp and the shadow of the mountain was already falling onto the bowl of the valley, lowering the temperature further.

"So where are we going?" I asked as we passed Icicle Road and the slope flattened considerably as U.S. 2 made its two-lane way through town.

"No idea. Didn't look it up yet."

"Did Rice tell you where the house it came from was?"

"No. I had the impression the salvage wasn't quite on the up-and-up, so he didn't have an address—covering his ass in case anyone complained and identified him. He said it was in an orchard outside town."

I looked around. Everything that wasn't houses or quaint Bavarian shops was either apple trees or ski resort business. Even from the business-choked confines of Highway 2, I could see the fruit trees climbing the hills surrounding the town. Late blossoms covered many of the visible trees in mantillas of pink-tinged white. Brighter white or pink splashes marked out the occasional pear or cherry tree in the congregation.

"Yeah . . . that's going to be easy to spot."

"We'll start with the address we've got for Christopher Drew—the guy who bought the puzzle ball. The writing's a bit hard to read, but that seems to be the name. If I can find some WiFi, I can look it up."

It didn't seem likely we'd get any signal in the middle of the road, but it wasn't going to be easy to park: The streets of the town were thick with cars and pedestrians. Over the sound of engines idling, a loudspeaker squawked something about Apple Blossom Royalty and beer gardens. A lot of the cars ahead of us peeled off to the right in front of a restaurant named Gustav's that sported an onion dome on a steeplelike extension and gingerbread deck rails cut with fanciful tulip shapes.

Quinton shot a wary look at the throng turning right and stayed to the left. "Let's not go wherever they're going."

I took a longer look and saw the branching road was much more ornately built with unrelenting Bavarianisms on both sides. A block or so away the road curved abruptly and I could see a bright yellow banner hung high across the street on the dogleg beyond. It wasn't close enough to read but I got the gist.

"I doubt we'll be able to avoid it," I said. "There's some kind of festival going on."

We crept past a hotel dressed up like an Alpine ski lodge that sported a smaller yellow banner with the words "Welcome to Maifest!" right under its Howard Johnson logo. I grimaced at our timing.

"Better park and walk," Quinton suggested.

I rolled my eyes at the thought.

It turned out not to be so bad, though it did take fifteen minutes to find a parking place. I figured that dinner was approaching for some of the locals and they might prefer to eat at home rather than at the tourist-quaint biergartens and rathskellers. A bit of walking on the less popular highway side of the main drag brought us back into the center of town. Quinton spotted a familiar green logo near the park in the middle of the village and we headed for it, though the heavy German script made it difficult to make out the small carved sign on the building's side that read "Starbucks." We hunkered down with the dark sludge they call coffee while Quinton poked at his handheld.

Leavenworth was an odd place. On the south side of the highway it was conspicuously a themed tourist mecca with cute Alpine architecture straight off the slopes of Disney's version of the Matterhorn. North of the highway, the Bavarian theme continued but in patches, interrupted with much more prosaic American buildings and ordinary houses beyond that. The Alpine architecture wasn't entirely out of place since we'd only come a few hundred feet down from the ridge to the valley floor: The area was still mountainous and would whiten with thick drifts in the first snowfall. In the Grey I could see the bland, busy railroad town it had once been. But the rails had moved north to take a shorter route though the pass and this town had nearly died.

I stepped outside for a moment and glanced up and down Front Street—the main drag—looking at the pretty little buildings that hung their present happy colors over the sad, shuttered businesses that had once dominated the place. That was depressing, but as silly as I thought the current incarnation was, at least it was thriving. I had to applaud whoever had come up with the idea. Other towns abandoned by their primary industry hadn't fared so well.

Quinton came out onto the railed porch that overlooked the street and put his arm around my waist. "It's a little weird, isn't it?"

I nodded.

"Did you know they have their own German-language newspaper here? They're really into the Bavarian thing."

"Seems to be working. Though it must seem a bit sad and strange when it isn't Maifest."

"It's always something out here. Next week is Spring Bird Fest. Can you imagine what it must be like in October?"

I shivered at the vision of thousands of beer-loving tourists flooding into the tiny town to celebrate the traditional German brewfest. I wondered if they had to chase the visitors indoors and hose off the streets every night, though at that time of year, hosing might lead to icing; the seasons turned cold quickly on the eastern side of the state. I didn't like the way my thoughts kept coming back to the negative, so I changed the subject. "Did you figure out where the address is?"

"Yeah. It's close, but it's on the other side of the river, so we'll have to drive. The nearest bridge is a two-mile walk and we'd have to walk about the same distance on the other side. I don't relish that sort of hike with the mountains already cutting the sunlight."

Quinton was right: Snuggled up tight to the valley's

western wall, the shadow of the mountains had already cloaked the town, casting it into a long blue twilight scented with apple blossoms. We'd have to get moving if we were going to get much done before full darkness.

Quinton had his map on the palmtop and I drove to his directions, continuing down Highway 2 until we crossed the Wenatchee River, then doubling back on the other bank, looking for a house set back from the road. We nearly missed it, overhung as it was by trees and pushing its back door almost up to the riverbank. It wasn't an interesting house, just an old one and quite plain, painted a muddy green that vanished into the trees and overgrown yard.

There was nothing sinister about it, yet as I got out of the truck, I felt a chill creeping over my skin that had nothing to do with the oncoming night or the rising chatter of the grid. In the Grey, a brilliant line of clear blue energy sizzled along the river behind the house while spikes and coils of red and yellow formed an ornate fence around the property. I'd never seen anything like it. The closest thing I could think of was the gold tracery of Mara's perimeter spells around the house on Queen Anne Hill. This wasn't the same shape or color: The lines and curves were much more pointed, thin, and sharp, more like barbed wire than the vinelike weaving Mara made. Although it was red, I didn't get the same nauseous sensation from this cloud of energy that I did from vampires. It was unpleasant in a different way and I was not pleased that the puzzle ball was in the possession of whoever had raised that fence.

Quinton noticed I was looking askance at the place. "What?"

"Something magic. I don't know if it will let us pass or not."

"Magic like a monster, or magic like a spell?"

"Spell. Boundary markers, I think. How do you feel when you look at that house?"

Quinton turned to study the building. "Like I shouldn't be here; this is the wrong house. Whatever I came here for is pointless and I might as well go home." He started to turn away and caught himself. "Ah . . . I get it. It's some kind of . . . 'leave me alone' spell. Must keep the kids out of the yard pretty well."

I hummed to myself. That wasn't quite the reading I was getting, but then I didn't see or hear things in the normal way. The energetic border was definitely sending out a "go away" vibe, but more specifically, it was a warning to other magic users: Don't try it. Looked as if I was in for a bit of dismantling, though I couldn't imagine that was going to make the spell-caster pleased. I glanced around the property, searching for a place to take a shot at the magical fence without being in direct view of the street or neighbors. This was not going to be fun and I preferred not to do it in public, though it was growing dark so fast that that might not be an issue for long.

As I was staring, Quinton gave a sudden twitch and dug into one of his pockets as if it were on fire. He pulled out a mints tin and held it out to me in two fingers, as if it were hot or infected with something. "I think you want this."

"What? Why?"

"Your ghost is giving me shocks. Maybe it doesn't like this place, either."

I took the tin, having momentarily forgotten about Simondson's ghost. Flipping it open, the ghost of my killer emerged like a red-orange smog. "Earring."

"What?" I asked, peering at his thin form.

"I don't know. Something says 'earring.' You need an earring."

"And whose errand boy are you, now?" I demanded.

He grew thick and solid, then winced and writhed away in pain, falling back to his shadowy state. "I don't know! I just want shut of you! Of this. Something says 'get the earring' and I say 'get the earring.' I don't care if you do or not. Go get yourself killed for all I care."

I felt the urge to laugh at him, however nuts that sounded. "If I get killed, you'll be stuck here forever in this candy box."

"No, I won't. You'll come back, like the damned bad penny that you are."

"Says who?" I asked, but I, too, had the feeling that I wasn't quite up to death-the-last yet. If I was, Wygan wouldn't have been continuing to push me; he'd have given up on me as he had on Marsden in London. But if he wasn't there to push me, who knew what I would become in the Grey? Or what I might lose . . . ?

"Says . . . them," Simondson replied. "Those . . . voices. They say so."

Them. The voices in the Grey. He didn't identify them as other ghosts, just "voices" the same as I did. I nodded. "All right. I got the message. Are you ready to go back in the box now?"

"No! I want to leave! You said—"

"When I'm done, Todd. Not before. Now, in you go."

I shoved his incorporeal self back into the tin and snapped it closed. I turned back to the truck for a moment, stuffing Simondson's box into the glove compartment while I looked around the floor.

"What are you searching for?" Quinton asked, drawing close behind me. He was still rubbing his fingertips as if contact with the tin had given him a shock or a burn.

"That box of Edward's that the knife was in. It had an earring in it. . . ."

"Why do you want that?"

I'd forgotten Quinton couldn't hear the ghosts. "Simondson says I need it."

We scrabbled in the accumulation of bags and belongings stowed in the back until we found the carton I'd slit open outside the FedEx building. I extracted the earring from the collection with care, feeling a bitter pain as I touched it. I tucked it into my pocket with its twin from the puzzle ball and turned back to the house.

I started back along the property line toward the river. Quinton followed saying, "What are you thinking?"

"That I need to find a way past this magic fence and then I can do whatever it is I'm supposed to do with this earring. . . . I have a bad feeling that just walking through is not as easy as all that. And once I do break the fence, whoever made it is not going to be pleased."

"Maybe you don't have to break it. Could you bypass it?"

I turned back under a weeping willow tree and frowned at him. "I'm not sure I know what you mean."

"Magic seems to be a bit like electricity. Electrical circuits can be bypassed—jumpered—in some places. You run a piece of wire from one part of the circuit directly to another, which cuts part of the circuit out without the rest of the system noticing since current is still flowing and all other parts are functioning. So long as the bit you bypass doesn't set off an alarm on its absence, you can go right through the circuit at that point. That's how burglars used to get through simple wired perimeters: Just make a jumper wire long enough to slide under, connect your wire from one side to the other of the hole you need, cut the original wire, and go through the hole while the electricity keeps on flowing through the system as if nothing happened. Most magic things seem to be pretty simple circuits, so maybe some kind of bypass would work without disrupting the spell enough to set off an alarm."

"If it were that easy, I think witches and mages would do it all the time," I replied.

"Maybe it's not easy for them. Magic users have to address the system through the interface they have; they don't just grab hold of the system itself. But that's not the way *you* see it. You see magic in the raw, as it were."

"But you're not talking about seeing; you're talking about manipulating. I don't do that."

"Why not? If you can pull magical things apart like you did with that alarm spell outside the Danzigers', why not this? It doesn't make you a mage," he hastened to add, cutting short my objection, "but it seems to be in line with other things you've done recently."

That startled me. The idea was dangerously close to the one advanced by Carlos: that I could potentially bend the fabric of magic itself. "I . . . really don't want that power."

"You don't seem to have a choice, sweetheart." He pulled me into a loose embrace under the willow with its long strands of leaves like a curtain between us and the world. "I know you're afraid—"

"Not afraid, more like horrified. I don't want to be Wygan's tool for . . . whatever it is he's got planned."

"I understand that. But he's going to keep pushing until you're his or you're dead. I don't want you dead, not even hurt. It's hard for me to see the things that happen to you, the things that are happening, but—and I never thought I'd say this—Carlos may be right: The only way to stop Wygan is to take the power and use it against him. If you understand it and control it before he has a chance to control *you*, it's not his power or his choice anymore: It's yours." Even in the gloom, I spotted a suspicious moist shine in his eyes. Quinton cry? Surely the world had turned upside down.

I didn't get to reply since a voice from the other side of the willow arras cut into our conversation. "Touching. So touching, in fact, I may be sick. I thought that sort of sentimental dribbling went out of style when Andy Jackson was elected."

The hanging fronds of the willow parted and the magic perimeter line wavered and flashed a moment, curling toward us as the speaker stepped through. She was about five foot five, neither round nor thin, with a heavy mass of silver-streaked ringlets piled on her head with a plastic clip. In the thin light from over the mountain, it was hard to guess her age. Her posture said thirty, but her hair and the powdery quality of her skin said sixty—or a hundred. I couldn't guess at the color of her eyes; the darkness masked all but a ruby gleam of magic in their depths.

She continued her comments as we blinked at her, the arms of red and yellow energy that branched from the Grey fence circling us as she spoke. "Still, it was an edifying conversation to eavesdrop on, my little burglars. I shall have to make some changes to my spell next time to keep out people like you," she added, glaring at me.

"We're not burglars," Quinton objected; his voice sounded a little strained and I noticed that the tendrils of red had twined around his legs. They must have been exerting something—pain or pressure at least.

"Callers ring the bell."

"You don't seem to have one," he retorted.

"Indeed. Possibly because I don't *want* any callers in the first place! And especially not those of your sort."

"Pardon me, ma'am," I cut in. "What sort do you mean?"

"Stalkers or supplicants from that enclave of fools in Seattle. Since I heard your dislike for the Pharaohn, I assume you're with Kammerling's party. I've done quite enough for that spendthrift fool. Tell him to go to hell and shut the door behind him."

"I'm not here on anyone's behalf but my own," I replied.

She snorted in derision. "You're a Greywalker and it's clear that you haven't gone completely insane yet, so you must have someone's help. Which means you're someone's slave."

I snapped at the haughty bitch. "I'm not anyone's anything and I want to keep it that way. Is it a fair guess that you're Chris Drew?"

"Did you imagine I would be anyone else? And you're backward. It's Drusilla Cristoffer."

"What I *imagined* was that you bought a puzzle ball from Charlie Rice because it came from an old house out here that you had some attachment to."

She barked a laugh. "Quite an attachment: It was *my* house! You go away for a few years and someone tears your house down! I had to move into this common shack until I could make arrangements to remove my stakes and leave more permanently."

"Your house. Then you know how the puzzles work and where the maze is."

Her eyes grew narrow and cunning. "Oh, so that's what you want." I could tell she was thinking very hard: The red threads around Quinton's legs drew back and slithered toward her, as if offering their substance to fuel her mental process. Finally she spoke, dropping each word on me with careful deliberation. "I made it to protect Kammerling. I should have taken more care with it. It was never meant for a prison." She spat the word.

My breath caught in my throat as I understood she was confirming that the puzzles somehow led to my father's arcane cell. It wasn't what they were meant for, but it was what they did now.

"When the labyrinth is gone, my last tie here will be broken, but for this." She put out her left hand and closed her eyes a moment. Blood welled in the palm of her hand though she had no cuts there. She murmured and a whiffling noise rose and rushed toward us. The other puzzle ball slammed into Cristoffer's hand as if thrown from a great height, but she didn't move from its impact. She let her breath out through her nose in a gust and opened her eyes.

"And what would you give for it, Greywalker? I can see your desire for it, see the mark of its twin upon you. What will you give . . . ?" Her hand made a lazy turn toward Quinton, curling inward. . . .

He shivered, rooted to the spot.

I plucked the first, quiet earring from my pocket. "I think I have something of yours." I held the garnet drop up so it swung, sparkling in the river's light that crept and darted through the willows.

Cristoffer cast an assessing glance at me and the bauble that dangled from my fingers. "That— But of course you've opened the other door. I wondered where it had gone. . . . Edward's doing, I'm sure. Overly clever of him. He always was. But it's of no moment. Just an ornament. Do you suppose me moved by sentiment?" Her laughter made the river falter in its banks. Quinton ground his teeth and shut his eyes until she gave him a glance and then looked back to me. "More."

I dug into my pocket and held up the second earring, its gem gleaming with unnatural light the color of dark venous blood. Brought together in the free air, the earrings sang a chord that made the grid thrum and spark.

Cristoffer's eyes shone as hard and glittering as the facets on the garnets. I could see her breath accelerate and she leaned, just a hair, toward the chiming earrings. "Oh . . ."

"Do you want them back?" I asked. Of course they were hers: her puzzles, her jewels, her labyrinth—wherever it was. I could see her hunger for them reaching out like discorporate hands. As I stared at them the garnets seemed to run, turning to liquid blood that dripped slowly toward the ground, vanishing into red mist and river fog before it struck. I shook them, making the earrings cry and bleed. "Make up your mind."

"You think I care for such baubles . . . ?" But her voice quivered. The red creepers of her power scrolled across the ground toward me and an answering glow reached out from the earrings.

I threw the live earring down and put my foot over it, pushing it into the mud with my boot until I felt the unyielding rock below. "I think you do."

I shifted my weight down, a bit at a time, feeling the frangible gem grind and groan against the riverbed rock. Dru Cristoffer's face tightened in pain and she seemed to suck her chest in as if I'd struck her in the center of her rib cage. The words came up through the muttering in my mind: "I could crush this more easily than your heart. . . ."

Her lips thinned to a frustrated line. Then she gave a sharp nod and sucked her tendrils of power back to the edge of the willow's curtain. "All right."

"The earrings for the ball."

"Yes, yes. Give them to me."

"Say it: The earrings for the ball."

She growled. "The earrings for the ball."

The world seemed to shiver and the grid flashed, throbbing under us, the voices shouting with its energy. I stooped and dug the buried earring from the muddy ground. I held them both out.

She turned the ball over into her right palm and spat on the bloody blot that marked where it had hit her. She chuckled quietly in her throat and drew a figure in the blood with the middle finger of her left hand. Then she blew on the figure, making the wet surface sizzle and smoke as if her breath were fire. Once it satisfied her, she smiled and lobbed the puzzle ball at me as I tossed the glittering earrings into the air near her.

I caught the ball and winced from the heat of the thing. It smelled of singed flesh and teakwood. Where she'd drawn on it, a complex symbol remained as if branded into the surface.

She snatched the earrings from the air and slipped their wire loops into her ears with a sigh. Then she looked at me, one side of her mouth curling upward. "Take it and go. You'll only need that one, once you open the way. When you're done, make sure they both burn to ash. The salamander's call will start the fire," she added, pointing at the symbol. "Be sure the other ball burns with it. You have three days, for I intend to raze the labyrinth to the very bedrock, and if the doors haven't burned by then, they will by my command. You won't want to be near them when they do, though I suppose it wouldn't hurt to add an enemy or two to the pyre if you have some handy to throw in. Such things like blood sacrifices."

She started to walk away; then she cocked her head and half turned back, the dark-red gems glittering at her earlobes even through the gloom. She regarded us over her shoulder as the willow branches lifted aside like a theater curtain. "One other thing: Your friend's trick might work on the wards I hung for Edward. It was quite a while ago that I raised them, so I may not have buried the tap as well as I would now." Then she chuckled and it felt like hail on my skull. "Good luck with them."

She stepped through the open willow swag and over the red line of her own magic, which drew back in as soon as she was across. Quinton sighed in relief and I lunged forward, thrusting my empty hand through the willow fronds before the red lines closed completely.

"Wait!" I shouted. The fiery marks snapped onto my forearm like teeth and I yelped in pain. "Where is the maze?" I gasped.

Dru Cristoffer laughed on the other side of the green veil. "Find it yourself, Greywalker. I've done enough—more than enough—to save that pesthole city. And more than enough for you. Next time I shan't open my door."

I felt blood running down the hidden side of my arm. The warm liquid seemed to loosen the clamp of the magical lines and I yanked my arm back, feeling invisible barbs scrape gouges in my skin as I withdrew. Cristoffer's laughter receded into the fallen darkness beyond the tree's swaying curtain of leaves. I didn't want to stay there, but at the moment I was shaking too much to move and I sat down hard on the ground at the base of the willow.

Quinton plopped down beside me. "Well, that was lovely, in a tea-party-with-Satan kind of way. You all right?"

"I'll heal," I observed, closing my eyes to the sight of my skin knitting up over pinpricks of light and lines of blood. "How about you?"

"I think I might have some welts, but I'll be fine."

"Welts?"

"Yeah, that magic of hers is like stinging nettle, only worse. Burning nettle might be more accurate. And that was just the friendly parts."

"Well . . . we did get the puzzle ball, and some useful information—maybe."

"But we still have to find the labyrinth."

I nodded, taking a couple of deep breaths and heaving to my feet. "I don't think we'll do it tonight, though. We need some sleep and we can start looking in the morning."

Quinton crept out of the willow's shroud behind me. "Got any ideas where to start?"

"Historical society. This is the sort of town where all the buildings are documented by someone, even the outlying ones and especially the interesting ones. I'd think a house with a maze would rate at least a mention."

"As long as we don't have to go back to that . . . woman's."

I saw the Rover still standing at the side of the road, trailing the tattered Grey rags that seemed to adhere to everything I owned for more than a week. Nothing had disturbed them and no new colors of magic clung to the truck.

"She's a blood mage," I said as I climbed into the safety of the Rover's front seat.

"You mean Cristoffer?"

I nodded. "Yeah. I probably would have guessed in a while, but that trick with the puzzle ball was pretty obvious. And she mentioned the wards in Edward's bunker—those had to have been hung by a powerful blood-worker, which would be her."

"She's got to be a lot older than she looks," Quinton added. "Not that I want to know. . . . Do you suppose she actually knew Andrew Jackson . . . ?"

"I think she probably saw him in diapers."

TWENTY-TWO

The hotels were full and we ended up sleeping in the Rover at a campground east of downtown Leavenworth—probably just as well since using a credit card for the deposit would have left a trace of our presence. Beside us the river gurgled to itself in the dark, lending a descant to the singing of the grid. The back of the Rover was a bit crowded and smelled of dog, but it was acceptable and Quinton fell asleep with ease. I lay on my side, tired and wanting to sleep but afraid to. The strange voices of the grid were increasingly present and increasingly loud. They chilled and compelled me, drawing me too close to the warp and weft of the Grey.

I was certain that anyone I asked would say, "Just don't listen to them; don't do what they say." But that wasn't so easy and the voices, singing in ever-closer harmony, hadn't always been wrong. If my dad's advice was what I thought, then I needed to listen—to "know" what they sang. And yet . . . those voices had urged me to kill Goodall and to do something to Will. One of those I had recoiled from and the other hadn't worked. I had destroyed Alice, but that didn't seem to me the same as killing Goodall. But it was difficult for me to articulate the difference and why one was acceptable and the other wasn't. I hated the hard shell of ice that seemed to be growing around me, dragging me away from compassion where it seemed most deserved.

And I wondered what was I going to do once I got to Dad. Supposedly he would tell me Wygan's plan and how to stop it. But what if he didn't? What if it was a trap, as

Mara had suggested? Or a wrong turn? Ghosts don't know much and what they do know may be wrong or incomplete. I wasn't sure why I assumed my father's shade was different, but I did and I hoped that meant I hadn't become a ruthless machine of some unknown retribution. "Paladin of the Dead" was what Carlos had called me. . . . What dread thing did that make me . . . ? In the dark, lying beside Quinton and yet feeling alone, I did not know what to do, which instinct or voice to give ear to. I felt I was not myself anymore, that my decisions were those of a foreigner in my skin.

I'd thought I understood who and what I was two years earlier, before I'd died in an elevator. I'd thought I had control of my life—at last—that I was the person I wanted to be, doing the job I wanted. Part of that certainty had been torn away from me when I ceased being blind to the Grey, when I became something I did not want to be and didn't understand. I thought I had regained some equilibrium since then. I had come to accept what I was and what I did and make the best of it. Sometimes I'd even gotten a little smug about it. But I'd still been wrong. I wasn't what I'd thought, nor had anything about my life been what I'd believed. Deceptions, manipulations, and illusions had shaped the fabric of my life and I had not been blameless in making it—I'd destroyed my own memories and lived in the bitter confines of my anger at my parents. I'd clung to my beliefs without questioning them and learned I was wrong. I'd reacted, rather than acting. I'd done the predictable thing and run the maze like a good little rat. Was I still a rat, still going where I was pushed?

Now I was further away from what I'd been—or thought I'd been—than ever. I felt something powerful and frightening coiling under my skin. This ability everyone pushed me to embrace would change me fundamentally. I knew this without any question; the rising, clarifying song in my mind and the cold electricity across my nerves told me it was so. It was one of the few certainties I had, and yet I did not think I had a choice to reject this power. Among the dozens of questions I couldn't answer, one occupied and terrified me most: Would I, if I survived this, still be human?

And if not, would I be able to stave off destruction of all that was dear? This sleepless horror held me until dawn.

By the time Quinton opened his eyes to the morning light, I was damned tired of being damned tired. He noticed I was dragging.

"Didn't sleep?" he asked, sitting up and putting his arms around my shoulders.

I rubbed at my eyes. "No. It's awfully noisy in my head these days."

"I keep thinking I should be able to help you, but I'm not sure how."

I gave him a weak smile. "You do. Just keep on doing what you already do."

He made a rueful face. "You say so. . . ."

"I do. Now, let's get moving and see if we can find this maze."

We were still a bit ahead of the Maifest crowd, and the Upper Valley Museum, which housed the Upper Valley Historical Society, wasn't open yet, so we were able to get some breakfast first and wait on the stonework terrace that surrounded the old house that was now the museum. It sat well back from everything else on the north side of the Wenatchee on a large swath of high riverbank land at the end of a small street that marked the eastern edge of Leavenworth's Bavarian theme. The building itself—a fieldstone craftsman bungalow with a low, arched roof and lots of wood and windows—predated the theme by at least fifty years. Most of the houses and shops on Division Street were plain late-Victorian clapboard structures and a few much later condos, so the gracious low lines of the museum stood out even more as it rested in green isolation at the end of the road. From the back terrace I could see the willow trees where we'd stood the night before with Dru Cristoffer, but there was no sign from this distance across the river, other than a thin red haze in the Grey, that there was anything magical on the opposite bank.

Quinton and I had done some reading up on the museum and historical society during breakfast. The building had been the summer home of the Lamb-Davis sawmill's owners, and then the local banker's house for many years before becoming a bed-and-breakfast, and then the museum. There'd been some information about it online, but not much else about any other buildings, much less one with a labyrinth—plenty about Spring Bird Fest, though, which was upcoming at the museum in a week. I couldn't say I was sorry to miss it, since I was just as glad not to be eyed by the wild raptors of the local bird rescue group or surrounded by children in songbird costumes. The old house was far enough removed from Front Street to still be peaceful that morning and the clear, constant babble of the river seemed to calm the chorus in my mind, so sitting and waiting suited me fine.

Two women in their late fifties arrived on foot at 10:45. They smiled at us and waved. "We'll be open in just a few minutes," one of them called to us. "Just sit tight a bit longer." They began unlocking and setting up the museum to welcome the day's visitors. One of them struggled out carrying a sandwich board events sign and Quinton jumped up to help her take it down the steps to the driveway. I drifted toward the door she'd left ajar and slid inside the building.

The house wasn't very large, at least not on the main floor, and I imagined the one basement floor didn't add much living space. I found myself in a wide, shallow entry with doors on each side and an open post-and-beam arch ahead of me. The remaining woman stepped out of the doorway on my left, which was labeled "Gift Shop." She was a soft-looking woman, a little round everywhere without being fat, her blond hair fading but not to silver. She was wearing a brown sweater set over camel-colored trousers and brown loafers that cost more than I made in a week.

She jumped with surprise when she saw me. "Oh, we're not quite open yet. . . ."

"Actually, I'm looking for some information about an old house in the area. It must have been torn down or otherwise destroyed about two years ago."

"Oh. A house. We don't knock down many houses around here, you know. Most are historic one way or another."

"This one may have been historic in its way. Apparently it was very old, at least two stories, in one of the orchards, and it had a maze or labyrinth on the property."

"Oh. A labyrinth. In the orchard. My, my. That must have been the Rose house."

"Rose house? Was that a family name or did that refer to roses on the property?" Maybe I needed to look for rosebushes as well as apple trees. . . .

"No, no. I'd have to look it up to get the family name of the owners, but the house was called Rosaceae originally and it got shortened over time to Rose."

An electric current seemed to run through me when she said the original name. That was one of the words I'd heard from the voices of the grid: "rosaceae." I could feel the humming delight of the chorus tingling over my nerves. "That's a funny name for a house," I said, coughing a little on the grid's excitement.

"It's the scientific name for the plant family both apples and roses belong to."

"Apples *and* roses?" I wouldn't have imagined them to be related.

She smiled a bit smugly. "Yes. Roses, apples, hawthorn, cherries . . . they're all part of Rosaceae. My family planted some of the earliest apple trees in this valley."

I noticed she didn't say "the first." I shook my head as if amazed. "You must know a lot about the area, then—and the fruit trees."

"Oh, I do!"

"Why did the owner give the house such an odd name?"

"I don't think anyone's sure. Except that he was very eccentric. He didn't lay out his orchard in the usual way, either—not in square rows but in a kind of crazy radial pattern around the house and the maze. So the most efficient way to harvest the fruit was to spiral out from the middle or in from the edge. Except you couldn't, since the house took up a big square in one quarter of the array. And the orchard wasn't all apple trees, either. Some pear and cherry were mixed in, too, though that isn't really wise if you're producing commercial fruit."

The other woman reentered with Quinton at her heels. Up close, she was plainly the subordinate of the pair: Her hair was cheaply dyed, her clothes weren't so expensive or well maintained, and her complexion bore the ruddy marks of a harder, more outdoor life, though they were otherwise much alike. "Janice," she puffed, "this young man—oh." She caught sight of me and came to a sudden halt. "Oh, well, here she is, then." She turned and looked at Quinton. "Here she is! This is your lady friend, isn't it?"

Quinton nodded. "Yep, that's her. Thanks for helping me find her."

The other woman blushed. "Oh, it's nothing. Thank *you* for your help with the sign and the garage doors—they're so heavy!" This last declaration came with a sharp look askance at Janice.

Janice ignored that. "Belinda, do you remember the Rose house?"

"The house in the crazy orchard on North Road? I sure do. They finally tore the old wreck down about two years ago."

I turned to look at her more directly. "Why was it torn down?" I asked her.

She rolled her eyes and made half a grin of shameful pleasure. "The upper story caught fire once—don't know why it didn't light the trees—but after it was put out, it just sat there for years. No one lived in it and it was turning into a real danger. The kids from the high school would come out and dare each other to go in at night and do something foolish like take something or paint their name on something. Crazy things like that. I did it too when I was a kid, but Nils and I—he's my husband now—we got chased off before we could get in trouble."

"Who chased you off if no one lived there?"

"Well, that's why it was such a big dare. People said the house was haunted. There was always strange stuff going on around there. Lights at night in the trees, wolves and bears and rabid raccoons running around. And oh my God, the crows! Crows used to nest all over the orchard, even when there wasn't any fruit, and they'd dive-bomb you if you tried to walk through it."

"Animals chased you off?" I asked.

She nodded. "Oh, yes. I think it was a bear—just a little bear, mind, but a bear all the same. I couldn't swear, because I didn't see it very well in the dark and it's been a long time, but it smelled bad and it growled and charged us, and we ran like the dickens!"

"Oh, Belinda, it couldn't have been a bear all the way down there," Janice chided.

Belinda dropped her eyes to the floor for a moment. "Well, I said I wasn't sure. It might have been a dog, maybe. . . ."

"I don't know," Quinton speculated. "It's not that far from the hills. If the deer come down, why not the bears?"

"Well, yes. Now, that's what I thought," Belinda said, shooting a defiant glance at Janice.

Janice sighed as if indulging a child, but said nothing.

"Where was this house?" I asked Belinda.

"Out near the old cemetery." This just got better and better, didn't it?

"Could you tell me how to find it?"

"Certainly!" She crossed the room in a few strides and grabbed a handful of flyers about donating to the museum and wrote on the back of one. "See, you go up Division here to Highway Two. Turn right. Then you go just a little ways to Two-Oh-Nine—that's Chumstick Highway—and you turn left, which is going to be northerly. Then you go on up Chumstick just a mile, past the county shop yard, and turn right onto North Road." Belinda drew and lettered a map as she talked. Her printing was precise and very quick, her demeanor entirely confident as she worked. I hated to interrupt her.

"What's a shop yard?" I asked.

Belinda looked up just long enough to give me a smile. "It's the county's equipment maintenance shop and storage yard," she explained before she returned her gaze to her map in progress. "After the yard, you cross the railroad tracks and then take the first left—that'll be the cemetery road. It's not much of a road and it's not marked too well, but you'll see the sign for the graveyard. Stay to the left, 'cause the orchard there is private property. Pass the graveyard and stay on the orchard road along the railroad tracks until you get past the end of the orchard boundary. There's a real small road there on the right—it's hard to see but look for a pair of lightning-burned trees standing side by side. That'll be the road. Go up that and follow it around the hook to the old orchard. You'll have to walk up from the edge of the property. You'll know you're there 'cause there'll be an alley of pear trees and then a lot of old stone lying around. That used to be the house foundation. And then the trees start up all around, like a big circle with a slice out of it, and you're there."

Belinda looked up and handed me the map. "Why do you want to go out there, anyway?"

"Uh, ghost hunting."

She paled. "Ugh. Well, better you than me. Be careful out there. There's still bits of that maze out there and you can fall into it if you're not keeping a sharp eye out."

That was an interesting caution—how could one fall into a maze? We thanked Belinda and Janice for their help and set out to find Rosaceae.

I drove this time, holding the noisy grid voices at bay a little more easily now that I was doing what they wanted.

Quinton was frowning and about the time I turned onto Chumstick Highway I asked him why.

"It's bugging me: What did Belinda mean about a circle of trees?"

"The other one—Janice—was telling me the orchard around the house is planted in a circle or circular area with the trees arranged in irregular radii, not in regular rows. Apparently, it was hard to harvest unless you worked in a spiral."

"Ahhh . . . that's what I was wondering. I'll bet the center of the spiral coincides with the center of the labyrinth."

"Why?"

Quinton paused, ordering his thoughts. "This mystery turns on keys, puzzles, and a labyrinth. But really, it's just the keys and the puzzles because a classical labyrinth is the visual expression of a key as a circle."

"I have no idea what you're talking about."

"OK, look—turn right."

"What?"

"This is North Road. Turn right."

I did and the road began to climb quite steeply. I had to concentrate on the grade. Even as we crossed the railroad tracks, the angle barely eased and the road curved sharply to the right. I made the curve and almost missed the road to the cemetery. The sign marking it was faded and small, but I saw it in time and made a hard left onto the steep path, not much wider than the Rover itself. The truck's tires were so close to the edge that they pulled on the ruts rather than falling into them, making the ride a thumping, twitching misery until we passed the neat rows of fruit trees on the right and found a grove of old oaks shading a small slope dotted with crumbling headstones and strange monuments enclosed in rusted iron fences.

Although it was quaint from most vantage points, I found the cemetery unsettling and odd. Most of the graves were old enough to lie quiet, but a few were literally giving up the ghost in spires of colored mist and restless shapes. A disproportionate number of the restless forms were tiny: evidence of high infant mortality. There was a strange cluster of shady forms around the trees at the north end of the small graveyard. The voice of the grid urged me to ignore them and I agreed. I kept my eyes to the right where the last row of graves on the orchard side petered out as the road took a sudden dip down. The Rover lurched a bit at the change of grade but had no problem keeping to the hard-packed dirt surface.

I tried to put the conversation back on track so it would be easier to ignore the curious stares the ghosts turned on us as we passed. "So . . . how is a key a labyrinth?"

"Not just any key: a Greek key—a meander."

Yet another chill of recognition rolled over me. "*Maiandros*" was also one of the words the Grey chorus had spoken into my dreaming ears. "Wait—what? A meander is a key? I thought it was a piece of a river."

"It is, but it's also the Greek word for an ancient, endless shape—the Greek key or fret. Mathematically it's a relatively simple structure of two connecting, single-turn spirals, one coming into the center and the other going back out, kind of like an outline of an ocean wave. But it's usually shown squared off instead of rounded, so it looks a bit like the wards on an old-fashioned key. You see it all the time on Greek and Aztec art; I think the Hopi and Anasazi used it, too, but that's off the point. You know the shape I'm talking about, right?"

I could see it in my mind, running down the hems of ancient clothing and along the edges of dishes at the Greek diner in Fremont, bordered in lines so the squared-off wave shape was contained. "Yes, I can see it."

"All right. If you think of the outer lines of the shape as solid bars and the inner ones as elastic, then you can grab one of the bars and swing it around over the top of the other so the two bars are now resting back to back. The lines of the spiral elastics will describe the path and shape of a classical, round labyrinth with a circular center, just like the famous labyrinth at Knossos where the minotaur lived. So a key and a labyrinth are reflections of each other."

A sudden flash of vision or memory made me step on the brake and bring the truck to a halt in a small flurry of dust. In front of me, formed in silver mist, I saw an image of my father's strange key flexing and twisting in and out of the shape of a classical labyrinth. Then it flew apart into glittering shards that re-formed as a smaller version of the puzzle balls that shifted and rolled across an invisible surface, leaving strange trails of color on the mist of the Grey. "That's a little freaky."

Quinton couldn't see it, so he continued on his own conversational course. "Not so much. It's just math. But here's an interesting detail most people leave out of the whole labyrinth myth: A *Lady* presided over the labyrinth at Knossos and she was viewed with such awe that she received the same tribute each year as all the other gods combined. She must have been a pretty powerful woman to be treated that way."

I shook away the Grey's persistent show. "Please don't suggest that Dru Cristoffer might be an ancient goddess. . . ."

"I'm not thinking so, but . . . it's an interesting idea and maybe that's part of the reason for this crazy system of puzzles and keys. Maybe she used that model, scaled down."

"So that makes my dad the minotaur?"

"That makes him the prisoner. The Labyrinth of Knossos was a prison for the Minotaur of Crete."

"If I remember correctly," I added, "Theseus slew the minotaur. . . ."

Quinton gave me a long, sober look. "You didn't think everyone was going to get out of this alive, did you?"

I snapped at him, feeling grief-stricken and unreasonably enraged at the thought, "Don't say that!"

He sighed, closing his eyes a moment before he said anything more. "He's already dead, and you can't bring your dad back. He's a ghost. Do you think he wants to stay? Given what you've told me, do you think that's a good idea? The best thing you can do is let him—and that poor bastard you've got tucked into your pocket—go. Maybe that's all it'll take, though I doubt it. Between Cristoffer and the vampires, blood's going to spill. If it comes down to saving a dead man or a live one, pick the one who's breathing."

I gaped at him. Not because he was upsetting me—that wasn't his fault—but because the voices were talking, babbling in swift and rising harmony that shifted the silvery mist of the Grey like an immensely complex game of Tetris, dropping images and pieces of sound and magic into a glittering mosaic of information. My silent stare unnerved him and Quinton started to reach for me. I held my hand up to ward him off, quivering and drinking in the growing fractal vision. Then it jerked to a halt, frozen and dangling in the ghostlight, silent until it broke apart in a thousand chiming pieces that fell away into dust.

I gasped and tried to clutch the shards and hold them together, but they had no substance and only stung my hands like ice and melted away. Quinton lurched forward and caught me by the shoulders.

"What is it?"

"I . . . don't know. I almost had it. . . . I almost knew something. . . ." I shook my head in frustration.

"Maybe you'll know more when we get to the maze."

"Maze?" For an instant I didn't know what he was talking about.

"We're heading for the maze in the labyrinth."

"In the orchard," I corrected, concentrating on calming my shaking and getting the Rover back in motion.

"No . . . I was getting to that. The classical labyrinth has a single long path that goes into the center and back out again. We use the word as if it's a synonym for 'maze' but it's really not. Mazes have multiple paths or multiple *possible* paths to the solution. But if the orchard is laid out in a spiral, then *it* may be the labyrinth and there's something else at the center—another way out. Possibly another maze."

"Then we'll have to find out," I answered, turning over the ignition. The Rover growled sullenly but started, and I drove on, looking for the lightning-struck trees that marked the path to Rosaceae and its labyrinth.

TWENTY-THREE

It was so narrow and weed-choked that I almost missed it, but I found the road that turned up the hill and away from the railroad track. Once we were on the path, finding the remains of the house was easy. The road went up through a slight fold in the hillside, twisting north and east of the cemetery into what was clearly no-man's-land until the trees appeared, like the fringe of a pale-green cloak on the shoulders of a giant. The track—it wasn't really wide or clear enough to call a road—ran along the edge of the thickening grove of trees and then turned suddenly to the left to end in a ragged dirt oval bordered on the east side with trees and on the west with scrub that fell away before rising again to hide the house from the railroad and the cemetery. No one would find this place by accident unless they came down the hill on the northeast, and that was covered in neat, cultivated rows of apple trees above the stark ocher rifts of the miniature valley's walls that cupped the Rose house in its weathered palm. A lane of trees came right to the edge of the oval and led straight back to a pile of fieldstone rubble and half-buried wood, charred and broken among the stones. I used the oval to turn the Rover, figuring it was better to be prepared if we had to leave in a hurry, and got out.

The ground whispered under my boots like distant earthquakes. I found myself narrowing my eyes, suspicious and expecting trouble. The avenue of old pear trees—their blossoms whiter and more translucent than the apple's—led directly to what had been the front steps. Now it was two broken marble slabs and a wasteland of ruin beyond the cracked front stoop. I stopped about halfway up the path and studied it. The approach was much too easy.

Quinton paused beside me, stuffing the two puzzle balls into his backpack. "What?"

"Something's wrong. Cristoffer wouldn't leave it this simple. Am I missing something? What do you see?"

"I just see . . . trees. Just a mess of trees."

I huffed a strand of hair out of my face and crouched down, changing my viewpoint, and let my vision open to the Grey. But I didn't slip in; if there was something there, I didn't want to meet it just yet.

In the silvery world of the Grey, the house rose in blocks with a round central turret like a finger pointing into the sky. The trees tossed their shaggy heads in a spectral wind and cast moving patches of colored light onto the fog-shrouded ground. The thick, vibrant feeder lines of the grid—the leylines and main trunks of magic—throbbed below the earth and arrowed for the back of the house. I couldn't see where they were leading from here, but I would have guessed they converged at the center of the labyrinth of moving trees.

Quinton had been right: It was a labyrinth. The apparently concentric rings of trees were strung with lines of light and mist, creating barriers that would confine and control whoever stepped into them, forcing them to wander a single, tortuous route until they reached the center. The ground was a sheet of silver marked with red, black, and white in scattered lines like runes or broken bones. I held Quinton back and inched forward, putting my hand against one of the barriers.

The broken lines on the ground stirred, rising into the air, and a shock wave of crows erupted from the nearest trees, plunging at us, shrieking and shattering the Grey. Quinton ducked, yanked his hat over his head, and turned up his collar, hugging his coat close against the ripping talons and clacking beaks of the flock. I turned my shoulder into the cloud of birds and tucked my head down until they lifted away again, circling into the sky and flocking to and fro as if waiting for my next move. A shadow shaped like a bear assembled itself from the clutter on the ground and roamed a restless path a few feet away, pacing just beyond the next wall of the labyrinth.

I looked at the trees and the ground, then back up and down again, studying the way the shadows fell and the returned detritus that lay along the labyrinth's paths. "So that's where the animals came from," I whispered.

"Are they real?" Quinton demanded, raising his head warily.

"They are, but they're not exactly normal. Did you get a look at any of them?"

"Hell no. Too busy hiding my eyes from their beaks."

"They're dead." The cloud of crows fluttered and fell from the sky, breaking into bones and feathers, scattering back into the years of leaf rot and weeds. "Every animal that ever wandered in and died here guards this place. Guardian beasts by the score, animated by the energetic forces under the house. Probably tied to it by blood—seems like the blood mage sort of thing to do, doesn't it?"

"Sounds like the creepy thing to do, you ask me."

"But effective. That's probably what attacked the kids who came here and thought they were chased by animals. These guardian beasts try to keep people out of the labyrinth or away from the house; cross the lines, walk in the wrong place, and they come after you. I'd bet that you encounter fewer of them if you stay on the right path. . . . You want to take the long way, or risk the dead things and run straight through?"

"To where?"

I pointed to the cleared place at the back of the tumbled-in foundation: a circular area of weedy grass about the size of a baseball infield. "There. The center of the labyrinth." It was as clear as water to me, and as I named it, the misty walls of the orchard labyrinth thickened and brightened, increasing the electric sensation in my body.

Quinton gave it and me a considering look. "Much as I tend to live recklessly, I think this might be a better time for caution. And I could do without any more encounters with skeleton crows."

I stared at the ground for a while, looking for the silver

fog that marked the lines of the labyrinth's walls, then led forward until we came to the first turn.

We must have looked insane, wandering around the orchard in looping arcs for no apparent reason. We were nearing the center and I was getting fatigued from staring at the Grey without vanishing into it. A thin silver fog covered the ground in my view and I was concentrating on the thicker shapes of the walls, so I missed the shadow bear, its tattered skin stretched over an incomplete skeleton of bones and twigs.

The eldritch creature grunted and charged us, rising on its back paws as it came on. Its breath was the scent of things rotting in the earth as it roared, swiping at me in the lead. Quinton grabbed for me, shouting, "Watch out!" as he tried to pull me backward. The massive, ruined paw of the shadow bear fanned over my shoulder, claws ripping into the leather of my jacket.

I threw myself sideways as Quinton tugged back, losing my footing and scrambling for a solid purchase. My foot descended on emptiness and I plunged straight down into a pit the Grey had concealed.

I landed on the damp-smelling earth with a thud and a burst of pain up my right leg. Quinton jumped down next to me and the shadow bear lumbered to stare down at us from empty eye sockets, too large to get through the narrow hole we'd come down. It pawed the earth a moment, thrusting its razor claws at us through the opening, snorting. Defeated, it finally shuffled off in disgust.

I let out my breath and leaned against the dirt wall of the hole. Jarred out of my observation of the Grey, I could see it was more of a ramp than a pit, a twist in the path that looped under the main way like a stream under a bridge.

Quinton pulled me to my feet, wincing in sympathy as I made a pained face. "You all right?"

"Yeah." My ankle twinged and throbbed, but well-laced in my boot, it held up fine. "I'll be OK, now the bear's gone. What about you?"

"All right. Couple of cuts and scrapes but nothing dramatic. How did you miss seeing that hole?"

"I wasn't looking for a normal trap," I replied, a bit ashamed I hadn't thought of it.

"The bear *was* a little distracting. You can't watch everything, I guess. And why did the bear attack us anyway? I didn't think we'd stepped off the path. . . ."

"Guardians are supposed to keep you out of things . . ." I started but petered out.

Standing under the path, we looked around. Even with normal eyes it would have been hard to detect the new path much earlier. The roots of the apple trees and decades of rain had camouflaged the entrance and filled it in slightly, making the hole smaller. I turned around several times, trying to get my bearings on the new elevation.

Another path took off under the bridge, heading off in strange twists and falls through the surface of the orchard labyrinth. The bridge wasn't so innocent either: From the top it looked like just more surface dirt, but from below, it was a stonework arch that opened into a new landscape of passages below and through the orchard.

"It's another maze," I observed. "A hidden one under the surface labyrinth."

"I don't think it's just 'another maze.' What if it's the start of the *real* maze? Should have realized a labyrinth—even with ghost-bears and skeleton crows—was too easy. That bear was trying to keep us out of here. I'll bet this leads into the center," Quinton speculated.

Studying the visible part of it, I agreed. "I guess we'll find out."

"Can you make it?"

"Yeah. My ankle's a little sore, but the boot's as good as any brace. Let's go."

He shrugged and walked closer to me as we passed under the arch and into the new maze. This was different from the labyrinth above; the paths branched and twisted, rising up to the surface and falling back below it, ducking under more bridges and coming to sudden ends that turned us back again and again. But the closer we moved to the center, the stronger the sensation of electricity coursing through me became while the harmony of the grid grew—louder and more like a single great voice.

We'd been in the maze nearly an hour when we saw a shaft of light from above. We were passing through a long, turning corridor choked with roots when we saw it cutting through the gloom ahead, plunging down from an opening above. The light was brighter and stronger than any we'd seen since entering the maze and we moved toward it with caution. It seemed too good to be true and that made us both wary.

At the base of the light, we came to another arch, this one leading to a cylinder of rising stairs. Going up them, we emerged into the edge of an empty circle at the heart of the original labyrinth, about a hundred and fifty feet from where the back door of the house must have stood. I paused at the top of the steps, looking through the Grey again before stepping out onto the weedy grass. Bright blue lines of energy crossed just to the west of the stairs at the center of the circle. Dru Cristoffer had enclosed a power nexus for herself in the secret walls of her labyrinth. A spiderweb of rich green and golden-yellow energy spun out from the crossed spokes of the nexus. One color I did not see was red.

I had a bad feeling.

I checked my shoulder where the shadow bear had hit me, but only the jacket showed any damage. If it had cut me, the wounds had already closed. I looked back at Quinton, blocking his path up the stairs. "Hey, how bad are those cuts and scrapes of yours?"

"Not bad. Kind of oozy, but nothing to worry about."

"You have any bandages in those pockets of yours? Because I think this might be a very bad place to bleed."

He frowned and squinted. "Why?"

"Cristoffer is a blood mage. This is, essentially, her workroom. What do you think?"

His face lit and then clouded with unhappy recognition. "Ah. Yeah. No bleeding here."

I left him on the stairs and stepped cautiously onto the lawn, half expecting something to attack or flash or change, but nothing did. "Power must be off," I muttered to myself and thought I heard the voices of the grid giggle. I walked to the point where the colored lines of energy crossed, figuring that was the most likely place to start with whatever came next.

"OK, Dad, I'm in the labyrinth," I thought aloud. "So . . . what do I do?" I supposed now was the time to open one of the puzzle balls. The doors, the voice of the grid reminded me. Just one at a time. . . . But I didn't have them. Quinton did. I called out to him. "Can you throw me the puzzle balls?"

"Sure."

They were a little bigger than croquet balls, not as large as volleyballs, and well within my ability to catch, but while the first one was easy enough, the second spun off-center, wobbling as it came toward me, making an odd, thrumming counterpoint to the chorus of the Grey. I made a scooping motion to catch the ball, but it seemed to slide across my fingers with a slithering, impossible shimmy to fall willfully to the earth. The dark blotch of burned blood that Dru Cristoffer had made touched the ground with a clash that shook the foundations of the collapsed house behind me until they growled and grated together. Red light flashed across the lawn with a roar, sealing the center of the labyrinth in hot energy. I heard Quinton shout, but the sound seemed to come distantly, as if from behind a steel door.

"No!" I yelled, and darted for the stairs, but they were gone, hidden away behind an impenetrable shield of light. I grabbed for the crimson-glowing barrier, concentrating, reaching with all my will for the living fabric of the Grey, and felt the earth groan and bulge as the searing shock of the grid burned through my frame.

My ears rang as if I were surrounded by noise, but the silence was absolute with the rushing feeling of something pushing through me. The voice that wasn't a voice but a million whispers told me to stop trying. To let go of the seal. Yes, I could break it, but not now. Stop. Stop and open the first door—just one—and all will be well.

I shuddered at the invasive sense of knowing. Something that wasn't me—that wasn't even a single thing but a collective of knowledge—spoke to me, not in my ear but directly. I raged around the room of red light until I was too tired and dizzy from its endless sameness. I didn't slip out of it; I didn't tear it apart. I could have. Knowledge hovered nearby, taunting me with the way but not allowing me to do it. Dragging my feet, I came back to where the two wooden balls lay on the ground, hovering on the scarlet surface like bubbles on water.

I picked up the first puzzle ball, the one Will had given me and in which I'd found the quiet one of Dru's pair of earrings, and rolled it around in my hands until I found the odd slit in the surface into which my father's key fit. I didn't have to fumble around with the funny little wire puzzle this time. Once in my hand it shuffled into the right shape on the first try, adding its satisfied humming to the song of the grid. I was filled with disgust at the smug noise of it all.

The puzzle ball folded outward, opening wider and larger, moving away from me as it pushed a passage into the Grey. I started to step into the passage, but a distant voice shouted and made me pause:

"Theseus had a ball of yarn to mark his path through the labyrinth."

It didn't look like another labyrinth, just a hallway, but so far very little of this had been what it seemed. I didn't have any yarn, though. I put my hands into my pockets, searching for anything I could use and finding only the hard, cool tin in which I'd stuck the strand of Todd Simondson. I pulled it out and looked it over. The writhing end of his energy fluttered from under the lid.

I opened the tin and Simondson flowed out, confused by his surroundings but still pissed off. Before he could start demanding anything, I shushed him and caught a twist of his strand on my finger while I stuffed the second puzzle ball—Cristoffer's puzzle ball—into my jacket.

"Stay right here," I ordered the ghost of my murderer, and I started into the doorway, trailing his angry color behind me. Nothing and no one seemed to object.

The red illumination of Dru Cristoffer's labyrinth faded until I was able to see only by the shifting ghostlight that defined the hallway I was walking down. I cast a glance back over my shoulder, but though I'd never made a turn, the way behind me bent and vanished into darkness. The deeper I moved into the mist, the quieter my head became.

I could feel more, feel the energy of the grid running through me as if I'd bled out completely and my veins were full of the living fire of magic. But of the chorus that had invaded my mind both dreaming and awake, I could hear almost nothing. I twisted to the left and found another, smaller round room with no other entrances or exits.

This had to be the center of whatever labyrinth I'd just run. Keeping Simondson's thread looped around my finger, I dug the other puzzle ball from my jacket even as I felt the grid nexus below my feet as strong and loud as before; I had moved and yet ended up in the same place. I fiddled with the key and felt it click into shape. This time it only made a dull whisper and opened the next ball with a grating noise.

There was a stink of recent, bloody death, burned gunpowder, and the ice-blue odor of anesthetic. For a moment the silence was so profound I thought I'd gone deaf. Then came the distant sound of bone spines chiming against one another and a train wreck's screech moving sideways and away from me. I recognized the strange underwater babble from a dream, and still trailing the red light of Simondson's ghost from my fingers, I stepped into utter darkness that unfolded from the second puzzle like a blanket of night.

TWENTY-FOUR

Beyond the portal of the open puzzle ball, the darkness brightened slowly into the silvery mist of the Grey, but not quite as I'd seen it in a long time. This was more chaotic than I'd become used to. The mist itself writhed and swirled as if things churned unseen below its surface, things that pressed incomplete impressions of their form into the dark fog, turning up glimpses of faces and limbs that then sank away into the restless steam of the world between. Walls made themselves evident, the form of the maze composed of passing roils of gaping, half-formed heads and writhing limbs. The grid had ceased to sing and only the vague burbling remained. Here the power lines of magic had gone quiet and reverted to the empty wire-frame grid I used to know. Here was a corner where the Grey was hidden even from itself.

I followed the walls, staying to the left for two turns, drawing closer to the gut-wrenching odor. I came around a corner and into a small open circle: the middle of the last labyrinth. Here the faces in the walls made shrieking, gibbering expressions of torment and madness, but no sound came out of their twisted mouths. Off to my right, about the three o'clock position, a human form protruded from the wall, mostly free but not entirely. Part of the head, one arm, and the side down to the hip were undifferentiated from the cloud-stuff of the writhing wall that appeared to be splashed with dark-red gore. I recognized the odd medicinal smell under the death-stink: lidocaine, a contact anesthetic my father had used in his dental office. The figure in the wall turned toward me, twisting in an impossible way through its apparent skin.

I recoiled a step: It wasn't that the head was embedded in the wall, but that part of it was missing. And I recognized the too-fine hair and doe-brown eyes just a moment before he said, "Little girl . . . you made it."

Part of me wanted to run to him and part of me wanted to scream and hide, but I just stood still and stared at him and felt my eyes grow hot and wet.

"Oh, no . . . oh, little girl, don't do that. Don't cry. There's already plenty of blood and plenty of tears here."

I stumbled a step toward him. "Dad?"

"I'm sorry you have to see this. I never wanted you to."

"I understand that, Dad," I said, wiping the ruddy tears off with my sleeve.

"Be careful. You've been clever—and lucky. You were always lucky, but now you have to be wise. Listen up, little girl—there's not a lot of time. Don't cry. Don't bleed. It heals you, but this close to the web the power wants to flow freely through you. It'll push every living thing out of you if you let it. I don't want that for you."

"Dad—" I started, but he cut me off with a glare that sent ice into my chest.

"Listen up! It's the Guardian Beast he's after. He'll take its place—that's what he means to do—but he has to have you to make the way. He needs someone to call it and someone to kill it and you to trap it between the Grey and the normal. And after that he has no use for any of you."

"But . . . why would he want to *be* the Guardian . . . ?"

"He doesn't want to guard anything; he just wants to take its place—that's not the same thing. He's like you: He's becoming part of the living grid. But he doesn't want to be sucked away into the song. He wants to *own* it, to control it. If he can displace and destroy the Guardian—"

A clattering and bubbling started up beyond the wall of silently screaming faces. My father's eyes bulged and he looked panicked. "Oh, no. . . . They're coming back. . . ."

The mist-world began a gentle heaving.

"You have to go. I don't want you to see . . ."

"But Dad, how do I get you out—"

"You can't. They'll know. You mustn't tip your hand until the last minute! This place is hidden, but if it's empty, they'll know." He twitched and pulled into the wall a bit, letting out a gagging sound. "Please go! Now! Listen to the song. Don't trust it, but listen. It will tell you what it needs, but you must know when to refuse or you'll be swallowed up. Draw close; command it; then turn it on him when he's vulnerable. Don't let him become the Architect of the Grey. Use the second door—this puzzle—from wherever you are. It will bring you straight here so long as the first door is still open and then . . . and then you can do what you have to. Carry the ball and key with you until then and protect them well. Anyone can use the door but only you can stop the plan. Oh, no. . . ."

He jerked back into the wall until only his left side and the destroyed top of his head remained. All the faces in the wall opened their mouths and screamed as the blood above them began to run. . . .

I wrenched myself away and bolted back the way I'd come, blind in sudden darkness, reeling up the scarlet gleam of Simondson's thread as I ran.

I fell out of the portal that had been the second puzzle ball, tumbling and spinning to swipe at the misty shape of the opening, trying to force it closed and cut off the shrieking that roared out behind me. Desperate, I stabbed the key at the incorporeal door and twisted as if locking the thing closed.

The mist slammed shut with a red gust of magic that knocked me to the ground as the chorus of the grid shouted back to life in my head. The puzzle ball, now closed again, rolled against my side, and I scooped it up, turning and looking for the next door while shaking my head, trying to clear the ringing in my ears that the voices made.

But the first door was gone and I was crouching on the weedy grass of the Rose house's labyrinth as the red light of Cristoffer's magic seal faded. Simondson's tangled red shape glowered from where I'd left him beside the other puzzle, which lay open and scattered into a strange figure that gleamed with every color of the rainbow and showed the flickering phantom of the shape Dru Cristoffer had painted on the ball in blood and fire, hovering in air. If I turned just right, I could see the door.

Thinking of my father's instructions, I left the puzzle ball and its weird door as they were and tucked the other one deeper into my jacket along with my father's key. I would want them later. . . .

At the distant edge of the clearing, Quinton turned away from staring at the trees and ran toward me. "Harper!"

Simondson spat an ember of fury into the ground even as he twisted with pain. "When—?"

"Soon," I snapped back at him. "One more trip and you're out of here, but first you stand guard over this. Anyone comes to close this door, you scare the hell out of them."

"Me?"

The clamor, the fatigue, and my fright made me snappish. "You're a ghost, damn it! Don't you think you can haunt someone here with all this power to use? Just look! It's like a dead-guy playground here. Just fade back and wait."

Simondson peered around and spotted the shadow bear in the distance. He grinned, an expression that was truly disturbed. I snapped the tin closed on the end of his red strand of existence and buried the other in the ground at his invisible feet, feeling the surge of the grid into my fingertips as I did. "If I call you, you come; otherwise, it's all yours." I could see him wiggling into the banked fire of the nexus and tugging the monstrous bear around like a toy. The sound he made in the unnaturally still air carved a frozen track of horror into my guts.

Quinton pounded up and swept me into his arms. "Thank God. I thought you were lost!"

"I had Simondson to get me out."

"He makes an ugly guide."

"He makes an ugly guard, too. Let's get out of here before the bear notices us. I think Simondson has plans for it, and I don't want to see them."

This time we simply ran through the ruins, didn't even bother with care or delicacy; Dru Cristoffer's traps were designed to drive people out, not keep them in. We stayed a hair ahead of the storm of dead avians and animals that rose to pursue us. I was glad of the foresight that had made me park the truck pointed toward the road.

Quinton and I dove into the Rover's front seats, slamming the doors behind us, and the cloud of reanimated birds splashed against the truck's metal and glass, dissolving into dust and feathers. I started the engine and jerked the truck into gear, pulling away fast enough to raise the litter and dirt into the air in a plume as the remains of ghastly crows and jays sloughed away on the wind of our passage, the bones of dead deer, cougars, and bears scattering across the road.

I tossed the puzzle ball into the back as I drove, needing both hands free. I wanted out of the town of Leavenworth as quickly as possible. Quinton divested himself of his pack, coat, and hat more slowly, putting them behind the seat and frowning all the while.

I felt wound tight and ready to break. My mind, my thoughts, seemed to have been tossed into a blender with the emphatic blaring of the Grey to chop it all fine. At the bottom of North Road, Quinton urged me to pull over.

"Why?" I asked.

"I know you didn't get any sleep. If you're ready to head straight back to Seattle, it might be better if I do the driving. The trip out wasn't a picnic, remember?"

"True."

"Besides, you haven't filled me in on what happened in there."

I'd become so used to Quinton's presence by my side in the past few days that I hadn't given much thought to the fact he'd been locked out of the ghostly labyrinths. My father had implied that non-Greywalkers could use the second puzzle ball as a gateway to the hidden bubble of Grey just as well as I could, but Quinton had been cut off behind the wall of Cristoffer's magic.

I unbelted and swung out of the driver's seat. "All right. You drive and I'll talk."

I gave him the details of what I'd seen and what I'd garnered from my father—so far as I could since a few points about the possible living, collective nature of the Grey and the grid still refused to come out of my mouth. Quinton looked concerned when I got to the bits about Wygan's intentions and my guesses on why I was suddenly crying blood.

"So . . ." he started, keeping his eyes on the mountain road we were traveling. "According to your father, you're sort of . . . becoming part of the flow of magic. And you think you cry blood and bleed light because the . . . pressure of magic pushes into your system whenever there's an opportunity. Because it's trying to flow through you."

"Roughly, that's what Dad seemed to be saying, and if he's right about what Wygan's up to and my part in it, that kind of makes sense. Carlos said I was starting to warp the fabric of magic, or would, and that fits with what Dad said and . . . with what I'm observing."

"Run through that again. I'm not sure what you've observed and what's just my guess. You said you hear voices. . . ."

"Maybe I'm just losing my mind. Cristoffer wasn't the first to suggest that Greywalkers go crazy. . . . Marsden gouged out his own eyes. . . ."

"That's a little extreme. And while it's possible that you're cracking up, it's not a complete explanation. I saw some of this stuff myself and I met that . . . woman, Cristoffer. I can still feel those things crawling up my legs. . . ." He shuddered.

"I wish you hadn't had—"

He put a hand on my knee for a second before driving demanded it back. "I don't blame you for anything I've seen or experienced. Don't take it all on yourself. You know what they say: Shit happens." He made a silly face at me and I huffed a laugh.

"All right, all right: It's not all my fault. Some of it's Wygan's." I could hear the hate and disgust in my voice for a moment, but Quinton said nothing about it.

Instead he said, "And a lot of other people's. So . . . voices, doorways, dead dads, and Wygan wants to be the Guardian Beast. Sounds like a pretty crappy job. . . ."

"Only if he plays by the rules—and you can bet he won't. Dad said something about his becoming 'the Architect of the Grey' and I'm not sure what that means, but it sounds like it's not a good thing."

"No, I'm pretty sure it wouldn't be, not if it means no more Guardian Beast to keep the nasty stuff behind the veil. Any ideas on freeing your dad?"

I shook my head, eyes closed against both the shocks of passing ghosts and the plain weight of sleeplessness. "None. I think I'll have to work that out on my own. He doesn't want me to attract any attention by letting him go, but that implies there's a way. I can always try it on Simondson first. Oh! Simondson . . ."

"What about him?"

"I left him . . . standing guard on the labyrinth. So far as I can tell from Dad, I can use the second puzzle ball as a direct jump back to my father's bit of the Grey labyrinth as long as the first stage remains open. I'm not sure how it works, though. . . ."

"Some type of magical entanglement would be my guess. I suspect the puzzle balls have a similar relationship once they're open and operating that entangled subatomic particles do. And there may be a series of points between them that are congruent in space-time, effectively making the puzzles doorways to all of those as well as any point one of them occupies. It's possible that other paths in the second ball's maze lead to other points of congruence in the Grey. Good thing you had that little skein of ghost to mark your way or you might have gotten lost and popped out in the wrong place."

"I owe you for suggesting it."

"I didn't."

That gave me a hollow feeling inside. I'd heard a voice distinctly and imagined it was his. . . . I shivered and didn't want to think more about what had spoken. I would have to be very careful about which advice I listened to in the Grey from now on. But I did have an idea. I'd have to discuss it with Carlos, but I thought I had a way to put him out of Edward's—and therefore Wygan's—control without their knowledge that it had happened. I didn't like my part of it, but if I was going to stop the Pharaohn's plans, I needed Carlos on my side, free to act, not compelled to obey.

In spite of the sun suddenly piercing into the Rover as we headed down the western slope of the pass, I fell asleep somewhere east of Monroe and stayed out until we were past Edmonds, just north of Seattle. I woke up to the smell of hamburgers.

I blinked and rubbed my face, trying to clear the sleep and soften the noisy babbling of the grid in my head. "What's this? Where are we?"

"Outside a McDonald's in Mountlake Terrace. I thought we'd better figure out where we're going before we hit Seattle." He held a sack out to me and pointed one finger at a drink cup sweating in the console cup holder. "And eat, since it's now almost six and breakfast was ten hours ago."

I grunted as I adjusted my posture in the passenger seat and unlatched my seat belt. "I didn't mean to sleep like that."

"It's all right. You needed it. You need food, too. 'Cause I was thinking that if you're being drawn into the Grey's power system, then blood may not be the best conductor, and maybe you're replacing blood every time you're injured with something . . . non-blood, and you might be a little anemic. Thus: hamburgers. Rare meat might have been better, but I couldn't find a drive-through steakhouse in the area. See: That's something the U.S. really needs. Cow-n-Carry: for steak on the run."

"What's it on the run from?" I asked grabbing a wrapped burger from the bag. The smell of hot, greasy ground chuck, usually a bit off-putting, was making my mouth water.

"Probably from these guys. Also all manufacturers of gelatin, leather products, and dog toys."

"I'd say you're killing my appetite, but right now, I could probably eat at an autopsy." I folded back the wrapper and took a large bite of the steaming burger.

"Now you're ruining *my* appetite. Autopsy? My delicate sensibilities are offended."

"This from a man who accepts payment for work in mystery beer."

"By its nature, beer is safe—it's alcohol—so long as it's still sealed."

"Beer. I wonder if a couple of beers would make these

guys in my head shut the hell up. It's like living downstairs from a rehearsal hall." I smacked the glove box in a four-four rhythm. "Smile, smile, keep the line. Three, and four, and do it again!"

"Do choreographers all sound like that? Or is it just in movies?"

"Yes. They all want to be Bob Fosse or George Balanchine."

"So . . . you're feeling a little better . . . ?"

I smiled in spite of the clamor in my head. "Yes."

We finished up our food and I took over the driving to head back into Seattle.

"Where are we going this time?" Quinton asked.

"Remember how Dru Cristoffer mentioned Edward's wards?"

"Yeah, something about using the bypass idea to get around them."

"Yeah. I figure, even crazy as she is, she's not wild about having the Pharaohn in charge of magic—which is what it sounds like he's chasing—so she gave us a hint on surviving long enough to stop him. If we can get past the wards, Edward's bunker is the most secure place for us and the least likely to be under any attack by Goodall or anyone else. Goodall's burned his bridges with TPM as well as Edward. By now, he's on the security blacklist, so he won't be coming to visit and Wygan pretty well can't. But we can. I'm still on Edward's pass list, or I was the last time I went there and it's unlikely the head of building security would take me off it on Goodall's recommendation. So we go to TPM and see if we can get into the bunker. It should have almost everything we need, except food."

"What about the ferret and the dog?"

"Better off where they are. If we go to fetch them, we may pick up a tail, and unless the Danzigers are in trouble, they're safer without our presence. I'll need to contact Carlos again and make some plans, but I can do that from TPM."

"If we can get in."

"I have a key, but I don't know if it will still work to get into the building. And after that we can only know by trying."

TWENTY-FIVE

It wasn't quite that simple. The key did get us into the parking structure and the building. Getting past security was a little more complicated: I was still on the pass list, but the key cards I'd taken off Goodall were dead and I didn't have an appointment with anyone. Finally, a late call to one of Edward's many secretaries produced a pissed-off young woman with interesting marks on her wrists and blood in her eye. Her name was Carol Linzey, and she fixed a glacial glare on the current chief of security and signed me through. Then she handed me her own card to the lower level and elevators before turning back to flay the man with a whiplash tongue and language you don't expect out of the mouths of executive assistants for making her come downtown to show him how to do his job right. She dressed him down about everything from his lack of protocol or common sense to his hairstyle and he cowered as she did. I've heard milder manners from felons and parents in custody battles. I'd prefer the felons.

Down below, the elevator lobby in front of Edward's bunker was empty. It was not, unfortunately, any quieter in the Grey. Normally I found the magic in that area muted, but as we faced the inner doors the chorus of the grid broke into a warring cacophony of advice and warning. "Shut up," I muttered.

Quinton cut me a curious glance. "What?"

"Them," I replied, shaking my head and tapping on my temple.

He frowned. "Have to do something about that."

"That would be nice. . . ." I said, distracted by my study of the problem before us. I had Carol's card to open the door, but I knew the wards hadn't been told to let me in. The card alone wouldn't get us past them or the other nasty things that had been twined into the protective magic around the portal. I doubted I could shut down the wards on the door itself, but I could get the door to open automatically if I could reach the key reader.

A secondary loop of protective magic circled the doorway and the card pad. I'd seen an invisible eye above the reader and the snapping teeth of something hungry under it the first time I'd come with Goodall. That monstrosity was right where I'd have to put my wrist to use the card, exposing the vulnerable skin, veins, and tendons to the horror beneath. Whether the card worked or not, I thought that the dreadful biting thing would rip open the arm of anyone it didn't recognize or hadn't been told to admit, and I wasn't sure it felt friendly toward me. I'd seen it take a chunk out of Goodall while he was still on the security pass list. Since I also qualified as a potential threat in both the normal world and the Grey one, I was more than a touch reluctant to put my flesh near the disembodied thing in the wall.

"What did Cristoffer say about this again . . . ?" The noise in my skull was making it hard to recall anything but what I was staring at right now. This time, the voice of the grid was not so much a song as a hooligan rabble.

"She said she probably hadn't buried the tap as well as she would have now," Quinton replied. "I would guess that's sort of the power line feeding whatever magical alarm she put on the door for Edward."

"It's a little more complex than that. There are at least three linked systems here: two magical and one mundane. We have the card for the normal system, but we have to get past the others: recognition and defense. At least one of them took a bite out of Goodall—and I mean that literally."

"OK, door bites man. I'd like to skip that."

"Then don't touch the door or the wall near it." I crouched down to look harder at the bottom of the wall where it met the floor, searching for the power line up from the grid. I hoped Cristoffer hadn't been teasing us with her hints. She had seemed angry and annoyed more than cruel, but I wouldn't have put any sort of mean-tempered joke past her.

Even sliding deeper into the Grey, I found it hard to get a clear look at the spell around the door and card reader. The magical structure was almost Byzantine in the degree of twisting and doubling back that it displayed. I wondered how much of it was really necessary and how much was there to disguise the important parts. I wished I had Quinton's knowledge of circuits, but I couldn't show it to him and describing it seemed impossible. Along the edge of the carpet that touched the wall, I could see a narrow, dark gap, as if the carpet hadn't been stretched as tightly as usual when it was installed.

I eased out of the Grey so I'd have a better grip and, keeping my hand away from the bright crimson lines of the spell, I dug my fingertips into the carpet edge nearby. Something sharp poked my middle finger and I gasped, jerking my hand away.

"Are you all right?"

I looked at my fingertip, seeing a small, dirty puncture. "Just a carpet tack." A single drop of blood squeezed out of the skin as it reclosed. I sucked the injured finger, thinking it would be a bad idea to let the blood escape and land anywhere near the chittering red lines of the spell. I tucked my fingers back into the gap with a bit more care and caught the edge of the carpet. As suspected, it wasn't tight to the wall or the strip of tacks as it should have been—the installers hadn't been allowed close enough to do it properly, or whoever finished up the job wasn't experienced with the technique. Either way, lucky for me. The edge of the carpet pulled up and away, making a sloppy pocket at floor level on the right side of the doorway.

In the shadow of the lifted carpet, the strands of magic gleamed like neon threads. One was quite a bit thicker than the others and it split about an inch up the wall into four other lines that described the whorls and arabesques of the spell. Of the four lines, one was slightly thicker and brighter than the others. Among the knots and twists above it was difficult to pick out, but so close to the split it was obvious. Warily, I touched it.

A jolt of pain shook my spine and a snapping doglike head thrust out of the wall below the card reader. The creature was bright red and gruesome, furious as it pushed into reality.

Quinton took two fast steps backward. "Jesus! What in hell is that?"

I twitched my finger away from the thick line and the monstrosity recoiled into the wall. The voices in my head screamed conflicting insults and remonstrations at me. "Shut up!" I barked at them.

Quinton stared at me.

"Not you." I put my hands over my ears for a second, but it didn't help. "I don't know," I whispered, tucking my head down. "I don't know what it is, only what it does."

"Eats people?"

"Pretty much."

Quinton sounded shaken. "I wasn't really expecting to see anything like that. . . ."

I groaned from the rising noise in my head, like pressure in a balloon. "Don't say you didn't believe there was really something there." My voice sounded hollow in my ears.

He stepped close and crouched down, putting his arms around me and pulling me back a little from the wall. "No, sweetheart. I just didn't think I'd be able to see it. There's no physical sign of any . . . animal or cage here. Where did it come from?"

"I think . . ." I felt sick to my stomach, sorting the noise and my own thoughts as I spoke. "I think someone sacrificed a dog."

"You mean Dru Cristoffer."

I nodded, spasmodically. "That's the dog. In the wall." If I sorted the images that were flooding into my head from touching the line of its imprisonment, I could see what had happened to the poor animal and I didn't want to describe it to anyone. In light of what she'd done, I reevaluated Dru Cristoffer: She was evil. And I painted Edward with the same brush for letting her—telling her—to do it.

I didn't want to simply go around this monstrous security system. I wanted to destroy it, wards and all. It wasn't my place to make that decision—it wasn't my property, and Edward wouldn't thank me for ruining it—but knowing what had been done to safeguard this place made me sick and seething with anger. I didn't want to know what Cristoffer had done to make the panels on the doors throb as they did—didn't think I could ever sleep again with such knowledge in my head.

The Grey chorus tried to give me the information and I screamed at them, "Shut up! Don't tell me!" I couldn't block them out with my hands so I tried to beat them into silence rocking violently forward in Quinton's embrace to strike my head against the floor. "Shut up! Shut up!"

Quinton hauled me hard against his chest, locking me to him and pushing away from that wretched wall. "Stop it! Harper, stop!"

I couldn't. The insidious whispers of the grid would not go away. They persisted and echoed, telling me horrible things that had happened in these rooms, reciting a litany of horrors that lay ahead. I panted and gulped my breath, thrashing against Quinton's grip because there was nowhere to turn that they did not come, invisible and unstoppable, into my mind. I felt myself shaking, convulsing as if the voices brought the electric shock of the grid with them. I understood why my father had killed himself, why he had blown out his brains rather than live with this. . . . I wished I could. I wished I could stop—

Quinton clamped one arm hard across my body, crushing the air from my lungs. I felt a jab against my side and then a jolt, a violent yank as if I'd been hit in the chest and thrown across the room. I buckled and collapsed onto the floor, facedown, huddled like a hurt child.

But the silence! The blessed silence. I wanted to stay in it, curled around myself in the quiet.

I felt Quinton holding me against his chest, panting and sweating. Or was that me? Breath came hard, in gasps, into my lungs and a ringing started up in my ears, but just an ordinary buzzing noise this time. We were on the floor. Were we on the floor? It seemed we had to be since I couldn't feel my feet touching anything.

"Harper? Sweetheart?" He breathed the words against my neck. "I'm sorry. I had to. I didn't know what else to do. Harper?"

I pressed my face against his shoulder and tried to say it was all right, but it came out a weak mewling sound.

He sagged under me, relieved, and shifted his grip so I slid lower into his lap. "Thank God. Baby, I thought I'd killed you for a second there. Oh, sweetheart, I didn't know what else to do."

"S'all right," I mumbled. Or I think I did. My mouth wasn't working very well. Actually, nothing was. I was a big, limp lump, but everything was wonderfully quiet. I didn't think it was permanent, but it was fine for now. I'd have to do something about the spell and the dog in the wall before the noisy voices of the grid came back, but for a few more seconds, I only wanted to cling to Quinton.

"Wha—where . . . ?" I tried, not sure where I was or how long I'd been gone. I couldn't feel him touching me now. . . .

"Still here. Basement. Had to shock you. Only thing I could think of to make you stop. I think you lost a couple of minutes there. Are you . . . all right?"

I couldn't answer that. It wasn't just that I was messed up—I was more than that—but that the flow of the grid had risen over me in a rapid swarm of flickering light and awesome silence. The same whirring, pale-blue energy that had settled on me as I'd escaped from Wygan's lair under the broadcast tower clothed me and moved me up to my knees. Then forward, lurching a bit as my limbs tried to coordinate the signals of this power with the familiar firing of my nerves.

Without any desire for it, I pushed myself out of Quinton's embrace and sprawled across the rug, bringing my face closer to the gap I'd made between the carpet and the wall. My vision should have been weak from the electric shock but it was sharp as a sniper's, and I stared into the complexity of the spell that painted its light up the wall with a terrifying, alien understanding. I could see which of the loops and whorls acted like a retainer or cage for the angry spirit of the dog, which held the eye that had been separated from the animal, and which was the subroutine that connected the card reader to the spell. I'd have to cut that out of the magical circuit and push the guardian aside so it wouldn't take a bite out of me or Quinton on general principle. The eye was no threat alone, so I could ignore it and reinforce the cage or rip it out altogether, but I didn't care to at that moment. Just didn't care, didn't feel the emotional coil and turmoil of being human. I knew I could simply . . . change it, move whatever I didn't like aside. For now.

So, this was what Carlos meant by an ability to warp the fabric of magic—my ability for the moment. I could have this all the time if I stopped resisting the changes happening to me and just . . . took them in. I'd held back so long that, this time at least, touching the power lines and shapes of the Grey would be agonizing. This I simply *knew*.

I started to slip deeper into the Grey, closer to the grid that flared and sang, reaching for me as if I'd been lost such a long time . . .

"Harper?"

I paused, balancing between the normal and the paranormal, glancing over my shoulder at Quinton. He was chewing his bottom lip and trying not to look frightened, but the energy around his head had gone a solid, unhappy shade of orange with jagged sparks of bile-green, a combination I'd always thought of as "scared sick."

"Don't worry," I said, my voice echoing up from a distance well below me, filled with the chorus of the grid. The hollow look Quinton returned should have sent a pang through me, but I felt nothing beyond the necessity of rearranging the elegant abomination around the doors. Some distant, silly creature said I'd have to deal with the consequences and his distress later, but that was later and somewhere else. Not here, in the fine-lined world of the grid that spread in all visible directions and outward past what any puny human eyes could see.

The whole world was a fiery network of colored lines in the darkness, so thick and numerous that they cooked the air white. It sang the voices of nymphs and selkies in the vast ocean of luminous mist. I focused past the distracting beauty of it, closing my eyes to all but the gyre of the spells and the thick, blue stream they sprang from.

Cristoffer had picked a strong line of neutral blue that turned red only as it entered the coils of her spell, the influence of blood. This was the first time I'd ever studied the structure of a constant, dynamic spell. Most of the ones I'd seen before were static things, powered by their creator's personal energy or some stolen energy and doomed to eventually fade and die out. This was live, drawing power continuously to keep it up and active, ready to respond to whatever happened near it. The lines of the spell split into four parts: the main circuit that sustained the slaughtered animal, a second heavy line that composed the restraints and camouflage over its furious remains, a third thread not much wider than an eyelash and very slightly blue-tinged by the mundane electrical connection of the card reader, and a fourth bloody-red strand that fed the unblinking eye above the card plate—the magical half of the recognition system. With the brightness of the three red lines that coiled around and over it, the thin, orchid-red line was hard to discern. Even with the right key card in hand, the wrong hand holding it would still be bitten—or even ripped right off—by the fury of the guard dog embedded in the wall. The baroque loops of the three other lines made it nearly impossible to reach for the card pad's line without touching one of them. It was very clever and would have been difficult to dismantle, or even bypass, without injury. But that wasn't going to be a problem for me. Not now.

Standing up, I looked for a place well above the pad and eye, where the card reader's line was exposed and found a tiny loop near the upper hinge plate. I could tear it all apart if I liked, but there was that other person, Quinton, to think of. He needed the pad to work without worrying about the teeth of the door's guardian. I'd have to shunt the beast and its support aside but leave the rest, and the wards, intact.

I puzzled over it for a minute. I just needed to pull the unwanted bits away, as the mage had done to power her spell and much the same way I had teased Simondson's thread up from the ground. It was convenient that I was tall and could reach the loop without standing in front of the spell itself. I pushed both hands into the wall, feeling invisible resistance from the material things that composed it, finding the action more difficult than I'd anticipated. It should have been easier . . . but I wasn't familiar with this power yet. I knew I could do much more and with very little effort once I was truly part of the grid, but for now, I'd have to try something more limited.

I remembered the way the edges of the hole around the Hardy Tree in the old London churchyard had torn at my touch and whirled off into tiny vortices. I could tear the edges of something exposed and ragged. It seemed to me that the tap Cristoffer had pulled up must have a ragged edge to it somewhere, like a rough spot where it had come away from another feeder line.

I reached below the red color of the spell and closed my fingers on the blue line of magic. My seeming-distant body twitched involuntarily as the power line seared into my fingertips, sending pain and electrical shock into the nerves of my hand and up my arm. I bit my lips against an impulse to scream. I concentrated and pushed the feeling aside. The hot pain dropped down to a lower intensity, still burning and miserable but no longer of concern. I pulled steadily until a strand of cool blue energy spooled out from under my fingers, about two feet long.

I pinched the free end and stood, pulling a longer filament of energy free. I knew the loop wouldn't last long once I pulled it away from the feeder line it came from. If it withered and died, I'd have to start again. I'd have to make the connection quickly so I could let go as soon as possible. The pain was growing, and holding two live ends simultaneously might be more than the body could bear.

I snapped the energetic thread off, like breaking the yarn on a raveling sleeve. For a moment, it pulsed; then it began fading. I knew I had very little time. I pinched the nearest end onto the lowest part of the card reader's red thread. Then, from below the gaze of the disembodied eye, I shoved the fiery container of the dead dog aside a few feet with one hand before I rose and pinched the second end on at the loop above the hinge. The watchdog snapped at nothing as I passed its eye, reached, and turned the small, unblinking organ to see only the emptiness of the space inside the wall. Then the dog fell quiet.

The new strand slowly flushed red while the strand it bridged paled to lavender. I reached out and snapped off the original line just above the floor. Shock jolted through me as the line faded to pale blue, then withered and vanished.

I jerked backward, thrust away from the calm sea of the grid, dazed by the sudden return of normal pain and the ripping loss of knowledge.

The card reader was out of the magical circuit.

I breathed hard and stumbled back a few more feet, becoming more painfully normal with every difficult tread.

Quinton stepped up behind me but didn't quite touch me. "Harper," he breathed. "Are you all right?"

My breath shook in my chest and my limbs felt burned and leaden, but I nodded. "Good enough." Remarkable in the Grey. A total wreck in the physical. My electrified mind gibbered and shrieked while the grid chuckled to itself at my expense. My spine had already begun buzzing, and the singeing sound was swelling back up with the residual pain from handling the grid that I had ignored at the time—ignored, since human concerns such as pain and loss were outside my world. My gods, if this was anything like what Wygan expected me to do, there was no way I'd do it, even as a bluff. I could feel my muscles and joints stiffening from the sensation of electric shock still lingering on my nerves. I could never let myself be subsumed into the inhuman power of the Grey's magical grid as I'd just come very close to doing. The potential had been awesome, but the divorce from feeling was too chilling. I wasn't very good at emotional expression, but the sensation of removal was too terrible. Even so, I couldn't fall into contemplating that now; there was still something to do.

"Just need to put the card on the reader," I gasped, breathless, enervated, and ready to collapse.

I tried to retrieve it from my pocket, but my fingers were too senseless and burned to feel it. Quinton got the card for me and held it out toward the reader's plate at arm's length.

The spell throbbed brighter but the monstrosity stayed quiet behind the restraining bars of the casting, now out of line with the card plate. The door clicked and swung a few inches open. Quinton started to move forward.

"Don't touch them," I panted, crumpling to my knees, unable to stay upright any longer. "The wards on the doors are still active. They're worse—even worse than the dog."

Quinton glanced at me and started back to pick me up, but I waved him off. Scowling, he looked around the foyer searching for something to shove the doors wider open.

A pretty, spindly-legged console table stood under a painting on the wall to the right of the elevator, distracting the eye from the hidden door to the observation room on the opposite wall. A large vase of wilted flowers stood on the tabletop, and at first I thought he was going to snatch it up and throw it at the doors.

Quinton picked up the whole table instead and shoved it hard into the gap between the doors. The red-shining panels on the door surfaces let out a gonging sound loud enough to make us both flinch and cower as the table exploded into flame. The force pushed the doors back on their hinges as the burning bits of the table flew away, cutting through the air of the room with whistling sounds.

Quinton snatched me up and threw me through the gaping opening before the doors could rebound and snap closed. He didn't follow and the heavy portal slammed shut again.

Inside the room the hush was intense and made the resurging babble of the grid in my head all the more noticeable as I fought it down. Still, I limped to the doors and tugged one open: Edward hadn't warded the interior, and even though the malevolence of the wards seeped through, the discomfort of visions and the cold pain of touching the handle weren't enough to stop me. Quinton dashed through the doorway and kicked the door closed again behind him.

Then he turned and grabbed me and hugged me so hard I squeaked with what little breath I had left—it hurt, but it was a pleasant ache. He was breathing very fast, sweat making his face and hands sticky.

"That—I don't ever want to do that again. I don't want to see you do it again. There was—ugh. It was like all those tapes from 9/11 going off in my head. Screaming and fire . . ." He shuddered.

"I know." Yes, I knew, like I'd been split in two: one half looking only at the numbers, the other burning in the wreckage.

TWENTY-SIX

It took some time to get settled in Edward's hideout. First I had to find the magical odds and ends that might cause Quinton trouble and mark them or cover them in some way. The seals Edward had had installed at two corners of the conference room area were easy: one was shattered and the other I simply toppled a chair into upside down. There weren't a lot more problems but I still had to spend the time searching to be sure. We also ruled out spending any time in one of the small rooms near the elevator shaft which seemed to be Edward's sleeping space. I felt uncomfortable anywhere in or near it.

The suite had a small kitchen that didn't seem to get much use, even though it had everything and the fridge held several bottles and containers that argued that someone—I was guessing Goodall or Carol—needed to eat once in a while. Aside from that, one would think only alcoholics ever came into the basement, but I'd noted long ago that vampires have no problem drinking alcohol. The extensive facilities in the bathroom made me think there might be things about vampire habits and hygiene I didn't know and really didn't want to. Quinton found it all rather unsettling, but he had no complaints about the security or the speed of the computer and communications equipment. He looked at it with speculative avarice while he settled me on a couch with a blanket we found in a closet.

"You look like you never took that nap," he commented.

"I feel like I've been trampled by elephants wearing electrified cleats."

He looked contrite. "I'm sorry. I should have asked how you were sooner."

"Stupid to ask when you can just see it."

"Well, yeah, but it's . . . graceless of me."

"I can skip grace. I like practical. Though I could stand to hear a little less of whatever's bugging the Grey world at the moment."

"Is it getting worse?"

"It's . . . different."

He knew I didn't want to discuss how it had changed. Instead, he just said, "I need to work on that. . . ."

"I'm doubtful there's much you can do."

"I can try though. Electric shock seems to knock it down. . . ."

"You can't keep on zapping me." And I wasn't sure that the zap hadn't somehow facilitated the sudden shift in my connection to the grid. The ordinariness—for us at least—of the conversation was odd after my experience with the Grey a few hours earlier, but welcome.

"No. That would kill you. Eventually, maybe, but no thank you all the same."

"Yeah. I think I'll skip that option."

"Still, it's a datum and that's a start. I wonder if it's a field effect, like the Grey detector flux. . . ."

"Maybe I just need hearing aids that turn the volume down instead of up," I joked.

"Noise canceling, maybe. Have to find the right frequencies though. . . ."

"Have I mentioned that you're cute when you're obsessing?"

He smiled at me, but it wasn't quite the irrepressible grin he usually used. "So are you. You bite your lip. It's very Marilyn Monroe."

I couldn't say that comforted me since she was dead, so I didn't say anything except, "I'll have to call Carlos before this gets worse."

"About what?"

"How to get him off Edward's hook." Not to mention figuring out a few other angles on this thing. . . .

* * *

Contacting Carlos proved easier than usual and he returned my call himself about nine o'clock. Quinton had been poking at me with weird implements and taking various electronic measurements whenever I said that the noises in my head were louder or more distinct. I wasn't sure he was getting anywhere with the research, but at least it kept him busy and both our minds off the problems ahead.

"Blaine," Carlos acknowledged me. I'd never heard him on the phone before and his voice did odd things to the line, causing strange echoes and screeches I wasn't certain were coming from my head alone.

"I can do it. I found the back door."

"Resourceful. Are you certain of the other?"

"Not really. But I . . . have warped the fabric. Reluctant as I am, I think it can be done."

He was silent a moment. It came off brooding, even over a phone connection. "Even so, assurances of our alignment will be needed. Of our . . . helplessness," he spat. "And a diversion from what we do. His eyes must look elsewhere."

"On that account I'm afraid I have no ideas," I said. I could barely keep my mind on track enough to think of how to remove the knife tip from Carlos's heart and catch up to my father long enough to ask him what had become of his old receptionist, Christelle, and then get him free of Wygan. And I had to free Simondson, too. I'd made a promise, after all.

"I do. My protégé troubles me. . . ."

"Cameron?" I was aghast. Cameron was nothing if not loyal to Carlos. He'd spit in Edward's eye before he'd go against his mentor, so far as I could tell.

"He may require some talking to. And more than that. See to it. Tonight he goes to visit his sister."

"Sarah? In Bellevue?"

"I believe she has moved to this side of the water. A condo in Belltown. Call him. He will see you." As if he wouldn't see Carlos. Something odd was afoot and I wasn't going to ask: The whole conversation felt like something from a spy movie in which we knew we were being bugged.

"I will," I agreed, and cut the connection.

I plucked at the collection of wires and sensors Quinton had decorated me with. "I have to go soon."

"I had that impression. Why?"

"Honestly, I'm a little confused by it, but I suppose Carlos feared someone eavesdropping on him. I can't imagine any other reason for that obtuse conversation. I'm to meet with Cameron at his sister's condo in Belltown. I assume he'll somehow know what's going on. But I have to call him first: I don't know which building she moved to."

Quinton made a sage face. "Ah, the politics of vampires."

"I think it's more the maneuvering of a double cross. And as long as I'm not the victim, I'm fine with that."

"I wish you weren't going anywhere. I'm worried about you and, much as I hate to say it, this place gives me the willies."

I laughed. "You're not the only one. But it's safe. The biggest threats to us are never going to come here, nor will they be sending any little minions to do their dirty work."

"Still . . . it's a vampire's lair—damned nice one with some really terrific toys, but all the same. . . ."

I nodded. "Yeah, I understand. But you can't come along. It wouldn't be safe for either of us."

"What if you have another problem . . . with the voices?"

"I think I can manage for as long as this will take."

I held his further comments at bay while I called Cameron. He answered the phone as if he'd been waiting for it.

"Hi, Harper."

"Hi, Cameron. Look, I need to talk to you right away."

"We're on our way to Sarah's."

"We?"

"Me and Gwen."

"Skinny Gwen?" Lady Gwendolyn of Anorexia she'd called herself the first time we'd met. The only vampire I'd ever seen fading away from lack of giving a damn. Though the last time I'd seen her, she'd seemed much scarier, back in Edward's fold and becoming sharper and more predatory in his care. "You're taking Gwen to Sarah's?"

"They get on all right. Sarah understands Gwen, and with Edward missing, Gwen needs friends." He sounded a little defensive.

I found myself puzzling over that one. Vampires needing friends?

"Well. If you're coming," he continued, "you can meet us at Sarah's." He rattled off an address—a rather swank building on Second Avenue that had originally been a fancy public bath, and then a synagogue before the developers tore down the old building, preserving only the historic terra-cotta facade.

Surprised, I agreed. "All right. Fifteen minutes."

"See you then."

Quinton disliked my leaving, but he watched me call for a cab and leave via the elevator to TPM's lobby. It was safer that walking back to my truck, which we'd moved off-site on the assumption that Goodall still had some moles on the building staff.

As I was crossing the lobby, the security man on the night desk called out to me. "Ms. Blaine. You expecting any visitors?"

"No, why?"

"Been someone lurking around outside since you got here. Not making any moves but persistent. Figured he's watching you."

"Really? What's he look like?"

The guard waved me to his monitor and flipped through several screens until he got to a camera that pointed to the far northern corner across the street from TPM's lobby. The guard froze the frame and zoomed in, pointing to a pale blob that resolved into a familiar face.

"This guy."

Will. I shook my head in exasperation and didn't even mind the chorus of annoyed little voices in my head. "Ex-boyfriend."

"You want we should run him off? Call the cops?"

I sighed, closing my eyes against the vision of Will arrested again by Seattle's finest. "No. . . . I'll handle it. Hold my cab."

I walked out of the lobby and straight toward him, straight for the uncontrolled flashes of wild color and chaos that surrounded him, only taking time to scan for traps and other watchers. What the hell was Will thinking? Whatever it was, I had to warn him off for both our sakes. I stopped less than a foot in front of him, glaring up into his unbalanced smile.

"Stop it, Will. Go away. I can't help you."

"It's all right. I know I upset you last time. I can be patient."

"Apparently you can't. And that's not the problem anyhow. You think I can do something for you, but I can't. Not won't. *Can't.* You have to stop thinking that way. How did you even find me here?"

"I knew you'd go to Leavenworth. I just drove there and looked for you."

It hurt me to be so cruel to him, but nothing seemed to get past his insane belief that I could save him. I glanced at him with his damaged limbs and avid eyes. I shook my head, appalled at the implication of what he'd pushed himself to do after the ghastly things that had been done to him by vampires in London—and those were my fault: his beautiful hands smashed into permanent claws, his feet slashed and crippled, and his mind shattered into disjointed fantasy and fury. Why would he want anything to do with me? To even think of me anymore? And how could he hold the steering wheel or work the pedals of a car without suffering? "You drove yourself . . . ?"

He raised his eyebrows in an encouraging smile, nodding. "Michael wouldn't. It's all right. It was hard to catch up to you, but I did and I followed you home. I don't mind the pain: It's real; it's like a friend. It only hurts me to help me. But it's not enough. I need you."

He started to reach for my shoulders, but I drew back with a warning look and he stopped, his broken hands still in the space between us, supplicating. "There's so much darkness here. You're my light. I need you to banish the darkness. I need you to keep them away."

My heart was wrung like a rag. "Oh, Will. I can't. I can't even keep them away from me." I brushed his cheek with my fingertips and felt a frisson of jagged cold and terror leap from him and rime my skin in goose bumps. "I'm not the solution to the problem: I'm the source. You need to stay away from me or something worse will happen to you. Go home. Go back to Michael and let him help you."

"No. He won't help me. He only wants me to take pills and go back to the hospital, but they don't help. They only make it worse; they only let the darkness come closer. They want me to sleep, but that's when it's worst. They want to banish the pain, but they don't understand: I can't *feel* anything but this." He wrung his hands together and I could hear the half-healed bone and tissues pop and tear. The energy around his hands flashed dark red and the freakish void in his aura momentarily illuminated with white sparks. He let out a shaking gasp mixed of suffering and perverse satisfaction.

Horror nauseated me and sent trembles through my body. I grabbed his hands, forcing them together, palm to palm, between mine, letting the chorus of the Grey cry for compassion. "No, Will. No. Don't do that. Don't fall in love with the pain." I wished I could make him better. I wished I could push away his torment and confusion, repair him, restore his elegant hands and make him forget monsters and terrors in the endless night. "That's something they gave you—something from the darkness. It's not good for you. Don't embrace that. Don't let them have you."

Touching him ached and the voices of the grid bound into a single cry as sharp and clear as breaking crystal. His hands were cold but mine were warm around them, and I held on tight for the few seconds' paltry comfort I could give. He closed his eyes, and for a moment the tension in his muscles slackened, the riotous energy around him easing down to a small halo of blue and red and green. It wasn't my doing: I was only grounding him enough to let him do it himself.

He let out a little sigh, just an ordinary one this time, followed by a longer, slower breath. "That doesn't hurt."

"No. You shouldn't hurt. Remember this feeling. When the dark things come, reach for this, not for the pain. Breathe just like you're breathing now—"

"Blue."

"What?"

"It's blue."

I was startled. I saw the gentle, neutral energy as blue, too—the clean, clearing breath taught in Yoga classes and meditation. I didn't think Will had any ability to see the paranormal, but maybe things were a bit . . . different now. "Yes. Blue," I agreed.

He opened his eyes, his gaze steadier but still disturbed in its depths. "Harper . . ."

I backed off slowly, letting his hands slip out of mine. "That's all I can do for you, Will. Take that home, now. Please, go home."

He nodded, but he didn't move away. He just stood still and watched me go back to the TPM building and get into my waiting cab. He was still standing there when we pulled away.

TWENTY-SEVEN

"I'm late. I apologize." I seemed to be doing that a lot lately, contrary to my usual habit. And here I was doing it again in the doorway of Sarah Shadley's condo. It was after ten.

Sarah shrugged and let me in. "Cam and Gwen are in the living room."

I touched her on the arm, stopping her. "Why did you move?" Last time I'd been in touch with Cameron's older sister, she'd been living with their mother in a middle-class suburb of Bellevue and trying to patch up their strained relationship.

"Oh. Mom's doing OK and . . . I needed some space of my own. I sold the house. Lucky timing: The market collapsed right afterward, but I did all right. And Cam . . . well, I missed him."

She looked remarkable, a complete change from the defiant, confused girl I'd first met: hair badly dyed and growing out, clothes in-your-face instant Goth with an aesthetic meant more to appall than engender any community with her fellows. Now she stood up straight, her light-brown hair shining and smooth. Her makeup was still pale, her clothes still a touch Goth but in a subtler, softer style that owed more to the romantic side of the movement than the punk. She seemed happy, content with herself, and confident.

"You know vampires aren't the healthiest friends to have," I said.

She gave me a half smile filled with secrets and clasped her hands without thinking, rubbing one thumb against her inner wrist under the long, fluttering cuff of her blouse. "Yeah. But he's my brother. And . . . I guess I don't really mind some things. With the right person. I've always been a freak, anyway. At least now I'm a useful, happy freak."

I followed her into the living room, feeling a little ill from more than the presence of vampires. When she sat down next to Gwen on the long, chocolate velvet sofa that faced the view of Seattle's lights tumbling down to Elliott Bay, I felt only slightly less squicked. Yes, I knew vampires needed blood and they had to get it from a living human—preferably someone they had an ongoing relationship with and could trust, or at least control—but since Sarah had been through that before and escaped, I hadn't expected her to voluntarily return to it. At least it didn't look like the same abused-pet situation she'd been in with Edward. Gwen leaned against Sarah with casual intimacy. So, maybe not lovers, but extraordinary friends. It could be worse, though from my feeling about vampires in general, it wasn't exactly good. I just wasn't sure that being a milk cow was something to be pleased with.

The roiling red miasma wasn't as bad as usual, or maybe I was getting used to it after all this time. I couldn't deny I was drawing closer to the Grey. I repressed the desire to swear at the smug little voices in my head.

Cameron was at the other end of the couch. I'd met him as a frightened boy who was trying to come to grips with his transition to vampire and his problems with Edward over it. I'd helped him and it was through my mediation he'd ended up under Carlos's protection. Gone were the long angelic curls, the hint of a mustache, and the artfully ragged sweaters of his university student days. Now he lounged like a blond leopard, sleek and dangerous, all coiled energy and patient knowledge of terrible things. He didn't project any of the anxiety I'd caught in our phone call before I went to Leavenworth, only power that hung around him as a bright nimbus of red and black. He gazed at me, studying me as if I'd changed since the last time we'd met. I suppose that was true since it had been more than a year since we'd had any in-person contact. Something about me brought out a crease between his eyebrows. He wasn't quite as good at keeping his emotions off his face as his teacher was.

"So," he drawled, "what is Carlos up to?"

"That depends on where you stand," I replied, taking a seat at right angles to the sofa on Cameron's end.

"Behind him, if possible. Beside him, if he'll let me."

I raised an eyebrow. "Really? I thought you two might have had a falling-out since the last time we talked."

He shook his head. "No. But he's more guarded lately, even around me. Ever since Edward disappeared . . . he's very wary. And I did ask him your question about the process started by one vampire and finished by another. He says, 'Yes.' That would be exactly what happened and it makes the current situation all the worse."

For a moment I was confused and had to think hard on what he was telling me. What had I asked him to ask Carlos . . . ? Oh yes: about Goodall.

Cameron went on, knowing I would figure it out. "Bryson Goodall must have started out under the Pharaohn's influence, but subtly. Sent to Edward for the security job—naturally Edward would . . . want a more personal connection. Something like that," he added, nodding toward his sister and Gwen.

I glanced at the women. Gwen, her sharp chin tucked down so her long strawberry blond hair fell over her face, watched Sarah with intense eyes while the other talked in a low voice, her face glowing and her eyes animated with excitement. It wasn't love—at least not a sexual kind of love—but it was a deep connection that wove a flexing net of magenta and blue lines between them.

"Goodall is like a cuckoo," Cameron said. "He may be raised in another bird's nest, but he's still a cuckoo in the end. As soon as you were out of the way and Edward was in his power, Wygan didn't need to leave Goodall in Edward's nest. Now that the information is out, it's gotten worse for any of us loyal to Edward. That he could have sheltered and embraced a cuckoo—the Pharaohn's ushabti at that—makes everything he ever did suspect and cause for gossip. Or worse. It's very bad for Carlos. He's not a fan of Edward's but . . ." He trailed off, one hand eloquently touching his own chest a moment, then rolling outward as if to say "you know."

"Then you're aware of the complication between Edward and Carlos," I observed.

"Oh yes. He tried to teach me some way to repair it, but I simply don't have any such power. It was you who gave him hope it could work at all. But it doesn't. At least not with me."

"What? What idea did I give him?"

"Remember back with the organ?"

I nodded. Yes, I remembered the organ that had been the vessel and prison of a vengeful ghost. The case had come to me at the same time as Cameron's because of my fresh awakening to the Grey.

"You suggested that vampires, being creatures who live in the power of death, might have some ability to channel that power. You remember?"

"Uh . . . yes, I do." I had to think hard on that point. I'd been very tired and confused by that stage in the investigation and I'd only made the suggestion on an idiotic impulse. Sometimes my unconscious is a lot more clever than my conscious mind, and more prone to blurting.

Cameron's mouth lifted in a smile that didn't go any farther than his lips. "And it's partially true, but we can't direct or control that power. We tried, he and I. But it's passive. Only a powerful necromancer, like Carlos, can make anything of it. So we failed and he continues to be at Edward's mercy."

I nodded, knowing that much from Carlos and my own experience. "But surely the situation between them is different now. I got that impression at least."

Cameron shrugged. "Yes, but how does it matter? In the current upheaval, he's unable to move in any direction. He can't reject Edward and secure his position with another faction because of the tie between them, but he can't do anything to support him either; they've been enemies for too long. Who would believe it? So he's suspect and under attack himself. Not that he's worried about most of the other vampires; it's only the Pharaohn that scares him."

"Anyone should be scared of the Pharaohn," I said.

"Most of us are. The ones who aren't are either his own or too young and stupid to survive. But we cleave to power and most would rather be under his protection than on his hit list. They're just squabbling to prove who's good enough to be second lieutenant."

"So, without Edward, Seattle's vampires are currently in a power vacuum with Wygan poised to topple the dominoes he's been putting in place for . . . how long?"

"Centuries," Cameron replied. "And at the moment, he's the only option we seem to have, outside of willful naïveté. There is no one else capable or in the right position. As far as Carlos and I have been able to determine, that, too, was part of the plan. And we've all stumbled blindly into it like sheep."

"So you two have discussed this in the past few days."

Cameron nodded, grim-faced. It appeared he knew most of what Carlos knew and I guessed. He probably had a much better idea than I of what Carlos wanted from this conversation. That granted me some relief, but only a little. I still felt a bit like I was walking through a darkened minefield, fighting the pull of the grid and the holes in my own knowledge, but I pushed forward with the idea I was getting about what Carlos expected from us, hoping for confirmation in Cameron's response.

"What if Carlos could stand against the Pharaohn . . . ?" I suggested. It wasn't entirely an original idea of mine: The more fractious of Seattle's sanguinary brotherhood, not privy to the reason it was impossible, had muttered in favor of Carlos toppling Edward for as long as I'd known them. As terrifying as the necromancer was, his evident power was attractive to them over the suave manipulation of their now-missing leader.

"That would be a battle worth seeing," Gwen's voice floated from the far end of the sofa.

Cameron and I both turned our heads in her direction.

She gave us a thoughtful smile. "He'd lose, but it would be interesting. And terribly sad." Her voice was still as soft as ever, but the timbre of it had turned to steel in silk. She still dressed like the subject of a Waterhouse painting, but she no longer drifted through her un-life, it seemed, but floated with a disguised will. Underestimating her would be foolish beyond measure, and yet most people probably did. She had become a frightening monster, indeed.

"Why?" I felt compelled to ask.

"It would be tragic to lose Carlos. Ned, though I love him, is too much a fool and too fond of his own ideas. Any strongman among the Seattle pack could replace him with less impact than the death of a mayfly. They are none of them as clever or charming as they imagine, none of them so well equipped for the job as Alice was. But . . . she's gone and no one has the power to destroy the Pharaohn alone. It would take cunning, power, and a perfect opportunity. So, unless Carlos can defeat the Pharaohn through craft and subtlety, Seattle will fall to Wygan."

"Which is worse than you know," I added, thinking very fast on what I knew of the Pharaohn and his abominable children. "Wygan doesn't intend to *rule* Seattle—why should he when it's chaos and fear that he really craves? If Seattle was all he wanted, he'd have killed Edward already. It just happens that everything he needs to gain control of the flow of the Grey is here. And that includes Edward, and Carlos, and me."

Cameron scowled. "Carlos said as much, too. But he won't tell me what the Pharaohn means to do."

"He doesn't know; I do," I said. "Our conversation on the phone was too short for me to tell him." I had difficulty continuing; the chorus of the grid shouted at me to keep silent, to protect it, to say anything other than what lay on the tip of my tongue. But I had to tell them: It was the only way we could do anything to stop Wygan's plans, and though I was sure they had the parts, only I—and probably Carlos—had the whole picture, even if my view of it was a little fuzzy here and there. I had to force words out, like cold molasses drawn through a straw. "You know . . . your world . . . is . . . separate. Protected. . . ."

"Separated from the normal world, concealed. Yes. Protected by a guardian beast—the ultimate Guardian, actually," Cameron finished. "It keeps the normal world from flooding in, and ours from . . . being exposed."

I nodded, mentally thanking Carlos for teaching his protégé well, but selectively. It made my words flow a little easier, but only a little. "Wygan's plan. Is. To change the role. To replace. That Guardian." Some of it was an informed guess, but the heart-stopping difficulty in saying it confirmed I was right.

For a moment they waited, expecting me to go on, but that was all I had.

Cameron figured it out first. "With himself?"

Another nod from me and I could feel the angry constraint of the Grey loosening on my chest. I sagged, catching my strangled breath again.

Gwen finished it. "And from there, magic itself falls into chaos and all creatures such as we are swept up in it. Not just our world, but everywhere that magic flows will become the maelstrom and food for his kind."

I nodded at her, hating that vision, and offered the only solution I could think of: "If Carlos and I can stop Wygan," I suggested, "Seattle would be his for the asking."

"But Carlos has no interest in claiming the city," Cameron said.

"Are you sure?" I asked him, not turning my head away from Gwen as I glanced from the corner of my eye at Cam.

He gave an adamant nod, also keeping his eyes on Gwen. "Oh, yes."

"Could it be forced on him?"

Cameron laughed at me. "You try it."

I shook my head in despair. "So that leaves no one, even if the Pharaohn's plans are defeated. Which they have to be."

"Unless you can rescue Edward," Sarah suggested.

Gwen stroked the other woman's arm, shaking her head with a woeful expression. "Even then, Ned's reign is over. He fell to the enemy; he left the city to the mercy of the mob and the Pharaohn. They won't have him back. Carlos is the only chance we have—and only if he can act independently of Edward."

I took a deep breath before I said, "I think that can be taken care of."

All eyes turned to me. Cameron's gleamed and he nearly smiled. "He said you could do it."

I cut my eyes away from them, not wanting to meet the gazes of two vampires or even Sarah's half-hopeful stare. "I'm not certain, but I believe I have the resources. There is one problem—well, two, really. The Pharaohn can't know it's happened, so we need to divert his attention, convince him that even if Carlos is free, he's no friend of Edward's and more likely to do as Wygan wants."

"Why?" Sarah asked. "Why would Wygan want Carlos to do anything for him? And why would Carlos do it?"

"I don't know the details, but I've been told that the Pharaohn will have to call and trap the Guardian in some kind of spell before he can . . . kill it, I suppose. He can't do it himself since he means to take its place—or maybe the process is too complicated for him alone, I don't know—and he needs the . . . elements, I guess you'd say, that led him to this stage: Edward seems to be one of those. Carlos is the only dark mage powerful and near enough to do the work. If he's become Edward's friend, he would refuse the Pharaohn's request. We don't stand a chance of stopping the creep if he thinks we have the ability to oppose him, to hell with the drive. So long as he thinks we're all his tools or too weak and divided to stop him, we might stand a chance. He is an arrogant bastard, and I think that's the only viable weakness to attack him through. We may have to get very close to the endgame before we can destroy his plans. He'll have to believe we are at his mercy, distracted, naive, or too weak to stop him until it's too late."

They all nodded, which made me feel giddy with nausea. I was making plans with vampires to save the world from monsters even worse than they were.

"For this to work, there has to be someone . . ." I continued, but I couldn't finish; my head was too noisy and my throat clogged with disgust and inarticulate horror. I had to bite my lip to hold back the urge to throw up or start screaming. The emotionless separation I'd experienced before hovered near the back of my head, but even that didn't pull me away from the loathing I felt at what I was saying.

"There has to be a new Prince ready to lay claim to the city," Gwen finished. "It will not be Carlos and it cannot be Ned. It must be someone strong enough, but not of concern to the Pharaohn. Someone he discounts . . ." She looked at Cameron. "You."

Cameron reared back, recoiling from the idea. "I'm no one. The rest of them would tear me apart—I'm a child to them. I have no power, no influence. Without Edward to protect me, and Carlos to teach me, I'd already be dead. And I can't front for Carlos." He made an angry gesture, pointing into the north and then chopping downward. "He doesn't want the job, and as a figurehead to a reluctant Prince, I'm still nothing but dog meat. I don't know enough to keep this pack of animals in line, even if I could convince them I had Carlos or Edward behind me."

Gwen began laughing, a sound both musical and menacing. She clapped her hands, tossing her hair back and jumping to her feet in excitement. "Oh, but *I* do!"

She danced around the room, laughing and talking in spurts. "No one worries about poor, silly little Gwen. No one is afraid of sad, stupid little Gwen. They talk and talk and never guard their tongues; they never hide their dirty little secrets and nasty little plans. And I know them all. I know them all! But they'd never let me be Prince—no, no, not Lady Gwendolyn who couldn't slay anyone, who could never beat a necromancer like Carlos in a battle. But Cameron of Edward? Oh, yes! Cameron who studied at Carlos's knee? Oh, yes!" She threw herself down on the floor in front of Cameron, ignoring me, and reached up to grab his hand. "My Prince, dear Prince, say yes! I'll be your hidden consort and I'll whisper in your ear. I'll tell you everything and they'll all cower like dogs and wonder how you know. Take pity on me, poor, sad little thing that I am, the last of Ned's sorry, sorry mistakes, your warm sister's cold friend, an ineffectual nobody whom no one will suspect."

He pulled his hand away from her, startled and appalled by Gwen's outburst. "It's crazy!" He glanced at Sarah and then at me. "I'm still no one, doubly no one with you as my only supporter. I'd have to have Carlos's backing at the very least, and I'm only his student!"

Sarah gave a "don't look at me" shake of her head. I didn't have a chance to say anything before Gwen chimed in again.

"Then defeat him! If you beat Carlos in some combat or contest, then he's your vassal. He has to support you, but he doesn't have to support Edward!"

"Me? Beat Carlos at . . . anything? Impossible."

"Not if Carlos throws the fight."

Cam and his sister stared at Gwen in dumbfounded silence.

But I nodded, further thinking aloud. "Which, I think, is exactly what he means to do. He said you needed a talking-to . . . that we needed a diversion and commitment to show Wygan. . . . Not a commitment to the Pharaohn, because he wouldn't believe that, but against—or at least not in favor of—Edward. I'm not sure this is exactly what he meant, but it could work. . . ."

Cameron still looked a bit unsure. "He said something like that, but I thought it was insane."

Gwen smiled at me and it flipped my stomach over cold. Then she turned back to Cameron. "If you and Carlos have a public falling-out about Ned and who's going to hold power while he's missing, that's not a move against him on Carlos's part. If you come to blows and Carlos loses—even for a ridiculous reason—no one else would want to challenge you after that. The city *would* be yours! And the Pharaohn will believe Carlos is on his side if only to harm you and Ned." Her eyes gleamed dreadful red. "Then Carlos can get close to the Pharaohn and destroy him. Before he can take the Guardian's place. It will work. It will."

I felt a little less sanguine about it but confined my comments to saying, "Now we just have to figure out the timing of everything else."

Cameron looked at the rest of us, his expression hardening from dismay and incredulity to cold determination. "Tomorrow." He gave me a hard look. "You'll have to get to Carlos immediately—now!" He glared at Gwen and Sarah. "And we'll have to start agitating tonight so it will look as if Carlos is coming after me as soon as word reached him." He checked his watch—an expensively understated thing. "We can get to the After Dark by eleven if we leave now." He glanced back to me, as if he heard the objection forming on my tongue. "It has to be now. Enough time's slipped by us already, and the longer we wait, the closer Wygan gets to his goals. Our activity tonight will help mask yours, but there's no margin for error. I can see you're tired, that things are falling apart for you, but all the better reason to move as soon as possible. I'll work out the details and send you the plan for tomorrow by e-mail."

Then he paused, a moment's uncertainty crossing his face. "I owe you my life—such as it is. I can't give that back, but . . . maybe I can return the favor. The longer we wait, the less likely that becomes."

Cameron stood up in a sudden fluid movement, pulling Gwen with him to her feet and holding his other hand out to his sister. "Come on, then."

There was a flurry of grabbing coats against the summer's moist night wind—vampires don't need coats, but they do need camouflage—before Cameron herded us all out the door. He paused to give me one more odd look as Sarah and Gwen went down the hall. "Be careful, Harper."

"If I were careful, we never would have met."

He only gave me a sardonic smile in return and followed the women.

I called Quinton on my way to pick up the Rover and left him an undetailed update on my situation. I mentioned Will's appearance and told him to keep an eye on the monitors for anything else that might lurk in the urban jungle nearby. I didn't tell him exactly what I was going to do. In theory the line was clean, but I felt paranoid enough to speak in generalities and hope he would fill in the blanks.

TWENTY-EIGHT

I didn't know if I hoped that Carlos was home or that he wasn't. The street through what had once been a cemetery seemed as dark as ever and possibly more haunted. The ghost mist seemed to hum now, and it glowed in lambent colors as the voices of the grid muttered in my head. The névoacria crept across the landscape, flanking me like an honor guard, flickering in and out of existence as we went on.

I passed through Carlos's hellish garden and found him glowering at me from the open darkness of the front doorway. He waved me in without a word.

I passed him and stopped in the living room, shuddering a little as the heat and cold radiating from the magic circle below brushed over my bones and added its voice to the chorus in my mind. I still had the broken Lâmina carefully wrapped up in my pocket, and the circle seemed to reach for it and want it. Perhaps it was drawn to the blade because it was similar to something that was part of the circle's creator, or maybe it was just the nature of Carlos and his magic to want dark things.

"Did you have any idea Gwen was a devious mastermind?" I asked as Carlos entered the room.

He raised an eyebrow. "You met Cameron at his sister's home, then."

"Don't act like that wasn't what you intended."

"I left that to Cameron. He has an interesting friendship with Edward's other renovated error. Perhaps near-starvation made her sharper—she was certainly unremarkable when she walked in the daylight."

I gave him a narrow stare. "You're going to just love her plan. You get to publicly pick and lose a fight with Cam over who has Edward's best interests—and those of the city's vampires—at heart. Cam gets to be Prince of the City, with Gwen behind the throne, and you get to help me foul up Wygan's plans and kill him before he replaces the Guardian Beast. All in the next twenty-four to forty-eight hours, depending on how fast the Pharaohn and his henchmen react to the rumors Cam, Gwen, and Sarah are busy spreading right now."

"I'm impressed. Cameron exceeds my hopes for him."

"He seemed to think you were a little disappointed that he isn't much of a necromancer."

Carlos snorted. "Only initially. Edward had an excellent eye for potential—it's too bad that he's usually only wasted, perverted, or destroyed it. He brought Cameron and Gwen into our community, and they have both proved to have exceptional depths no one yet recognizes."

"No one but you."

He made a half nod of acknowledgment, keeping his hands clasped low in front of himself and his stance as solid as a tor. He reminded me of a bouncer or a bodyguard when he stood that way, but the only thing he was guarding was himself. In the ghostlight, with the illumination of the grid's whispering in my head, I could see that the black weight of his magic and his past pressed him hard onto the earth. "They'll do well together."

"Cam and Gwen? Maybe. But only if the rest of this works. You'll have to pick the fight in a way that makes it clear to Wygan that you're not on Edward's side, while not putting Cameron there either."

"I understand the situation," he replied. "You will have to witness it yourself."

I shook my head. "No one said anything about my being involved in any vampire dominance games."

"A witness, Blaine. You are the neutral party everyone trusts. They know you've helped all of us and have no personal stake in who rules. I'll make it easy. Trust me: I have learned how to lose in all the centuries of my existence. You'll have no difficulty with that. It is this other that may challenge you."

"This," I said, pulling the silk-wrapped bundle from my pocket.

Carlos swayed a half-inch away from the iron knife in its black shroud. The buzzing and chattering in my head swelled to a dizzying volume. I could not help bringing my free hand to my face to wipe the sudden cold sweat that broke over me.

"I wish it didn't have to be now," I muttered. I was afraid of what might happen, of how close I would have to come to the grid and whether I could stay separate—I won't pretend I wasn't. The emptiness and inhumanity of it repelled me, but the overwhelming power pulled like gravity. And I was tired, perhaps too weak to resist. . . .

Carlos raised his left hand and touched my shoulder with a single finger, as if he saw something on my jacket. The light pressure of that one finger reverberated through me as if through a timpani. I clenched my teeth until it passed. Then I looked at him through narrowed eyes.

He seemed to have expected my reaction, but he didn't show any satisfaction in it. "I know, but it must be now. You're shattering, coming close to the edge of the web itself. That is the moment the Pharaohn will act. We must act first. If you die without his control to hold you in place, all this may drain away and you will be useless."

I pushed my suddenly damp hair off my forehead and glared at him. "I wish people wouldn't keep talking about my dying like it's no big deal. It's a big one to me."

Carlos laughed at my grousing tone. My temperature fell again as the sleet sound of it swept through me. "If you die before I do, I shall miss you, Blaine."

"Like a favorite lab rat, maybe."

He didn't respond to that. He just looked past me to the cellar door. "Let us be about it, then. Before you grow too weary. I trust you have everything you need?"

"I think so." Knife, ball, bad attitude, and all, I thought. Oh goody: magical surgery for amateurs. The idea made me sick. The act would probably be worse.

I followed him once more down to the basement. This time I knew enough to keep well to the edge of the room and watch where I put my feet. The foundation stones left ashen marks on my clothes as I passed. Carlos moved to the circle without hesitation, snatching something off one of his workbenches as he passed and crossing over the singeing red and black lines with no qualm—but it was his circle and still unclosed. I doubted it would be so friendly to me. He stopped in the center of the open space within the glowing arcs and swirls.

"How do you intend to shield this action from the Pharaohn's knowledge?" he asked.

"In part that's why Cameron and the others are starting their whisper campaign—to give the other side something else to pay attention to tonight. But I did find my back door and if it works as my father says, we'll do it there."

Carlos looked wary. "This back door . . ."

"It leads to a sort of maze inside the Grey. The doors are one-way unless you have the key. Dru Cristoffer made it, if that's any recommendation."

Carlos looked intrigued and much less worried. "Recently?"

"No."

"And I've never heard of it. Clever of her."

"Given the way she hid it, I'm sure keeping *anyone* from hearing of it was exactly what she had in mind."

"Did you meet her?"

The question was too casual. Knowing the twisted way Carlos's mind tended to run, I wanted to say "no," but I was sure I couldn't lie to him in this room. Instead I said nothing at all while the noises of the grid clattered in my head. In a moment he cut his glance aside and the sound eased.

"Step into the circle, there," he directed, pointing to a place on the floor where the design was thinner and darker. "Bring all you need. Once the circle—"

"Yes, I know how a magic circle works," I interrupted him, irritable and rubbed raw by the constant hot and cold sensation across my nerves, fed by the babbling voices in my head and the growing draw of passionless silence. I put down my bag, grabbed the ball from it, checked my pockets for the key, and transferred the knife from my jacket to my hand. I thought that should be everything. As an afterthought, I turned off my cell phone—it just seemed like a bad idea to have it go off while I was trying this—and left the jacket behind with my purse. It was cold in the cellar workroom, but the ease of movement would be more important than warmth. Besides, no amount of clothing had ever negated the chill of the Grey.

With the wrapped Lâmina and the puzzle clutched to my chest, I stepped, cringing inside, over the darkened line of Carlos's containment spells. The lines of the circle throbbed but remained quiescent.

Carlos glanced at me and cocked his head, frowning. "Are you afraid?"

"Wouldn't you—" I started before I realized how stupid that idea was and shut up.

He made a sound in his chest that wasn't quite a chuckle and a quirk at the corner of his mouth that definitely wasn't a smile. "Yes." Then he threw something hard at the ground where the circle was dim. The small, dark thing shattered on the smooth black floor in a chime of breaking glass, spreading a spill of red liquid that ran into the lines, flowing into the dim voids, to complete the shapes and close the circle with the iron scent of blood.

Carlos caught my startled expression and gave me an amused glance. "It's hard to close one properly from the inside. That's sloppy but effective. Nothing from the outside will interrupt us. Let us hope nothing from the inside will, either. Proceed," he added, stepping as far back as the circle would allow.

I was leery of letting Carlos anywhere near the puzzle ball or the key that would make it into a doorway to the Grey's hidden places. While I knew we were bound together by the geas, that didn't mean I could trust him, and things of power were always of interest to Carlos. These weren't dark artifacts, but they were magical.

I didn't have much choice, however. I shoved the knife awkwardly into my back pocket. Then I unlocked the puzzle ball with the odd little key while Carlos watched, frowning. The inner door of the ghost labyrinth spilled open and filled the room, wiping out the solid appearance of the walls and ceiling in the shimmering maze of the mist-world. This time there was no barrier between me and the man with me; I could still see Carlos, though it seemed he was distant in the fog.

"Oh, little girl, no. Not yet."

I turned around and looked down the long bending corridor of mist to the spectral form of my father, half eaten by the boiling wall of tormented faces. "Dad?" I glanced back at Carlos, who hadn't moved, though he was getting clearer, which I thought meant he was getting into the labyrinth somehow. I returned my attention to Dad. "I know. I know it's not time. But I need to be here for a little while and . . . I need to ask you something while I can. What happened to Christelle? Your receptionist? Did . . . did you . . . ?"

"Kill her? I thought I had at the time. In a way I did. But it wasn't quite Christelle anymore. The Pharaohn's ushabti . . . took her over in some way. That one was a puppet master—the ushabti are all different just like you and I are different from each other. I didn't know what any of them were, didn't know about vampires and asetem and that they aren't the same. I didn't know about dhampirs, or that the ushabti can walk in the daylight. I couldn't know or guess. . . . I only saw Christelle and knew she wasn't really . . . normal anymore. I didn't know she was a shell, animated by something inhuman. I didn't want to hurt her. . . . I let her linger too long, spying, keeping the real Chris from leaving. Do you know—does she haunt the office? I thought she might, but . . . I can't go there."

"She does. She's confused. She doesn't know you're gone."

"Oh, poor girl. If you can, tell her what happened. Maybe she'll go on."

"What did happen, Dad?"

"The ushabti killed her. The Pharaohn used to tell me about it: He smothered her, so she wouldn't have any marks I could see, and when they were done with her, they buried what was left in a landfill in Torrance."

"Torrance? On the hill heading to Palos Verdes?"

"I think so."

"That's a botanical garden now."

"Oh. Thank God it's not a dump anymore. I hated thinking of her like that."

Carlos's voice came from a distance, buzzing with red noise from the Grey. "Blaine . . . ?"

"I have to go, Dad. I'll let you out of here soon."

"You mustn't. He'll know."

"I'm not going to leave you in this place for eternity. I just need to know how to undo what the Pharaohn did."

"Ah, that's the easy part: remove anything crossing the core that isn't blue. But you'll never get to help me without dooming yourself. Just leave the doorways open. We'll all go up in smoke together."

"I won't—"

"Oh, my little girl, don't make my death useless. I can still save you from some of this, from giving way to the grid forever. We're fluid when we die. Some things we gain; some things we lose. Some can be carried away forever. I was a terrible father and I can't make you what you were never meant to be, but . . . I can make you safer." And he pushed on the living Grey, making a wave of pressure that shoved me back.

"Dad!" I screamed as he forced me away from him, slamming a door between us.

"Blaine!"

I turned and ran through the sudden twists of the maze to the center and into Carlos, who was glowering at me.

"Where have you been?"

I was surprised that I wasn't crying or shaking. "To visit my father. I don't think I'll have a chance again."

The necromancer growled at me and my skin crawled with goose bumps. But I glared back at him. "Don't rush me. I needed some information. He's been haunting the Pharaohn since I was twelve and, like Gwen, no one's been paying him any attention while he listened to everything they said. Sometimes it's useful to interrogate the invisible man. He told me what Wygan is planning."

"Did he."

"Yes," I snapped back. "And I'll tell you as soon as I get that . . . thing out of your chest. Because, frankly, I would like out of this place as soon as possible."

"It is not a pleasant place," he agreed and I goggled at

him. Never would I have expected such a sentiment from him.

I took a steadying breath. Carlos sat down on the misty floor, crossing his legs and bracing his arms behind him.

"What are you doing?" I asked.

"Reducing the distance I'll fall when you pull that wretched fragment out. Don't imagine it will be painless. For either of us."

I hadn't thought of it at all and that bothered me: Was I becoming callous? Was the unemotional distance of the grid taking over? I preferred to think I was sure of Carlos's lack of feeling rather than any of my own, but in truth, it hadn't occurred to me to worry about it. If Carlos hadn't been a vampire, would I have? I hadn't given any thought to this process. I didn't know what to do or how it would work, if at all. I assumed I could do it because I had the tools—the power—but what if I couldn't . . . ?

Carlos grabbed one of my wrists and yanked me all the way down to his level. The furious cold of his touch froze my lungs and bound up my chest in ice and agony. "It won't be complicated: The Lâmina wants to be whole again and you've only to help it come together. Just be sure the smaller part comes to the larger and not the other way around. And slowly, or what blood I have will spill like water. You will not wish to be the only warm, human thing within reach if it does."

I knew what any animal would do to maintain its life and I knew he would do the same and more. My choices had gone the moment I'd walked through his door and now I had to do this right. I felt a moment of panic like smoke in my chest. I yanked my arm back from him, fighting his superior strength without thinking. My shoulder popped and creaked, near to dislocating before he let go. I fell back, the hard, silk-padded bulk of the blade in my pocket jabbing into my buttock. I was panting and the shrieking of the grid in my mind drove my fear into tightening circles, but the sudden hard thump of the knife startled me and shocked the last of my breath from my lungs in a sad little squeak.

The seconds that I lay in the mist, breathless and stunned, silenced the voices and I took my first new breath quivering but not afraid. I gulped in a few more lungfuls before I could look at Carlos again. He made no move, no indication that anything was amiss. He just sat where he was and waited.

"All right," I told myself. "OK. Let's do this and get it over with." Carlos didn't make any acknowledgment of my muttering.

I crept across the silver fog that obscured the floor, the lines of the circle gleaming like dim neon miles away below the ghostly maze.

I pulled the wrapped Lâmina from my pocket as I knelt in front of Carlos.

He held one hand out flat, palm upward and thumb tucked across it. "When you hold the knife, hold it in your palm like this, your fingers flat under the blade. Your hand becomes the knife, your arm the tang. Then cut. Like this," he added, his hand curving upward and toward my own heart. "But slowly."

He unbuttoned and opened his shirt so I could see the dusky amber of his skin marked with a thick scar nearly as broad as my own palm. The scar curved a little, raised into a long ridge that gleamed like oily water in the ghostlight. Low and to the left of his sternum, the uneven crescent made me think the blow had come from below, underhanded. Just like the urge that had driven it.

I nodded, tucking the still-wrapped knife into my hand as he'd shown, letting the silk fall away to a single layer between us. Carlos shut his eyes as a tremor moved under his skin. I sank down toward the grid, letting the color swell and burn out the mist of the labyrinth until there was only a thin smoke of substance clothing the lines and tangles of power in the world. The energy seemed to rush up, much hotter and more urgent than the cold steam of the Grey had ever been. The fearful silence stayed at bay this time, but I felt it nearby.

In the blazing net of the grid, Carlos, a smear of tangled threads wrapped in shadow, looked dim and weak but for a burning ruby ember at the core, gleaming like one of Dru

Cristoffer's earrings. A dull void of light or color—triangular and sharp—stirred across the face of the ruby that pulsed once, slowly, and shuddered as the dark thing scored across it. I wanted to stare into this fire wrapped in darkness and watch the gleaming heart of it as it trembled against the black shape, beautiful and horrifying. Then the voices were crying in my head that it was a heart, his heart, this burning thing was Carlos's heart. The black shape was the broken tip of the Lâmina, stirring toward its missing part, cutting as it moved.

I tasted bile as I forced myself to action, pushing my hand toward his chest, toward the cloud of blackness that shrouded the fiery heart. I felt cold pressure against my fingertips, but I could barely see them. I put my other hand out flat against him, feeling the scar, the shape of his rib cage and muscles, invisible but solid and shockingly cold beneath my palm. I felt his shudder and the whispering told me to press with both hands, flat with one and forward with the other, press. . . . I felt the scar part at my fingertips as they sank into his skin. . . .

I had reached into zombies and into ghosts, into the warped and furious constructs of human madness, ambition, and anger, but never into a solid, living thing before. Though he was undead, as a vampire, Carlos still had the solid flesh of a live human being, cold as it was. One would have thought he didn't need a heart and could feel nothing in that dead organ, and yet apparently he did. As my hand holding the knife pushed into his body, I tried to shut off my mind, tried not to gag as he tensed and shivered and the slow substance of his body resisted my cutting. I pinched the fingers of my other, flat hand into the trailing silk and let it pull away as the blade on my palm sank into him, drawing my hand into the cold flesh.

The naked blade sang to its missing tip and the dark triangle twitched toward it, cutting a path by centimeters across the vampire's heart. Brilliant golden light oozed in the wake of the black shape and wrung a sound of suffering from Carlos's throat.

I trembled also, every movement was so slow, hard fought for every half-inch, that my muscles ached with fatigue and knowing what I was doing sickened me. I wanted it over with. I could barely stand any more of this creeping torment. The perverse chorus in my mind teased me that I could kill him at any moment, if I wanted, that I did not have to follow the route already made. . . .

I eased the blade sideways, cutting further to the inside of his chest than the original path and pressing hard on the plane of his upper chest as he jerked against the sudden change of motion. A growling cry boiled out of him as the broken point wheeled sideways, nicking a deeper golden line in the blazing scarlet heart as it moved to align with its parent blade. I tightened the muscles of my arm and thrust harder into the new incision. I cut into his body, urging the knife to meet its missing part sooner.

The bloodless meat below his ribs gave reluctant way and the jagged edges of the Lâmina yearned toward each other. The point turned a bit further, making one last bright line, thin as a hair, across the surface of his heart as it pulled from it. A slow golden haze slid over the ruby fire, gleaming as Carlos shivered and buckled backward a little. I shuffled forward on my knees to keep the blade from ripping out of his unseen flesh and felt the Lâmina quivering like a tuning fork in my grip.

I looked down, setting myself into position to continue, and saw the glitter of gold fade off his heart's surface. I froze in terror, thinking I'd miscalculated and destroyed Carlos, but he shuddered, not yet truly dead. I stared at the black shape of the blood blade within the skein of red fire and black smoke and noticed the point had cleared the bright knot of his heart and changed shape. The broken edges of the blade seemed to reach toward each other, thinning and elongating until they touched and bound. The blade lurched in my grip, as if it could not wait any longer to meet its missing part, and I hauled backward to stop its hungry lunge.

The separated pieces rang together and the Lâmina vibrated, tolling like a bell and surging in my hand. I braced myself and pulled against it, hoping I was guessing right. The knife drew reluctantly from Carlos's undead flesh. I lurched backward, back into the ordinary Grey, as the blade came free. I wrapped the black silk scarf over it at once, hiding it and binding it tightly, afraid it might move on its own. I scooted back, away from Carlos, keeping the knife bundled in my hand as I groped for the key that would shut the maze and dump us back into the cellar.

The moment I touched the key to the walls of the maze it collapsed as if it, too, had been impatient to escape from my nightmarish work. Even the bloody red lines of Carlos's magic circle seemed comforting after what I'd just done. I shivered and hugged myself against the incorporeal cold as I sat on the glassy black floor, tucking my head down against my knees.

I could feel Carlos stirring before I bothered to look for him. He was back on his feet, if a little less steady than usual, his shirt already buttoned. He glanced at me and the dark gleam in his eye frightened me to the bone.

He stepped close to me and put out his hand. "May I have the blade." A demand, not a question.

I started to hand it over but paused, clutching it in its silk swaddling and holding it aside. "Only if you promise not to use it on me."

He raised an eyebrow. "I do so swear. Never on you." His sharp white teeth shone in the gloom.

"And no fangs either. I'm not a blood donor."

He chuckled. "Very well."

His hand remained where it was, still waiting for me to hand over the Lâmina. I wondered if there was anything else I should say before I gave it to him, but no suggestions came to mind. The grid's chorus was suddenly quiet.

I put the black-wrapped knife into his hand. His lips curled into his wolf's grin. Then he flicked the scarf away from the dreadful object and looked at it in the ruddy light from the circle.

He tilted it back and forth, his gaze running over the restored blade like a touch. "Perfect. Now it *is* mine—of my blood, undying." His smile was cruel and showed his sharp teeth to the darkness. He turned and slashed the knife through the circle, felling the protective barrier.

He stepped out and I was quick to follow, however ungracefully from my sitting position. I scrambled to my feet as he wiped the blade clean on its wrapping.

"You've done excellent work, though I thought you meant to kill me."

"You trusted me," I replied. "I don't betray people."

"Yes, generally. But you didn't do as I told you. You changed the path of the blade."

I started gathering my things, more than ready to be out of his house—forever, I hoped. I didn't look at him as I moved around, not sure I could stand the sight right now. "If I'd let it come out the way it went in, the tip would have had to travel most of the way through your heart from top to bottom. Once I knew the path was immaterial, that the pieces would take the most direct route to each other, I pulled the blade to the side and shortened the path the tip would take. That's all."

"You could see the tip moving through me?"

"Yes. I could see everything. I'd like not to see it again." I shrugged into my jacket.

He was behind me and I didn't know how he'd gotten there. "The voices trouble you."

"Not right now. They were helpful this time, but mostly they wear me down."

"Do you understand what they are?"

"It's the grid—the weft, whatever you call it."

"It is the collective of souls, born and unborn, the consciousness and body of the power. You cannot lie so close to the warp of magic without hearing it. You cannot banish it. It is the material of the Grey, the ghost body, the mind that does not know itself. That is why it requires a Guardian. Or two. You are the Guardian's hands and eyes on the hard side of the veil. It could not recognize you until you accepted it. You belong to the Grey and it to you."

"Why are you telling me this?" I asked, turning.

"I owe you for this." He let the dim light of the room play over the dark blade of the Lâmina.

"You won't be so pleased when I tell you what Wygan plans to do."

"Ah. Yes."

"He's going to take the Guardian's place. He means to kill it, according to my father, and become a sort of . . . Anti-Guardian, I guess. 'The Architect of the Grey,' Dad said—

the creator of a new purpose for all that magical potential. Someone told me the asetem thrive on chaos, pain, terror, and other strong negative emotions. You said the Pharaohn yearns to be like a god again and strengthen his brood. What could be better for that purpose than turning the power of the Grey loose on the world and letting his spawn feed as they like on what would happen after that? No restraint, no Guardian Beast to stop him, and all that power, pouring into the world like the flood from a broken dam. . . ."

Carlos became thoughtful, his gaze wandering to some dread vision as he contemplated my words.

"It would be hell on earth."

The words rolled on, mine and not mine, unrestrained and cold with truth. "You still want to stop it? Edward has no more hold over you and therefore neither does Wygan. You don't have to do what he wants, nor do you have to stop him. In fact, you don't have to do anything for anyone, if it doesn't please you." There was the geas between us, but in the gleam off the Lâmina and glow of the grid, it was as fragile as frost flowers.

The glare he turned on me was black and painful. "The warp has turned your mind. What feeds the Pharaohn does not suit me. And I also don't betray my friends."

TWENTY-NINE

I didn't understand what Carlos had meant. I could barely keep myself upright enough to leave and was too exhausted to puzzle around with it for long. Which friends? Me, Cameron, Edward? I felt broken by the long events of the day, the horror, difficulty, and revelation. Not to mention being half crazy and all tired. I longed for the reassuring clutter and familiarity of my condo, with the ferret living up to her name by burrowing in the bookshelves and tossing paperbacks onto the floor—that was the only sort of chaos I desired. After this I might change the furball's name. . . .

And Quinton. I was surprised that I missed him after only five hours apart. We didn't live together and I normally didn't mind my solitude—preferred it in fact—but now I wanted the comfort of his presence, a warm body wrapped around mine, not some cold construct of undead flesh like a cadaver that won't lie still. I couldn't understand why normal people fell for the glamour of vampires. Even cloaked in magic, the fact that they were the living dead should make an impression at some point *before* you shucked your clothes or bared your throat. Shouldn't the atavistic lizard brain kick in and let you know there's something deeply wrong with the thing you're snuggling up to, magic or no? Ugh. . . . Even thinking about it made me queasy and in want of something warmer and more reassuring.

It was nearly three in the morning when I got back down to Edward's apartment in the TPM basement, but Quinton was still up, pottering around with the computer suite. Some people drink when they're worried; Quinton tinkers. He got up to let me in since we still couldn't touch the doors themselves from the outside, but after a brief hug, he dragged me with him back to the monitors embedded in the conference table.

He pulled me onto his lap and reached around me to type. "Look what I found."

I collapsed against him with only enough energy to mutter, "Oh, rotten, dear. How did *your* evening go?"

He squeezed me and kissed the side of my neck. "I know. I'm sorry. I know you did hard things and you want to go to bed, but I found something I think is very useful here. Tomorrow's Monday, so I think we'll be able to track Solis down and get him to bring the info to the investigators."

"Huh? Why would we want Solis? Are we having someone arrested?"

"No, not 'we' as in you and me. Carol and me. And it's Goodall we want nabbed. See, this footage should have been wiped, but Goodall's not an alpha geek: He didn't completely destroy the image, only the file system information. That's probably what he was doing down here when you came to see El Jefe Sanquino. Now tell me this doesn't look like a digital image capture of Renfield Jr. kidnapping Seattle's favorite bloodsucking entrepreneur."

Contrary to popular film and fiction, most vampires show up just fine on video, so long as they aren't making an effort to obscure themselves by hiding in the Grey. They do look a little out of focus most of the time, however. This particular recording did look awful; it hurt my head to try and watch it.

I was so tired I didn't even pick a fight about Quinton's going to Solis with Edward's secretary Carol, and I wasn't sure the crappy image was due to damage to the electronic file or if it was me. On the center screen, hazy, low-quality video of the bunker's elevator lobby jerked forward in a storm of digital snow. Goodall was recognizable—his size and bearing were distinctive, even on a video screen where the color was messed up and no Grey auras showed. He put his card on the reader plate while he kept his other hand clenched at his left side and waited for the door to open.

Edward stepped into the doorway, holding out both arms to keep the bronze-covered door wide open for his security chief to enter. But Goodall didn't pass through the door. He took a step forward, swinging his left fist up into Edward's ribs. It wasn't a hard blow, but the static bloomed in a white flash where he struck the vampire and Edward collapsed in a heap. Goodall bent down, tossed something behind him onto the foyer floor, and then grabbed Edward under the armpits to drag him out of the doorway. He never touched the door itself and got out of its way as quickly as possible, dragging the downed bloodsucker along the carpet another yard or so before he snatched up the dropped object. Then he crouched, dead-lifted Edward, and flung the unconscious vampire onto his shoulder before he vanished from the scene.

I blinked at the snowy screen. "What the. . . ."

"Want to see it again?"

"I'm not sure . . . what happened? I mean he can't have taken Edward out with a single punch. Vampires aren't that fragile."

"He didn't; he stunned him." Quinton typed and poked the mouse a bit until he had a close-up of a frame where Goodall hit Edward. Even through the white confusion of the electric arc, I could see the small black horns of the stun stick protruding from Goodall's hand. Quinton advanced the frames so I could see the small device flung across the room. Then he zoomed in on it and tweaked the still a bit until it was a little more clear.

"That looks like one of yours."

"Not quite, but similar. You know you can't buy one in this state unless you're an officer of the law or the court. If you need to back someone off, you have to use another method or make your own. So what I'm thinking is all that craziness in the underground with vampires zapping other vampires was Wygan's guys experimenting to see what voltage they needed to use and what happened if they got it wrong. They didn't steal any of my stun sticks; they just started working on the idea themselves—maybe they even thought they could blame it on me and you. Whoever's building the stunners doesn't know as much about the technology as I do, so they had to do a lot more calibration and experimentation. They probably had to find out if Edward really was immune—he always implied that he was—before they even tried it. It probably took a while before you left for Goodall to get that information. And as soon as he had that and confirmation that you were in England and too far away to help—bam!"

"And Edward's reclusiveness helped cover up his absence. Why did Goodall come forward with the missing boss story at all . . . ?"

"Edward's secretary reported it. Carol. The one who let us in. I called her. Edward had her phone numbers on the desk phone speed dial. All of them."

I blinked and rattled the information into place in my brain. "Oh, *that* Carol. You call innocent secretaries in the dead of night to ask about their missing bosses?"

"I learn from the best: Get 'em while their defenses are down. Besides, she wasn't sleeping and she's not innocent. She's an insomniac, which I think is how she met Edward in the first place, and she was his favorite blood donor until Goodall showed up. I guess they were 'sharing the love,' so to speak, after that."

"She could be pointing the finger at Goodall out of jealousy."

"She didn't say much about him, actually. And that clip isn't doctored that I can see. Goodall bumped him, all right. Also, I got the idea that something Edward does or something about the bite itself helps her sleep. She's effectively addicted to him, but like any drug, too much would have killed her. So she didn't mind that her . . . doses of Edward were smaller. But she did notice when he didn't show up at all for a couple of days."

"Did she tell the investigating officer?"

"Only that he'd been missing for a couple of days and that she normally saw him every day or two on business. She never claimed Kammerling had been kidnapped and she didn't accuse Goodall of anything. She assumed he's like she is: some kind of addicted donor. When she started working with the police and FBI on the disappearance, she started hiding things from them—the sort of things a vampire's buddies usually hide from the daylight world—and finding a few herself, like doctored security logs for key access to this floor. My guess is that Goodall changed the logs and wiped or doctored the security recordings for the cameras and monitors in the room down here."

"But not this one? How did he miss it?" My brain was sluggish. I felt I was missing something. . . .

"He didn't. He tried to wipe it out but he's not the hacker I am, and this recording is from one of Edward's own backups, which Goodall didn't have direct access to once the door locked and Carol had him taken off the security pass list. He tried to get at it through the remote backup system, but . . . he's an end user and he doesn't know how to really make a computer record disappear. And if it's not wiped out in binary hash or physically destroyed, I can find it. Especially with direct access to said computer."

I nodded and scrubbed my face with my hands, trying to shove away the muzzy feeling that had settled on my brain. Quinton pulled my hands down and kissed my cheek. He tucked me tight against him and pressed my head onto his shoulder. I wanted to fall asleep there.

"Sweetheart, I'm sorry. I'm trying to make things easier, but I guess I'm just making them more complicated. And here I am running off at the mouth about my end. . . . I don't know what you've had to do tonight—don't even try to tell me now—but it couldn't have been easy or pleasant, what with Novak and the vampires and Carlos. You go to sleep and I'll take care of this."

"Take care of it . . . how?" I mumbled.

"I'll get the files cleaned up and together, and Carol and I will take them to Solis in the morning."

"No. You can't go: He'll arrest you."

"For what? For supposedly being a homeless drug addict who's cleaning up his act and being a Boy Scout? He won't. He'll suspect me of something, but not this. Solis is a fair guy. He's the only one I can trust, but he's not the point man on this case. He'll need more than Carol's word to believe the information is good and take it to the team. This is the evidence that can bring the case out of the darkness and into the real world. Carol will give it weight to keep me out of trouble. And it's one less job for you to do, so you can sleep in while I'm talking to Solis. Then I'll show you the Grey dampener I've been working on and we'll take care of the rest of this mess tomorrow night."

"Why you? Can't you just give the recording to Carol and let her deal with Solis?"

Quinton shook his head. "Convincing the cops will take some technical expertise and that's my bailiwick. If it works, the feds might arrest Goodall before Wygan can put the last of his plan into motion and that may buy you some time. It's a little risky but trust me: It'll work out."

I made a grunt of protest; there was something wrong with what he was telling me and it would hurt him, I was certain, but I couldn't put it together and I couldn't keep my mind working against the pull of sleep to say so. I needed to tell him about tomorrow night and Carlos and all the rest, but it floated away before I could make the words. I tried to shake my head, but with me cuddled up against his chest, it just turned into a dopey nuzzle.

Quinton kissed the top of my head and stood up, keeping me clutched against him. He carried me to a couch and tucked me in to sleep under the blanket, and I don't remember what he did next. It didn't involve any naked snuggling, though, which was disappointing.

I know our bodies do most of their healing while we sleep. While we're inactive, our brains sort through our activities and anxieties, making dreams and cleaning up the mental litter while the rest of the system goes into repair and restore mode. It's also when most people die. Accidents and violence aside, it's while asleep that most people shuffle off their mortal coil and leave the physical world for whatever lies beyond the far side of the Grey, where even the Guardian Beast doesn't go.

It was well after noon when I finally woke up, and Quinton was gone. The buzzing voice of the grid pulled me out of sleep and I woke up, blinking, into a world ablaze. The colors of the grid had bled up into the world overnight, or I'd stopped holding them back, and everything I looked at was brighter than I could stand. As I walked across the floor, it seemed to ripple silver and blue under my steps, little waves breaking outward as if the surface of the world were a thin membrane stretched over luminous water. Every movement I made seemed to whisper across the burning threads of the grid. I might have been able to push them back, but I just didn't care to expend the energy and find out. This was the state Wygan had pushed me toward for so long and I'd fought it once, but that had only left me weak and unable to use the state to my advantage. I didn't care to be in that position the next time I was deep in the Grey—and I would be unless something in the current situation changed more than I could imagine.

Showering felt strange: My skin was too sensitive and the water felt effervescent and sharp. Every step of my usual routine was fraught with oddity: scents that were too strong or out of place; sounds that came too clearly to my ears; touches and sensations on my skin and fingers that were too rough, too cold, too hot. Even the taste of an apple I found in the kitchen was too sour and too sweet at the same time. I wore the softest clothes I had and kept the lights low.

I read my e-mail, including Cameron's instructions for the evening, with the screen dimmed nearly black. Beside the computer, I found a note Quinton had left for me—handwritten on a single sheet of paper—saying he'd gone with Carol to talk to Solis. He thought he'd be back about two. But it was just passing that and he wasn't back. I tried calling the numbers for Carol on Edward's phone but only got voice mail and had to leave messages asking for updates. Finally I left a long note for Quinton myself, telling him what had happened the night before and what was going to play out tonight.

Beyond the facts, I had to include my speculation, too. I didn't know if we had one day left or only tonight until Dru Cristoffer's deadline for the puzzle balls expired. Guessing based on her personality, I suspected she'd be literal and give me seventy-two hours exactly from when she'd declared it. That meant I'd have to act with Carlos as soon as the matter of vampire succession was settled. I didn't know where Wygan would stage his Grey coup, but if Carlos was right about the timing, it had to be ready to go the moment I was, so it had to be someplace nearby and already prepped.

I'd already touched the fabric of the grid and bent it to my own designs—badly and in a limited way—but that would be all Wygan was waiting for and I was pretty sure he already knew it had happened. His own connections to the grid weren't the same as mine, but it was clear to me that he could sense or hear things happening there, too. So far, he'd had only one chance to grab me and that had been too soon after my experiment with the power lines of magic in the walls of Edward's bunker to give him much time to come for me. The easiest thing for him to do now would be to let Goodall catch me and take me himself to wherever the Pharaohn's plans were meant to play out. I didn't like the role of goat, but I didn't see a lot of options, and I knew that no matter how much Goodall disliked me, his master wouldn't let him harm me at this stage. I imagined that my presence at the After Dark club would bring someone around if I lingered long enough.

After that, it was a matter of action and, whatever the result, it would be over by morning. Live or die, I had to succeed in stopping the Pharaohn's plans for good tonight.

I wrote another long letter, folded it, and put it in my purse. Still no sign of Quinton or Carol and the time was now four thirty. I didn't have much of a window left to get the last of my business done before night fell and things got crazy.

My first stop was Nanette Grover's law office downtown. I worked for her once in a while, doing backgrounds on witnesses and investigating their stories before Nan went into court. She also acted as my lawyer on the rare occasions I needed one. It was an easy walk to her office from TPM, though I had to wear sunglasses under the overcast sky: The grid was too brightly present without them. Her secretary, Cathy, came out to meet me and it took a little discussion before she agreed to hold on to my holographic will for forty-eight hours. I said I'd come back and tear it up if everything went well, but I didn't explain why it might be necessary in the first place. Mostly I wanted to be sure the property and pets scattered across Seattle got back where they belonged if I wasn't drawing breath in the morning.

I had a feeling that I'd bounce back if something fatal happened to me, but that hadn't been the case for my father. There were a lot of things that could, potentially, go wrong in a permanent way and I didn't know how to mitigate any of them. The close harmony of the grid, its strange way of taking me over and then leaving me at a distance, only confused my sense of survivability. And there was the seductive call of the grid itself. You didn't have to be dead to fall away from the world and not return. Or return altered. I thought my father had hinted I could lose these odd powers, but to what extent? And what would my shape be if that were true? For all of these reasons—and for Quinton—there had to be something left behind.

After that long, depressing thought, I found a quiet spot to call my mother.

Funny that a month earlier I wouldn't have considered calling her for anything—not even a matter of life or death—but here I was, poking her phone number and hoping she had a few minutes to talk. She had been the monster of my childhood, but lately I'd begun to see her differently: as a desperate and lonely person I almost pitied. Almost. She was still responsible for her own misery, but at least she wasn't truly responsible for mine.

She answered her phone and I wondered if she ever didn't. "Sweetie!"

"Hello, Mother."

"I was worried about you! You had to leave LA so quickly and I thought there must be something wrong."

"Yeah. A little. I went to London on some business, but I had to come back to Seattle to finish it up. While I was gone, my employer was kidnapped." If anything happened to me tonight, chances were good I'd be connected to Edward's disappearance in a bad and public way—at least by the press—and, in spite of years of indifference, I didn't want her to think that badly of me.

She gasped and judging from the dramatic sound, I guessed she had an audience. Probably her fiancé. "Oh, my goodness! Is he all right?"

"Not yet. I'm . . . helping out with something this evening," I fumbled, uncomfortable with my ragged half-truth. "If it works out, everything will be fine. I just . . . thought I should let you know that I'm fine."

She was quiet for a moment. "Harper, be careful. Obviously you're not going to change your mind about doing . . . whatever it is you're doing. But . . . you're my baby. And you promised to come to the wedding." Her voice quivered a little, but she stamped down on that and finished strong. "And I'm holding you to that! You hear?"

I smiled. Gods, she was transparent. "Yes, Mom." And she had not abandoned me, even when I thought my father had. I was wrong about that, too, but as much as she infuriated me, at least her reasons for the crazy things she did were human.

She sniffled. "You never call me Mom. . . ."

"Well, I do now. And I have to go." Before I started getting weepy myself and bloodying my clothes in public. "Send the invitations early, OK?"

"All right, sweetie. You take care."

"I will. And you too."

I hung up and looked at the phone a moment before I put it away. That had been awkward. . . .

I killed the last of the sunlight eating dinner in a restaurant at the top of a glass tower and staring at the city below as the lights came on, arc-bright in the Grey I couldn't shake off. The voices of the grid grew louder as the hours passed but less comprehensible, the words chopped up like I was standing in the midst of a large party that jerked in and out of time. It made me irritable and paranoid. Quinton didn't call. I didn't like admitting that I was worried, and more than that: I feared I'd never see him again.

THIRTY

I wasn't dressed for the place, but the doorman at the After Dark let me in anyhow. I suppose being alive in a vampire club is all the cachet you really need to get in. Staying that way may be trickier. But they know me, which is my real ace in the hole.

It was still early for the bloodsucking fraternity and there weren't very many customers in the place yet. A lot of the early birds were demi-vampires, donors, and subordinate turns waiting for whoever pulled their strings or strung them out. The room was always cold, but now the chill was my sense of the Grey clinging to me like a wet coat. The white marble floors seemed almost reflective in their brightness, and once the room was full, the red-and-black clouds of vampiric auras would give it a stygian cast. I spotted two asetem near the back door, their uncanny glowing eyes free of the usual contact lenses and gleaming orange like hot coals. I imagined the news of my presence would be in Wygan's ears in minutes. The broadcast station had plenty of phone lines, even if there wasn't a more arcane method of communication between the Pharaohn and his children that I didn't know about.

I sat down at what was usually Edward's table, making a small stir in the thin crowd. I put my sunglasses back on and waited, schooling myself to be still, not to fidget with my bag or look for something to do. It wasn't too hard: With my shades on, I could close my eyes against the battering light and sound and let the noise of the grid, humming and babbling with every change in the room, be my alarm system.

The one positive angle I could see to the increasing apathy I felt as the grid tried to bind me to itself was that I didn't yet feel any anxiety about this situation. And that made me less interesting to the watching asetem as well.

The crowd was denser half an hour later when Gwen arrived. She slid next to me, as light on the strings of the grid as the stroke of a feather, but I still felt her presence like a cold finger drawn up my spine. "You look ruthless," she whispered.

"Ruthless?" I asked, opening my eyes and glancing at her.

She was as pale and ineffective-looking as ever, but her eyes gleamed and she gave a tiny, hungry smile. "Yes. Dangerous with an air of power held in check."

"Hm," I muttered. The strange change in my perception of the Grey seemed to have an outward expression as well, and that intrigued me a little. Or maybe it was just that the brightness and the noise made me scowl.

I could feel tremors and flutters in the Grey. It was like being a spider in her web the way every disturbance traveled to me. The impression of Cameron's arrival rippled through the room just a moment ahead of his presence with a gust of Grey whispers. I wondered if psychics felt something like this. It was interesting, but overall, I didn't care for it. The asetem in the opposite corner were a different matter. They thrived on strong emotional emanations, so they must have been having a delicious time with the hors d'oeuvres of anticipation radiating from most of the people in the room.

There was a palpable wave of anxiety and excitement that rang discordant wind chimes on the grid when Cameron and Sarah walked in. A sussuration of speculation raced and spread like flame, leaping high when Cam paused by the table, looking it over before he chose to sit down in what was usually Edward's chair.

My phone vibrated in my pocket and made me twitch—I hoped the vampires would take it as a sign that I was as surprised as they about Cameron's move. Without looking, I squeezed the silence button and sent the call to voice mail. I hoped it was Quinton, but this was not the time to be checking my phone.

Two of Edward's usual hangers-on sidled close, plainly hoping to talk to Cam about what he was doing and looking askance at Sarah, who had taken the seat on his other side, putting him between her and Gwen. I, the foreign creature with the scary aura, sat at the free end of the group, where I could move at any time. The setting projected "Prince in his court" with the subtlety of a brick through a window.

Cameron gave the two curious vampires a bland "Yes?" that served as opening enough for them to sit down and start whispering at him. The sound grated on my ears, distorted by the noise of the grid into sharp squawks. Cam looked bored and a little annoyed by the two supplicants, but he leaned forward and listened. I wondered if they'd been put up to the scene or if it was just a natural extension of the usual jockeying for position. I let my attention float out into the room on the power lines of the grid, wide enough to thin the noise in my head, but it only helped a little as everyone was focused back toward Cameron's entourage.

The other vampires and kin in the room stirred and muttered. Some left or moved to new tables, breaking and forming alliances as I watched; most stayed as they were, acting as if nothing going on in the room was important to them. A few sent Cameron glares of open hostility. Cam ignored it all and went on with his conversation.

The place was full and the murmurs and adjustments were dying down when Carlos entered and blew the latent emotions in the room into brilliant flame that roared through the blazing grid. He stopped a single pace inside and studied the scene. A slow boil of black fury rolled off him and he strode toward our table. He did not seem to look at anyone other than Cameron, but I knew he was aware of us all, from the asetem looking avid and excited in the corner to me, playing stone-faced in my personal madhouse while Gwen cringed beside me.

Carlos stopped at the edge of the table and glared at the two whispering vampires next to Sarah. They scuttled away without another word, leaving an insectile chittering on the threads of the Grey.

Cameron looked up, his expression one of pleasant surprise and confusion with a touch of fear that I didn't think was entirely feigned. He stood up, smiling. "Carlos!" Then he bridled and winced as Carlos redirected his glower to him.

Carlos's voice was not loud, but it rumbled through the Grey and set waves crashing into one another. "Presumptuous whelp. Do you think you're Edward's equal because you are my student?"

Cameron shook his head. Tiny flashes of white and gold exploded in the energy nimbus around him. "No. Of course not. But there's a void without him and it needs to be filled. I seem to be the only person willing to step in temporarily rather than try to grab it all for myself."

"Are you? And what if he never comes back? Will you step aside for someone else?"

"I would if it were you. It ought to be you as—"

Carlos hit him, the movement visible only as a black blur. Cam went backward into the wall hard enough to dent it as Sarah tumbled to the floor in the oversweep of Carlos's strike. Gwen and I both flew to our feet—as did many of the audience—in an instant. Gwen made a slight whimpering noise that echoed in my head as she backed up.

I held my ground, not knowing how this was meant to play out once I'd said my piece but sticking to the short script I had. Cameron's note had not told me exactly what to expect—there hadn't been time and, had we done otherwise, the asetem would taste the falseness of our fear and anger. It was all the most desperate kind of improvisation. I hoped. "Carlos, this isn't necessary. Maintaining peace in this community—" I started.

He whipped his head around to glare at me and his expression was almost a blow. "This is none of your affair, daylighter!" he roared. Even holding fast to the knowledge that it was only an act, I had to clench my jaw and shut my eyes against the buffeting pressure of his voice.

He turned his attention back to Cameron, who'd pushed himself forward off the wall, using his momentum to drive a flat-palmed strike into his mentor's face. Gleams of gold and silver energy rushed ahead of the movement; Cameron was putting more than his physical strength into hitting

Carlos. He'd been only twenty-one when Edward turned him, and his slender frame offered insufficient muscle against the bulkier, older vampire, even with the paranormal advantages of the undead.

Apparently taken by surprise, Carlos was flung backward about two feet and came to a hard stop against another table, knocking it sideways with a crash. "Oh, very nicely done, schoolboy," he spat, regaining his balance and running his fingers down the crooked length of his broken nose. The cartilage crackled and popped as he moved it back into place.

Cameron's punk-short hair hadn't been mussed, but fury disarranged his features into an unrecognizable mask. "No one touches my people," he hissed back.

"Ah, 'your people,' " Carlos repeated in a sardonic tone. "So it comes out. You *are* usurping the position of your patron."

"I wouldn't have to if you'd do it yourself! You're the most powerful of us all. You could hold this city in the palm of your hand in your spare time!"

Carlos moved closer, his chin down so his black stare bored out from the shadow beneath his brow. His aura flushed a vibrant red among the death black, and the sound in the grid became a banshee wail. "I am *bound* to Edward. He commands my fealty so long as he is on this earth."

"How is it disloyal to preserve what is his until he can reclaim it? How is that against your oath?" Cameron shot back. He made no allusion to the real reason for the uneasy centuries of detente; neither Carlos nor Edward had ever wanted to expose that twisted betrayal.

Carlos raised his head in a rush and looked down his nose at the younger vampire. Cold seemed to roll off him, damping everything in a sudden pall. "The depth of your ignorance astounds me. I wash my hands of you. And I'll leave you to the mercy of 'your people.' " He turned away.

Cameron was not going to let it go. He reached out and yanked the bigger man back around. "You're a coward and you call it loyalty. You'll challenge me and lecture me, but you won't stop me." Cameron, less than a full step away, spit in the other vampire's face.

Rage ignited around Carlos, flushing the Grey a glittering scarlet that chimed and shrieked all the louder. His voice ground out between his teeth, ice-cold and implacable. "I *will* stop you, treacherous brat. I'll show you what it is to be obedient, to bow your head and bend your knee while you seethe with hate. Bound by the flesh of your flesh and the blood of your creation, you will know what torment is." He snatched Sarah to his chest and stepped back in one impossibly quick motion.

Cameron froze. The necromancer held a small, glittering knife to the young woman's throat, flicking it against the edge of her vein as she trembled, wide-eyed, in his grip.

Gwen cried out as blood flowed from between Carlos's fingers, "No! Sarah!"

Carlos muttered in quick liquid syllables as the blood hit the floor and rang on the Grey like a giant bronze bell. Sarah rolled up her eyes and went limp as the vibration rippled through the room. I knew she was acting, but even I thought it looked real. Carlos let her fall, his right hand coming away from her neck smeared red. He drew on the air with her blood, whispering quickly and making a hard gesture that flicked the precious fluid toward her brother's face.

Cameron snatched the blood from the air between them and leapt forward, pressing his bloody hand over Carlos's face and taking up the weird language of the false spell in a rapid shout. The last word dulled the sound in the room as if someone had closed a sealed door and sucked out the air. It was impressive, even though the weight of it in the Grey was next to nothing. Only the breathless, sinking feeling was real: The rest was magical sham and fireworks, and I was one of only three people in the room who could tell the difference. Even the asetem would only feel the ripple. Carlos flinched as if Cameron had struck him much harder but kept to his feet.

Gwen scrambled over the table to scoop Sarah off the floor as Cameron knelt down beside her. He stroked his bloody hand over the dripping wound on her neck. Then he turned his head away. "Gwen, you do it. I—I can't. She's my sister."

Gwen seemed to coil around her, hiding what she did as she bent her head down over the young woman's neck.

The Grey sounded hollow, waiting, whining like a clockwork thing wound too tight.

Carlos had not moved except to close his eyes. The fallen set of his shoulders and the darkness around him looked like despair. The bloody handprint on his face faded as if his skin drank it in.

Cameron stood up and looked at him, his face full of pity and sorrow more than anger. "Did you think I didn't learn anything from you? *You* taught me that blood binding. *You* taught me how to break it and how to avoid it as well. Now you're bound to me, by your own words. And by that blood I was born with. And since she's not dead, you're also bound to Sarah. I know you know all this, but I'm saying it so all of our kind here know it, too. You're mine." Actually, most vampires wouldn't know a binding until it bit them. But the show wasn't for them: It was for the Pharaohn's spies. Cam glanced side to side as if a little nervous about what he was doing. "I think it might be wise for you to kneel."

Carlos opened his eyes, his face devoid of expression. He spoke without emotion or force, in the same sort of floating emptiness I had experienced the night before. "I will not."

The strange golden sparks welled again in the palms of Cameron's hands as he brought them up, open, to chest height. "Don't make me force you, sensei."

It was a strange word to choose, freighted with respect and tradition, and it reminded me that Cameron had been studying Japanese when he was still an ordinary college student. An age of knowledge had passed since then, and though he didn't look much different, here was ample evidence that everything had changed. He leaned closer, resting his clean hand on Carlos's shoulder, and whispered something into the bigger man's ear. Then he took a step back.

He didn't quite let his hands relax, keeping them poised just a bit in front of his body, but he didn't do anything. He just waited, his brow shadowed with anxiety.

Nothing stirred. A roomful of creatures who don't breathe make an unsettling silence.

Sarah let out a quiet little moan. The sound seemed to break Carlos, and he sank onto his knees, letting his head fall forward. He shuddered as he settled all the way to the floor, putting out his open hands, palms up, on his thighs. The bloodstained penknife clattered onto the marble tiles, spinning a scarlet smear. "I submit."

The high-tension whine of the grid wound down, and the harsh carmine of the Grey drained back to a few splashes of uncomfortably bright color in the glaring silver mist of the world. Cameron relaxed and an ordinary shuffling and rustling of impatient bodies warmed the silence.

"Will you support me and defend me, aid me and advise me, with your best will?" Cameron asked. It had the feeling of something formal and old that had been translated poorly.

Carlos raised his head, looking at Cameron a little sideways with a sarcastic expression. "Yes, damn it all. Can we get this over with? I am your man, your sworn supporter, by blood bound. Is that good enough?"

Cameron blinked. "Um . . . yeah. I guess that'll do."

"May I stand up now . . . my lord?" The snark was thick enough to gag on. "And if you tell me to 'rise,' " he added in an undertone, "I may have to 'advise' you to do otherwise in future."

Cameron rolled his eyes. "Oh, jeez, just get up."

A ripple of amusement spread through the room and gave cover to my relieved sigh. I'd had no idea if this sketchy plan would work, but even if they didn't buy it completely, none of the vampires could argue that Carlos hadn't sworn to support Cameron. That alone would give anyone other than the Pharaohn pause, and Cameron's loyalty and reasonable treatment of his teacher would give them hope for the same themselves. Benevolent dictators are much harder to depose.

I remembered the rest of the evening's responsibilities and hoped Carlos and I would be able to leave soon. I needed to talk to him before anyone else made any moves and let him know we were far from done tonight. And I hoped that away from the bloody rage of vampires, I might be able to think without so much noise in my head for just a few minutes.

Once Carlos was back on his feet, the patrons of the After Dark seemed to know the show was over and drifted back to their tables and conversations, speculating, no doubt, on what Cameron would do first as Prince of the City. Only the asetem acted disinterested. Gwen and Sarah had retired back to one end of the table, bent toward each other like parentheses. I frowned as I glanced at Cameron, but he was busy with a sudden press of admirers and sycophants.

I looked for Carlos—no one would think it odd that I did, since I was there as a neutral party and I could talk to whomever I pleased—and spotted him near the door. Just one more scene to play. . . . I twisted my way through the moving kaleidoscope of bright colors and cold bodies to catch up to him before he went outside. Once out of the club, there was nothing to stop the asetem from closing in.

I met him at the entrance. He gave me a chilly glance with one lifted eyebrow. We hadn't discussed this bit of business, but he was even more the experienced performer than I was and I was sure he'd pick up my cue and play along. I made only a small twitch of my head toward the door before I spoke, but I knew he caught it.

"I wouldn't have expected that of you," I said, not modulating my voice down. I wanted to be heard, after all.

"Obeisance?"

"Betrayal."

He narrowed his eyes but made no other reply.

"Everyone knows you hate Edward and you took Cameron only because you couldn't refuse—"

"A situation you engineered."

"For Cameron's sake. Not Edward's. But he's been a loyal student. He's been your friend—if that's possible. And you were going to kill his sister and bind him to you so you could . . . what, watch him twist in the wind while you abandoned him? That's not any better than what Edward—"

He clamped his hand onto my biceps and jerked me close. "Enough, Greywalker!"

"No," I protested, "it's not enough."

He growled and pulled me into the cold of the foyer, letting the black doors slam shut behind us. Sounds came down from the street in ice-blue trickles and leaked thinly from under the door like water. The area was built like a well, all white marble with a curving, iron-railed staircase going up the circular shaft to a gate on the street. It wasn't an ideal place to talk, but it would do for a moment.

Carlos let go of me at once and kept his voice low. "An unpleasant evening's work."

"Yes, but now the little kingdom is secure and you're Cameron's sworn right-hand man."

"So much mumbo jumbo. None of those would know the difference. There is no binding. Only my word."

"Which is as good as, I recall."

"Yes."

"You won't betray him, not after what Edward did to you."

He nodded, his mouth pulling down in distaste.

"What about the magic? What about Sarah?"

"Special effects." He spread his fingers and I could see white cuts and lines in his flesh between the index and middle fingers of his right hand, knitting up as I watched. "One learns a lot of tricks in such a long lifetime. She's in no danger. I took care to feed well on waking."

"I hope it'll last: We're not done."

The interrogative eyebrow rose again.

"The labyrinth portals expire tonight and after that, there's no back door."

"We don't need it. Only the right knife and you. The Lâmina I have with me. And you . . ." He peered at me in the darkness that was bright as Broadway to me. He pulled his head back and frowned. "Already?"

"If I were any more in touch with the grid, I'd disappear into it."

"Exactly."

"Do you think he knows?"

Carlos snorted. "No doubt he's known for hours. We shall have to let them take us."

I disliked the sound of that, but it was the same conclusion I'd come to myself since I didn't know where Wygan would do his dirty work.

"Are you ready?"

I shook my head. "I . . . need to make a phone call first."

He laughed at that, but he let me walk a few feet away and do it. I noticed the earlier missed call was from the phone in Edward's bunker. It must have been Quinton and that pleased me at the same time it made me sad. I'd only have time to tell him the bare bones of the situation before I'd have to go, and my chances of coming back weren't good. I called anyway.

Quinton answered at once. "Harper?"

"Yeah."

I could hear his sigh through the phone, and it slid over me, soft and warm. "I was with the police and the FBI all day—"

A finger of concern touched me. "The feds didn't suss you—?" I started.

"No, no," he reassured me. "But things didn't move as fast as we'd hoped. I was worried. . . ."

"It's almost over. We've settled some things and now . . . it's just up to the bad guy to come get us."

The door opened from the club and the two asetem stepped out. They stared at us with baleful, glowing eyes.

"Ah, the escort is here," I said.

"Is it Goodall?"

"No," I answered. "Why?"

The asetem were walking toward us, trying to herd us up the stairs without actually touching us and causing a scene. Carlos glowered at them but let himself be moved, though he kept them away from me so I could finish my phone call. It was what we wanted after all, but we couldn't make it look too easy.

"Goodall is bad news. Ex-military, ex–black ops. The Feds wouldn't even say which group, but they got quiet and worried when we showed them the recording."

"But we knew he was that sort of trouble. He won't hurt us. He's on Wygan's leash."

The asetem hissed at me, and one of them darted in my direction, forcing me toward the stairs a few steps. I could see the shape of someone at the top. . . .

"Stay away from Goodall! He doesn't want to capture you; he wants to kill you! And I mean in a not-getting-backup-this-time way. The bullet hole in the Danzigers' doorway was at head height. Head height, do you understand? He had all the time in the world to take the shot; it's not a mistake. If he'd just wanted to knock you down and drag you to Wygan, he'd have chosen to shoot you anywhere else, but he was aiming to blow your head off. That's what took out your father. That would kill you, too. He is not playing by Wygan's rules: He means to take you out permanently!"

The light was odd, but it illuminated the waiting figure better as we rounded the first few steps.

"Ah," I said and closed the phone, slipping it back into my pocket.

That was Goodall at the top of the stairs.

THIRTY-ONE

Run like hell. That's what my brain said. Even in the strange, broken light through the gate with the glare of the Grey welling up, I could see the dark, squared-off shape of a pistol in Goodall's hand. Parkerized black. He had no reason to harm Carlos—and a gun certainly wouldn't do it—so that was for me.

One of the asetem grew impatient and pushed on my shoulders, urging me up. I let the motion take me forward at the waist and kicked back hard with one foot. Even as strong and fast as the asetem were, a boot to the chest will knock almost anyone down those slippery marble stairs.

Goodall cursed as I grabbed on and swung over the stair rail, rolling and dropping to the floor. The impact jarred through my body and I heard the crack of a shot. I ducked and ran back under the staircase, cutting for the door into the club. There was a scrambling and banging on the stairs behind me but I didn't turn around to see what it was. The stair and its shaftlike opening blocked a good shot at me as I bolted, but that didn't stop Goodall from taking some. Shards of marble ricocheted around the dark space as I plunged through the door.

The host usually stopped everyone, but he stood aside this time and pointed. "Door at the back."

I ran through the main room at my best late-for-rehearsal speed, dodging bodies and jumping tables. It wasn't graceful and I had to shove a few vampires and their friends aside. None of them moved to stop me, which was amazing. Vampires aren't slow or weak, and just two or three could have caught me easily. I heard Cameron shout for someone to "stop those two!" which explained a lot. I spotted the discreet white door to the back room and pushed through it.

Vampire kitchens are not a sight for health inspectors. It's not that they aren't clean but that they aren't really kitchens that's disturbing. I dodged a lot of things that could have been prep tables but looked more like cots as I went through.

Nearly every building in Pioneer Square has a basement or two, and most have a door that leads into the underground—the network of abandoned sidewalks that ring the buildings at what was once street level. The downside is that there's no way to cross the street without coming up to the surface. I had to assume Goodall had some more of Wygan's asetem with him and they'd be spread out around the street—what else did they have to do now that their Pharaohn's big night was at hand but roll up the competition? I'd have to come up where I could check for them before they could see me. That would mean the staircase by the old record store.

Bud's Jazz Records had been in the basement near Temple Billiards for ages, but it had finally given in to declining sales and closed its doors. Now the old space was empty and I'd spent enough time in the underground with Quinton to know where the original back door was. It would be locked and alarmed, but at that moment, I didn't care if I pulled in every cop in the district. It was pretty likely I'd get out before anyone arrived, but even if I didn't, there's little more secure from most bad guys than being surrounded by pissed-off patrolmen. Suicidal villains are a different problem, but I didn't think Goodall or his asetem friends were willing to trade themselves for me just yet. They might be if they didn't get me to Wygan tonight, but I didn't plan to miss that party; I just meant to arrive my own way. I didn't know what that was going to be, but I'd figure it out when I stopped running for my life.

I skidded around a corner on the filth of a hundred years' neglect and slammed into a set of steel construction doors. Someone was doing work in the underground, and to secure the area from people just like me, they'd put up a barrier. Damn it! I didn't hear anyone behind me, but that meant nothing. I was humped.

Except that I wasn't. I was a Greywalker, and this was about as Grey as Seattle got: the depths of the old city where ghosts were as common as dirt and the layers of time slid and chimed over one another like slices of broken glass. I started to put my hand out by habit to feel for the temporaclines, but I didn't need to. The bright glow of the grid as I now saw it turned the ripples of time into colored banners fluttering horizontally in an uncanny wind. And I didn't need to slide onto one; I simply reached and it bent. I stepped through.

It was a miserable day I'd picked: pouring rain, the streets so muddy that cart horses bogged in it up to their fetlocks and had to be hauled up onto the wooden sidewalks while their wagons were cut free to sink until someone could come back for the goods. The ghosts of the early shopkeepers paid me no attention at all as they tried to save their stock of one kind or another. I slogged through the phantom mud, which felt as slimy and sticky as the real thing, to the waterfront and down the length of Yesler's wharf toward the sawmill. The old dock area had long ago been filled in and made into the land on which the current waterfront and Alaskan Way stood within inches of the old level. That would be well out of the zone any of the Pharaohn's henchmen would be watching and safe enough to appear in. I'd never exited a temporacline below the present world's street level and I didn't want to find out what would happen if I did.

I stumbled a little as I came out not far from Rice House Antiques. The warehouse was locked up for the night, even the red London phone box tucked away inside. I checked to be sure I wasn't wearing the haunting of hundred-year-old mud and crossed the street to the ferry terminal. A few lonely cabs stood at the curb waiting for anyone returning on foot from Bremerton or the islands. I got in one and directed the driver to the Westin Hotel. It's a big building near TPM, but not so near that you can see it from there, and I thought I could find a place to lurk long enough to figure out my next move.

And call Quinton to let him know I wasn't dead yet.

THIRTY-TWO

My phone buzzed as I walked into the Westin lobby. I didn't stop to look at the number, I just opened it up and answered. "Quinton?"

"H-Harper?" The voice was shaking so hard the word barely came out, but I still recognized the speaker.

"Will?"

"Run . . ." he started, but his voice trailed away as someone else snatched the phone. " 'Ello there . . . 'little girl.' It appears your friend 'as dropped by to play. . . ."

I swore. "Haven't you had enough fun torturing that man, Wygan? You won't get anything from him and his mind's already too broken to be much good."

"Oh, but there is still blood in 'im and, as you say, the fun of it. And of course there is your father. . . ."

"Why hold on to him? He's dead. How much satisfaction can you get from tormenting a ghost?"

"Not enough, that's true. They really are somewhat unsatisfac'try. But you do 'ave quite a few other friends. I'm not overfond of witches, so I might take a particular delight in the anguish of that cozy little family. They are quite nearby. . . ."

Broadcast tower. That's where they were. The idea came into my head illuminated by another: I still had a back door. Wherever Wygan was, the ghost of my father was nearby, which meant that the door opened to within a few feet of the Pharaohn. It was behind a barrier in the Grey, but I thought my current affinity for the grid might allow me to tear through that barrier. I just had to get close enough to use it unseen and I could step out almost on top of him. Then I would have Carlos to help me destroy the Pharaohn for good.

"That's enough," I said. "I'm coming."

"Ah, good. I knew you'd want to play your part."

"What I want is to rip your head off." And I did, but it had a distant, intellectual kind of appeal at that moment. I didn't feel the burn of hate I would have expected, just a clear, steel-strong certainty that he needed to be removed from existence. Now.

"I suspect you shall be disappointed."

"I don't think so." I hung up on him. It was a small, cold satisfaction, but at least it was mine. I wasn't completely lost to humanity yet.

I called Quinton again, cutting in the moment he answered. "I'm all right. I slipped Goodall but I have to go stop Wygan—"

"No, you don't! He can't force you. If you don't cooperate, he can't get what he wants."

"I don't intend to cooperate, but I can't let him hurt people. He has Will, he is threatening the Danzigers, and you know what he will do once he has his way. He has to be stopped for good. What's happening to me is almost finished. If it goes on to the end, I believe I will . . . I'll just disappear into the grid. It is pulling on me, singing me into it, and my ability to remain separate is failing. My father suggested there's a way to stop that, but putting an end to the Pharaohn is the only chance I may have. And the only thing that matters. You said someone's not coming out of this alive. I would rather choose who and how this ends than hope for the best."

"Harper, don't—"

"He's somewhere around broadcast tower two—maybe the park or the buildings nearby—and so is Goodall. You'll know when you spot it. But don't come too soon: The cops wouldn't like what they'd see."

I wasn't being entirely truthful: I wasn't going there to save Will or anyone else, not myself, not even my father. That would be nice, but I no longer had the luxury of pity, or even the fleeting sense of it, and that wasn't what was moving me toward the towers on Queen Anne Hill. This had been my intention since London: to destroy that which had manipulated and ruined my life. Now the need was greater than me and mine. Gwen had been right to call me ruthless. In the dispassionate influence of the grid, compassion—perhaps humanity—had died in me. Only the job remained: Paladin of the Dead, Hands of the Guardian.

THIRTY-THREE

Of course I couldn't just walk into the monster's lair and give myself up to whatever he had in mind. I had given Goodall the slip, but that didn't make me much safer here; Wygan meant me no good either. Another taxi dropped me off near the towers, and I walked through the shining Grey to the screen of shrubs near the old gym buildings, searching for a blind spot that was near enough to fall within the compass of the labyrinth. When I found it, I opened the ghostly door, but I didn't step through.

I pulled the tin that had contained Simondson's ghost out of my pocket and opened it up, dumping the last bright thread from it. "Come here."

The troubled red mass that remained of him materialized with a crackle of sound. I stared into it, not bothering with the normal view of the world. In the middle of the red threads and black shadow of death, I could just spot a bit of bright blue energy. I thrust my hand into the cold light of him and groped for the burning red torment that struck through that blue luminescence, disregarding the howl of shock he gave as I did. When I caught the hard strand that I wanted, feeling it only remotely as it seared into my palm, I looked toward where his face would have been. To me it was the thinnest mist now, barely a face at all.

"Shut up. In a moment I'm going to pull this. Then you'll be free. You might go immediately to wherever it is the remnants of the living go, or you might stay—I don't know. But if you do linger, do me a favor: Go to the man who killed you and wreak screaming havoc." I pointed toward the broadcast tower with my free hand. "He's in there somewhere."

I didn't wait for a reply; I just yanked the scorching knot of energy loose and tore it apart. I saw the ghost streak away into the yellow wire frame of the broadcast tower, a blue comet trailing a cloud of blackness that turned suddenly and dove into the tangled skein of the earth below us.

I didn't care which way Simondson had gone. I'd be there soon enough. I turned and stepped through the misty doorway into the labyrinth. Then I started running toward my father, down the ethereal corridors that twisted on themselves as I went, tangling behind me into snake's coils and endless tesseracts of empty space. I kept to the left, always, just like the classical labyrinth, turning counterclockwise until I came to the center.

My father moaned, thinner and less material than ever, half-embedded in the wall. "You're too late, little girl. There's something loose already."

"That's just a friend of mine, making an entrance. You know they can't start the wedding without the bride."

"Perhaps you should run. . . ."

"Everyone keeps telling me that, but I'm done with it. You screwed up. You didn't stop him. I will. But you, Dad . . . your job is to stop *me*. Before I disappear into this forever. Can you?"

He sobbed, his eyes hidden behind the opaque memory of his glasses. "Only—only if you die, little girl. And I don't know what will happen to you; if you live, you'll still be a Greywalker, but not like this." He writhed and churned in the wall of tormented ghosts. "I can't do this! I can't let them hurt you: You're my child!"

"You have to. Because I *am* your daughter. I always loved you, Dad, but you owe me, and I don't want to be like this. If I die here, you can make me better. Come on, Dad. Be my guardian angel one last time."

I didn't give him a chance to waffle or worry. I reached past him, reached for the walls, for the ghost substance that hid this cell from the rest of the Grey, and plunged my hands into it. It was easier than the walls of Edward's bunker. It felt softer than Carlos's body and gave way with more ease, tearing into silver shards as the grid lamented and blazed bright through the falling walls of the labyrinth. The tumbling Grey flashed and burned, loosening the ghost of my father from his prison as the phantom structure crumbled away.

I emerged into a room I had never seen before but which was unpleasantly like Carlos's cellar, marked in swirls and rings of magic, but these were indigo and black, looping together into three smaller circles within a larger one. At the center of the circles, a shard of suspended temporacline glittered like ice. Colored lights flickered in sconces at the corners of the room—lights to confuse and keep the Guardian Beast at bay. Behind me, I could feel the slipping, unraveling presence of my father as a passing breeze that could not last long. But he was there.

I took in the rest of the room at a glance. Will, waxy pale and bloodstained, huddled in a corner, weeping, with the colors of his aura a shattered mess of violence and fear streaked with smoke-black. Carlos was several feet away from Will, restraining a wasted and half-mad Edward, who struggled weakly toward the terrified man with his eyes staring and fangs exposed as if the skin of his face had shrunken away. Wygan, his twisted white snake shape more prominent than ever, waited on the other side of the joined circles, closest to me and farthest from Carlos. Goodall was turning in tight arcs, swiping at the trailing coil of black that swirled around him in furious rushes. It seemed I had interrupted the preliminary stages.

Sometimes the solution to a problem is simple. I didn't think this would be, but I would be a fool not to take an opportunity that presented itself. I strode to Wygan, drawing the HK from under my jacket and squeezing the cocking lever as I shoved the muzzle up under the Pharaohn's ophidian chin. He started turning toward me. He was huge in this form and I had to reach high to press the barrel into his skin. The gun seemed laughably small and inadequate as I pulled the trigger.

The shot exploded against the ceiling, raining glass and concrete on us as the illusion of the massive snake collapsed. The smaller, corporeal Wygan rammed his fist into my chest, shoving me backward.

I fell into a crouch, my ribs aching and breathing difficult, and launched myself at him.

He whipped aside as quick as his illusory form. Then he snapped out a hand and caught me by the neck. Squeezing until my vision dimmed and my fingers went limp, he pulled me around to face him and shoved me to my knees. The grid roared in my head, calling for me. The pistol tumbled out of my grip and skittered across the floor.

He let up only enough to keep me breathing and the noise receded a little. "Dramatic entrance, Greywalker. I admit I did not expect it. You're full of surprises."

Without any apparent effort, he dragged me toward Goodall and snatched the fluttering remains of Simondson from the air. He shook the black shroud away and consumed the dimming blue light that remained of the ghost.

Panting with annoyance, Goodall glowered pure hate at me. Then he punched me and pushed me backward so I tumbled and sprawled into the closest circle. He slapped his hand down on the edge of the lines and spat out a word. The dark blue cage of the circle flashed upward, surrounding me. In the hum of the circle the grid rose in burning voices and smears of misty color.

I could almost touch it . . . the gleaming stuff just beyond the circle. But the whispered voices counseled patience. I'd have a better chance to destroy Wygan if I just waited a few minutes, let him think me weak or stunned. . . .

Outside the rushing sound of the indigo circle, Goodall still glared murder at me, but the Pharaohn wasn't interested in the petty anger of his ushabti. "Start it," he commanded. "We have the gateway," he said, gesturing to me. "Now bring the Beast."

Goodall shook himself and turned to flick off the colored lights, leaving the room bathed in only the diffused cones of work lights far above that glittered on the substance of the Grey like dust motes. Then the screaming started in the grid and a sound like a train bearing down with failing brakes came from the air overhead. I remembered that last sound from two years before in the burning disaster of the Madison Forrest House: the shriek of the Guardian Beast, enraged and rushing to destroy a threat to its domain. Colors flickered and surged in the hot lines beneath the city. Without the colored lights to confuse it, the Guardian saw its enemy and the razor-edge of destruction he represented for the Grey's thin barrier that kept the worlds of the normal and the paranormal apart and safe from one another. It could not care about any threat to itself; it only came on.

I remembered what my father had said: call it, trap it, kill it. As I stared into the grid, I got the whole shape of the plan. I was the gateway into the trap, a bridge between the normal world and the Grey; Carlos was the knife; and Wygan himself both bait and replacement. My living connection to both realms would hold the door open between them while Wygan caught and destroyed the Guardian, leaving the things of the Grey free to rush out into the normal world. But what would compel the Beast into the trap . . . ? I studied the shape of the magic circle, looking for the way to ruin Wygan's plans, to use any moment where he might be vulnerable as he threw off one form and strove toward the next. I couldn't resist the grid's pull, but I might be able to reshape it to my own purpose. . . .

The Pharaohn glanced at Carlos. "Speak, Ataíde. Bring the Beast here for slaughter."

I had never heard that word before—was it an insult or a name? Carlos narrowed his eyes but said nothing, gave no clue. I thought Wygan was going to strike him, but he reined in his temper, stepped around the necromancer, and crouched down next to Edward.

"Order it done, Kammerling." Wygan didn't know Carlos was no longer bound to Edward. But I was still unsure what further role Edward might have. . . . Carlos could defy Wygan, but he wouldn't do it yet.

Distracted by his need for blood, Edward had difficulty pulling his attention from Will. His voice was a cracked whisper. "I call my own death if I do." That puzzled me. Unless Wygan shattered the already broken tie between them, Carlos would be bound to defend Edward from whatever threatened—including Wygan or the Guardian Beast.

Surely Edward knew the connection of the knife was broken. But perhaps some older bond still clung between them. . . .

"You're dying as it is. But you could go more comfortably. . . ." Wygan stepped across the gap in the circle to Will and grabbed ahold of his nearest extremity. He began dragging Will, feetfirst and screaming and thrashing at the floor with his crabbed hands, toward the fallen vampire Prince.

Will's terror galvanized me for a moment and I jolted against the magical barrier, ready to rip it apart and go save Will—the voices screaming at me to wait, wait, wait—but Carlos spoke and stopped me.

I didn't know the language or what the words meant, but they trembled on the air and then turned liquid, echoing in the grid and running into the circle, flushing it a deep purple. Something made of bone spines, spiderweb, and ghost sinew began to form in the second circle. The roar of the Beast issued from its shadow jaws of dagger teeth. But the circle around it wasn't quite closed. . . .

Carlos shot me a warning glance. "You cannot imprison a Guardian with the paltry blood of a mad human."

Wygan dropped Will's foot and turned around, watching the necromancer with narrowed eyes as his victim scrabbled away. The Pharaohn twisted up a smile as he looked at the two vampires. "What would you, then, Ataíde?"

"The blood of a magical creature is required."

The Pharaohn laughed and it came out a long, strangling hiss. "We are out of unicorns, I fear."

Carlos shrugged but there was nothing casual in it. "One of your own will do." He let his glance shift to Goodall. "Even that abomination. You do not need him to close the spell now that I am here."

Goodall scowled and swayed forward as if he would break from his place and attack Carlos.

Wygan shook his head, the reflection off his ghostly scales scintillating in the air like snow. "Ah, Ataíde. Not quite so clever as you think you are. I still need him to keep you from my throat. And the Greywalker would not volunteer even if she could. But the blood of a vampire will do. Kill Kammerling."

Edward tried to thrash away, but Carlos held on to his arm with no effort and shook him a little, saying, "Peace now. I am no threat to you." Edward subsided into a weakened heap. Then Carlos returned his attention to the Pharaohn. "You well know that is one thing I cannot do, no matter how I crave it."

"Oh, yes: the tie that binds. . . ."

He kept his gaze on Wygan's, daring the hypnotizing stare of the White Worm. "If you would have it, then you must free me to do it. As you promised."

Wygan knit his thin white brows and shot rapid glances at me and Goodall. The ushabti growled and took a step before another glare put him back in his place.

"Kammerling's too weak," Goodall suggested. "Cut the Greywalker. Her part's nearly done."

"But nearly is not completely," Wygan muttered back. "You let your jealousy and greed for power run away with your sense. No, Edward will do."

I kept my mouth shut, still studying the circles on the floor. I could see the weak links, the open gates, even as the gold, blue, and red lines of the grid began weaving into me, pulling my substance and will toward it. I sank to my knees to get closer, risking the connection between normal and Grey, letting the warp and weft of the grid be extra eyes and ears as I moved toward it.

The Pharaohn turned his gaze back to Carlos, evaluating the necromancer before he stepped close. The set of his head told me he was bothered by something but unable to pin it down. He put his hand out toward Carlos, and in the blaze of the grid I could see how his shape slid into the tangled lines of power around them, brushing into magic in a way that was chillingly familiar. He didn't encounter the thread he expected and twitched back, angry.

But the asetem aren't as fast as other vampires and Carlos was already thrusting the Lâmina up toward the Pharaohn's gut. Only the intervention of Goodall and the luck of the devil kept the uncanny blade out of Wygan's eldritch flesh. Goodall jumped and yanked his master backward as Carlos moved and the whispering knife slashed through cloth and air.

The nearly solid shape of the Guardian screamed in the circle, but Wygan would not be distracted again. He shoved Goodall back and stepped close behind Carlos, plunging his hands into the dark vampire's neck and shoulder, holding him in the grip of his fury and power. He shook the bigger man violently and I could see Carlos arch and buckle as the shape of his own life and magic twisted under the Pharaohn's grip and the blade clattered from his hand.

"I do not know how you've freed yourself, but there shall be no more tricks, Ataíde. Do it, or I'll scatter you to the wind."

It was not an idle threat, but I could see his power strain. He could destroy Carlos, and it would ruin him in the process, but the urge to survive was too strong for the necromancer, whether he knew the odds or not. And there were still chances to stop the Pharaohn. . . .

The dark vampire nodded. "All right." Wygan pushed him down.

Carlos crouched beside Edward. "I'm sorry for this," he whispered. "I meant to forgive our past." He picked up the Lâmina from the floor and let it touch the base of Edward's neck. His eyes sought mine for just a moment. Then he looked away again.

The other vampire twisted in pain, clashing his fangs, before slumping over, exhausted, muttering, "Our past and I are too broken. Finish it."

The room shook and the shrieking of the Guardian Beast made the Grey dim and flicker as the tip of the blade sliced upward, flaying open the artery in Edward's neck. The blood didn't flow: It dripped, dark and thick, from the wound. Carlos said a few more words in the weird tongue and let Edward fall into the edge of the circle. Wygan hissed and darted to the crumpling vampire, scooping him up and tossing him all the way into the center of the main circle as he threw himself into the remaining small open circle between me and the nearly captive Guardian Beast. Now Wygan was locked with me into the accelerating motion of the spell.

Edward struck the ground where the temporacline glittered. The floor shook. Slow blood spattered and ran outward. I could see the lingering shadow of his existence shatter and stop, frozen in the instant he expired, borrowed blood still dark on the glassy floor. Goodall slapped his hand down on the lines of the outer circle once again, and another inner ring slammed closed, sending up a curtain of dark fire as the monster of bone and mist surged into it, corporeal and vulnerable as a lamb. The Guardian Beast was captured.

Popping sounds came from above us, punctuating the noise of the grid with unexpected flashes of white light and confusion that barely penetrated to us. I wasn't sure what it was, but it seemed foreign and removed from what went on here.

The Guardian Beast screamed in frustration as it was caught, dragging my attention back. Then the circle began tightening around it like a noose. I could see Goodall hauling on the threads of it, pulling them somehow *through* Carlos, drawing the dark lines closer to the construct of the Grey's wrath even as Carlos fought him. The first touch of the deep purple fire crumbled the Guardian's spines like rotten wood.

The world screamed around me as the grid burned brighter and brighter with the dissolving essence of the Guardian Beast pouring back into it. The silvery ghost-stuff of the Grey boiled and rippled as if pocked by gunfire. The Beast dwindled and Wygan seemed to unknit, loosening form and essence, giving up his ancient body to reshape himself. . . .

Now, now, now! the chorus screamed. A deeper throbbing note rolled the floor beneath my feet, calling me, and I leapt toward it, diving into the world between. Digging myself into the grid, I heaved on the circle, my own energy flowing into it and tearing at the weak links. I could taste the work of Carlos there, corroding the marks painstakingly prepared by Goodall and Wygan. I could feel true names like sharp stones tumbling away beneath me.

The gleaming fog substance of the Grey stretched all around me, falling away into depths that rippled with color like a lightning storm. Above us, a squall churned the surface, but nothing more. Distant sparkles and sheets of light flashed and vanished, reappearing elsewhere as racing lines that curled through the rolling, constant clouds of ghost-stuff. It was vast and empty, lonely and yet so close, touching and supporting me amid the matrix of its power. The bright-burning wire frame of the energy grid plunged and soared in every direction, sending throbbing lines and curls of magic outward, some thick as sewer pipes, others mere whispers and strands like fallen hair. My heart seemed to expand in my chest, pressing the breath out of me as I stared into the profound and terrible beauty of it. It reflected a sense of satisfaction at my wonder.

The brightness flexed and twisted, throbbing with intensity and engendering a pleasant anticipation. It rippled—the nearest, broadest conduits of power arcing toward me—and I reached for them with open arms. I almost laughed as I stared into it all, seeing the thin threads of the magic circle around me as fragile sketches. I knew I could simply step out of them if I wanted. They were pulled from the grid, and all of that was mine to move as I pleased. I could just . . . disperse into it, out of my restricted physical shell of a body, and be gone. . . .

Then the Grey shrieked again, heaving like a stormy sea and shaking me in my fragile, mortal skin. I could see the Guardian in the coil of the shattered magic circle, reduced to a thin rope of color, twisted too tight, nearly to the breaking point. I reached for it, drawing it toward me by lines of colored light, but I was too late and the rope, pulled in two directions, broke, unwinding and spreading its threads to sink into the grid and scatter like windblown sand across the waves and ripples of the circle, sliding toward Wygan.

As the Guardian Beast unraveled, the Grey broke on the edge of reality and surged outward, battering me back to the surface of the normal for a moment before it tried to suck me back down, back into the depths of the grid. Wygan laughed as the roiling chaos of it washed over us all.

I could see Carlos pushed back by the wave of power flooding the room, shattering his connection to the circle. He fought against the tide, the Lâmina still in his fist, as he turned his attention toward Wygan. Goodall threw himself across the vampire's path, grappling him down and sending the knife spinning across the floor as the door behind him swung open. Quinton darted in and snapped to a halt, searching for me. But I was hard to see in the rioting, wild magic and fog of the room.

The bloody blade cut through the edges of the circle, destroying the curtains of indigo and purple light. Wygan shivered as the directed power faded and joined the rest of the rampaging energy in the room. "The hard way, then," he said, chuckling and fixing his gaze on me through the layers of fog and magic.

He was fast, barely corporeal, fed on the Guardian's death, the rampant noise of the grid, and Will's terror. He caught my shape easily and hauled it in, taking my head in his ghostly hands like he meant to break my neck. "Now you'll have to die, my dear. Sometimes we must break our tools."

"I am not your tool," I whispered, sinking down toward the grid and away from his flickering physicality. "I'm your doom."

I'd had a lot of practice in the last twenty-four hours and it was easy to slide away from him, luring him deeper into the Grey, toward the raw surge of magic. He would have more power there, but if he wanted to catch me, he'd have to pursue me toward the grid, shrugging off the physical strength of his body. I would not. And once this confrontation was done, I would not mind dying.

We slipped through the ice storm of the Grey, sinking into the live fire and swell of power lines that shouted and sang into my head. Wygan's form shivered and lost solidity, but still snakelike, he flowed after me. We twisted as I hunted for a corner of time hard enough to trap him in, racing through the sharp edges of temporaclines as he clawed and bit at me, tearing pieces of my weirdly expanded self away, whittling me back to only body and will.

Each wrenching wound cut through me like a knife, pain I had not expected manifested in the shrieks of the Grey. I thought I grew smaller, shrinking like Alice as she plummeted down the rabbit hole.

But we fell not into Wonderland but into light: light living, crying, mourning its protector while it flooded up and overran its banks, devouring and searching for a shore. It threw me into the whiplash stream of black and red that Wygan had become, and I swam sideways, wound in his lightning grip, dragging him into the tide of shifting time against the slashing edges of temporaclines and monstrous things too old to name.

I cried in agony, growing desperate for the moment I could turn and pin the monster that laughed red-and-gold horror into me. I could feel the Pharaohn's delight in the treacherous depths of the Grey, his exultation, anticipating my tormented, useless death.

"Here, little girl," came a whisper of white sparks. "Here."

I spun, twirling streamers of gold across the silver ocean of mist, and thrust through the black-snake coil, diving toward the voice of my father and towing the Pharaohn with me. To the reflection of normal eyes that the Grey fed me, I knew I looked a tiny figure, turning like one lost in the fog, fighting a ragged shadow of white smoke and ethereal flesh still just recognizable as Wygan. Up and sideways, into the black center of a blazing ring within a ring, each burning too hot for flesh to stand with the shattered sliver of temporacline glittering at the center. I could see the edges of rooms superimposed on rooms, trees, fires: Dru Cristoffer's apple orchard maze, my father's office splashed with his blood and brains, the Hardy Tree, the puzzle balls falling outward/inward . . . into the fiery circles of the oubliette and ethereal labyrinth doors as they blazed. The puzzle balls and their unfolding magic gates to the hidden parts of the Grey were finally burning and we would go with them in a moment.

I could have stayed there and held Wygan to be immolated together into nothingness, but I yanked myself into searing air, my body protesting, bleeding, gasping for breath. And the Pharaohn rushed from the cold blackness beneath our pyre, struggling for shape where there were only fiery recollections and ghosts. For a moment, his memory of himself coalesced, drawn from the ash and flame: the ancient snake god writhed before me, gaping its fangs and striking. I let it come, taking the bite in my back, the fangs sinking in. I held the monstrous thing against me, forcing him to the gleaming surface of the temporacline, as I hooked my fingers into the slowing, knotted energy of his ethereal form and pulled the core of him apart. It burned and struggled, his fangs biting deeper, tearing at me as it loosened. First memory falling away, then shape, and then the scorching tangle of energy, magic, knowledge, self . . . so many jackstraws in my hands. I sank, exhausted, toward the dark center as the fires of the labyrinth doors burned out. I struggled away from the grid, back through the mist and chaos of the Grey toward the surface of the normal world, scattering the dimming threads of the Pharaohn and the falling ash of his children into the fog.

The world seemed to gasp and quiver, dozens of voices crying into the grid at once, lost and terrified. The voices of the asetem, the grid told me, those too weak and old to continue without him, falling into oblivion with their father-god. The half-mad unconscious of the grid raged at me in mindless despair; I had destroyed a god. . . .

This time there was no emotional chill to insulate me from the horror and pain of what I'd done. I stumbled back into the normal, bereft and bleeding, trying to get to Quinton and get out of the room before things got worse. Pandemonium still reigned in the concrete basement I fell back into; the rift had not healed with the destruction of Wygan. I could feel the furious Grey hungering, trying to devour me as it searched for another Guardian, for anything that would hold it in shape, stop it from raveling out into the wide world.

My vision was still dazzled by the ghost-stuff of the Grey and the raw burning of the grid within. With it storming around me, I couldn't find my way. I crashed into someone and grabbed on to him. He was shaking, slim, too tall to be Quinton and too insubstantial to be Goodall or Carlos.

"Will," I breathed. "Can you see the door?"

"Oh, yes." He wasn't shaking with fear: It was excitement. "It's beautiful."

I turned to look back the way I had come, back toward

the center of the circle that was now only ash and flickering fire, back where the single glassy temporacline shard had sparkled, where time had stopped under Edward's ruined shell.

Yes, there stood a door, much like the one I'd seen the first time I'd gone into the Grey, back what seemed long ago. Made of cloud and light, it beckoned and pulled us toward it. The door. The mouth of the starving Grey, seeking something, someone, to guide and protect it.

"No, Will. You shouldn't go there. That's a dangerous place."

"It's lovely. It wants me to come." He planted a soft, absent kiss on my temple and pushed me aside, moving crabwise and crippled through the doorway. The raging power of the unbound Grey unwound his physical form, leaving a fleeting Will-shaped skein of bright blue and gold that sparkled away into the light and fog of the world between the worlds.

The clouds of Grey and magical fire drew in as a new Guardian began to take shape beyond the door: the long, elegant form of a Beast spun of spiderwebs and ghostlight into animate runes and twining Celtic knots, flickering silver like reflections on glass and strands of platinum hair. The door whispered closed and the storm ceased.

Footsteps pounded across the floor as I stood, staring at the misty portal that faded toward the colors of the grid through the retreating silver fog of the Grey.

"Harper, Harper!"

Even through the ringing in my ears and the diminishing mutterings of the treacherous grid, I heard Quinton and started, once more, to turn.

And something ripped into my back and through my gut, driving me onto the floor.

Warm wetness spread under me, bringing new pain with it, covering me, and making the world darker at the edges.

"Little girl. Let me take this. . . ."

"Dad . . ." But he was gone and I felt sorrow, compassion, despair, and joy flood in as the inhuman remoteness that had tortured and sustained me disintegrated, leaving me. If ever I woke, I would not be the same, I would not hold and move the power of the grid again. The humming of it died and the bright lines slid away from me, growing further distant as darkness closed in. Even the Grey turned thin and cold, mocking me with voices I almost remembered, until it sparkled, dying. . . .

EPILOGUE

He had run. He had not waited. Carol had tried to stop him, but he fought and made it to the elevator before she caught up to him again. He dragged her in with him and rushed through the best explanation he could make.

"Harper knows where Goodall and Wygan are—where they have Kammerling—but I think she's going to try and stop them herself. I think—I think—"

"That she's going to do something kind of stupid," Carol suggested.

"Foolish. Honorable. . . . OK, yeah, stupid!"

Harper had been growing stranger and more upset since she got back from London. He knew she wasn't always saying everything she thought—that was how they were together—but this was a distant fear and despair that pulled her away from him. He wanted her to tell him, but what she had said was horrible and incomplete. He tried to help. He comforted and supported and looked for information or ways to help her silence the voices that had plagued her until she beat her head against the floor.

That had upset him. It wasn't like her to hurt herself. But she had and she seemed to be heading for worse pain.

He hadn't meant her when he'd said someone wouldn't walk out of the situation alive. He'd been sure Kammerling was already toast, but no one else seemed to believe that. But it sounded like she hadn't expected to walk away from the broadcast tower at all. Not for Novak or her dead dad—neither of those made sense—but for something she couldn't express. She'd said the Grey was swallowing her and he wasn't sure how that could be true, but maybe it was and he couldn't let it happen.

Carol had driven them to Queen Anne, to the broadcast towers, where they saw nothing that indicated anything amiss. They drove back and forth across the crown of the hill, checking each one. . . . Maybe he should have gone to the Danzigers', but time felt too short.

Finally, he pointed at the place they'd found Wygan the last time: the tower in the middle of the hill, alone on the edge of a park, across from the condemned gymnasium. He got out of her car and stared at the place. Something wasn't right . . . a thread of light out of place, a reflection maybe. He turned until he was facing the old gym building. One of the chained doors wasn't quite tight in its frame. But there shouldn't have been anything in there at all.

He leaned in through the car window. "Maybe you should call Solis. I'm going to look around."

"Not by yourself! I'm going with you. My—my boss is in there."

"No. If Harper is right, it's going to be dangerous in there, and if she's in trouble, we need backup. Which is why you are going to call the cops and wait here. I don't want anyone else dead."

Carol clamped her mouth into a hard line and her bottom lip quivered a little, but she didn't argue further.

Quinton slipped off into the shadows, skirting around the streetlamps and bushes until he got to the streak of light. He could hear people talking in low voices that seemed to rise from the ground, and there was a smell hanging around the place like turned earth and new cement. New construction under the cover of the condemned building. Why hadn't he noticed it before? Aside from not looking for it in the dark last time and being too busy running away.

This was just a bad place, bottom line. Rotten shit happened here and he was sure it would happen again tonight.

He touched the door and felt it give a little: Someone hadn't pulled it all the way closed or . . . He ran his fingers lightly over the edges of the frame until he found a pebble that had wedged itself in the hinge. Should have cleaned up better, but if they'd been in a rush, one little rock was easy to miss. Lucky for him.

He thought he should check for an alarm, but with the door ajar, it would have gone off already if there was one.

He patted down his pockets and found a dental mirror. Then he opened the door a bit more and pushed the mirror in, looking for anyone inside. Empty little room, lockers. He went in and shut the door until it stuck on the pebble again—after all, it's not breaking and entering if the door is open. Empty, empty, empty, but he could still hear the mutter of voices somewhere.

He went carefully through the rooms, but he didn't find anyone and that was just weird. People had been there, but they were gone now. One room looked a lot like a jail cell except it didn't have bars, just a strange metal bench thing—or a box, depending on how you looked at it.

He found a set of recently poured cement stairs and started down one at a time. The air in the stairwell seemed too thin and he felt like he couldn't get enough oxygen. It might have made someone else panic, but Quinton was used to strange airless places and he just moved with more care.

Noise, much louder, came up the stairs—something like a tree falling and then a gunshot. He startled forward but caught himself in the return of silence and went on, creeping down.

Someone screamed, hysterical with fear. Not Harper's voice, but it made Quinton move a little faster. The staircase was long, way too long. . . .

A noise like a train wreck ripped through the building, sending a shot of adrenaline into his blood that got him down the next six stairs in a run. The clatter of his own feet made the noise worse as something screeched and choked until it stopped. Then a blast of air knocked him back, icy cold and carrying a sensation of horror so strong that it turned him around.

He froze. He could hear more noise now, from above as well as below. The sound of cars and men in boots. The police. He'd have to get downstairs before they did. God knew what was down there, but he wanted Harper out of it before Solis and the Feebs showed up. The need to get to Harper was stronger than the wash of things unclean and dreadful that roared up the stairs.

He bit his lip and charged down, letting his feet clatter all the way to fight the noise of something down below that screamed with a thousand, tormented voices at once and froze his blood. He felt like his innards were turning to water, but he kept going.

The bottom landing had a locked door on it, but he braced himself against the wall and kicked it just above the lock. The door buckled but didn't quite spring open. He put his shoulder against it and pushed.

The door swung open on boiling fog and light, spiked with the scent of blood and something rotting. He couldn't see well, but he thought he saw Harper in the haze before she faded and vanished, grappling with what looked like a giant white cobra of smoke. The snake screeched and unraveled, dissolving into the strange vapor that filled the room.

He could see other people moving in the fog, but the sense of something threatening, sinister, and hungry held him at bay a moment longer. Brightness bloomed in the center of the room and he could hear feet coming across the cement above.

Then the gleaming cloud sucked itself away with a whispering sound, leaving a nimbus like a double rainbow around the middle of the room. There was a door there and two people. One of them turned and went through the door, bursting into light and falling apart into golden shapes that tumbled away, leaving the impression of some huge, lithe shape that faded with the brightness and left only quiet and the smell of something burnt. Only the other remained. Slim, brown-haired . . .

He ran toward her, calling her name: "Harper, Harper!" She started to turn toward him. He saw bruises, wounds, blood. . . .

From the edge of the room something moved, and Harper jerked, slamming forward onto the ground under the concussion of a gunshot. Quinton wheeled toward the shooter. Fucking Goodall.

He couldn't hear the words on the other man's lips, but he knew "bitch" when he saw it and the man kept walking forward, raising the gun again. . . . Quinton leapt at him, twisting to clutch for the heavy automatic still smoking in the other man's hand. Something shoved him away, pushing him toward Harper. The dark thing moved too fast for a human and stunk of carrion. Jesus, another vampire. Another shot went off behind him—smaller and lighter than Goodall's—but he didn't turn back, just scrambled along the floor to Harper, past something dead that wasn't too human and something that looked like cremated remains scattered through a tangle of ruined clothes.

He tried to turn her head, but she wasn't moving and her face was scraped and oozing blood where she'd hit the floor. Her shoulders and back were lacerated with weird marks that closed up as he watched. He rolled her over, pulling her head into his lap. She sighed, staring up at him, but he knew she didn't see him. There was a ragged hole in her midsection, an exit wound the size of a fist, a foul stench, and a sea of blood where she'd been lying. She wasn't bleeding now. The big hole seemed to sparkle, and he thought it was knitting up, pulling itself back together the way the cuts in her shoulder had.

Then it stopped. Breath slid out of her mouth and she seemed to get heavier in his lap, her staring eyes seeming to dull as he watched. Something felt like it cracked open in his chest. He wanted to scream, but men don't, and he wanted to cry, but he couldn't. He just held on to her body, which already felt too cool, and listened to feet pound down the stairs too damned late.

Something loomed behind him, but he didn't give it the satisfaction of a glance. "She will come back." Carlos. Scariest bastard in the bunch and he hadn't helped her.

"How do you *know*?" Quinton screamed. "What if she doesn't? She said there's always a last time and what if this was it? All this is for nothing. She didn't save anyone, not even herself. And you didn't help!"

He hung his head and now the tears came. Carlos made a scoffing sound deep in his throat. Quinton wanted to kill him.

"Oh, ye of little faith. It appears Ms. Blaine shot Mr. Goodall before she went down. She is much too stubborn to die."

Men with guns scrambled through the door and Quinton could feel Carlos step back, probably sliding into shadows or some other damned vampire trick so he wouldn't have to explain anything.

In the distance, someone was talking. "Who are you?" Solis, maybe . . .

"Carlos Pires Ataíde. I accompanied Ms. Linzey and Mr. Lassiter."

Solis grunted and said something in Spanish.

"No, only Portuguese and the sort of words your mother would blush at."

Shuffling sounds barely penetrated his mind as he blinked the stinging water out of his eyes, trying to see Harper's face for as long as he could. He kept fooling himself that she'd twitched or shivered, but he knew it wasn't true. She felt so cold and heavy. Didn't they always say dead people were lighter? What was it . . . twenty-one grams? The weight of a soul. Or a breath.

Someone was kneeling beside him, pulling on him, trying to get to Harper, but he wouldn't let them take her. Busy hands worked around him and voices floated past, unheard.

Quinton shivered, breathing too roughly around the heavy constriction in his chest and throat. His hands trembled, brushing the fallen teardrops off Harper's face. How would he ever draw another breath with this feeling in his chest? It was like dying himself.

Then Harper blinked.

AUTHOR'S NOTE

I made up several terms and creatures for this book and the previous one since I couldn't find good words to describe what I wanted or monsters to take the roles I needed. In two cases I worked from Portuguese roots, since Carlos, who introduces both terms, is originally from Portugal. In vetting my terms I got some help from two native Portuguese speakers: Nelia Chalmers, and Guilhermes Damian. Errors and misappropriations are all mine and not their fault. I tend to take vile liberties with languages, so I hope native speakers and scholars won't be too upset with me for what I've done here.

Névoacria: "Mist creature." Created by me from two Portuguese terms: "*névoa*," meaning "mist," and "*criatura*," meaning "creature." I shortened the term to make it easier to read.

Lâmina que Consome as Almas: "Blade that consumes souls." A suggestion in Portuguese from Nelia, and one I just couldn't resist.

Seraphi-guardi: "Seraphlike guards." This is a passive creature made of numberless, ethereal eyes, suggested by the seraphim described in Madeleine L'Engle's Time Quartet books. Another term I made up, but this time from the Latin roots.

Kreanou: A vampire subtype with shape-shifting abilities, driven by ultimate fury and despair to destroy its creator and therefore itself. Each is tied to its vampiric creator by an incompletely severed link which stops it from ever being sane or free. This is another creature I invented; the name is bastardized Greek.

Asetem-ankh-astet: Ancient Egyptian vampires who thrive on emotional pain and turmoil. They are the "children" of the Pharaohn-ankh-astet and depend on his existence and power for their own. As his power wanes, so does theirs. They cannot long survive without the Pharaohn.

Ushabti: A daywalking demi-vampire type specific to the asetem. Closer to human than most demi-vampires and dhampirs, the ushabti acts as a servant to the Pharaohn and has magical abilities that are unique to each ushabti. The term comes from the Egyptian funerary figures of the same name that were put into ancient graves to assist the dead in the afterlife.

Pharaohn-ankh-astet: The god-king of the asetem, he is the dwindling remains of an ancient serpent god—which I cobbled up from the numerous snake gods found in legends throughout Asia, Africa, and the Middle East. Only the Pharaohn can make an asete, and with his death, the remaining asetem must either find another god, learn to make one, or die (quickly or slowly).

The previous book, *Vanished*, had no author's note even though I did a lot of research for it, including some on-the-ground work in London. But since nearly all of the research did make it into the book, a note didn't seem as important. What didn't make it may have its day another time.

For *Labyrinth*, there was a lot less external research than any previous book. I did go to Leavenworth, Washington, and do a lot of driving around and reading up to find the perfect place for Dru Cristoffer's house and labyrinth. The actual location has never been built on and is, in fact, just a fold of empty land up behind the cemetery. The Leavenworth graveyard, however, does exist right where I said it does. It's an interesting place to look at and people are still being buried there once in a while.

The ghosts Harper sees on the road are memorials to documented modern and historical accidents. One in particular, the two women and a boy, is a sad, strange tale that began with the death of a Seattle mortician on Thanksgiving night 1944 and ended with the death of his family exactly four years later. It's the sort of thing you'd half expect Harper to find, and if you want to know more about this tragedy, the article at HistoryLink is very good: www.historylink.org/index.cfm?DisplayPage=output.cfm&file_id=8229.

The ladies at the Upper Valley Historical Society have no idea how much my tour of their museum and bookshop helped in the writing of the Leavenworth scenes and my understanding of the town's current and past incarnations. All the museum volunteers were helpful and sweet, and they never knew what dreadful things I was contemplating. Also, the maker of some of the tastiest chocolate in the world is located in Leavenworth so the trip wasn't *all* work and no play.

Some of my research into math, mazes, labyrinths, and their relation to Greek keys led me to the fun webpages of programmer Jo Edkins. You can find a nifty animation showing how a Greek key becomes a labyrinth on this page that Edkins designed: gwydir.demon.co.uk/jo/greekkey/origin.htm.

I got some help from my sister, Elizabeth Rose, and her husband, Armando Marini, with the Lâmina's possible origin and construction as well as some of the ceremonial magic and magic circle information. As usual, I tweaked a few things to match my needs rather than sticking strictly to canon. Clay quenching is a real process in weapon forging and several legends mention quenching magical blades in the blood of enemies, but I don't suggest trying this at home. Or anywhere else.

I also must apologize to residents of the Nob Hill district in Queen Anne for putting a nest of asetem in their midst. I had to muck about a little with the actual geography of the hill and its towers to get what I wanted for the story in place, but I tried to keep it to a minimum. For instance, the Queen Anne High School gymnasium building wasn't actually closed until September of 2009, but it was too good a location to resist. I would have used the original high school building, which is said to be haunted, but it's now been renovated into very classy condos and I just couldn't see Wygan living there. . . .

The asetem-ankh-astet and their Pharaohn are entirely my creation. So far as I could discover, there aren't any legendary vampires in Egyptian mythology, but I'd already gotten started on the tale and pretty much had to leave it in. I ran across a few references online to the Church of Astet-Ka but was never able to get any substantive information about this group, what it is, or its origin in the time I had. I borrowed part of the name and then twisted and played with it to my own ends (and just in case there are any copyright issues), but the vampires and their details are all mine and not extracted or borrowed from another source.

The hardest thing about this book was pulling all the strands together from all the previous books. I did try to keep everything consistent and look things up when I didn't have them already in the series bible, but I may have missed one or two details or gotten them wrong. My editor, copy editor, and beta readers did their best to keep me on track, but where things went wrong, that's all my fault.

I really didn't enjoy killing off characters. I'm kind of attached to most of these folks since they are my very first creations, and doing any of them in wasn't fun. But not everyone can live forever and sometimes in fiction it's necessary to cut someone out and do horrible things to perfectly nice people.

I also hope readers will forgive me for allowing time to slip a bit in these stories. Harper's tale to date has only spanned a little more than two years, though it's taken five years to tell it, and details have been matched to the time of writing rather than my attempting to keep Harper in strict chronology. If that had been the case, the current book would have been set in May of 2002, but it takes place in May of 2010 instead. I plan to continue with this habit as long as the series is still in production, since it not only makes it easier for me, but readers seem to relate better to a character who is active in their own time.

And in spite of having killed the poor woman off yet again, Harper's not done yet. I hope you'll stick with me and see what happens next.

—KR

Read on for an exciting excerpt from
Kat Richardson's next Greywalker novel,

DOWNPOUR

Now available in hardcover from Roc.

There was something deeply wrong with Lake Crescent; I knew it even before I saw the accident that wasn't there. The ground seemed to hum and mutter as if there were a current raging beneath it. Cobwebs of colored light leaked from the Grey—that slippery place between the normal and the paranormal where ghosts are real and magic gleams like neon reflected in wet black streets. The unreal light stretched in patches and strands over the soil and low-growing plants or dripped from trees like Spanish moss. Sudden bolts and globes of the same transient energy darted across my vision, apparently unnoticed by anyone but me. Standing under the wan February sun, I could hear the whispering ghosts that I knew would appear as solid as living flesh once the sun went down, and I hoped I wouldn't have to come back for them.

I could have written off some of the weirdness as the result of my altered interaction with the Grey since my most recent death, but I hadn't seen anything quite like it anywhere else since I got out of the hospital. It wasn't just me: The Grey itself was different here.

I'd come out to the Olympic Peninsula to work on a pretrial investigation for Nanette Grover, a lawyer who's a regular client of mine. I'd had to drive up in to the mountains and try several sites around the lake before I caught up with the potential witness—an itinerant handyman/sometimes-carpenter named Darin Shea—whom she'd wanted me to talk to. A man of indeterminate age, race, and origin who spoke with a New England drawl as untraceable as the rest of him.

By the time I was done talking to him, I wished I hadn't started. He seemed to say little of value but took plenty of time to do it, his slow molasses voice wandering off the subject in long, meandering asides as difficult to break through as a wall. We stood on the deck of the Log Cabin Lodge, where he was working for the day, on the Piedmont end of the lake, and, though I should have been paying more attention, his speech was so boring that I found my attention wandering out to the cold expanse of Lake Crescent as it lay behind him, struck with orange and pink by the fugitive sunset cutting through clouds above and illuminated from below by hints of the Grey's power grid in the depths of the dark, clear waters.

I listened to him with half an ear, taking notes while watching something burble out of the lake near the western shore—something dead-white and man-shaped that seemed to slog ashore with the reluctant, spastic movements of a creature yanked forward by an invisible rope. I thought I saw a second figure on the shore, beckoning and calling in a voice that seemed to pluck the strings of the Grey and that sent a tingling electric sensation over my skin, but I couldn't be sure. . . .

I started to peer sideways at the strange scene, looking by force of habit for the eerie and hearing the hum and rattle of the grid swell as I did, but Shea waved a hand in front of my face. "Hey there, you listenin' to me?" he asked.

"Of course, Mr. Shea," I replied, and I reminded myself that I wasn't here in search of ghosts but of reliable testimony for Nan's case—not that I was feeling positive about Shea's reliability by then. I pushed my attention to the Grey back and focused on the handyman instead.

It was cold and dusk was descending fast by the time I was done with him. The ghosts around the shore began showing themselves as silver mist that moved in human shapes, with voices like the sound of wind that breathed icy words. The uncanny queerness of the place made me anxious to get home—or at least down into the flatland and streetlights before full-on darkness hit—with the hope that I could let the strangeness lie for once. Of course, that is not the way my job works.

The road on the northeastern shore of Lake Crescent was narrow, twisting, and prone to dive down suddenly into unexpected gullies and through shadows of ghost light. But even without the disturbing persistence of the Grey the route was treacherous. Deep shade beneath the cedars and firs harbored dirty piles of snow between patches of bare ground and slicks of black ice on the asphalt surface of the road, so my spotting a car rammed up against a tree beside the tarmac didn't even seem unlikely. The flames coming from under the hood didn't look quite right, but when a normal person sees someone struggling to exit a burning car, their first thought is not "It's just a ghost," but something a bit more visceral, like "Holy shit!" which was exactly what went through my own mind.

I steered my Land Rover onto the frozen loam at the roadside and bailed out of the front seat to run for the other driver's door and wrench it open. But my hands passed through the flame-flickering material of the Subaru Forester with only a phantom sensation of heat while someone else's terror and pain washed over me. I flinched back from the melting face that stared from behind the unreal glass and backed away—was it my own fear I felt or his?

The ghost wafted out of the memory of his fiery death, following me, mouthing words without sound and bringing along the odor of searing flesh and melting rubber, hot steel and burning cedar. I retched at the smell. I couldn't fall back any farther without standing on the road, so I put up my hands as if I could hold the smoldering specter at bay with the gesture alone. The ghost stopped, just touching my out-turned palms. A sparkle of gold and a flicker of Grey bent between us where his searing memory of fire struck against the shield I had unconsciously raised. I held my ground at the ragged edge of the asphalt.

The ghost's voice trembled off the Grey surface between us as if it were coming through a speaker: "Not an accident. Not an accident."

I could feel the vibration of it in my head and chest. I nodded but still held him away. "All right, I believe you. What happened to you? What's your name?" He was not the first ghost I'd seen and he wouldn't be the last, but he was the first willful spirit I'd encountered in the nine months since I'd been shot in the back. This ghost felt horrible, exuding terror and fury and need while his memory burned in icy flames and remembered agony, resonating through the barrier between us and slicing into me.

"Steven."

The smell and sensation made my stomach flip, but I swallowed the lump of revulsion and held still. "What's your last name, Steven?"

But he didn't seem to understand me, or at least his answer didn't sound like a last name. What he said was: "Blood Lake. My family . . . We should never have let them. . . ." He started fading away.

I forced my protections aside and pressed my hands into him, trying to make a stronger connection, even though the feel of him made me gag. I couldn't grab on to him as I should have been able to do, so I let myself slide deeper into the Grey, closer to his own plane. He firmed up a little, but I still couldn't get much of ahold on him. He was thin and weak, as if whatever gave him substance was fading or distant and only his ardent need for help allowed him to manifest at all. "Steven. Steven, listen to me. Tell me your whole name or where you're from. Anything. Help me find you or I can't help you."

"Le . . ." And he fell apart in a drift of dust and smoke.

The burning car remained a moment longer, sending memories of flame and sparks into the silvery air of the Grey. I stared at it, hoping to memorize the license plate before it vanished into the mist, but I only got part of it. I tried backing out a little and reaching for the temporaclines—the layers of time and memory that accrue in the Grey like silt—but they were slippery and knife-edged here, and I couldn't seem to find the right one. I eased back out of the Grey and into the normal, looking for any sign of the accident, but I found nothing of it in the near-dark. It was long gone.

Disturbed, I returned to my truck and headed back down the road that would connect to Highway 101 to Port Angeles and then to the ferry back to the Seattle side of

Puget Sound. I felt haunted all the way home even after the strangeness of the area had faded away.

I spent the next morning finishing reports for Nan, but I couldn't get the ghost's words out of my head, and from the corner of my eye, I continually caught a flicker of something Grey that almost looked like a charred skull. Before I took my reports to Nan's office, I gave in to the phantom harassment and ran a search through the Department of Licensing database. From the partial plate number and the first name, Steven or Stephen, I got about two hundred hits; when I filtered for the make and model of the burning SUV, I got three.

A bit more poking got some additional background information on the three names, and I printed the pages out to read at Nan's office. Since she was prepping for a trial that looked to be lengthy, it was hard to guess how long I'd have to wait for her to be free to talk to me.

I walked from my office to Nan's, liking the feeling of moving through a familiar place again where the Grey seemed less volatile and dangerous. After some chitchat and paperwork, Nan's secretary set me up to wait in the firm's library. The space was about twice the size of Nan's office and lined with floor-to-ceiling shelves filled with mostly outdated law books and periodicals. Most firms have no need for an extensive library anymore—they just subscribe to the LexisNexis system online and do their research from their computers like I do a lot of the time—but Nanette's firm kept the room intact, using it as an additional meeting room. The acoustic deadening of a foot of leather-bound pages lining the walls made it an ideal space for recording depositions and discussing sensitive matters. No sounds penetrated in or drifted out of the room once the door was closed, and the few spooks around the place were as dull as tax law. I huddled over my printouts and drank coffee until Nan came in.

"Is that my report, Harper?" She was as uncreased and unemotional as a slab of ebony.

I looked up, tidying my pages into a pile and pulling out the folder full of reports from my bag. "No. This is your report."

I slid the folder across the table and watched her read it. Nan reads frighteningly fast. In a few minutes she looked up at me. "So, what are your thoughts on this witness?"

"He's a problem," I said. "I can't get a background on him so far—he won't even supply one himself. The best I could get was that he'd been in the area off and on since he was sixteen, but he wouldn't say how old he is now, and he doesn't have a driver's license—though he does seem to have a truck that isn't registered to him. He feels unreliable to me, even though he's got a solid reputation as a worker with the locals. He's overly chatty in a way that made me think he'd been coached, so I don't feel confident about his information, and his manner of speaking would drive the judge and jury crazy. He volunteered some additional data I was frankly suspect of. Because he has no fixed address or verifiable status, I think you'd be hurting your case if you put him on the stand. If your opponent wants to use him, all that might be in your favor, but he still feels shady to me."

Nan arched her brows barely enough for me to notice. "*Feels* shady. Expand on that."

I gave it a moment's thought before I obliged her. "Well, to be crude about it, you can't tell what age, race, or region he's from and, unless he cleans up really well and changes his speech and mannerisms, that lack of identity will make a Seattle jury distrustful of everything he says. And at this point I can't say they'd be wrong. He talks around the point pretty well, but when you tear it down, his information just isn't solid."

Nan nodded. "So you'll need to confirm or eliminate his facts and nail down his background."

"If you think he's worth it, I'll keep digging on Shea, but that's going to take me away from the King County side of the investigation."

"True. How long will it take?"

"I'm not sure. It's going to be legwork and combing the ground every step of the way. There's also another case that's come up out there—a cold-case missing person that might be a homicide."

"Related to my case?"

"Doesn't look it, but it'll be a lot of the same interviewees and I'd like to dog it down as long as I'm there."

Nan's face could have been sculpted from ice-cold bronze for all the emotion she usually displays. She didn't even raise an eyebrow this time, but I knew she was annoyed from the way ragged orange spikes flashed in her aura for a moment. "We'll be in court in less than a month, Harper. How long do you think the additional Clallam County investigation will take?"

"I'm not sure," I repeated. "I'd like to get David Feldman to take over the King County work. You know Feldman's solid. He did a lot of the background on that body on the freeway case a few years ago."

Nan nodded. "I've worked with him." She stopped talking and studied me a moment in silence. The wisps of blue-and-yellow energy that always coiled around her office stirred a cold draft and I shivered. "Tell me about this other case."

Relief spread through me: She hadn't decided to take a hard line with me about her own case taking precedence, at least not yet. I took a sip of my cold coffee and returned the cup to the table with care before I looked back at Nan. "Sometime in late 2005 or early 2006, a Lake Crescent area resident named Steven Leung and his 2001 Subaru Forester disappeared. He was sixty-seven years old, retired from the Clallam County Assessor's office, widower, two surviving daughters. A witness claims Leung was killed in a car fire on East Beach Road and the details he provided point to vehicular homicide. I can't find a record of any similar accident in that area in the past ten years, but the telling thing—the thing that persuades me this isn't a hoax—is that all information about Leung just stops by April 2006. There's nothing. It's as if the man stepped off the planet and no one cared—not even his survivors, who never filed a missing person report."

"Could Leung have moved out of state or entered some kind of medical care?"

"There's no forwarding address for him so far. Even if he was in a nursing home all this time, his mail would have to go somewhere. There's no death certificate or record of cremation or burial in Clallam, Kitsap, Pierce, or King County and no record of his car being sold or the registration renewed by anyone. There's no release of interest to indicate he'd transferred ownership to a wrecking yard or charity, either. The only other lead I have is that the witness said something about an area called Blood Lake. It sounds like a local place-name, but I didn't have time to look for it before this meeting today."

"I don't find this missing person case that's five years cold particularly compelling."

She didn't ask what I wasn't telling her. She just fixed her commanding gaze on me and waited. I wasn't sure how to persuade her; I couldn't say that I had it from the ghost himself that someone had done him in and that there might be a lot more to the situation than a simple disappearance. I made up my mind and leaned forward.

The motion made me wince as the muscles in my back and abdomen pulled unevenly. I still hadn't rebuilt all the tissue destroyed by the passage of a .45-caliber bullet through my middle, and I didn't move as fluidly as I once had. "I think it's murder, Nan. You know that every delay in pursuing something like this lowers the chances of solving it. And yes, I know it's five years old already, but how long should anyone have to wait for justice?"

She studied me for a few long seconds before she replied. "Are you sure you're in the condition to pursue an undetected homicide?"

"Am I in shape to chase down an unprosecuted corporate malfeasance complaint?"

Nan gave it some thought. "All right. Chase Shea for a few more days while you work your case, just to see where it leads. If you turn up enough to justify continuing, so be it. If not, I'll expect you back on my pretrial work immediately. In the meantime, call Feldman and brief him on the malfeasance case to date and get him to work before you leave town." She stood up and took the report file off the table. "Is there anything further on this witness?"

"Not from me."

"Good. I need a report Monday." She turned and strode out, which is pretty much the only way Nan walks. She was disappointed, but she didn't give any outward demonstration. She never showed an emotion outside the courtroom that I knew of, and I wouldn't have been able to guess what she was feeling if I hadn't had the ability to see the colors of energy that cling and swirl around most people.

Auras and energy lines didn't seem as blazingly bright or vibrantly colored to me as they had before I was shot. But they'd been getting a little out of hand by then anyhow, and I was just as glad that—except around Lake Crescent—the colors had faded a bit and I no longer heard a constant, inescapable singing and whispering in my head. It made me feel more human to know there were limits to what I could do and see.

There had been moments during that last, horrific investigation when I'd felt I *wasn't* all that human anymore. The power to sink into the grid itself and to move the threads of magic, to tear them apart and push them around with impunity, had been too seductive, too alien. I would have been just as glad to have lost that, though I hadn't really checked the limits of my abilities yet. As I'd been warned, dying without direction had been like slamming a fist down on the magical reset button, and I believed I'd reverted to a lower, weaker state of interaction with the Grey, or at least something on a less godlike scale. That was fine by me.